THE
FIRST FIRST
GENTLEMAN

THE
FIRST FIRST
GENTLEMAN
GERALD
WEAVER

LONDON
WALL
PUBLISHING

ISBNs
Paperback: 978-1-911195-23-8
eBook: 978-1-911195-22-1

Published by London Wall Publishing

200 Aldersgate Street
London
EC1A 4HD

www.londonwallpublishing.com

For my wife, Lily

A silent look of affection and regard when all other eyes are turned coldly away – the consciousness that we possess the sympathy and affection of one being when all others have deserted us – is a hold, a stay, a comfort, in the deepest affliction, which no wealth could purchase, or power bestow.

Men who look on nature, and their fellow-men, and cry that all is dark and gloomy, are in the right; but the sombre colours are reflections from their own jaundiced eyes and hearts. The real hues are delicate, and need a clearer vision.

In the little world in which children have their existence whoso-ever brings them up, there is nothing so finely perceived and so finely felt, as injustice.

Change begets change. Nothing propagates so fast.

Charles Dickens

BOOK ONE

HIS STARTLING BEGINNING

As with so many epic love stories that end in the White House, this tale has its beginning in a bullet-ridden drug deal gone bad in a crack house in a seedy neighborhood of Boston.

There is a certain implacable gloom that settles over this great New England town and its harbor, often with the fog and many times without it in the fall and winter, or in the other seasons as well. This gloomy quality seasoned the sternness with which Boston and the rest of the world came to be viewed by its Puritan settlers, and it is the same gloom that then settled into the fates of the Patuxet Wampanoag who inhabited it when the white men arrived. Gloom in a very practical manner inhabits this coast of the North Atlantic Ocean. It stares out of the cold gray water and the sea mist and into the faces of the workers at the Charlestown Navy Yard, into the windows of the homes on Beacon Hill, and into the moods of the town's sports fans and politicians. Gloom hovers and then settles into the coffee of the office workers in Back Bay and into picnic baskets of summer visitors to Boston Common. There are gloomy roads and mornings, gloomy traffic and dispositions, gloomy birthday parties and politics, and a certain amount of gloom suffuses and puts a bit of a glumness even into the hearts of the denizens of this region.

There are in London, another great North Atlantic seaport, entire neighborhoods and suburbs composed of buildings made of many differing colors of brick, red, yellow, beige, ochre and even white, which have over time become essentially all the same color, a variation of brown and gray, a shade that would find its chromatic equivalent in a dirge, a color that looks as if it took much more of its nature from centuries of fog, mist and smoke rather than from its manufacture. The Massachusetts seacoast gloom has infused this same funereal London pigment into the red brick buildings of Cambridge and even into appearances of the students who pass through Harvard Yard, but not into their aspirations, which may be seen to suddenly wink a little sparkle here and there in the pervasive and stolid grayness.

It was on one such gloomy evening that Garth Teller realized there something about street corner drug dealers; that they all dressed as if they were about to join each other on a hike in the Cascade Range in Oregon in the early fall, except for the ball caps, the fact that none of the pants had a belt or were being worn on any man's waist, and that each article of clothing was brand new. Had Garth Teller stepped out onto that corner he would have been instantly identifiable as a white man, not only by the color of his skin but the fact that he was the only one not dressed like some upper-middle-class white kid standing in winter outside of a suburban mall in upstate New York or Minnesota. Garth was wearing a black leather jacket, black slacks, a black jersey, a black stocking cap and a pair of black rubber soled athletic shoes. If it wasn't for the shoes, he could have been mistaken for a policeman and one would have to look closely to notice the shoes.

One other thing shared by the young men on the corner was a look that was poised between casual indifference and utter watchfulness, like poker players at the high stakes tables in the gambling palaces of Las Vegas or as if they had each been a jealous wife observing her flirtatious husband wandering too far away from her at a cocktail party. They would not show their certain concern about his observing them if it should arise, other than to drift away from the corner one by one, and they were unlikely to do that right away since most of their business came from young white men who looked not unlike Garth did and who drove cars like his. These late model sports utility vehicles and foreign-made sedans would circle the block once or twice, allowing the dealers on the corner to catch a glimpse the first time and make significant eye contact the second time. If the eye contact was maintained and the car slowed down then one or another of the dealers would go to speak to the men in the car. And there was rarely only one man in any car, as it was uncommon for a young single man from the suburbs to be so bold as to drive into this neighborhood at night without a friend unless he was desperate. The entire street corner pageant was far more organized than it appeared, and the reason that Garth wasn't surprised by the fact that none of the drug dealers were ever dressed to take off on a run, as he was dressed, was that none of them had the drugs on them. In each case the cocaine or the marijuana was stashed somewhere nearby, and the entire process of each dealer taking turns making eye contact with each successive passing car and the subsequent trips to the planters and hallways and trash bins nearby was actually carefully regulated by a well understood agreement.

Ben appeared at the passenger side of the car. Garth unlocked the door and Ben let himself into the car. It was only the second time Garth had met Ben Dessous; the first time was when he was introduced by their mutual acquaintance, Earnest Dapple, for the purpose of putting together tonight's deal. Even on this second meeting Garth was startled by Ben's appearance. He was very dark, but with striking Caucasian features and a long scar on his left cheek and another shorter one on his forehead that caused an interruption in his right eyebrow. It looked as if Ben had once been beaten lifeless and again had been strangled to death and each time had returned to the world of the living. This apparent and intimate exposure to that mystery, in which we will all have our equal share, had lent hardness to his long face with its straight nose and to his lean and tall body that was also reflected in the directness of his gaze, which was now fastened on Garth. Earnest had introduced Garth to the idea of meeting Ben by saying, "Ben is from St. Croix and if you have ever met any of those crazy Jamaicans, let me say that the Crucians make them look like kindergartners." The apprehension that such a statement caused was still present as Garth examined Ben and took in all that he could, including the fact that, as before, he detected dignity and intelligence in that damaged hardness. Garth was also aware that he was being similarly examined and he hoped with positive conclusion.

Their first meeting had been brief. Several of Garth's friends and classmates at Harvard had decided to put together some funds to buy cocaine at something other than the retail level and at a lower price per unit and to do so for an upcoming party. It was natural that within that group, Garth would be volunteered for putting the deal together. He simply was the only one among them who had not been made effete by the privileged upbringings they all had in common. Unlike the others, he did not lack observation and judgment or empathy when it came to the world beyond their social set. Whether or not this also made him bolder was beside the point. He was simply going to be more attentive when he was placed into a novel situation, and he tended to seek such settings. Garth in this case had sought out Earnest, who had been able to sell him smaller quantities of the drug. Earnest also had gone to a private preparatory school and had more in common with Garth's other classmates than Garth, except that by being of African American descent himself he could make contact with local people of color without the same barrier that would have faced Garth. In this way Garth was passed along to Ben, who was local, older than the students by a handful of years, and a resident of the neighborhood in which they were now parked. At that first meeting Garth had determined that there was something to Ben that was more solid than in Earnest. There was also something inexplicable and deep.

"So, are you ready to do this?" Ben asked.

"I believe I have prepared for this my entire life, from the excellent education I have received, to all the observations I have made in my numerous trips into the demimonde, to the many books I have read and the tight spots from which I have escaped, and not forgetting that I am locked and loaded, strapped up and ready to go," Garth said.

"No. I meant do you have the money?"

"Oh, that, yes, I have it," Garth said. His nervous bravado made him feel foolish but he knew enough to not now reach into his pocket and pull the money out or even to touch it.

Ben focused his attention on the young men on the street corner.

"I think two or three of them have marked me," Garth said.

"Which ones?" asked Ben.

"Well, the guy in the blue coat has looked in this general direction about three times and in a way that was timed rather too regularly to be natural. He was checking each time and shortly after the first time he said something to the guy in brown. And after about two or three beats, that guy looked down the block this way. I also think that the third guy said something to the second guy right after you got into the car."

Ben now focused his attention more on Garth. Ben took him in more than he had previously. He noticed that Garth had particularly dark eyes, so dark you could not see where the pupil ended and the iris began, at least not in this light. It gave them a grave and deep appearance and his eyes were deep set into Garth's face below thick black eyebrows and a high forehead. Garth had a long straight nose and a long face, and a mouth that was a bit small and well formed for a man and gave the appearance of being sensitive. There was more to Garth than was apparent at first, and perhaps there was a touch of some kind of ethnicity that might have made him not just your standard order Harvard white boy.

Ben could never have known that the Teller family was nominally Jewish. Garth had never been to a synagogue and his Lutheran grandmother had taken him to her church more than several times. His family had not been very observant for at least a few generations. And they had been on American soil for over two hundred years, having migrated to Charleston, South Carolina from Holland around the time of the American Revolution. A distant ancestor of theirs had served as a Confederate general in the Civil War. The family had a history of civic and business involvement in Charleston and had prospered for generations. But all that changed at around the time of a very remote event, the beginning of the massive immigration to the northeastern United States from Germany and Eastern Europe at the turn of the twentieth century. Garth's grandfather's great-grandfather took his family one summer to the River Hill Hotel in Aiken, South Carolina, just as he had done every year. Post Civil War Aiken was the end of the rail line that ran south from New York City, and a lot of old New York families had established Aiken as a place to summer, bringing their horses and their money and names such as Vanderbilt, Winthrop, Pendleton and Welles. South Carolina had developed a tradition of religious tolerance since well before the Revolutionary days, and some of the Jewish families of Charleston had summered in Aiken for many years before the New Yorkers had arrived. In fact, there had been much the same sort of early American religious tolerance in that northern city formerly known as New Amsterdam. But with the mass immigration from Germany and Eastern Europe in the early nineteen hundreds, the social and economic gatekeepers had decided it was one thing to tolerate the handful of the sons of Abraham who had been in their midst for generations, but quite another to leave open the doors for their striving brethren fresh from the European continent. The Tellers suddenly found themselves barred from checking into the River Hill Hotel.

Garth's great-great-great grandfather then echoed the famous words of Davy Crockett, "The Hell with this place. We are moving to Texas." He moved his family to Texas, where they had lived ever since. In Texas, family members had operated hardware stores and dry goods stores and served in local governments. For the first generation or so after the move they had made the effort to blend in and to conceal their religion as well as they could and fit in to the local communities. Garth's grandfather had not been observant and had even married a woman of Scottish and German descent who thought nothing of taking Garth to her Lutheran Church. The last generation of Teller boys had attended local private schools and then colleges outside of Texas. The Teller family was still conscious of their heritage, which was coupled with watchfulness toward outsiders and a wariness of other people of Jewish descent, particularly their relatives.

Garth had attended a private preparatory school in the Northeast, among many of his future college classmates, but he had always had these extra dimensions which boiled down to a lack of comfort that he expressed toward all of his many privileges, and toward the other institutions that supported the comforts of his life, such as the police, the government and civil society. And there was that watchfulness, which was what Ben was observing at that moment without being able to know its origins.

"That second guy . . ." Ben began.

"The one in the brown and tan jacket with the brown boots . . ." Garth said.

"Yes." Ben paused. "He is the one who will take us to the meeting. We will have to get out of the car."

As Garth got out of the car, he tried as much as possible to blend in to the street. He minimized all motion and developed what child psychologists refer to as a flat affect or lack of facial expression. He watched Ben and slowly and subtly mirrored his movement to Ben's, but not in style of walking or motion. He stayed as utterly unremarkable in movement as he could. He just moved when and where Ben did, almost like a shadow. He did not stare straight ahead but he did not look anyone in the eye either. He stepped lightly and was part of the street, or so he thought.

There is a kind of bright sunlight that for a fair-skinned blond man will wash out all his color and for a man of darker color will make his features stand out. There was no such sunlight here on this gloomy Boston winter street at night, but the dark had a similar but inverse effect. The darker men and women sort of moved along the edges of the light. Garth's white skin had a glare to it. And his spare and limited manner of locomotion and his absence of any flourish made him look like the one sick or dead bird in the aviary.

Ben's approach was premeditated to thwart Garth's design, since Ben knew that the perception of a white man and a black man together in this part of town would mean only one of two things to the insightful observers. They were either together solely for the purpose of transacting a drug deal or they were police. Since the former prospect might invite notice and intervention and the latter would discourage it, Ben was doing what he could to be visible and direct and apparently unafraid to be observed. Ben's plan was having the greater success but as they walked down the sidewalk Garth thought that he was successful at being invisible. No one looked directly at him and many people failed to notice him when it seemed likely that they might.

In fact a sort of a path opened up as they walked down the block past the Chinese take-out place with the Plexiglas window that enclosed the counter and past the check-cashing store with exactly the same precautionary set up. No one really crossed their path and people standing in doorways seemed to slightly recede from the street as they passed. Children on the street, but only the smaller ones, looked directly at Garth and they would stare. His notion of his apparent invisibility began to fade with this and as they approached the corner the dealers began to drift away, one by one. By the time they had arrived only the one Ben had arranged to meet was still standing there. He was looking directly and warily at Garth during the entire conversation that he was having with Ben. Garth's efforts at being unseen at this point had evolved into an intense kind of self-consciousness that became so acute, it prevented him from paying much attention to what had been said or to what he was then doing. He only knew that he and Ben had left the corner and walked down an alley next to the boarded-up building in front of which the young men had been standing.

"Are you going to be all right?" Ben asked.

"What? Yeah. Oh, yeah. I will be fine. Just give me a second."

What had come over Garth was something like shame or guilt, although he had done nothing wrong. It was an accusatory kind of self-consciousness that had a habit of floating in the back of his mind and which occasionally would rise to the fore of his thoughts at the oddest moments, and rarely when he was actually guilty or had a reason to be ashamed, times when his pride or his instinct for self-preservation would keep him from blaming himself. But at other times, in social situations, or in a class, or getting off of an airplane, he would just feel as if he were the only person who had been singled out in some way, or that he did not belong, and that it was his fault. Often this feeling would manifest itself at school at times when he had the feeling that everyone else had been given some kind of preparatory memorandum and he had not been given or that everyone but he had attended some orientation. It would also arise when he had made a call or had written to a friend and the lack of a response would make him wonder if he had done something to offend the person. And, as at this moment, it would surface when he had misjudged something.

Gerald Weaver

Fifteen or twenty minutes later, he would run back out of the building and would stop to find himself standing in exactly this same spot. This same feeling would come over him again and he would have to react to it.

HER EQUALLY STARTLING
BEGINNING

At this same point in time, Melinda Sherman was six and a half years old
and living in London, Kentucky with her mother, father, and her brother,
who was five and a half years older. Even at this young age Melinda was
particularly sensitive to all the sacrifices that her mother had made for the
sake of the family and she also appreciated them and was grateful for them,
especially the ones of which she had no knowledge, those that had been
made before either she or her brother had been born. Her mother, Angelina
Sherman, had been born Aniolek Bol in Poland several years before the
outbreak of World War Two. Melinda understood this fact and all that it
meant in two ways. It was quite beyond her and in a way was subject to often
unsupported flights of imaginative embellishment and as such it resided in
the realm of something that she knew she could never fully comprehend.
Yet, she also understood it completely and deeply and in a way she could
never consciously reach. We each have something like this inside of us and
inside of Melinda it sometimes spoke Polish.

"Siedzimy," she heard her mother say.

Melinda heard this from the living room and knew instinctively that
it meant that her brother was enjoying the warm and loving nightly bath,
a ritual of their earlier childhood that her mother had suddenly undertaken to reintroduce in the case of her brother. This was another of her

mother's many tender sacrifices, to give up this part of her evening to the affectionate care of Melinda's gentle older brother. She was certain that her mother was kindly suggesting that her brother, Porter, simply sit still so that she might take better care of washing him. Melinda knew to be prepared at one moment's notice to dash into the bathroom in order to help. She kept the appearance of this readiness deep within her and would not let it reflect in a way that might be noticed by her father, William Sherman, as she sat with him and talked, and read to him from her books. In a relatively few years after this time, at some point in the middle of the night when all in the Sherman house would be sleeping, Melinda's understanding of her connection to her father would turn on a silent and unseen fulcrum and it would mean that in her mind their roles must be reversed. Even at this earlier point there was a glimmer of this larger later shift, a change that had already flickered to a flame in the way she was beginning to see and treat her older brother.

William Sherman was one of those gently amusing, warmly intelligent men of the kind that most people imagine all elementary school teachers ought to be. He actually was such a teacher and the parents of his pupils uniformly appreciated his ways with their children. He would often stop teaching in the middle of class and tell them beguiling stories, after which they approached their studies with renewed interest and intent on pleasing their teacher. He treated his students as if they were his own children. Since his wife was not in the classroom with him, that guidance was different by manners of quality and quantity from that which he provided at his home. To reach this charming part of her father that she rarely saw at home, Melinda had begun to enact the role of his pupil, reading and discussing, storytelling and learning, as she was doing at that very moment. These lessons always took place around that same living room chair, the one in which the teacher sat during most of the time he was in the home, afternoons, evenings, weekends and the entire summer. Whatever apprehension she might have had at that point about potential events in the family bathroom were withheld from her father's notice, in order encourage him to remain more or less her personal teacher.

Crushed at first by his marriage, Melinda's father had soon found a dull relief in it. He was figuratively under lock and key but the same barriers that kept him in had kept a number of his possible troubles out. If he had possessed the gumption or the will or the wildness to have struggled against his strictures he might have become heartbroken or a drunk or divorced, but his choice or perhaps his fate was to slip with a spiritual lassitude into his slowly arcing descent that eventually and inevitably landed him in that chair and found him beginning to be under the care of his younger child. He had been relieved of so many other concerns that he could at least now enjoy the less thorny pleasures of his life, such as those provided by his daughter whose approach to him was uncomplicated by demands or agendas or anything other than unconditional love. He was a soft-spoken man of about medium height and forty-seven years, who seemed a dozen years older, with graying brown hair, rounded features and about twenty extra pounds. It seemed that he had at several different times opened his mouth when he was alone with his daughter, as if he had something on his mind; but he often just shut it again, without saying anything. Melinda talked and read with him, one ear trained on the bathroom.

Her mother had once been the most beautiful girl with the sweetest disposition in her small town in Poland, which her elders believed to be the oldest in the country. For Angelina's entire childhood she had given the impression of being much younger than her years. Her diminutive figure and her small features and her fair skin and blonde hair had combined with a retiring and gentle goodness in a way that would never quickly draw the attention of the men and women of Kalisz. But once they had noticed her she was easily and speedily a favored child, a "Little Angel." She had soft hazel eyes and a quick, lively expression. Her movements were delicate and smooth. She greeted the German shopkeepers and Polish farmers and Czech workers of her town with an equal grace and a quiet smile. In some ways she was an emblem of Kalisz, sunny, with the red-tiled roofs of a more southern town, open and prospering, friendly alike to Catholic, Jew, Orthodox Christian and Protestant. Kalisz had been a crossroads of agriculture, industry and culture, beautiful and clean, and poised without any natural borders to protect it from the determined arrogance of the Germans or the expansionist imaginings of the Russians. The prosperity of the town and the buoyant mood of its people during Angelina's youth were a reason for and a reaction to the growth that had occurred since Kalisz had been almost entirely destroyed in August of 1914 by German artillery at the onset of the First World War. The resilient town had always returned from such blows, dealt by the Mongols, the Prussians, Napoleon, the Russians, and in a way these incursions and rebounds had made it one of the most diverse and open towns in all of central Europe.

The Little Angel, Aniolek, knew nothing of this past. She only knew that there was a town hall that her mother and father told her was brand new, and that the diversity which she saw on the street and in the variety of places of worship she passed from day to day spoke of an innocence which she also carried in her heart. Then, one day when she was eight years old, she noticed that her smiles were only met with despondency and averted looks, that the town was now filled with men in black and gray uniforms who spoke German, and that she had been told that her father had gone away. None of this had come with a warning. This time the Germans had not needed artillery.

The Bol family was not unusual in that Aniolek's father had worked out of the house for long hours, for six days a week, and the matter of the children was left to her mother. The sudden absence of her father removed another light from the bright room of the young girl's life, and her mother's emotional withdrawal from the new circumstances cast the entire family into a profound darkness. Her mother became sharp and suspicious and guarded, and when she was not particularly depressed she took great pains to train her children to be on their guard. She never did so more than before their family was about to receive a visit from its own personal German soldier. The young girl greeted these visits with a mixed blend of anxiety and enjoyment. The soldier seemed silly to her and he was relaxed and told jokes and stories in Polish and always brought gifts. But her perceptive children did not misunderstand the girl's mother's mutedly anxious and pained expressions. There was real danger in these jokes and stories and in the gifts of bread and cheese and wine and medicine.

Nature had taken to the features of this man with a set of unusual instruments, pressing in his cheeks and temples with a spoon, flattening and squaring his head with a vice and pulling at his nose, cheekbones and chin with a large set of diabolical tweezers. His hair had been sprayed on in brown and gray mottles that gave his blocky skull a kind of patchwork of short and upright hair follicles. Nature had placed inside of his eye sockets a set of dull mirrors that gave him the impression of never really looking at anything, which was not quite corrected by the fact that his left eye had been graced with an extra set of ball bearings that often caused it to scrutinize the wall next to whatever was the object of its partner. He had also been blown up a bit to a size quite larger than the men of the town. He was in his late twenties and while his one eye clearly was of the wandering variety, the other one had a figurative way of being so.

He was on the lookout for something and the little angel could have had no idea what it was, whether it was for traces of her father who may have been in the Home Army and secretly in touch with the family, or if it was for signs of the Bol family participating in any other resistance activities, or if it simply was personally related to her mother. Nor could Angelina at her age have any idea of the magnitude of the evil he represented, even if such a thing were possible at any age or by any person. During the six year time span that this man was her family's personal jailer and spy, she had not been able to fully grasp the full import of the fact that every Jewish person in her town, a full one third of its population, would be exported for extermination, or of the fact that the majority of its Polish inhabitants were to have been relocated to slave labor camps or to other parts of the Nazi occupied lands or to new homes beneath the surface of earth. Nor could she fully grasp the fact that her mother's enmity toward the soldier had become decidedly personal and that some of that animosity leaked over onto Aniolek. Beyond feeling her mother's anxiety, the Little Angel only felt in a personal and direct way the manner in which the human heart and in particular the innocent soul contains provinces within it that will simply flourish in response to gifts and to compliments and to small kindnesses. She did not fear or hate the soldier.

There are degrees of hardened evil, tones in the palette of blackness that are inexplicable, so that even in the way this soldier viewed this inmate family of his and everyone else in Poland, there was a slight deviation in the way he saw the little angel. Men of this kind well learn to mask what it is that puts them at risk of not only violence from others, but at risk of simply being ignored by people who upon apprehending them only sense horror and revulsion. So his kindnesses and his idle comments and his gifts of food contained only a miniscule hint of malice and foreboding, except that this slight gradation in his approach to the girl could possibly have been interpreted as bearing none of that stain. Angelina had almost lost the memory of the feeling of her father's clasped hand, and the remembrance of her reception on the inviting and lively thoroughfares of her town, and the understanding of what it was like not to feel a shade cast over her mother's love. She would only think of these things from time to time and the soldier knew it and he acted on it. Soon she became fond of the fact that he took her out on walks to see the flowers in the fields, to visit the German women who held administrative or hospital positions at their military base and who would fawn over her, or to go to the few shops in town that still sold candy and sweets, each time holding her by her small hand. She sat by him on his visits to her home when no else would go near him. She even came to call him by his name, Helmut. So, hand in hand with murder and rapine, with no family or friend who would dare to try to guide her, and with no understanding of the common habits of the members of a free community, and drinking for most of her childhood from a well that carried this singular and unnatural taint, the Little Angel came to begin her womanly life.

What may or may not have been the plan for her, harbored in that sliver of difference in the heart of her soldier as it turned to her, or that may have lain more slovenly and hidden in the larger waste of his soul, was never to be known. Helmut was simply battered and bayoneted in front of the fourteen-year-old girl and the rest of her family by Russian soldiers who had conceived of the display as a spectacle of redemption and retribution for the Polish people they were liberating. While this had temporarily and largely elicited a cascade of sympathy and approval from Aniolek's mother and siblings, it was for her like losing another father and learning at the same time that this second father had been the serpent in her family's bosom. This loss was compounded when her real father, who had only returned home for a few weeks, and most of his Home Army companions met with their Soviet Russian liberators in the dark forests of western Poland in that late winter and came then to be put on more intimate terms with its rich, black soil. And at this age and from this second army, the Little Angel's visits came from not only one soldier, and her trips to the fields were not to see flowers.

Then came a time when eating was a novelty and amusement was a dream and only the steely reserve of the Little Angel's mother, several months of running and hiding, and the help of some men from what remained of her father's comrades in the resistance, were able to get them out of Poland and through a string of refugee camps in western Europe to land in a program for displaced persons in America. Passing through New York City, the girl and her family found all of it very little better and only slightly less unsettling than from where they had fled. The impersonal bustle of the throngs caused them to uniformly cower. They fled the approach of strangers and recoiled from the sounds of the massive city. The cars, the trucks, the streetcars, all bore down on them like infernal machines. The kindness of the people assigned to help them filled the family with suspicion and dread. They only found some comfort when they had been relocated to the American countryside.

When the gentle and unassuming man of London, Kentucky, who was so good with children, finally stood within Angelina's view, there is no need to explain what happened to her or certainly to this man. Long overlooked by his countrywomen, he found himself suddenly in the focus of the alarmingly intense and ethereally beautiful, child-like young woman for whom he was more than she could imagine.

This same man was now showing their daughter, Melinda, one of his favorite passages from the Book of Job when she heard from the bathroom a change which was that for which she had been listening. It was simply a reduction of the sound level she had been previously hearing and the fact that fewer of the words could be clearly heard by the girl and that many of those words were now in another language.

"Podatny," her mother said. It was the Polish name of her brother, Porter.

Melinda glided out of the living room and down the hall swiftly and quietly. She was in many ways the physical opposite of her mother. She was boyish and more gracefully strong than most girls her age and her size was slightly above average. She had athletic shoulders and was a handsome girl with a strong nose and good bone structure. She had those hazel eyes but had thick wavy brown hair. Her playmates had always been her older brother and his friends.

It was not long before she had slipped into the bathroom behind her mother in time to see her holding Porter's head under the water and muttering in Polish that he was too close to his friends, that her twelve-year-old son liked other boys too much.

There had been numerous culprits in the life of Angelina Bol Sherman, almost too many to count. These culprits had been spread as broadly as the steppes of Russia and the forests of Germany and had been lodged as deeply in her as the spiritual presence of her own late mother. There had also been an incident that had occurred a little over seven years before this time in which there had been another culprit, another man who had placed a mark on Angelina's life. There were just so many people to blame. The only problem was that none of these culprits were readily available. She was limited to dealing with the culprits who were now in front of her.

"He likes me, Mommy. See, he likes me. And I am a girl," Melinda said as she slipped quietly into the bath water with her brother. She had swiftly and silently undressed and as quickly and quietly had slipped around her mother and into the tub.

The Polish continued, "O, Miodladny," her mother muttered, and said it again, "Oh, Melinda," in English, as she let Porter up from the water and his sister hugged him as he gasped for breath.

"See, Mommy. He likes this girl. He likes me a lot."

Porter was holding onto her as if she were a life preserver.

"I see, Melinda," her mother said, returning completely to English. "I see," and she wandered out of the bathroom.

Now Melinda's thoughts began to turn to the teacher in the other room. She worried that a change would come to him, and how it might be anything but a service to him. She hugged her brother, quickly helped him out of the bath, dried him and began to help him dress. She even more quickly dressed herself and glided back into the living room, where she found her father, alone.

"You have abandoned me a bit too long, little one," he said. "I was beginning to wonder."

Her brother had wandered into the room quietly and he sat on the sofa next to Melinda, and he asked, "Will you get me something to drink, Mindy?"

"A glass of water for me too," her father added.

Melinda edged her way into the kitchen and as suspected she found her mother standing there, smiling and brooding in almost the same breath. Then her mother suddenly sat down, as if the air had been let out of her and her arm fell to the side of the table and her head dropped to her shoulder. Melinda quietly now took it upon herself to get three glasses of water, one each for the males in her care, and one for her mother. She handed it to her.

"You're a good girl," her mother said.

Her father echoed the same praise and so did her brother when she had returned to them with their glasses of water. Had there been a guest in that house that night he might have imagined that he had heard in these phrases a certain tone of custom that contained an inward current of resentment. It was not that the praise was ever withheld or that they were ignorant of her merit. It was more that they were habituated to her goodness, that it was just another part of their overall condition. It was as if there was a tenor of an expectation or of a right to what it was she meant to all of them, every day. Their voices reflected that whatever comparisons they had made between themselves and her had been merely to render her as necessary, as a part of the place in which they were all held in custody, because none of her cares or ambitions moved beyond that condition of their confinement. They could not have been mentally or emotionally prepared for the changes that were about to come.

THE POSSIBLE REQUIREMENT
OF IMMINENT ACTION

Time for Garth Teller had begun to telescope in the few short moments since he had managed to escape from that building and for the brief seconds as he caught his breath. While he stood on the same spot where Ben and he had begun their conversation with the dealer, he had been able to consider an extensive line of events and histories which seemed to have elongated those moments by the sheer size of what it was he was remembering. In the thirty seconds it had taken to run out of the building he had directly considered and reconsidered and had digested all that had happened in the previous twenty minutes while he had been inside. But, as he stood panting for only a few brief moments on the sidewalk, an entirely different and much longer and older memory made its way through his mind at a rate and with a clarity that defied the scale of its content, and which reflected events having had occurred long before the characteristic Boston gloom had been noticed by him on this night.

The men of the Texas Teller family, including Garth's father and grandfather and their ancestors previously of South Carolina, had always owned guns and had served their country in wars. For some reason and well before the adolescent years when such a thing normally will happen, Garth had developed a desire to begin to see himself as distinct from his father. It was hard to tell if the effect of this was that he had grown close to his father's father or if that in fact was the cause. It was difficult to know if this ambiguity may in itself have been the product of a similar development that had occurred between these two older men, or if it might not have been a trait that had run on the male side of the family for generations. But for this then eight-year-old youngest Teller male, the company of the handy older gentleman who took him fishing and hunting and who still wore his First World War service revolver on his belt began to be preferable to that of the other man who had served in World War Two, and who owned and operated a string of dry goods stores, and who kept his guns in a locker or on the wall, and who was Garth's father.

Garth preferred the gaunt older gentleman and could often be found lounging along the echoing precincts at his side. He would hear these echoes of an older time, a period that was littered with bits of minor romance, unfathomable otherness, quickly comprehensible and timeless verities, and the flashes and small eruptions that hinted at the larger untold stories of the family lore. They represented a large lost library and lexicon that had moved beyond the range of Garth's use once the older man had passed away, or since even before then when the adolescent Garth had turned away from both the older Tellers to focus on girls and sports and other diversions.

The gun was itself evocative. It was a revolver, but it was unlike any revolver any of the boys Garth knew would ever see on TV or in the hands of their fathers and grandfathers. It was not a six-shooter and it did not have an external hammer. And at .32 caliber, it was smaller than the relatively more common .45 caliber pistols. It spoke of the places beyond Texas to which his grandfather had traveled. It had five chambers instead of six. It loaded by a top opening mechanism and not from behind. It fit a smaller hand and it was sleek and shiny and streamlined, making it unique for a revolver manufactured at the end of the nineteenth century by the Smith and Wesson Company of Springfield, Massachusetts. Grandpa Teller would sometimes let Garth shoot it into the side of a hill or the empty old barn, only when Garth's parents were not around. When the old man would take Garth to his fishing camp on the bank of the nearby Guadalupe River the gun would accompany them. At eight or ten years of age, Garth would see this as a kind of initiation, the memory of which would never leave the boy and which would lend a sharpness to the regret he felt later for not having mined the old man for much more information and history. This gap in information would always remain unknown to Garth and would make that old man a much more important part of his life than could have been guessed at the time.

"You shoot like shit," the grandfather would laugh, his large ears and his skinny neck somehow waving like sunburnt standards on the dusty plains. "The damn thing is jumping out of your hand." Garth did not learn until much later that the long pull trigger and the short barrel are what made this gun do this. He only knew that he liked that it fit his small hand better than the bigger guns.

"Did the Army give you this gun to fight the Germans with, Grandpa?"

"No, Garth, they gave us officers the Colt .45, but I found it to be too heavy and hard to manage in tight quarters, which is where you want to use your pistol and not your rifle. I got this from a British gentleman, a cousin of your grandmother. The English used the Webley pistol, even bigger than the .45, but he showed me the virtue of the smaller gun. I learned a lot things fighting over there in France. I also brought back your grandma from that war, Garth. She was a nurse over there. She and I infused this old Levantine stock of ours with some more fresh and lively blood."

Grandma Teller and her daughter-in-law were the living distaff symbols of the differences between Garth's father and grandfather. Garth's mother was from Baltimore and a little bit more than nominally Jewish, having married into this family of non-observing Jews with the secret hope of bringing them back to the covenant. She was a dark and tensely quiet woman who by merely fingering her necklace and looking straight forward in a way that was only half staring could greatly unquiet any of the young ladies that Garth would later bring around as dates. But Grandma Teller drank scotch and swore back at her husband and laughed out loud at jokes and was at least five-foot-ten and could speak French and German. She was a lanky, tall woman with good bone structure and a wide and open face. She certainly had changed the family bloodline.

It was right now at this moment on this street corner in New England that Garth remembered that old man and was glad of his early associations with what the old gentleman had taught him and, more importantly, all that he had given him, because as Garth stood there he considered what he had told Ben Dessous earlier and which Ben had sort of passed over in order to get to the issue of the money, which was now still in Garth's pocket. There was something else in another pocket, something small for what it was and sleek. The old man's Smith and Wesson .32 revolver had been repatriated to its home state.

In the same way that the Boston gloom had permeated the night and particularly the room in the building that Garth had just vacated, the idea of the gun was in every thought and memory he now had about the past twenty minutes. The young dealer had led them to the door of the building in an alley behind the corner and had left them there. At the door a short and gaunt forty-year-old black man had greeted them. He was wiry and sharp-faced and prematurely graying. Much of him was prematurely something, as it seemed that for his forty years he had been looking at unfortunate events and now his face shone with a sullen reflection of them. He took them through a hall and across an abandoned warehouse floor, up the steps to a room above the floor. In that fifteen by twenty foot room there were two other men. The sullen one stayed and stood at the door behind them. This bothered Garth only slightly less than what he saw in the room.

The gloom was everywhere there, on everything, in the air and on the walls and in the lights and lying on the desk and table and chairs like worn upholstery. Standing behind the table was a shaggy large man of about twenty-five. His lighter brown skin was mottled and he had a large natural haircut. His arms and hands were too active and not at all nonchalant and he put his hands to his face and hair a lot. His eyes had little depth to betray them, but were sharp and bright and looked as if they had been fashioned by the best of doll makers. He seemed to use their blank charm as a kind of weapon, one fastened now on Ben and his companion.

"I know why you have come here," he said, "and you have come to the right place. I am exactly the man to see about this and I always aim to please my customers." He touched his hair. "Yes, for sure, when you deal with Tiger Mike you have made the right choice. Don't nobody say different, for Tiger Mike always is righteous."

The third man was inexplicably and quietly lying on the bench along a side wall.

"Get up, Rank," the larger man, Mike, said.

The thinner, smaller, darker man, also about twenty-five, slowly sat up but did not look up. He wrapped his jacket more tightly around his shoulders, reached into his shirt pocket, pulled out a pack of menthol cigarettes, removed one and lit it. He ran the thin fingers of his other hand slowly over the top of his close cropped scalp, very slowly, the way an old woman will gently pet a child's head.

"What time is it, Rank?"

"It is eleven twenty-five PM," said the other man with a strange mix of compliance and real mastery, as if his submission were merely calculated.

"He always knows the time, even without looking at his watch and even when he has just woke up," the larger man said smilingly. "He often just knows a lot of things like that, just knows them. See, I told you. You come to the right place. You all gonna be okay with Tiger Mike. Ain't nobody ever said different." The smaller man on the bench scratched behind his ear and then finally looked up at Ben, but not at Garth.

This Garth noticed, and he too was also watching Ben now as well and it became clear to him that he and his companion of the evening had somehow attained an instinctive way of understanding one another, based on each man's power of observation. He could see that all of Ben's awareness and expression had settled down into a very deep and ancient place within him, one from which there was little reflection. Garth recognized this as an atavistic place associated entirely with the acute awareness of the possible requirement of imminent action. Even though he and Ben had only had a few minutes of conversation, the college student could now recognize in this man his acknowledgement of Garth's own awareness and understanding. He could see this simply from one short sidelong look Ben made in his direction, which was the only momentary departure from the metaphysical crouching and gathering that he was still doing. The effect of this on Garth was difficult to comprehend or to explain but it combined elements of pride, fear, enjoyment, increased focus and awareness, dread, intensity and exhilaration.

Garth became aware of everything. He knew that Rank also was aware of Ben's poise and that Tiger Mike was not.

"We just did a deal here a little while ago," Mike went on, "some kids from Brookline. They got the best price possible. They were able to make a big profit, for sure. Isn't that right, Rank?"

Garth noticed that the smaller man did not speak, but only nodded his head. He also saw that there was little credibility in the story Mike had just told. The sullen older man, behind them at the door, was remarkable for his not moving at all. Ben had moved his chair slightly backward. And then Garth saw it all. It flooded into his mind as palpably as a certain memory.

He saw what Ben was communicating to him on a silent wavelength that was generated in that ancient place inside of him where he had lodged his consciousness and which came to Garth through his own power of observation. Behind Ben and now within his reach was one of those old style metal sets of shelves that would be found in a warehouse office such as this had once been. Ben and Garth were seated in chairs about ten feet apart on the door side of the table. Tiger Mike was on the other side of the table and the lean, quite smaller man was on the bench on Ben's side of the room. The stack of metal shelves was on the door wall behind Ben. Garth already saw what was going to happen and he knew that the next move was up to him. As Mike rambled, Garth raised his hand like a school child in a classroom, literally waving it as if he had a question to ask. Mike looked at him and the sullen older man looked at him and the quiet man on the bench looked at Ben. But it was too late. Ben had reached back and had pushed over the shelves and they toppled onto the man at the door. In an instant Garth turned and leaped over the fallen shelves and man. He was soon was out the door, catching a glimpse out the corner of his eye of Ben being grabbed by the smaller, younger man.

Out on the street there were one or two remaining memories of Grandpa Teller that had yet to flood through Garth's mind and they were of a secret trip to Mexico that they had taken when the boy's parents had been away for the weekend. The two had gone to a bullfight and had done some other things, but the young man remembered only the bullfight because it had struck him with a thrilling disgust.

"The Spanish, kid, as a race, know what the rest of the civilized world refuses to understand. They know that death is in our heart and that killing is in our nature. The Spanish gave us Cervantes, the discovery of the New World, Velasquez and Picasso. Yet their high civilization has never once caused them to turn their backs on what is really inside of all of us."

Garth also remembered the time that the old man had gone away for a few days and had left the gun in a drawer, almost so that the boy could sneak it out of the house one day on his own and feel the power and freedom of holding death in his hand.

By the time Garth had finished with all these remembrances he had glided back into the warehouse building and had quietly mounted the stairs and had taken a quick look inside the room. Ben was now in a chair behind the table on the other side of the room. The sullen and hardened older man was behind Ben and had pinioned Ben's arms. Tiger Mike was to the side and was rambling on about how Ben and the white boy should never have thought they could get away with this particular stunt. Rank was sort of leaning forward a bit with his back against the table and was punching Ben in the face. Garth charged into the room and it was exactly like when he was a boy and the gun would jump in his hand. His intent at this point was to scare the three men into not doing anything while he got Ben out. The first shot hit the ceiling and the second and third shots hit the wall above Ben. Tiger Mike fell to the floor, unhit. Garth put the fourth shot just above the shoulder of the sullen man and he released Ben.

Gunfire is far more exceedingly loud than is or can ever be depicted in movies. Given the volume of a movie sound track, if the sound of gunfire were to be accurately recorded and played back everyone in the theater would be temporarily deafened. Movies also show fights lasting far too long, with men trading blows over and over again. Ben knew differently. He knew that most men will not remain standing or be effective after only one solid blow and that such desperate fights are always ended and won by the man who successfully follows the maxim of getting there first with the most. And in these tight quarters the most was not a fist or a foot or a knee. It was the head. In an arcing and twisting, almost balletic move, Ben had spun and had plowed the front and top of his head into the nose of his captor, knocking him flat and unconscious to the floor not far from where Tiger Mike lay quietly but awake and unhurt.

No one can really know what calculations were clicking up and down the balance sheet inside the mind of the Rank at that moment. Perhaps he was acting on instinct or on prejudice. He had pulled his own gun but did not fire at the young white Harvard student. He quickly put the gun to Ben's head and spun himself around and behind the man from St. Croix.

"Drop the gun," he said to Garth, who by this time held his left hand under and cradling his right hand, as it held his grandfather's gun.

The Smith and Wesson .32 caliber in Garth's hand was small and light and had only one bullet left. And it had one other thing that few handguns like it had. It had a very small and very exact sight. It had a small separate rear-sighting element that was fastened onto the gun and a similar small front sight, both made of a finer grade of steel. And the gun sight was directly on Rank's right shoulder, the only part of him that was not now behind Ben. As Garth exhaled he slowly squeezed the trigger.

Momentum is measured by the equivalent of mass multiplied by velocity squared. The roughly seventy grain slug that hit Rank in the shoulder at roughly the speed of sound, about nine hundred feet per second, did so with a momentum of about one hundred and seventy pounds per square foot per second, per second of acceleration and where it hit was concentrated on a spot far smaller than a square foot. Rank would never throw a rock or shoot a basketball again and the small bullet did not pass through him but piled into the man's shoulder. In the second balletic move of the night, Rank spun around and down. His arm flew over his head and to the side and he fell to the floor, screaming at Tiger Mike.

"Shoot that motherfucker! He is out of bullets."

Tiger Mike looked at Rank's gun on the floor next to him and then at Garth. Garth then pointed his grandfather's gun at Mike and smiled, saying, "You know I only shot five."

He watched the puzzled look on Mike's face as Ben sped to his side, turned him around and they ran out of the building.

They quickly and quietly moved down the street and got into the car and drove down the street and around the corner and Garth kept driving without asking where to go. His heart was in his throat and as that feeling subsided he needed to let go with some of his adrenaline-powered enthusiasm. He was waiting for accolades.

"How did you know the little guy was in charge?" Ben quietly asked him.

"I just felt it, I guess," Garth answered.

"Are you worried about your safety, about possible retaliation?"

"I suppose, yes. Now that you mention it, I am."

"I don't think you need to be concerned about the possibility. Your Wild West constitution doesn't fit into their paradigm of what a Harvard white boy is. They may consider that you are some Italian kid from the North End or some black Irish guy from Chelsea or Charlestown, not that they would want to go looking for you in those places either."

"So, you think I am safe."

"I can think of no safer place for you than the Harvard campus. Rank simply could not get his mind around the fact that I was not the one he had to worry about. You are an enigma to them. And they wouldn't feel safe going over there to Cambridge anyway and would be anxious about potentially being rousted just because of the way they look. No, you are safe. Just don't come into this part of town again."

"But what about you? Will you be all right?'

"Thanks for asking, Garth, but I will be all right. We Crucians stick together and they know it. What mystifies me in all of this is how they thought they could pull this sort of an exploit on me. My friends will disseminate it on the street that they have done this. And they will be the ones on the run for a while. Then it will all find its equilibrium. It always does."

"Oh, okay, then I guess we can go somewhere to cut loose and relax then, huh?"

"Certainly not, as I am confident that you have your plans as much as I have mine. And feel free to let me disembark right here."

Garth slowed down and edged the car to the curb.

"So, where are you going now?" Ben asked.

"I have a huge party to go to, at my, um, club. It sure ought to be interesting tonight."

"That is perfect," Ben said, "so this might be of some assistance then," and he laid a plastic bag that contained about an ounce of cocaine on the seat, adding, "I am surprised that they brought this to that ambush."

"You know, now that I think of it, I know this party is going to be even wilder than my evening has been so far."

"I am sure of that," Ben said, "and I would tell you to get rid of the gun but I know there is some personal reason that you will not. So just send it away, somewhere safe. I also would tell you not to say anything about this, particularly to our friend Earnest, but I already know you won't say anything. So, just take care, kid."

"Just one more thing I guess, or two. How did you know I had the gun and that I would come back for you?"

"I just felt it, I guess. But you already know that. That party of yours tonight is going to be one rollicking revelry. Of that I am certain. Have fun." And he closed the door and walked away as Garth drove off to what was going to be the Harvard party of the century.

REFLECTIONS ON THE WATER

The small, three-bedroom bungalow in which the Sherman family lived on the outskirts of London lay slightly aslant on its foundation, the product of subsidence either from a local mine or of otherwise settling some bit away from the dauntless skill of the Kentucky men who had designed and built it several decades earlier. It leaned its sallow bricks into the vectoring force of its decay and fell small piece by small piece before this pressure. An unhealthy and cheerless patch had fallen over its gray roof. The house had seemed to go in mourning for the death of the sun. The sun or the moon might occasionally shine on it, but a baleful dusky mantle attended to it far more devotedly. Rain and frost and mist and cold lingered with casual apathy on its brown lawn for days after the other houses on that street had long warmed and brightened. The wind that ventilated or cooled the neighborhood in summer lost its breath before reaching the Sherman home, and shadows and webs filled its nooks and rendered the edges of the house less distinct. A light or a bright sound that might on occasion emanate from within it would quickly be dampened. The birds chose to nest and sing nowhere within several dozen yards of the porch and lawn. Other houses heard laughter and opened to send forth gamboling and laughing children or became the location for parties and music. This house did not. It was the home of not.

Melinda and Porter were not set loose to gambol and to laugh. Their sojourns from the home were launched not in freedom, but with admonitions and directions and hard tales of potential problems. They did not find a warming and welcoming peace when they would return, not like that a traveler long on the road might feel as he first opens the door of his home to the familiar smells and sights. It was not like the homes of London or of the rest of the area, as its soul was woven with threads borrowed from the spirit of Nazi Germany and Communist Russia and of the great millennial sufferings of the Polish people. It was not anything more or less than has already been seen, a place of confinement.

One month in the late spring of Melinda's eighth year, William Sherman had been asked to attend a seminar of elementary school teachers in southern Ohio and he was planning to take the bus and spend four days in Dayton. The father of the Sherman home did not want to leave it, or maybe he did.

"Something has gone wrong here with your mother. She is not as obliging and attentive as she usually is. I am so dependent on her many kindnesses. It really puts me out, to think of how her natural warmth and compassion might be afflicted by my leaving," he said.

Melinda stood by his chair and her arm settled onto his shoulder as she leaned over to embrace him.

"Something has given her offense, Melinda, and I am certain it is my leaving. Nothing can at all be done about it. I must stay."

Her head bowed down and both her arms wrapped around his neck as he went on.

"What does it matter what I do, really? What does almost one week away matter so much or not? What am I worth to these other teachers? What good am I here at home? I can be of no help to anyone."

"Father," she said, "Father, just let it go, please. Take your trip and assist the other teachers to help the little children. I will look after Porter and Mommy. Don't blame yourself. I should have begun to prepare the family better for your departure. I have been too slow to prepare the way for you. It is my fault."

"I wish you could have seen me when I was a younger man and your mother first met me. I was not so broken down as I am now. I was a fine picture. You would have been proud."

"I am proud of you, father. I will do anything for you." She hugged him tightly.

"I am not sure what I could do, either way. I am not in a position to ask anything of you, my younger child. I am sorry that I cannot do more for you. It is another one of the problems of my situation. I would give the entire world for you, buy you new clothes, take you to Europe, and send you to the best college. I have let everyone down."

"No, no, you have done everything for me. You are everything."

"I have done my best, I know. Weak as I am, I have always given you what I can. Haven't I?"

"Oh, yes, you have, father. And I will take care of mother and Porter. I really will. I have already begun. I started making a nice packed lunch for Mom every day before she goes to work in the mornings, so she does not have to worry about doing it. I will clean up more and do all I can to help her more. And I have been with Porter as much as I can be. It will be all right. You must go to Dayton and to talk to those other teachers and show them how you teach and why the children love you."

Then he leaned back and patted her arm with his hand and kissed her arm there.

"Bless you, Melinda. You will miss me when I am gone, won't you?"

"You know I will," she said.

There is a woman driving north on US Route 25 and approaching Mt. Vernon, Kentucky, in the middle of a morning not long after this. She is very thin and her fifty-year-old hands shake a bit on the wheel. She is wearing a designer business suit and blouse but they are from a period of twenty years before this time and although they are neat the patches of baldness on her gray and brown head offset their condition and expense. She has a lit cigarette in her left hand and does not appear to be actively smoking it, or the one in the ashtray that is also lit. She is driving her old station wagon slowly so as to not cross the middle line or wander off the shoulder or get too close to anything at all when she sees two boys on the road, hitchhiking. The taller one is a lanky boy with sandy hair and the shorter one is compactly built with brown hair haphazardly cut. In order to safely squeeze past them, the woman would have to drive entirely into the oncoming traffic lane. So she stops.

The two of them jog to her car and climb together into her back seat. At least the way is clear in front of her. She starts to drive again. The shorter boy looks furtively at the taller one and he recognizes the meaning of that look and he speaks.

"Thank you, ma'am, for picking us up. We are going to Dayton. We appreciate whatever you can do to help us get there."

"Oh, it is all so confusing," she says, "the whole thing, the dials and buttons, the dogs, the deer, the people on the road, and the road itself always changing and going up and down. And, I mean, where is the line going to be next? Sometimes my late husband tells me I should not drive. But I have to drive since this is not Philadelphia and you never know when the buses and trains will run anyway. And they don't go to Dayton, or whatever. You kids look queer, the little one, the hair, not what I would do. I have to be careful with my hair. Do you think I should drive? I guess so. That's what Ronald would tell me. The coast is clear. It's clear sailing. That's what he would say. I am only going to Lexington. You kids, you kids, hitchhiking and your hair. I think I can drive now. You are in the back seat, of all places, and I have only just had breakfast."

"Thank you, ma'am," the taller one said.

The car began to inch forward as the lady looked nervously at the road and then briefly in her rear-view mirror. She soon began to pick up speed, and within a few minutes the children were moving toward their destination at about five or six times the rate at which they had been walking for the last hour. Soon they were inching up on Berea, Kentucky. It was better than walking, which they had been doing for an hour previous, in the brisk cool morning. The road had been empty and the taller boy had wandered along the shoulder of the road, kicking rocks and whistling. His little brother, who was wearing some of his old clothes, was more watchful. When a car would at first come up the road, she would pull him fretfully off into the trees, where they would huddle quietly for a while before resuming their roadside trek. As long as kicking rocks and whistling had remained an amusement, Porter had kept up pretty well. But then, he became querulous about the brisk breeze, the walking, and the entire enterprise. Melinda had reluctantly decided then they must try to hitchhike and the novelty of the idea caught Porter's attention. She was aware of every sound and shadow. Though she appeared to be in the lee of the larger sibling, she had more or less of a tie on him, like a tug pushing a larger ship into harbor. She was no less watchful now and still kept her tug-like prow connected to the larger child, ready to give one more guiding push.

"My, my, when are these surprising days ever going to end," the driver continued, "with children on the road and in the car, children. Mine are not from here. They are from Philadelphia and we had to leave there, Ronald said. Children in the back seat again, and what funny hair. Could there be a reason that this light is on here? Where did I put my lighter? Light a cigarette to calm me down. Children. Children, where are you from?"

"I suppose you know that my sister and I come from Ceylon, ma'am, having just escaped indentured servitude there. It has been hard and we are very grateful for the ride," Porter said.

"Ceylon, Ceylon, I have never been there. I am not sure I know where that is, but I am certain it looks like a nice place. There are such pretty places and children are pretty. Ronald always told me that and told me to always remember that. He wore dentures too, in Philadelphia, you know, which is not Ceylon. She's your sister with the queer hair. Well, this is an odd business."

"You drive very well, ma'am."

"It is very difficult, I mean to tell you, and now I have to talk to children and children from far away who are in my back seat again, talking. The driving, you know, I have not always done it. Ronald used to do all the driving and I just took care of the children. And here there are deer in the roads and they eat my tulips and my daffodils and you do not want to hit them, not with your car you don't. And I have to keep the car between the lines and the lines keep moving. They actually eat the tulips but not the daffodils, not really."

Melinda had known that she must dress as a boy in order to make this trip and had cut her hair with the scissors that were in the utility drawer in the kitchen. Some of it she also trimmed with a pocketknife that she had won once on a dare with one of Porter's friends. She had left the house of her service for the first time. In another way, she left behind something else. If an objective observer were to describe her at this point he might say that she had more color and she was less tamed and there was something about her supple and resilient form that put one in mind of hunting or being hunted. Within her shy and helpful and considerate eye there had emerged something half like fierceness. It was this with which she now gripped that knife in her pocket, with which she firmly pressed her hip against the Ceylonese boy at her side, and with which she had first conceived of this trip.

Like a gypsy caravan setting up overnight, it arrives suddenly and noticeably. Or like a flock of birds passing rapidly overhead, or like the abrupt flush of heat and blood that harbingers lust or embarrassment or that heralds both lust and embarrassment, *le Mistral*, the famous wind of the south of France, blows the Provencal sky clear and fresh and dry with a direct straight constant force that has the power normally only seen in dark rain squalls. But *le Mistral* blows steadily strong and it will arrive suddenly and no one from Avignon to Arles may ignore it. It brings no rain or clouds and no real cold, but in the spirit of Mediterranean magic and mysticism it is reputed to bring love, good fortune and change. There are sudden and strong Polish winds too, and they blow in exactly the same manner, with the sole exceptions being that they arrive from across a thousand miles of frozen Russian steppe or from the dark German forests or from across the brackish Baltic Sea, and they blow neither dry nor clear and convey no magic. Such a wind had been blowing in the Sherman home since the father had left and Melinda had held herself and her brother well against it until it had blown through the phone line to Dayton and Melinda felt the need to go to protect her father.

"I don't see what is wrong with hitting a few tulip-eating deer. It seems like there should be a lot of sport in it," said Porter.

"The deer are such a problem, no natural predators. I hate that word, predator. But deer need them to learn to stay away. They need them. Children don't, not the dear children. I used to drive them in the car. Ronald told me to take care, not to send them far away. Driving this car this way and that for them, always trying to do as Ronald said. That is what he told the judge, that I always did as I was told. This is strange road with strange children on it."

Melinda took heed of these words and in a way that was almost against her will she also took heed of the skinny hand that now came to the woman's face and began to pull at individual eyelashes and to pick at imaginary blemishes on the face. This hand seemed to be fond of those activities, even while holding a cigarette, and it combined a certain dexterity with some passion as it had dislodged some imaginary blemishes and a few actual eyelashes before it moved on to the lady's hair, twisting and pulling several stands at once. It was this observation that moved the tug to nudge the larger craft out of the harbor.

"Oh, I am sorry, ma'am, I think we have to get out here," Porter said.

"I am sorry too, you two dears. I am not very good, nor very able to take that chance, to stop this car. It might go off the road. I can't . . ."

"Look, there is a huge pothole in the road right ahead. Don't you see it?" This time it was Melinda who spoke and the car came slowly to a stop, still in the road. Porter emerged from that port of call, his sister right on his stern. They turned and walked back down the road for bit before turning into the woods, from where they watched the station wagon slowly pull away. Then they got on the road and continued to walk. Several cars passed them, until one stopped ahead and backed up to them.

"Hey, Porter," one of them called.

The car was full of boys who knew Porter, who were two or three years older than he. These roaring boys who lived with one foot in the void were an indigenous species in these woods.

For Porter it was the highest affirmation. He climbed into the front seat next to two boys, without so much as a look at Melinda, who had to get into the back seat with two other boys. At least they were making good time, Melinda thought, as they sped up US 25 past Mt. Vernon, Boone and Farristown. It was an expensive, foreign-made four-door sedan. The boys gave the Sherman pair sodas to drink and potato chips to eat and were in a festive mood. Porter began to shine in the reflected light of this boyish camaraderie. He actively participated in the laughing and talking and was, for the first time to Melinda's notice, something similar to happy, only with a bit too much of an eerie glow. His playfulness and his joking irony were actually appreciated, or seemed to be. And these older boys, who were popular in school, took a shine to his particular sparkle. Melinda could not help smiling and being happy for her brother and momentarily she forgot that neither her hawser nor her notch were connected to the larger vessel.

When they neared Lexington they passed many cars going in the other direction, one of which was a police cruiser. Melinda may not have thought about it but she had long since developed an instinct for storms and for the lull that precedes them. It was part of her instinctive service to the Sherman home and its inmates to possess this sense of the weather, Polish or otherwise. Just such a lull had occurred in the boys' car when the police had passed. Porter was making a joke at the time, not that he would have sensed any change had he not been. Melinda suddenly felt nauseous and told the driver that she was about to be sick all over the car and that he had to stop. The two were quickly let out of the car. She did get sick.

"Melinda, I can't believe you did this to me," Porter said. "I was having the best time and those boys liked me. They liked me."

"I didn't mean it," she answered. "I just got sick."

"You never mean it. But you still always do it. But I could have never believed you would do this sort of thing when I was having the best time of my life."

"Oh, Porter."

"Don't 'Oh, Porter' me. Damn it, Mindy. Damn you. Damn you. I won't be able to show my face in school again. Why do I always let you do this?"

"I am sorry, Porter. I am sorry," she said, and she let none of what little irony she newly felt show itself to him as the police car again passed them, this time going in the return direction.

"You're always such a, such a . . . little mother."

The idea of such a thing had never really occurred to Melinda but the new intellectual and emotional distance she had begun to acquire only on this trip gave her a fresh perspective. She also saw that may have been why she had undertaken this odyssey in the first place. It was why she calculated now that hitchhiking rather than her original plan of walking was worth the risk, because it would get her to her father more quickly, so she could save him. In fact, risk was now less of a stranger in the neighborhoods of her mind. She was quick to get her older brother back onto the road with his thumb out.

This time they were picked up in the north end of Lexington by a very old and rusting four-door American sedan, the kind which has duct tape somewhere or other, in this case holding some of the upholstery in place, and a door handle, and the rear-view mirror. It was driven by a quietly beaming elf of a man, about thirty years old, whose smiling eyes and buoyant demeanor practically infected the siblings with relief and comfort and a relaxed sense of joy. He appeared to have walked off the set of a movie about seventeenth century British sailing vessels and adventures, as if he were a caricature of the happy seaman. His blue gray eyes twinkled on either side of his pug nose, which had a bulb on the end, before rising to a flattened upper part and ending at the bridge in a crease of flesh just below his unsmooth forehead. He had jug ears and wide fat face with a pleasant mouth that was a little too small for the cloud of flesh surrounding it. He was broad in build and a bit shorter than average and he wore cut-off blue jean shorts and a blue sleeveless tee shirt. He may or may not have been wearing shoes.

If this were not enough to delight the big brother and the little mother in the back seat of the car, the companion of the smiling sedan sailor was a glittering and ebullient small child in the person of a softly voluptuous fair-skinned young blonde woman of about twenty-five years of age who, befitting her true self, turned around and kneeled on the front seat and faced the children in the back. Her softness was palpable to such an extent that it seemed to Melinda that if one were to poke her flesh with a finger and then remove it, it would leave an impression which would only return to its original shape and surface very slowly as if it were a piece of soft foam. Her blonde hair was teased and tufted and gave the impression of cotton candy. She was pretty in the way a doll was pretty, with a playfully pouty mouth covered in red lipstick, small, bright features and eyes far bluer than her male friend's. She wore a low-cut peach colored blouse and calf length floral print slacks as she pressed her breasts into the back of the front seat. The number of exclamation points and question marks at the end of her sentences exceeded those in the speech of most people and it seemed that her verbs came in only one tense, the present.

As they approached the town of Georgetown they passed the expensive European sedan in which they had taken their previous ride. It had been driven off the road, up the small hill in the roadside field of tall grass, as if it had left the road at a good rate of speed. Next to it, but still on the side of the road, were two police cars with their flashing lights on and more than one or two policemen seemed to be running into that field in pursuit of the car's previous passengers.

"Oh boy, Benny, those kids are in trouble, aren't they? We don't have to worry about those cops. No we don't! They have their hands full now. That's for sure! We get a pass this time," the playfully pouty red lips said, with the clear, rounded, high voice of a nineteen forties movie star but without any of that flatness or the pattering cadence. It was a child's voice in a woman's form. Benny slowed the car to a gentle pace and kept smiling as he kept the beer he was holding low enough to remain unseen by any persons outside the car. And then there seemed to Melinda to be a slight shift in the light as occurs when a small wispy cloud passes across the sun and there seemed to appear a few frays in the peach blouse.

"I get Benny out and he says, 'It sure is great to see you, Brenda, after all these months.' And I tell him exactly the same thing and we are going to up to Covington to get us a room. Isn't that right, Benny?"

The man being questioned just smiles and he pops a candy into his mouth and washes it down with a beer before he throws the empty can out of the window. It is clear much of his cheerful demeanor is attributable to Brenda, or perhaps to the sunshine and fresh air, or maybe to the candy and to the beer, another can of which he opens with relish.

"Well aren't you two the prettiest little picture! And you look so much alike," Brenda added. "Why you must be brother and sister! And you, young lady, must be up to some mischief, dressed up like a boy with that wild boy haircut."

"She is actually a hermaphroditic bank robber and she is my mother, not my sister," Porter offered.

"And this boy, he is a smart one, Benny, he sure is! He knows some real big words. We know some bank robbers, don't we, Benny? And this sweet girl does not look like any one of them. Your mother is no bank robber either, and a woman bank robber is one we would sure remember. Tell him, Benny."

Benny beamed some more and washed down with some beer another one of the candies that he had taken out of the little round plastic bottle with the brown translucent tint and the white childproof cap. The frays that had just become apparent on the peach blouse seemed to be matched by some that began to show on Brenda's face as they passed through the town of Corinth, and now it seemed that her soft foam form might have been poked a little too hard more than once or twice in a number of places.

"Oh, Benny, this boy is a real rascal, he is, just like you, Benny. Aren't you a rascal, Benny? I don't mean it in a bad way, kids. Benny is good and sweet. He just plain loves me! And he doesn't mind one bit that I make some money for us. Some of those men though, they are worse than rascals. But we are together now, aren't we Benny?"

By the time they had passed through Florence, Brenda had bubbled on about her man and his patience and forbearance and his sweet disposition. She also began to ramble on about how he was as a man with her, about how he was not like any of those other guys, the ones who act like they own a girl because they give her money. Benny just ate more candies out of that pillbox and washed them down with a few more beers and kept smiling. He was smiling the inimitable and limitless smile of a man for whom the walls that had surrounded that mouth for some time had just come down and whose grinning eyes had for some time only seen the shadow cast by those walls. For the little mother and her older brother, all in all, it was a pleasantly zany change of pace after their previous ride.

But now they had been dropped off at the iron bridge over the Ohio River in Covington and picking up a ride there would have been a problem, so they walked. Below Melinda, as she stopped and stared for a long time at the view, was a great deal of very brown water that had begun clear and fresh where it had arisen in West Milford, West Virginia and in Ashford, New York. It had run from that first place past the coal fields and coke plants and steel mills of the Monongahela valley, and from the second place down the mountains and through the forests of the Allegheny valley to form the Ohio River, with a line down the middle of it at Pittsburgh, on the one side a clear green and on the other a murky brown. As it came down from Pittsburgh it carried barge after barge of coal past roaring steel mills, passing between Covington and Cincinnati and under the feet of Melinda and Porter as mostly river and partly industrial effluence. Porter stood patiently and watched his sister as she watched the river for several minutes.

It was here on the iron bridge, here above that changed and changing river, here where getting to another far off place was merely a matter of floating, here at a collecting point below the watershed above, and here where the transition from south to north crossed an even more transitional current, that Melinda had the first of what she would later call her visions. She perceived another man yet unknown, one who was also a bridge to some new place. She saw him in the brown eddies and shadows or among the flotsam and the barges or drifting with the watercourse or clinging to the banks like the foam and in the reflections on the water. She did not know if he was living or if he was drowning, only that he was there with her at that place and time and closer to her than anyone she had ever known in her short life or, she believed, she would ever know.

The final ride came from a very nice middle-aged man who spoke gently and sang along to the Broadway musical songs on the radio and who insisted that Porter sit up front with him and that Melinda sit in the back. It was not long before Melinda began to seem invisible and Porter and this man were having a spirited exchange with singing and conversation and funny observations about the towns of Monroe, Franklin and Kettering, Ohio as they passed them. The man patted Porter on the leg and called him words like "devilish" and "sweet" and at one point it was even suggested that they let "the girl in the back seat" out of the car and proceed on their own. The little mother tug boat had not become completely detached from the larger vessel. The big brother told the man that he was "taking her on the Underground Railroad to escape her enslavement in the South," so their separation was avoided this time and they eventually arrived in Dayton, Ohio and found the father of the Sherman home and several other things they would have never anticipated.

A LAMBENT GREEN FLAME

The Harvard Party of the Century at the Owl Club had already started but everyone knew that the best parties at the club did not really get going until around midnight and Garth knew that this one would not get into full swing until the arrival of the one club member who, unbeknownst to everyone, had actually shot a man that very evening. He pictured how he would arrive, be surrounded by his friends, and retire to the back room with his prize where he would be feted as the one among them who could navigate the demimonde.

As he walked in the door several people proclaimed him with, "Hey, Earnest, it looks like everything worked out as you planned." Indeed, Earnest Dapple greeted him at the door and took him by the arm and led him to the back room, waving to the small crowd as he did.

Earnest had a genius that consisted of a number of skills that were all largely different kinds of an expertise that existed at the interstices between the public and the individual. He had a way of feeling what the crowd wanted to know and how to get to the bottom of it, of knowing all the ways that the public would most likely be able to understand it, and of knowing how to frame it in the one way he would then choose. He was tall and lanky, six-foot-four and only about one hundred and seventy-five pounds. He was a handsome, with a long nose, short hair and a high forehead and light brown eyes that sparkled. His clothes hung on him like they would on a hanger, loosely and stylishly, without any apparent effort. His demeanor was similarly relaxed and nonchalant, in a way that appeared studied or calculated only to those who had observed it closely many times over a long period. Earnest had a way of lying to a group of people so that they were not only convinced it was the truth, but also that it was they who had actually uncovered the story as if it were the facts. This facility of his was so pronounced that Garth was convinced that Earnest would become a politician one day. He was mistaken. Earnest was a born journalist.

In fact this quality of being born was, as it were, quite the warp and woof of these young men and women, what made them sparkle. The gloom of Boston extended well across the Charles River and into Cambridge such that it really was the true ivy of the place, clinging to the buildings where the ivy did not, deadening the leaden slice of sky that drooped over everything, affectionately hugging the souls who walked, studied, disdained or condescended there. In Cambridge the gloom was partly illuminated and minutely dispelled like candlelight in a fog for a few feet around each of the thousands of brightly glowing points of light that made their way from class to library, to club, to dining hall. Much of this luminosity came from this quality of having been born, in a manner that was not unlike the way that the entries in Burke's Peerage had been to the manor or to title born. Earnest was a born journalist and Preston was a born oilman. Elliot was a born hedge fund manager and Leonard was a born banker. Jimmy Chazerman was a born doctor and born the husband of a nice Jewish girl whom he had yet to meet (but whom he had always known.)

Even though the lately arrived gunman had never had his own bar mitzvah, Garth knew that he possessed what he had always simply identified as the belatedness of his tribe, which consisted of a sense of ironic detachment. Contained within this was a generally suspicious apprehension, which in addition to being an inheritance had also been communicated to him and refined by his mother's teaching. Garth's general suspicions of this trait were heightened when he saw it in others such as Jimmy, who manifested it in a less guarded and a more complacent fashion. Garth had always known that by birthright, Jimmy's beautiful girlfriend could only ever be to Jimmy little more than practice, or some pleasant and preliminary revelry such as that which Prince Hal had shared with Falstaff before inevitably assuming that to which he had also been born. Jimmy's exquisite gentile sweetheart had never known any of this until this very night, the day after Jimmy had been accepted to medical school and had planned to move back to his hometown of West Hartford, where his family awaited with the yet-to-be-discovered mother of his children. There had been a man to woman discussion at that point and Jimmy's willingness to ascend to the medical throne and leave behind his college playmate had been made too evident for her to ignore any longer.

Garth had long expected this but had yet to learn that it had just happened. He was still in that back room with Earnest and some of the other Owls, each of whom the marksman felt were more owlish than he, and each of whom had been participants in the pooling of funds for Garth's excellent adventure. The question was what to do with the drug, and the other question that only Garth knew, was what to do with the unexpected additional amount of it. Five of them had only planned for and had funded the purchase of seven grams, or a quarter of an ounce. The unlikely shooter had returned with four times that much. Garth had presumed that Earnest, in his inimitable fashion, had been able to discover that he had successfully concluded the deal in one way or another but he wanted to find out how he had done that and how much more he might know.

"Well, I think we should each get one gram to keep and that we should leave the other two grams here in the back for communal use by our little group of investors," Earnest said.

In an instant Garth knew that Earnest had somehow tracked down Ben but that Ben had not told him the whole story, only that Garth was coming to the party with the drug. This had given Earnest the opportunity to promote the story that he had set up the deal and that the friends and the party would soon reap the harvest of his effort, which Garth had actually expended. For less than half a second Garth considered somehow holding on to the other three quarters of the ounce, but he would not be able to discreetly make that measurement and he also had the idea that he would put a dent in Earnest's contrived story, so he pulled out the plastic baggie containing the entire ounce and laid it on the table.

"Well, I just say we sit down and snort the whole damn thing right here," Elliot said, "and get rid of the stuff so it does not haunt us for the rest of the party."

The added irony to this statement that everyone had heard Elliot repeat many times before was a wit beyond the normal and caustic self-awareness it usually contained. It implied and understood that if they were to follow Elliot's advice at this particular time it would either take several days or it would kill them. It would have been a cliché to say that Elliot Barker had an addictive personality and far more insightful to see that he was simply too vibrant and excessively vital for the world around him. This led him to be quixotic and reckless and a bit too welcoming of destruction, and not only his own destruction but also that of things which mattered to him. This dash and daring was blended with worldliness disproportionate for a man so young and it played around the edges of the brightness of his gray blue eyes. The effect was to make him quite arresting in a dazzling and fatal way. The handsome blond Elliot might try to run through a wall or leap out a window; or he might destroy a relationship simply because it was a more attractive or interesting thing to do than the alternative. He was actually slightly older than the others as a result of having taken longer to complete preparatory school, due to some suspension or expulsion from Deerfield or Exeter or St. Paul's. But he was also younger at heart. Garth and most of his friends would later prove to have been wrong about Elliot, in that they all had assumed they would meet at his funeral at some point in their lives. They had misjudged the resilience of his northern blood. He would instead, at numerous points in the future, accompany them to the funerals of several other friends.

After the smiles and laughs faded from the end of Elliot's remark, it was Preston who spoke next.

"Well, shit, I suppose we ought to let old Garth here keep all the extra, or at least a larger share of it since he clearly went beyond the call of duty. Or else we can all buy it from him."

The word "buy" in Preston's speech sounded like the single syllable that a sheep emits, the indistinct vowel sound was elongated. Preston Cobalt's voice was baritone, his blue jeans were worn out, his stature was on the sturdy side of average, his features were plain, his flannel shirt was rumpled, his boots had lost all their shine, his blond hair was more or less brown and his skin was a bit weather worn. He had all the look of an oil wildcatter, which is what his grandfather had actually been, but with quite a bit of polish that was never far under a dusty surface, as if he were a fine piece of antique American furniture covered by Aunt Millie's worn out home sewn Afghan blanket. The notion of buying things was never far from his consciousness, nor was a kind of fiercely individualistic sense of fairness that was especially keen as it was turned to his fellow Texan. There was also third Texan in the room, Preston's girlfriend, who was a lively and luscious slightly older blonde woman, apparently imported directly from some Lone Star state honkytonk for the purpose of accompanying him through the parties at Harvard and whose own role as a Falstaff to Preston's Prince Hal was as well known to her as it was to everyone else.

The response of Leonard Rock to all this was to simply have his peripatetic fingers in the bag of cocaine, flakes and powder from it falling from his nervous shaking digits to the table. There were also traces of it under his nose and elsewhere on his face. He was the anxious genius of the bunch, and had once destroyed the ego of a science or math major by calculating in his head the product of two three-digit numbers more quickly than the geek he had challenged possibly could do so on his calculator. In fact, this product simply had arrived in Leonard's mind. He just saw it. And this remarkable faculty would one day in turn help to make him more or less of a high priest of a great religion, the pantheon of which contained compound interest, treasury rates, arbitrage, discount to present value and what Leonard would simply call the "vigorish." His mind was a dark, tightly wound, curly and unruly mass, or that may have been his hair. Either way, his owlish intellect was matched by an equally serious bent toward all manners of escapism.

Garth pulled a small vial out of his pocket, took what he considered to be a gram out of the bag, and suggested that each of the others do the same before they would conclude the debate and consider the question of what to do with the much larger remainder. He excused himself as if to go the bathroom but instead walked into the large main hall where the dancing had begun and the gathered crowd was beginning to grow.

In that large wood-paneled and high-ceilinged room, lined with the paintings of the club members' avian predecessors, glowering down on the gathering, Garth first saw Parker Askew standing near the door to the back room. Parker was a born sucker and by this it is not meant that he was a gull or a mark or any of the characters that were born every minute according P.T. Barnum's colorful apothegm. It simply meant that if there were a general quiet, as there was not in this party atmosphere, and if one listened closely when Parker was in the vicinity, there could be heard the faint sound of sucking. He was a very small man with a large chubby boyish head and long light brown hair, but his most noticeable qualities were metaphysical and were in the ways that he spiritually resembled a lamprey or a remora fish but only if those aquatic creatures could manage a constant smirk while using the same mouth to remain fastened to a larger fish. For the last couple of years this piscine smirk had been attached to Janet Tarlton, a voluptuous, erotically charged and strange-faced woman who was considerably larger than Parker and to whom no one ever remembered speaking, simply because they could never get past the sneering eel.

"There is a lot of free cocaine in the back room," Garth said softly to Parker, following it up with a nod.

Pairs and individuals and small groups trailed into the back room after Parker and his host creature, because Garth had moved from them to others in the room and had delivered the same message. Soon there was a general thoroughfare passing back and forth between the two rooms and the quantity of the dancing increased in the main room as Garth watched, while the quality of it decreased. Several minutes passed before Elliot had sidled up to Garth and spoke to him without looking at him as they both watched the dancing.

"That was a good thing you just did," Elliot said quietly.

"Do you think, really?

"For sure, and it was also the correct thing."

"How do you mean?"

"Many times doing the good thing is also doing the right thing, or the effective thing. It was good to share the bounty with the party and not to let some few individuals reap an unearned windfall. And it was effective because it made the party better. And it put the brakes on our friend, Earnest."

"I guess that was my thinking."

"That Parker guy sort of sucks though."

"You noticed that?"

"Couldn't miss it. So what are you thinking now? Are you thinking what I am thinking?"

"She sure is very hot," Garth said. They were both watching Jimmy Chazerman's former lover dance with her new steady date.

"She apparently did not wait very long to find another boyfriend and she did not go far to find one. That guy she came with and has been dancing with is Chris Katookie and he is one of Jimmy's inner circle, one of his best friends. I guess she did not want to go very far to find a new man and maybe she figures it would hurt Jimmy to see her with his friend."

"That is unlikely. Jimmy was never really serious about her," Garth said.

"She sure is willowy."

"If a willow tree could be like a cat in heat, I suppose, yes."

"Pussy willow."

"Now, that is funny."

"Not as funny as her name."

"You mean Tabitha is a funny name?"

"No," Elliott said, "Tabitha Vivenda is a funny name. What is that, something out of a Dickens novel? It fits too well. The way she is built conjures up every word that is a synonym for lithe or lissome or supple. She is thin everywhere except where you don't want her to be. She is very much alive, more so than most women. I can see that feline thing you see in the way that she dances and in her green eyes and her tail of long brown hair. It is too bad she has already paired off with another guy."

What was to follow from this point was a long series of nautical maneuvers. Garth set sail on the dance floor at diverse times with several different partners but at each point his craft was really beating various tacks into the Tabitha wind. Sometimes he would take a close haul to starboard and pass near enough to admire the lovely form and extent of her superstructure. Or he would sail across the wind on a beam reach athwart her stern, and admire her magnificent transom from a distance. Sometimes, as he was tacking, the wind would change and he would get a lift that would bring him close enough to see how slim she was at her waterline, or a header would come and send him farther off, and he would be able to observe the entire craft and watch the ways in which she would trim her genoa and fly her spinnaker. Every once in a while something would happen that would require him to come about or jibe or simply run before the wind until he found a mooring at the bar at the end of the room. Sometimes this precipitating event would be that the sounding line would show him in too deep water, but more often it was something more of a martial nature, as well as a nautical one. In those instances the two marines posted in her topsails would rake his deck fore and aft with their fire. Garth's mother, who had no facility for metaphor and even less for sailing, would later describe this particular phenomenon with a question that was as much applicable to Tabitha as to another woman who would enter his life at another time.

"Why do you always fall for the ones with the crazy eyes?" she would ask him many years later, while fingering her necklace.

Those eyes of Tabitha's, which would fire upon him and strafe him from forecastle to quarterdeck and scatter his mates and midshipmen, were like none he had ever seen. There lay behind them a lambent green flame that hinted at more thought and feeling than a single soul should contain. He was a long way from the point in time at which he would have to field his mother's question, but the notion that something wild and irrational lay in wait behind those eyes did not fail to occur to him, or fail to attract him. As if from some ancient galley out of Byzantium, they launched a Greek fire onto the deck of his ship, he being the infidel Turk. It would then distract his attention and divert his efforts from everything else, from his own movements, from his observation of the carnal eloquence of her dancing, from the perfect proportions of her silhouette, from his very thoughts. He just simply had to get out of their range once he had too long taken their fire amidships and he would then have to repair to harbor.

Garth possessed a brand of wisdom rare at his age that was again perhaps a part of that ethnic belatedness but was apparent to him as a kind of certain knowledge that there were many subjects about which he knew very little. He had only a little of that bravado of assuredness that his colleagues mistakenly had on so many matters. One topic on which he was sure he knew very little was the whole business of women, and that meant that he actually knew more than most of his buddies, who thought they knew a great deal. Garth had three sisters and a mother and his hard-working father had been largely absent from his upbringing. So, basically living alone among four women, the opportunities for him to have become ever more confused and in the dark on this question were numerous and manifest. And on the matter of this specific woman, he was fundamentally in irons and unable to engage his rudder. So it was an opportunity for him to mentally refit at the dock while drinking some grog.

He had plenty of unsettled subjects to meditate upon as he stood at anchor by the bar. He remembered his evening just a few hours before, in that Boston neighborhood, and how he had reacted. He recalled instances prior to this evening, moments of indecision and inaction. He considered his own story, his own history with women, his relations with his mother and his sisters, Agnes, Florence and Bella, his previous girlfriends, his best friend who happened to be female, his ties to them all, ties of respect and reliance on one hand and ties of affection on the other. Tabitha was a leading and constant subject of this rumination. Thinking of her and her recent release from the indenture of Jimmy Chazerman made him consider his relationship to her eventually in the same terms that he had thought of Ben when Garth had been standing on that street corner a few hours ago, thinking then of his grandfather and his gun. And the only change of circumstance he could foresee in his bearing toward this woman involved action, more or less along those lines.

He also considered Elliott, who had clearly kept a weather eye on Tabitha all the while she had been with Jimmy and had moved on to Chris. Normally, Elliott would have been the first to make a move. It could be that Chris had belayed him as he had said, but there was also another possibility. Elliott tended to stick to the prep school girls for whom his dash and daring was something totally new and different. There was something about the dark and sensual Tabitha that held Elliott back. It was not Chris. And on the surface, Elliott and Garth and Tabitha and even Jimmy were capital ships, or ships of the line, while Chris was a brig or a sloop or a caravel or a cutter. And Tabitha's glances at Garth had been the turning of her telltales, showing him which way the wind really blew. Contemplating the birth of Chris, Garth knew what Elliott must have been not mentioning, that Chris had been born vicarious. He had been born to stick close to shore and to set his sights no farther than his friend's girlfriend and never to set sail that way until the sailing was clear. And Tabitha must know this as well.

Garth's lack of understanding had been his sea anchor. Now it was time to set sail and drop his kedge and make a sharp turn. He saw Chris go into the men's room and he followed. Garth had stashed the gun but it was figuratively in his pocket as he approached Chris, who was standing at the urinal. He turned to see the taller, athletic Garth standing sideways and looking at him. There was no bluster to Garth, no menace or sneer, only an open sincerity that was engaging and direct.

"We both know, Chris, that you are not in her league. It was one thing to pine away for her while she was with Jimmy but it is another thing entirely to try to match what she is out on the open water. We both know that it is just wishful thinking on your part. It is time for you to withdraw from the engagement, don't you think? And while I am here, allow me to suggest that if you have a problem with what I have said that I may decide to simply tear off your head and use your neck as a urinal."

As Garth left the men's room and returned to the main hall he could sense those fell green female eyes on him but he did not return their gaze. He moved slowly toward the bar and watched as Chris hurried out of the bathroom, cast a glance at him, looked once at Tabitha, and then left the party. What Garth could not have known was that at that instant those green eyes flashed something new and different, something primal and feminine, something very much along the lines of an intuitive understanding of what had just happened in the men's room. And then Garth looked. The eyes now had lost some of their fire and had become as if they might have been if they had been used to looking at Garth for months, up close and a lot. There was something homey to them as Garth walked up to her and she and he began to set sail across the dance floor together. The wind fairly sang in her rigging. They were both on a lift of a close haul and her gunwales came close to the waterline as her keel began to hum with that unique sound of her reaching hull speed.

They danced like that, unaware that most everyone else was noticing them, until the party waned in the wee hours of the morning. Garth offered to walk her to her dorm room and she invited him in to her single. Garth came into her room and quietly talked with her there for a few minutes and refused to do more than that. He could not see himself making a move. But he had something to say.

"You know, Tabby, I have always been amazed by you. I always felt you were unapproachable. I still do. You are just so alive. You have an alluring excess of vitality. I have also found you to be unbearably physically beautiful. So, I wonder if you would do me one small favor. I am about to leave. I think we have had a nice evening and I would like it to end as it has been.

But before I go I want to take with me one last mental picture. I want to go home with the image of you naked, in my mind."

"What?" she said. "I am not sure what you mean. You want me to undress for you, before you go?"

"That is exactly what I want."

"That is sick and weird even for you, Garth Teller. There is no way I am going to do that."

"I understand completely," Garth said, still looking at her. "I had a great time and I will see you later." And he started to get up. But once again there was something cat-like about her as she was suddenly up, and quickly and quietly she was then in front of the door.

"If I undress for you, you will still just leave, right?"

"Absolutely," Garth said. He had truly meant it. He sat back down.

So, she began to undress for him. She was swaying almost imperceptibly as she unbuttoned her blouse. Garth was in awe of how trim and long her waist was compared to how high and large her breasts appeared in her bra. She was already barefoot and it was no problem for her to slip out of her tight slacks, unzipping them and sliding them down her long legs. Again, Garth felt a kind of reverence at the contrast between her thin waist and slender shapely legs and the fullness of her bottom. She was that willowy tree, laden with ripe fruit. She slowly removed her lingerie and the effect of that was equally as spiritual and religious. Garth's aesthetic wonder had overwhelmed his lust and the truth of his unusual original proposition was never shaken. He had been miraculously granted his impertinent request and he would have no trouble leaving. He thanked her and he stood up and started for the door. She stepped in front of him once more.

"Wait a minute. If you leave now after I have done this for you, I will be insulted," she said.

No skillful use of metaphor, nautical or otherwise, could do justice to the hours and days and weeks and months and even years that followed, except to say that respecting the capital ship Tabitha, Garth would never fully learn the ropes. Garth's mother had proven to be correct well in advance of her question/assertion. He had indeed fallen for a girl with crazy eyes. Only crazy was not exactly the operative word, even though there would be times in the years to come when that word would be the very one for which he would reach. It was not crazy, not really. It was simply the first time, but not the last, in which Garth would fall in love with a shine, with a glimmer, with an excess of vitality, with a lambent green flame that hinted at more thought and feeling than a single soul should contain, with what a neurophysiologist would later diagnose as a mental condition. The shine with which Garth would fall in love in later years would be different. In this first case, he had fallen in love with attention deficit disorder, specifically with the hyper-focus side of it, which was at the time trained upon Garth and which would later be replaced by distractibility and inattention. But he would not figure that out for many years.

The remainder of the winter and the following spring would find Garth sailing in the equatorial climes of Tabitha's unusually and intensely focused attention, in which it would appear to him that no man had ever been loved so much or so attentively and which would inspire and augment his own love. Following the spring would come graduation and for Garth that would mean a trip down Interstate 95 to Yale University to visit his best friend, Eakin Lambert, who unfailingly provided him a memorable experience, one worthy of a work of fiction.

THAT RESPONSIBILITY WAS FELT PRIMARILY BY THE PERSON WHO SPOKE OF IT

The Sherman children arrived in Dayton, Ohio and quickly found their way to the hotel that housed the teacher seminar where they found their father. As is certainly no surprise, they experienced a different reception than Melinda had expected. What Porter had expected was not to be known. There was however no astonishment expressed by the father of the Sherman house. He showed that he had expected to see them. What Melinda's pitying eyes saw there in her father and in her brother and in the situation, and how much of the whole truth of the matter she saw, lies shrouded in the many mysteries of childhood, of family relations, of the opaqueness of the souls of others and of ourselves. It is enough to know that she aspired to be different from those two, to feel responsible for them as much as for herself. She was inspired by her love and by her devotion and yet there was that growing new mechanism in the little mother that contained a severity that was allying itself with these gentler feelings at this moment, and more often than not. The odyssey that she had embarked upon with Porter had been precipitated by a fiercely protective urge she had felt toward her father which had been inspired by the one end of a phone conversation she had overheard, much of what she heard having been spoken in alarming Polish.

The happiness expressed by their father upon their arrival was not in seeing them, but in the opportunity to show them the respect he had received from his fellow teachers. The surprising unhappiness he expressed was for seeing his children. They had asked for him at the front desk and had been shown to his room.

"I have been held in some high opinion here, Melinda," he said, although he was looking at both of his children, "I really have. I am not so much of a lost cause. I am one of the chief persons here. You go out and ask the teachers here who has been honored, and they will tell you it is your father. They will tell you about the certificate they gave me and that I am not to be pitied. Here let me show you."

His voice died away, as if he felt it was a pain to speak or if it was uncomfortable for them to hear him. He showed them a piece of paper. It as a certificate of service denoting that William Sherman had been designated "a teacher of note" by the regional teachers' seminar, and that he had been a teacher who had given many years of excellent service to his students.

"You see, Melinda, here is something by which I will be remembered. Here is something of which you may be proud," he said, almost bursting into tears. Melinda embraced him. She observed him with something more than her usual devoted interest. It seemed that he was more worn down, more tired and lost. He seemed to perceive as well that she noticed this and that he begrudged her for it.

"You two should not have come here. I am extremely sorry that you did. It makes me look very bad. And it will cause me no end of trouble."

"We had quite a trip to get here," said Porter. "We got a ride from a lady; she was crazy, father. She really was. And we got a ride from a guy who seemed like he just got out of jail. And there were some boys from my school. They were very nice to me. They may have been driving a stolen car. And a man gave us the last ride who was very fine to me but not to Melinda."

"You should not have taken the liberty, Porter. It will not do me any good," William Sherman said. "What are you looking at, Melinda? Am I that pathetic? Do you not see how I have been honored here? I am doing fine. I need no pity."

Melinda had never felt the need to help him more than she did right at that moment. She felt it even more than when she had heard that phone call and was in fear not only for his well-being but for his life. She knew she could not open that subject now. She knew there were many things she did not understand, and would never understand, and that one of the foremost of these, as is the case for all children, was the relationship between the two adults in her home. She just continued to hug her father and to administer to him. She kissed him lightly on the cheek and then she stood back from him and looked at him and listened.

"I am sorry," he said, "so sorry. I am not sure what to do now."

It did not matter how young she was, or how small, or that she was a girl, or that she was the youngest person in the room, or how weary she was. It did not matter how much the trip had scared her or that she was now shedding secret tears, not for herself but for her father first and for Porter. She knew now that she was in essence the oldest of the three in all things but precedence, that she was the only one who bore all the anxieties and fears. As she looked upon their father now she was just as devoted and loving, but no longer as childlike or admiring.

Porter looked forlornly around the room. He turned his eyes downward. He was not sure he could deny some level of guilt in this enterprise, or what his implication in it may have been. His connection to the events was mysterious to him, and he was not sure whether or not the whole thing might have been his fault, or if he was not entirely responsible for the proceedings that led to his father's despondency. He kicked the carpet gently with his feet and continued looking down, and then he looked at his sister and looked at his father. Before long he was relatively certain that the entire catastrophe might have been solely his doing, and he was almost resolved to drag himself before the police and the proper authorities, and deliver himself up to justice and to be punished if that was what was found and was required. Melinda put her arm around Porter and hugged him as the two of them stood before their father. Porter found his entire attitude change for the better with this welcome and familiar bodily contact.

During this small physical exchange between brother and sister, Melinda noticed that their father had been more observant of her and attended to her with something more than his usual interest. He had an exquisite and delicate sense for his own dignity, and an acute sensitivity for perceiving slights against it, so much so that he often saw them when no one else might. He rarely missed them when they occurred, or when something that was closely related to a slight might have transpired. The minor change he noticed in Melinda's perception of him had not gone unnoticed. He felt that as she was looking at him she saw him as being more worn or tired. In fact he felt changed, more so perhaps even by her look.

"Melinda, what are you looking at and what causes you to look at me in that very particular manner?" he asked. "Do you think that I am not looking well?"

"I think maybe you look a little more tired. That's all," she answered.

"You are mistaken," he said and then he paused almost as if he had forgotten what he had intended to say next. "It is Porter who is not looking so well. Your adventure has not been very salutary for him. I recommend that he lie down immediately and rest."

The statement had the power of suggestion and Porter was beginning to look not only tired, fearful, and nervous, but weary as well. Their father addressed him.

"Porter, you look very feeble. I do not find you looking very well at all.

You are clearly not fit for all this traipsing over the landscape. The idea of it distresses me and I can see it has taken its toll on you. You should be more careful. You both should be more careful."

"I guess so," said the young man, who had no wish at that moment other than to not be displeasing to anyone.

"You have been wandering too much, and across two states. Your constitution is not fit for it. It is a wonder you can stand up."

After this, Porter began to sway and would have fallen down if not for the restraining grasp of his smaller sibling, who said, "Maybe we could get something to eat and then we might want to think about getting home. Someone should probably call Mother."

That responsibility was felt primarily by the person who spoke of it. Melinda went to the hotel room phone and placed an outside call to their home. Her mother was very reserved on the other end of the line, and only asked if they might be returning in the morning on the bus. Melinda answered in the affirmative.

They took supper in the hotel restaurant and were a long time over it. William Sherman lingered over his meal and only became somewhat animated when one of the participants at the seminar would walk past their table to stop and to offer greetings and to ask if his two companions were his children. He greeted each such person, and was particularly warm when his certificate was mentioned. Melinda always provided the answer to that one question. The father often referred to Porter's supposed condition and expressed a kind of unpleasant pity toward the boy. Porter was struck by these occasional references to the point that each time it happened he would let his drink or his food dribble from his mouth a little bit. Melinda was watchful, and on two or three occasions she noted that their father would stop eating and would simply look at her. Melinda somehow knew at that moment that she would remember years later how she felt that night at dinner and how he had looked at her. She kept up a cheerful manner and spoke to him about his certificate and she was dedicated to the effort of not giving either her brother or her father any cause for concern or unhappiness, but in that effort she was aware that her father seemed to require her to be like that while at the same time he also seemed to resent it.

Eventually he warmed to the prospect of telling his children more about how he had been honored by the seminar as one of the teachers of merit, and how he had addressed one of the smaller groups as part of a panel on managing an elementary school class. They slowly finished their supper and returned to the hotel room, which was a standard room with two queen size beds. Porter wanted to watch television for a little bit, so he did that while Melinda read to her father from the Gideon's Bible that she found in one of the drawers. She read chapter six of Ephesians to him, that children should honor their father and mother and that their fathers should not provoke their children, and in so doing each party was honoring the Lord. The two of them settled into their old way of being with one another and soon they were peaceful. Not long after that it was time to go to bed and they washed up and their father climbed into one bed and Melinda got into bed with Porter and held onto him until he fell asleep, then she herself entered the witch region of sleep.

She dreamed that night of another man, and not the same man of whom she had a vision in the waters of the Ohio River, but a different one, in fact a different father, one who was bold and strong and never weary even though he was quite a bit older than her real father. He was an outdoorsman and had a Western or Southern accent. She could not tell which, but it was clear he was from a different part of the country. She awoke from this dream to the light of a dawning day shining through the curtains of the hotel room and onto the pictures on the wall, giving each picture a different look as the sun's light moved over them down the wall. The faces in the pictures would thusly smile in the brightness and frown in the shadow, or appear to sleep and stare while their looks would move from passive to active or be shaded in a kind of desolation. Soon Porter was awake and the father too. They washed and dressed and went to breakfast, which was cheerful and bright. Porter was happy and made little puppet characters out of the rolls and forks. Then they got on the bus and went home.

Melinda remained steady and confident on the bus ride home and kept the spirits of her father and her brother at a high level. It seemed that her cheerful demeanor actually helped to propel the bus home at a more rapid rate. Porter made jokes about each point on the return road at which the two children from Ceylon had experienced an adventure. Melinda only really paid attention to what was outside the window when they crossed the great river. She never wavered in her sunny deportment even though a part of her did dwell on the suspense and anxiety of what might happen when they got home.

The topography of the part of Ohio around Dayton is relatively flat and open. This yields to rolling green hills on the northern shore of the Ohio River. Across that river and deeper into Kentucky, the fields and rolling hills rise over a thousand feet to evolve into the northern and western foothills of the southwestern tip of the four hundred and eighty million year old Allegheny Mountains, so in a way, the Sherman family bus journey that day was a trip back in time. The United States Geological Survey would have described this short voyage as one beginning in the physiographic region of the Great Plains, then passing through the Appalachian Plateau to end in the physiographic region known as the Valley and Ridge portion of the Appalachian Mountains. The great British musicologist, Cecil Sharp, simply described this last region as Southern Appalachia and in the early part of the twentieth century he recorded over two hundred songs that differed very little from the way that they had been sung and played in England hundreds of years earlier. To Sharp and to the United States Geological Survey and to the eyes of Melinda Sherman the mist-filled valleys and hollows were simply repositories, places where much older elements and forces could become lodged. The three of them rolled deeper south into Kentucky and soon they were home, in London.

Melinda and the Sherman men went into the home. The lady of the house was there to greet them. Both she and Melinda were extraordinarily composed and relatively indifferent to each other and to what they each knew of the events that had preceded the expedition and the return trip. They took little heed of one another and certainly took no more than might have been expected on any other day. It may have been that Angelina Sherman dreaded what Melinda might say or do, and might fear that Melinda knew this. She may have pursued Melinda with a dogged and secret attention, one that knew no rest or flexibility. It also may have been that Melinda would not have behaved any differently even if there had been a thousand watchful eyes upon her. She may have been strengthened in this by her youth and by her attractiveness, or maybe her usefulness to her brother and her father was a fortification for her, or perhaps her love for all the members of her family, now all safe and at home together, prevented her from seeing anything at all that could be construed as cold or cruel or implacable. It may be likely that she simply treasured being at home and on familiar ground with her mother and father and brother, or that something in her had changed, and had made it as if she were now stronger and older.

Whatever changes had actually occurred lay beneath the surfaces. Everything in the home ostensibly was as it had been before the trip, until such time only several days later when the Sherman home was to receive an uninvited visitor, one who would have an impact on the family and its future. It was not known by any of the Sherman family members at any time what had precipitated the visit and, in fact, this uncertainty was formed and half formed into unspoken opinions, which later came to lie within the practiced indifference with which Melinda and her mother came to view one another. These speculations may or may not have been strong enough to have found expression in another family or in another context, but half of the members of this family were capable of little more than indifference in regard to such things, while the other half were capable of a bit more than indifference.

What none of them knew was that the cause for the visit that was to transpire was what had occurred subsequent to the arrest of Porter's schoolmates who had taken a Mercedes Benz for a joy ride. Acting like little hardened criminals who are inured and immune to the interrogating techniques of the police, these boys had practically worn out their lips and tongues providing the authorities with the details of how each of the other boys had been the initiating mastermind and the driving force behind the grand theft auto. In those details, the names and actions of the Sherman children were inevitably mentioned. As if this alone were not enough to generate an imposing authoritarian visit of one kind or another to the Sherman home, the stories told by the youthful joy riders were augmented by a rambling report from an alarming woman, or an alarming report from a rambling woman, regarding the escape from indentured servitude by a pair of Ceylonese children, matching the description of the pair that had been picked up by the boys in the Mercedes.

SALAMANDER EXCOMMUNICATION AND GOLF CART ELOPEMENT

Garth's mother had often said that Eakin Lambert should have been born a boy. But Garth knew better, because he knew that in terms of what should have been, the world would be a better and more interesting place had all the boys been more like Eakin Lambert. She could ride a horse like few boys could and when it came to arrows or guns or speaking her mind, she was about as straight a shooter as could be found in the length and breadth of Texas. Those verbal arrows of hers that unerringly found their mark had the characteristic of being so well understood that they would often generate a great deal of apparent misunderstanding. The number of shafts in her quiver was augmented by an insightful and inciting intellect. A heart that had little regard for risk, but had an aesthetic appreciation for the beauty of a blaze, provided the potent thrust of those shots. It could be aptly said that some of her very accurate Parthian shots were made with flaming arrows.

A recurring theme in the plays of Henrik Ibsen is the sprite, the imp, the troll, and it is like nothing that is assumed about those things in popular culture, but refers more to the elemental Norse impulse that describes the part of us that wants to get there sooner, wants to set fire to things, enjoys going a bit berserk, and wants to go around problems rather than confront or solve them. It dances and drinks and drives fast and makes friends of monkeys. Its smile means more than anyone else's. The normative social impulse is to cage such a sprite, to limit the effect of it on the stolid and sensible world around it. The crowd works to do this for self-protection because that evocative smile is infectious, everyone loves to watch a fire, in our elemental hearts we were meant to drive fast, we all would love to have a hirsute homunculus home boy, and because chaos would result if the infection were to become a pandemic and everyone were to become such trolls. We love that sprite and identify with it. And that is the problem.

Eakin was a bit more of that particular imp than most people. And while those same people chose with high moral purpose to see the problem more than they felt the love, for Garth it was simple. He just loved her. There was never any problem for him with it, not even when Garth was excommunicated from the very expensive summer camp to which his parents sent him, for reasons due to the figurative marksmanship of his friend, Eakin. This love was never anything more or less than the love between a sister and a brother and, in fact, Eakin was more of a sister to Garth than were Agnes, Florence or Bella, his actual sisters. For one thing, Garth's sisters were six and eight years older and five years younger than he was. Eakin and Garth had been in the same kindergarten class and elementary school classes, had grown up among the same neighborhood friends and were sent away to that same summer camp, and even to the same large coeducational private preparatory school in New England, where she was captain of the girls' soccer team and he was captain of the football team. They were to only separate, if that may be the word, when she elected to attend Yale and he chose Harvard. All of this was so unusual or so coincidental as to seem like fate or a fairy tale, but none of those unlikely circumstances were any more improbable than the aforementioned excommunication, a term which makes more sense, once it is understood that the summer camp in question was one with a specifically religious essence, that being that it was the oldest and largest and most famous and most expensive and the only summer camp created in Texas for the purpose of giving a summer camping opportunity to the Jewish children of that state and the American southwest.

The Ricochet Hill Ranch had been founded only a few years before Garth's birth, in order to provide this opportunity, which had been denied to these same children by many of the other regional ranches and camps that would not accept them, simply for being Jewish. The founders of Ricochet Hill could not adequately or sincerely express their purpose if they too were just as exclusive, so at each session there could be found in the roll of the campers one or two children who were not Jewish. In one of the two summer sessions every year, for almost ten years, those very campers always were Eakin and Garth, although he was only not Jewish as a social matter, and his mother was very much so. Eakin's mother and her father were Presbyterians and were path-breakers, which made them not unlike the intrepid founders of Texas or its many other current inhabitants, except that the Lamberts were making new paths which were more socially unlikely in Texas than they would have been in New York City or Boston. Eakin was always given the broadest and most liberal parental tutelage so that she was the first student in the local elementary school to listen to the Beatles and to attend class in tie-dye dresses, which caused the very social ripples that were the secondary object of her parents' efforts. Their primary impulse was to make their daughter aware of the fact that there were very many different kinds of people in the world, and even in Texas. As a result few of Garth's contemporaries were as "different" as his best friend; the observation of which he was constantly being informed by those same contemporaries.

The tall, wide-faced, very blonde, athletic, blue-eyed tomboy with more than a few freckles and a very frank mode of speech, who preferred the company of Garth and the other boys over her fellow female campers at

Ricochet Hill Ranch, was more than just slightly different than those other girls at the camp. It could also be said that if any of those other young ladies had ever embarrassed as many of the boys as Eakin had by out-shooting, out-playing, out-swimming and occasionally out-scuffling them, they would have manifested enough of a difference that such a girl's parents would have quickly withdrawn their daughter from the camp and its perverse influences. As these and other of Eakin's dissimilarities had been introduced to the administration and staff and clients of the Ranch at the time when she and Garth had only been six years old, they had been accommodated. By the time the two of them were only a little older, they were more or less one of the attractions of the place, like the fishing and swimming lake, the stables, the archery range or the campfire. Each friend in his or her own right was an object of curiosity and discussion, a tall and athletic and attractive half-Jewish boy who was not observant and who had an odd taste in best friends, and that very friend who was an unreconstructed Gentile force of nature. But neither was so much an oddity as was their friendship itself. It was a strong and lasting bond that made perfect sense inherently, but did not lend itself well to interpretation, much like the very strongest and most insufferable marriages. But they were just the very best of pals and there was never any hint of romance between them, even though each was attracted to members of the opposite sex.

Members of the opposite sex were attracted to each of the two friends and this gave rise to the incident that was to cast into stark relief one of the many ways that the two friends' enrollment in that camp was consistently emblematic of their own friendship, the way they were close to each other and not like the people around them, the way in which they were often misunderstood or understood too well, and the way in which their friendship was defined as much by the smaller differences between the two of them as it was by their greater similarities. Each of the pair was bright and athletic and self-confident and even a bit iconoclastic, and one of the many reasons they loved one another was that the boy manifested this last quality with a kind of subversive charm that was actually rather politic while the girl, as has been said, was fond of flaming arrows.

Eight-year-old Rachel Rosenthal was inordinately fond of salamanders, so much so that her bedroom back in Port Arthur, Texas, contained salamander stuffed animals, books about salamanders, salamander slippers, posters depicting salamanders among other amphibians, a salamander toothbrush and salamander bed sheets, all purchased at some cost and found at some effort by her parents who wanted to encourage their young budding naturalist. It was on one evening in Garth's sixteenth summer that young Rachel had decided to take an unsanctioned late evening excursion alone along the shores of the Ricochet Hill swimming and fishing lake in order to look for salamanders.

Prior to that summer, Garth and Eakin had already spent one school year away at their private preparatory high school in New England, and as it was their final summer of eligibility to be at the camp they had each become a little bit jaded about its many wonders. While this was something that Garth approached with a certain social sensitivity, taking it upon himself to seem more like a counselor than a camper, for Eakin it was a curtain call, an encore for all the things she was at heart. For little Rachel, it was to become a naturalist lesson for which she would have been much better prepared in several years.

What drew her decided attention on that evening on that walk had definitely been the color of certain salamanders but what it, poor Rachel was unable to report later with any certainty, may or may not have been, was what had been customarily referred to in the Rosenthal family as an unmentionable, and it was specifically Garth's unmentionable, and it was doing something more or less rather amphibiously in the general neighborhood of the face of one of the older female campers. This same female camper, it was more accurately reported later, had formed a youthful romantic attachment to the tall, athletic, good-looking young man and, seeking an advantage over the several other girls whom she saw as competitors in this contest of the heart, had consulted his best friend, Eakin, as to what to give him so that he might like her better.

Eakin's response to this had been what might be expected by anyone who knew her. She directly challenged the basic intellect and understanding of the questioner, stated something along the lines that Garth was just a guy, and mentioned that this contender for his attention and his heart might simply consider doing something amphibious with Garth's unmentionable. This was conceived by the tall blonde sprite as a flaming arrow that she fully expected would immediately set fire to the ears and head of the other female camper, but which was met with less of a shock than with the kind of belatedly arrived at and simple understanding that is depicted by light bulbs over the heads of cartoon characters. It is almost pointless to report here that repercussions were felt as far away as Port Arthur. As Rachel's rambling reaction was as widely disseminated as it was confusing, there were also ramifications in Abilene, Lubbock, Beaumont and Brownsville, or basically in every nice home that housed people with the inclination to send their children to the Ricochet Hill Ranch, and who could afford to do so at a cost that was three or four times as much as was charged by other camps, which was how the Ranch managed to attain the effective religious exclusivity that it could not, and would not, otherwise or openly express. Even all this might not have been enough to generate specific and precipitous action upon the part of the Greenbergs, *monsieur et dame*, the worldly and tolerant founders of the Ricochet Hill Ranch, had not the older female camper in question been their daughter, Rebecca.

Garth and Eakin were sent home summarily. The Tellers and the Lamberts were disappointed and embarrassed, with the possible exception of the Teller grandfather. For both, the group of campers who were there that summer, and for those who heard the story in later summers, many of whom were to become leading citizens all over the Lone Star State and other places in America, the two friends were notorious to the extent that the story would come back to them on and off for many years afterward in the form of a surprised question. They simply and laughingly referred to it half incorrectly as the time they were excommunicated, and it was just one of the many such events that would come to characterize what would be their long relationship. They would even joke about it on this particular visit, the one that Garth was making to see Eakin at Yale, adding to it the possibly apocryphal detail that all of the amphibians were also subsequently and summarily banished from little Rachel Rosenthal's bedroom, starting with the salamander toothbrush.

There are some people who can never get enough of blonde beauties. Yale, to even the most casual observer, is on the order of such a blonde. This contrast with the gloomy place from which he had come was never lost on Garth, since he could never misplace the commanding view that every vantage point provided of the fair-haired and soaring beauty of Yale's Harkness Tower, or of the picturesque golden stone library and gymnasium which also rose above the plain of New Haven as if the entire campus were a kind of southern New England Salisbury cathedral. There was similarly a tall and flaxen openness to the architecture of Yale's student housing, since each building had its own great inner courtyard and elevated tower. Eakin was not the only blonde student there and seemingly to Garth almost all of them were blond; the Asian and African American students seemed blond. This fair-haired quality of the Yale men and women added significantly to that feature of the school seeming to be like the focal point of an English cathedral town. A visitor's eyes were drawn to them after passing through, and then standing on the periphery of the college among the drab and shady inhabitants of smaller and duskier buildings that girdled the university. There was a literal and figurative vacancy to these structures and people that simply forced Garth's attention to Yale and its students. It was completely unlike the importunate and hurried surroundings at Harvard, and which made Garth's university seem like just another urban patch in the greater Boston metropolitan quilt. There was only one thing to New Haven, and that was Yale.

Garth walked from the train station, up Chapel Street past the surrounding buildings and people and, as he crossed the Green, he began to confront all that blondness. On his way to Eakin's upperclassmen residence, he decided he would cross through the Old Campus, the large open quadrangle containing the freshman dormitories, where he was then literally run down by a golf cart. Such conveyances travel almost silently with their electronic motors, and this one seemed to have been aimed right at Garth, as it had so clearly failed to miss him. Lying sprawled upon the ancient and hallowed flagstone over which many American Presidents had walked, Garth suddenly began to notice that the golf cart now seemed less silent.

"Why don't you watch where you are going, Teller? Or don't they teach you that at Harvard?" Eakin said from the driver's seat.

Garth slowly began to pick himself up off the walkway as he remarked to himself that despite the fact that he had just been assaulted, and could have been wounded, he did not feel the slightest shred of pain or anger or injured pride or any of the normal reactions that might be expected, nor was this the first time that he had reacted unremarkably to such a mugging. He was simply happy to see his oldest and dearest friend in her element and being mostly who she was, and in this case, hauling a fully functioning keg of beer and a handsome young blond man with a pair of crutches. Garth recognized Dick Trent, who had been Eakin's boyfriend for that last several months, and he also recalled that Dick had been recovering from a knee operation and was on crutches. Since Dick had been a football player and since the Trent family had been a Yale family for generations, and since Dick's father had been the last Yale football player to lead the nation's colleges in rushing yardage, the athletic department had given him the use of a golf cart in order to get around campus more easily. Enter Eakin and the keg of beer, one with a long flexible distribution hose that could refill cups even as they were in the front cup holders.

"Hi, Dick," Garth smiled.

"Hi, Garth. Sorry about that," Dick smiled back.

"Not to worry. This sort of thing has been going on for years. I am used to it by now."

To Garth's way of thinking, Dick was not unlike Yale itself in the quality of resembling a rural English cathedral town. In this instance though it was not Salisbury but something more along the lines of Wells or Lichfield, and the cathedral was not Dick himself but was unmistakably and ineluctably what Garth could clearly see was Dick's love for Eakin. As this was something he and Garth more or less shared, it was impossible for Garth to miss seeing it, nor was it something with which he could fail to have great empathy. There were differences though. For instance, Dick also loved her in the way a man loves a woman, and Garth had treasured her with the resonance of time, having grown up with her. But the two young men had a palpable and lively camaraderie, which was based upon loving this oddly singular and preternaturally lively young woman. It was the differences in this love that allowed them to react to one another without jealousy. Garth had the longer view and this is how he could see Dick's love as Lichfield cathedral, and what he saw as outlying in Dick's personality was in comparison rather squat and dull and not at all of the high quality of his feeling for Eakin. In fact, this soaring and magnificent emotion seemed to arise astonishingly and in a way that seemed not to be reinforced by the surrounding buildings of Dick's personality. Garth had long tried to examine what it was that typified these more numerous, drab and low-lying structures that composed the cincture of Dick's abundant affection. He had considered that it was a kind of vacuity or a superficial quality or perhaps it was slow-wittedness or blandness. And though there were elements of these and other features that seemed to best describe the phenomenon, none covered all the bases quite so well as to describe these psychological structures as united by a kind of youthfulness. Dick was youthful and he always would be. Eakin would always be young at heart. There was difference.

"I suppose I should help you get up," Dick said, "but I think it will be easier for me just to pour you a beer," as he did just that, using the long hose from the keg and a cup in the holder in the front of the cart. "Easy" was also a word for Dick, Garth thought. It was very easy for Dick to accept Garth into his world. It had not been coupled with suspicion or resentment or even the kind of prejudice that Garth would occasionally still sense in some of his own classmates. Nor had it been the kind of treacle-laced condescension with which certain overt Christians or liberals might have embraced someone who was different from them. It simply was the grace that had been inherited from a couple of centuries spent at yacht clubs and board rooms and beautifully hollow Episcopalian church services. It was the graceful view accorded to wealthy Americans of English descent by generations of having seen things from the top. Garth felt that he was engaged in the same way that Dick or his ancestors might have taken a turn in the stock market or a failed business venture, with aplomb and a certain good cheer. These same ancestors hovered silently and invisibly at Dick's shoulder at all times, or that is the way that Garth observed it.

Finally getting up off the ground and sitting on the back of the golf cart next to the keg, Garth was spirited to Eakin's off-campus apartment where he learned that Dick had fully recovered from his knee operation but that he and Eakin had held onto the golf cart and the crutches mostly for their amusement. Garth put his backpack in the living room of the apartment and the three of them went to dinner at Dick's club, Mory's Tavern. Garth again noted how unusual it was that Dick and Eakin looked like brother and sister, from the same slight gap in their top teeth to their build, blond hair and occasional freckle. Dick was also, at five-eleven or six foot tall, only an inch or two taller than her. So, the three of them sat down to eat: Eakin, a young man who appeared to be her brother, and one who was her figurative brother.

At one point Garth laughed out loud, perhaps too loudly and with a certain hint of discomfort and Eakin glanced at him with a look he had seen before, the one that seemed to pass right through him.

"Oh, no," she said and smiled, "something is up with you. I can tell. You have been weird on the phone for months. And now I have it. You're in love again, aren't you? Our boy, Garth, is in love again, Dick. I should have known. This happens to him every couple of years. Like clockwork. It's that latest girlfriend, isn't it, that Tabitha person? I knew it. I knew it."

"What can I say?" Garth asked. "She is part of my existence, part of my self. She is in everything I see and hear and say and feel. These Gothic buildings around here are no less real to me than she is right now. She is all that is good in me and she makes me a better man. She is the embodiment of every graceful dream I have ever had. Her presence and influence are always with me."

"That is exactly what you said the last time. No, wait a minute. It is not exactly what you said. You said something else the last time, what was it, sophomore year? Oh, you said that you loved that girl irresistibly, that you loved her against reason, against peace, against promise, against hope, against all discouragement. What was that girl's name? Oh, I remember. Her name was Specter Void. Yeah, that's right. What a folly that turned out to be."

"Perhaps you ought to be a little less hard on Garth," Dick intervened. "After all, a little romance never hurt anyone."

"That is easy for you to say. You were not here when I had to pick up the pieces. It turns out that this woman was all charm and no farm. She could shoot a good handwriting. But there was no story. She was all yack and no shack. She had grown up in a strange house from a baby, and had her wits honed by sharp motherly intrigues. Her better instincts had been suppressed by masked paternal sympathies that were untoward impostures. Then she had learned at Miss Porter's School how to say to all the young men, or any other person, exactly what he wanted to hear, and to say it pleasantly. Our boy, Garth, here mistook that for genuine attention and he fell in love."

"Miss Porter's School?" Dick jumped in again, "Hey, I know that girl. Her name is not Void. It is Boyd. And her first name is something else. It is a family name, or something, like Draper, or Cooper."

"I don't want to go into it," Garth said, "because it was too painful."

"Yes," Eakin said, "it turned out that his sweetheart, Cooper or Specter or whatever her name was, could not say 'No' to any of these boy's innocent requests. She would simply just not show up where she said she would be. It was like falling in love with a very agreeable ghost; right, Garth?"

"This time it is different," Garth asserted. "Tabitha is intensely real. She holds me on a pedestal, and she makes me feel more loved than I have ever felt."

"And that's not a warning sign? Okay, I am not going to say anything more. I have to take your word for it and accept what you say. Congratulations, Garth. I am happy for you. What do you say, Dick?"

"I say, when do we get to meet this young lady, Garth?"

"Hopefully, the two of you will meet her when you come to my graduation, which is a week after yours. It is next weekend. By the way, is the whole Lambert family coming into town for your graduation? Have you met them yet, Dick?"

"I hear they are coming into town. And, no, I have not met them. My family will be here. It ought to be a great gathering, the Trents of New Canaan, Connecticut and the Lamberts of wherever the heck it is in Texas that you two are from."

"And what are your plans after college?" Garth asked.

"My plans are not as set as the two of you seem to have yours set. That is for sure. I think it is totally weird that you two will be trading places, that you will come here to Yale Law School and that Eakin will go to Harvard Business School. Your two lives are oddly parallel, like in a book or something."

"It sure is something," Eakin chimed in, "especially when you consider that almost no one from our part of Texas ever leaves it, and that we both went to Andover, and then one of us went to Harvard and the other one to Yale. It is pretty interesting, the way Garth seems to be following me around."

"That's rich," Garth laughed.

Yale's graduation occurred two days later. The most recent former President of the United States spoke at the ceremony. The convocation of the assembled Trent and Lambert families occurred at a rented side room at one of the nicer restaurants in New Haven, a couple of hours after graduation. They had planned to have dinner all together. It was something that Garth would retain for the rest of his life. He was sitting with Eakin's parents and grandparents and her brother and sister and all the Trent family when a waiter had called him into another room to take a phone call. The call was from Eakin.

"Garth," she said, "you have to do me a favor. Trent and I are already in northern New Jersey, and we are on our way to the Outer Banks in North Carolina. We have eloped. You have to tell our parents that we will not make it to the dinner."

"You what?"

"We eloped."

"What am I supposed to tell them?"

"Just that. Add whatever you want. I know you, Garth, you will say something clever and assuring. You're good at that. See you later. Wish me luck."

Luck was what Garth needed. The Trent family had no idea who he was, and would not take the word of a stranger on such an important and unbelievable matter. And the Lambert family was quite familiar with Garth and Eakin, with the pranks and troubles in which they had combined in the past, so they refused to believe him at first. Garth himself was not convinced. The whole thing was too out of the blue. Dick Trent's father was a successful businessman, and he reacted with the same compassionate understanding that was particular to that class of individual. The former college leading rusher forcefully demanded to know what was really going on, and was placing a call to the police just when Eakin's younger sister confessed that Eakin had shown her the marriage license the night before, and that she had not really believed it herself until Garth had made his report. The atmosphere in that room was like a minor dust storm on the Texas prairie; small bits of twigs and leaves and dirt flew high and around in small vortexes, obscuring any clear vision until they settled down onto the stark ground in a smooth blanket. After the calmness had arrived, the families and Garth had a very quiet dinner. There was tranquility, and a silence that was generated by the understanding that these two very different families were now related, and by both the increased familiarity and the genteel distance that such a realization entails.

That image of the dust storm described Garth's general inner reaction to the experience of the visit itself, from getting off the train to getting back on it. This often defined all his visits to see Eakin. Nothing was really calm until he managed to find himself alone. As he mentally composed his version of the story, he found that his powers of observation were limited and his ability to describe it was stopped. In his attempts to understand and to describe, as well as in the experience itself, something that was inherently depressing, but only slightly so and in that peculiar way of depression which is disguised by exhilaration. It made him smile, an arch and knowing smile, such as Eakin always gave him to have and of the kind that meant he knew this particular adventure was not exactly over. Eakin's precipitous actions were rarely conclusions. They were more often catalysts.

THE GOVERNMENT OFFICE
TO REPAIR EVERYTHING

The visit that was soon to occur at the Sherman home and change their family life had its origins long before this day. It had its beginnings at the very formation of the American nation and the founding of the Post Office, the United States Mint and the War Department. The original Articles of Confederation and Perpetual Union, which loosely bound together the thirteen former British colonies in America from 1781 until the ratification of the United States Constitution in 1789, left almost all governmental functions to the various individual states. The first very major problems faced by such a fractured nation were the mustering, pay and pensions of the armed forces, the standardization of the currency, and getting the mail from one state to another. Large-scale unrest among the Revolutionary War veterans, many of whom were not receiving pensions from their respective states, provided major grass roots support for a stronger federal government and the Constitution that was to create it. Businesses and commercial interests supported the standardization of currency, so that goods could easily be bought and sold across state lines. And to this day an American living in a small town in Georgia can get her private letter delivered to her uncle in a small town in Alaska for only a handful of pennies, something no private carrier would ever do, and something that had as great an appeal to every early American as it does today.

As everyone obviously knows, the federal government was outrageously successful in these endeavors since it inevitably could do no wrong, and only ever acted in the best interest of the American people, and moreover, because it always operated with tact and skillful precision. It was acclaimed as such, and was equally and as famously successful in all other endeavors that it was later required to undertake by the consensus of the American people, based upon the principle that the government is the only proper instrument for fixing any problem. This growing apparatus finally evolved into the great and wonderful agency that was to make a visit upon the Sherman family of London, Kentucky, namely the Government Office to Repair Everything, and specifically it was to send a representative from one of its departments, that is, the Family Division.

The ancient Romans were so uncivilized as to have never evolved beyond those types of government structures that existed only in the early history of the United States, which is why there are so few people speaking Latin today. As these ill-informed Romans spread and established their ignorance across Europe, North Africa and the Middle East, they brought the inhabitants of those places their overwhelming unawareness of the nimbleness and the acute skill of government to solve every problem. For the citizens of their far flung empire and for hundreds of years, these same coarse Romans had only been able to establish excellent permanent roads, the miracle of plumbing and sewers, a reliable and universal currency, architectural practicalities such as the aqueducts, museums, schools, the rule of law, sanitation, public order, peace and prosperity. It never had occurred to them the numerous ways in which the government could skillfully repair the problems that might exist in every single corner of their society, particularly within the homes of the families that inhabited it.

Those same ignorant Romans had an immoral and archaic concept or philosophy that they called *paterfamilias*. They called it that because they spoke only Latin, and because they were also ignorant of the way in which modern minds would justly recoil from such abhorrent words such as patriarchal, paternalism, and patronizing, and from all other words arising from the corrupt Latin root word for father, itself an outdated notion. Modern minds rightly and completely reject the idea of *paterfamilias*, because it gave the father of the Roman family sole power over all the other members of that family, even the power of life and death. The Romans also mistakenly paid attention to the second part of that concept, the Latin word for family, which was a thing so incorrectly sacred to their way of life that it was the one territory into which the unwieldy Roman government would never be allowed to intrude. Even the power of life or death over family members was pointedly not granted to the government, giving rise to the situation in which a son who was guilty of the worst crime against the state could not be tried by the government. His fate would first have to be determined by the leader of his family, the father. In the case of Lucius Junius Brutus, the government would do nothing until he expressly permitted the prosecution of his sons for treason. For these brutish Romans, the smallest social and political and indivisible unit was the family, and the Roman state would not cross the threshold of the family home under any circumstances. The civil and social contract was between families, and the father was each family's representative with the state.

Modern society has moved well beyond such clumsy and barbaric Roman principles and recognizes that the government can fix all the most particular problems, even those within a given family. This is such a universal truth that there is no debate upon the issue even between sides that normally are at odds on most other questions. American conservatives have recognized the duty of the government to cross the threshold of the family home in order to prevent a man or a woman from doing something in his or her or their bedroom that may be offensive to God. Liberals were so equally certain of the government's skill that they decided that only the government could determine the manner in which parents may raise their own children. The Government Office to Repair Everything had evolved to be able successfully fix problems with commerce, with health care, with what substances individuals might put into their own bodies, with admissions to private schools, with accommodating disabilities and with any number of other pressing difficulties. The professional politicians of both parties in the House and in the Senate and in the various state legislatures had at various points addressed the pressing needs for the Government Office to Repair Everything to repair issues related to protecting consumers, to educating children, to growing forests, to managing Native Americans, to looking after marine mammals, to saving the failing passenger railroad system, so that it very much had its finger in every private and public pie. Any and every thing even remotely in need of being repaired had at one point or another become the subject of protracted deliberation and action, thus not only giving the politicians something to do but also giving them various places at which to softly land once they were finished with their careers of deliberating.

For significant and understandable reasons that would forever remain unknown to the Sherman family, they were to receive a visit from the Government Office to Repair Everything, Family Division. Since the various subcommittees of the House and Senate would not be convening within the Sherman living room, and since a federal District Court would not be holding a hearing on their front lawn, and certainly since the principle that the government is the only proper instrument for fixing any problem could not magically manifest itself within the Sherman home and effect a repair to the problem, some other manner of skillfully and tactfully fixing the Sherman family would have to be implemented. As is most often the case, such an implementation would necessarily occur in the person of a government employee. In this case, the result of all this history and all this deliberation and all this social evolution was that this individual would be a one Brenda Cooter, twenty-three years old and a recent graduate of Somerset Community College, Laurel County Campus, London, Kentucky.

Brenda Cooter was an expert on abuse. She could sniff it out. Everything she had learned or seen or experienced in her six weeks on the job, in her two years of classes at the community college and in the two and a half years she had been a bus driver had prepared her for ferreting out child abuse wherever it might exist. And it was everywhere. After all, this was Appalachia, the fertile ground from which sprang thousands of country music songs about all the myriad ways in which a family can be broken. Brenda caught the scent of this abuse in the grocery stores, on the buses, in church, at soccer fields, at the movie theaters and practically everywhere she was certain it existed. And she could smell it in the Sherman house even before she got to the front yard. She just knew it was there. She knew it when she looked over the police intake forms, the one for the arrest of the joy-riding boys and the other for the statement of the strange middle-aged lady, even though the police officers in each case had specifically designated that they saw no reason for an investigation into the Sherman children and their parents. The police did not know half of what Brenda Cooter knew, and neither did the courts.

Melinda knew something too, and it was that she did not like Ms. Cooter at all from the first instant that she saw her. To Melinda's view, the social worker was a sullen and thickset and sulky woman with medium length, wavy, black hair. She even held her notebook as if the people about whom she had written in it had given her some personal affront. She did not have an agreeable air to her at all, not in her bespectacled gray eyes or in her thick unsmiling mouth or in any other aspect. She was as apparently heavy and disconsolate in the ways of her mind as she was in the manners of her body. Her comprehension, and even her complexion, were sluggish and awkward. And despite this stolid and impassive physiognomy and presence, Melinda sensed that there was something about her that was a false report, something that was a swindle, something that was an untruth and, as is always the case, something that was a lie that she told first to herself, and then which she foisted upon those with whom she dealt. All this caused Melinda to want to put herself forward in the best light, and the first thing she thought to do was to go upstairs and wash her face and brush her hair and put on a new clean outfit. Such is the way in life in which our greatest insecurities and our sincerest efforts are often most engaged for the benefit of people we despise.

The representative of the Family Division of the Government Office to Repair Everything had stated her purpose at the outset of the visit, which was that it was her intention to interview each of the family members and to determine what should be done. She handed her card to each adult, leaving William Sherman utterly confused, more so than usual. But Angelina Sherman simply became more reserved and reticent than was habitual. Brenda Cooter determined that she would interview Porter first. She had an affinity for boys even though she did not like them, and she knew that they could be less guarded and more forthcoming, and that the meeting with Porter might prove useful to her in subsequent interviews. She took Porter into the kitchen, and the parents stayed in the living room while Melinda went to clean and change. Sitting in that kitchen, they were two people who could not have been more in contrast. One was set up for theology and the other for frivolity.

"So, Porter, I understand that you and your sister went on a little adventure," she began.

"It is not uncommon," he answered, "as such things were constantly called for when we lived in Ceylon. We had been brought up suffering much travail and worked and lived among an abject and groveling race, laboring in the tea fields and in the ivory mines where we were stinted of education, liberty, opportunity and the very necessities of childhood. This may have been the third or fourth time my sister had directed us to decamp. Each time she has dressed as a boy and showed the daring of a man."

"I think they started calling that country Sri Lanka only a few years ago. And ivory comes from elephants, young man. So, I think you are pulling my leg."

"This only makes the ivory mines all that much more oppressive and dangerous. Such labor caused me to be utterly wanting in normal emotions and warm remembrances, and they make it unlikely that you will be able to work upon me in the way you have other young men to whom you are accustomed. Those elephants, as well, are ill-tempered, not knowing whether they are Ceylonese pachyderms or Sri Lankan ones."

"But you felt you had to flee this house. Is that right?"

"No. There is an unmistakable difference between this house and what we had been used to in Ceylon. Our new parents here are wonderful. But it is difficult to suppress such harsh memories of our life on that mysterious former colonial island off the coast of the exotic subcontinent. I can hardly think of those remembrances and not find that I am cowed by them, while my sister, well, she is much stronger than I. These flights have always been of my sister's planning, so there is very little I may add to your understanding of them."

"I find it hard to believe that a fourteen-year-old boy operates at the direction of his eight-year-old sister. I still think you are pulling my leg."

"Are you sure she is really only eight years old? Is it possible that you do not know that we are really twins? We communicate by telepathic pictographs. And her plans and directives arrive in my mind already fully formed. One minute I am playing baseball and the next minute I am on the road."

"So am I to believe that you cannot give me any reason for your most recent flight?"

"Not any non-Ceylonese reason, no, I cannot. But my sister very well knows what we are talking about right now as well as if she were sitting in the room with us. So you may begin your conversation with her exactly where this one leaves off. The twin thing, you know."

"I see. This entire investigation is of very serious matter, more serious than you seem to care to know. You may leave now, Porter, and please send Melinda in to speak with me."

It is a miserable thing to feel ashamed of your home. This already sharp feeling takes on a particular zest in the heart of a child, yet it is something that every child at one point or another comes to feel in some way. For most children it is more or less a rite of passage, and occurs in adolescence or later, when friends are brought home, and even then it is often a confused or an indirect feeling. Melinda felt it sharply at that instant and it made her miserable, if for the ingratitude of the feeling as much as for the perceived embarrassment. Home had never been a pleasant place for her, but it had been sanctified by her loving care for her brother and father, as well as for her mother, whom she felt needed her protection at this point. None of this was anything that she wanted to be detected by the stolid and disconsolate woman sitting before her. All of her joints and muscles were stiffened by the perception that she was under close observation.

"Your brother tells me that the idea to run away came from you," the young woman said to her, more in the form of a question.

"We did not run away. We just took a trip," Melinda said, without any show of emotion.

"He also says that this is not the first time the two of you have run away," the unsmiling one said, as she wrote "flat affect" in her notebook.

"Well, he also told you that we are from Ceylon, so you know what that is worth."

"Why do you think your brother flees into the realm of fantasy?"

"I think it might be just as fair to ask why you do not see that he likes to joke. He is a fourteen-year-old boy. He also likes to play in the creek and read comic books."

"How do you know he said anything about Ceylon?"

"It is certainly not because we communicate without words as if we were twins. I can tell you that much."

"Is Ceylon some kind of substitute or escape from his home life? Does he see your father as the foreman of a plantation?"

"We both love my father and he is an exceedingly gentle man. My mother is equally good to us."

"So why did you run away, and why does your brother say it was your idea?"

"We never ran away. We wanted to see my father get his certificate at the teacher seminar. It seemed like a good idea at the time. We are just kids, after all."

"Was it your idea?"

"I don't really remember. It seemed like something fun to do. No harm came from it."

"Thank you," the social worker said, as she made some more notes in her notebook. "You can go into the living room. I will be right in there in a minute to get your parents."

When Brenda Cooter walked into the living room, she saw that Melinda was sitting next to her father and that she had straightened his collar and helped him to his glass of water. Brenda thought again to start with the male half of the next duo and for the same reasons she had chosen to interview Porter before Melinda. She took William Sherman into the kitchen and began her examination. She left the three other family members in that living room with its same old faded floral wallpaper, its same worn furniture, and an added cool vapor.

"Why do you think your children would leave their home and embark on a two hundred mile journey to Dayton? Was it at your bidding?"

"I don't know what you mean. I am confused. I did not force them to make the trip and I would have forbidden it if I had known about it."

"Do you forbid your children to do a lot of things?"

"They are children. There probably are many things they should not be permitted to do. Maybe, I think, perhaps that hitchhiking should be one of them. They certainly have as much freedom as other children in this day and age."

"You mention this day and age. When you were a child, Mr. Sherman, were you abused in any way?"

"I certainly don't think so. I am not sure what you mean by that. I am confused by the question," the father of the Sherman household answered.

"I think you know what I mean. For instance, did your father ever strike you?"

"My father was an accountant. He collected books and butterflies. From what I remember, he loved me very much. He was born at the turn of the century. I do not believe he can be held to the standards of the current day. I think I do not remember him ever striking me in anger. And I have no idea what this has to do with anything."

"Child abuse is a very serious matter, Mr. Sherman. A great many people had been abused as children. The list is long. It happens all the time. We aim to stamp it out. Do you know of any victims of child abuse, like perhaps your wife?"

"My wife grew up in occupied Poland, which was a hardship all its own. I think about that and I realize I cannot get my mind around it. It must have been a painfully confusing time and place," he said as he paused. "The only victims of child abuse that I think I can recall are Rudyard Kipling and Virginia Woolf."

"Were they childhood friends of yours?"

"I think you could say that Kipling was, but only indirectly. He wrote *The Jungle Book* and other children's tales. I never read Virginia Woolf until I was older. You see, they are authors, ones I am sure you know. You probably were not thinking along those lines, so you were perhaps as confused as I am."

"Well, I am not confused about this. If they were abused, that was wrong and should have been stopped. In this day and age, we would have not let it happen."

"And perhaps then the world would never have had *Captains Courageous* or *Kim* or *The Common Reader* or *Orlando*, I guess."

"That will be all, Mr. Sherman," she said to him as she scribbled in her notebook. "You may send in your wife."

William Sherman may have been uncertain as to what to think about what was going on or as to what he should say, but the former Aniolek Bol was not. She was the only person in the Sherman family who had a degree of certainty that was close to that of their visitor. Porter had no idea perhaps of even what was going on, and Melinda only had her suspicions. But to Angelina Sherman, this visit in which the Government Office to Repair Everything had crossed the threshold of the family home was just another instance of the projection of state authority and not all that much different than visits she had personally witnessed, made by representatives of the governments of Germany and Russia. She knew what Brenda Cooter knew, and that was that such a visit was never made without a reason, and that if there were no reason for the visit, it could not be justified.

"I understand that you were born in Poland, Mrs. Sherman," she began.

"I was not born a fool. I can tell you that much. And that has been an issue for me because I have always been able to detect what other people have tried to hide. I might have had as calm a life as the fools seem to have, otherwise. I have always known that when people seem to be kind to me, they are often only patronizing me, and apparently open and warm feelings are really pity or condescending superiority. Others may be fooled by a sweet temper or by affection, but I know to be watchful among pretty smiles and kind looks."

"So you are a careful woman? The record here seems to show that you were married for well over ten years before you had your first child."

"I have had to be careful. My husband has a way of treating me with consideration and affection. That has always been a cause for concern and a reason for watchfulness. This has never been more the case than when I have been in a bad mood or have suffered some emotional disturbance. At those times he has always been most solicitous and says I have an 'unhappy temper,' from my experiences in the old country. I have always had to be very wary of such deceiving behavior. But in the end, I became pregnant with Porter anyway."

"So, tell me how your husband is with your children."

"This is the most alarming part. He ostensibly does everything that he can to support and to improve the love they feel for me. He leads them to me and coaxes them to share with me and gets them to tell this or that to their mother, to let their mother know something they think or that they did that day. He would tell them that their mother would know better what to say or to think or to do about some question they have. This was designed to show them that somehow their relationship to me needed his support, while their relationship to him was stronger. In their innocence, they would twine their arms around his neck, or climb on his lap in that chair. And when I would see that, it would cast me into a black and despondent mood and he would increase his efforts and seem to comfort me and would try to get the children to do the same."

"I think I am beginning to see, Mrs. Sherman. Thank you very much."

At the conclusion of this exhaustive investigation, Brenda Cooter told the assembled Shermans that they were now a G. O. R. E. family, that they were in the register, and that the findings of this office would soon be made clear to them. The report was to follow. It was to express the absolute certainty that the stolid and disconsolate social worker had felt from even well before she had begun the investigation. The problem in the Sherman family was where it always was in such cases; it was in the *paterfamilias*. Brenda Cooter was going to stand this folly of the ancient Romans on its head, if it were to going to be the work of her entire career.

William Sherman was found to be suspected of child abuse. The problem was not clear enough to rise to the level of requiring that he be removed from the home, but it was decided that regular and timely visits from the Government Office of Repairing Everything, Family Division must and should be made, in order to resolve the issues that existed within that family. And there would be no shortage of soldiers to undertake this task, since this agency has numbers of employees and their name is legion.

William Sherman was to compound his problem by making use of his right as an American to remove this issue from the frying pan of the bureaucracy, and place it into the fire of the local legal system. He had not the experience or understanding of an attorney, so he did not know that the law is a very sharp razor indeed, an expensive one to operate and which is quite uncertain in its application, far more noteworthy for its ability to cut and to slice than for its always carving in the right manner or even the correct creature. He hired a local attorney, whose skill and deep concern for his client was successfully able to publicize the case, but did not even get the barest attention of the judge who did not read the filings, and who only saw before him the government on one hand, and a local attorney on the other, and such a one as was unsure of the issues, the law or even the name of his client. So it was this client, Mr. Sherman, who received the very close shave. The publicity, however, was able to grant the father of the Sherman house a permanent administrative leave from his job as an elementary school teacher. Melinda gained a couple of lessons from this, one that would have a bearing on what would happen much later in this story and another one which would make an immediate change in her.

WHERE THE SINCERITY TRULY LAY

Dick Trent's and Eakin Lambert's elopement was followed by the sequel that came to be known by Garth and his best friend as the shotgun wedding. It was as if they had been Lydia Bennet and Mr. Wickham and had run away on an illicit and licentious adventure, and that Dick Trent's father then did what Mr. Bennet would have liked to have done, and that only Mr. Darcy had been able to do, which was to bring them back to be married properly in a church before either reputation could be irreparably damaged. It also had its aspects of a true shotgun wedding in which Dick might have seemed to have been forced to marry Eakin after having got her in a family way, even though she was not so, and although whatever force had been used had been applied not by the father of the bride but by that of the groom. In any event, Mr. Trent had obtained time at Yale's famed and ancient Battell Chapel and the two recent graduates were married again in a proper Episcopal ceremony and at some cost and only less than a week after they had eloped to North Carolina.

This scheduling meant that Garth was required to miss their shotgun wedding and that Eakin was unable to attend his graduation from Harvard. Although she was to be consistently present in his life, she was to have a tendency to miss some of his life events but this would never surprise him. He would also not see her that summer in Texas, since she would not be returning to live with her family but would simply move to Boston with her husband

and remain effectively in the New England sphere of the Trent family. They would still be only two and a half hours away from one another by train or by car, in their respective graduate schools. And Eakin would suddenly have the use of a car, which was a factor of that aforesaid compass of influence, and was a reward for acceding to the demands relating to the appearances regarding their matrimonial rites. It was in consideration of this affectionate care and maintenance that Garth knew would come in the direction of his friend from this family and from her husband that Garth decided to take one more step. He arranged to meet with Ben Dessous one more time.

"I am hoping you could do me one more favor," Garth said over a beer in a tavern in Cambridge.

"So, this is what this part of this town is like," Ben said, looking around, "but do not think of it, Garth. I more or less owe you a favor, or perhaps several."

"I am not sure about that. I am certain that I acted out of a kind of self-interest that night. And I certainly received a great deal out of it for myself."

"If it was indeed 'a kind of self-interest,' and I am willing to believe that it might have been, then it was of the enlightened variety. And I don't have to be all that astute in order to sense that you seem to have improved in some way."

"Have you always spoken that way?"

"What way, the way all your friends also speak?"

"Yes, I guess so. I am sorry. Maybe I was thinking that since French was your first language . . ."

"That I would speak as if I were any other African-American man?" He smiled.

"What you just said is an example of what I mean. You just used the subjunctive mood."

"Which in English is not even necessary, but weren't you just saying I had started out learning to speak French, which in St. Croix is really a brand of Creole?"

"Well, I am getting sidetracked. I had noticed it the night we met and had the sense then to say nothing. Now, I would like you to look after a friend of mine who is coming here to graduate school in the fall."

"What's her name?"

Garth stared at him, then spoke. "I was going to ask you how you knew it was a woman, but I guess you figured that out based on the fact that I implied that I would like you to be a little bit protective, so I will do no more asking like that."

"Yes, if you were to abandon that line of questioning and of thinking you would achieve certain economies of expression, as well as avoid the obvious social pitfalls."

Garth was still staring, but less intently. "She is very important to me, and I would like to know that there is someone on whom I can utterly depend, if there should be an issue."

"And since she is obviously not your girlfriend, you will not be in close touch with her nor will you be the one to whom she would turn. She must be a very close friend. So then there must be some other impediment, a boyfriend perhaps."

Garth said, "Actually, it is her husband."

"Well, I suppose we both know what you really think of him. And perhaps he might also be jealous of how close you and your friend are."

"That is not really the case, surprisingly. He understands that she is more like my sister and that we are close because we grew up together and were raised more or less as siblings. My own girlfriend, on the other hand, is jealous of her and always will be. So, that is another impediment. And she will also be here in Cambridge at least for one more year, since she is one year behind me in school. When I return here, it will likely be to see my girlfriend, and not my other friend."

"I see. Men are more or less oblivious of one another when it comes to women, or at least they can learn to be that way, while a woman will never fail to take significant notice of another woman's role in her man's life, even if that other woman is a sister or a mother. There is something else too, in you asking me to look after this friend and not at all after your girlfriend, even during the times when you cannot be around. I assume it is that your girlfriend would not be able to get her head around me, while your friend will be quite able to do that. I assume that has something to do with why she is your friend in particular, and why she is most likely your best friend. She is like you in the way that you are different from all these other Ivy League boys, including the one I assume that is married to your best friend."

"And that difference is not only noted in your words to me," Garth said, "but it is proven by you saying them. It indicates that I have had the instinct for which your words now give me complete understanding, and that is that you are exactly the right man for the job."

"That was the smartest thing ever said to me by a white man who speaks only one language," Ben said wryly. "And your friend's name is what?"

"Eakin Lambert, and even though her first name is pronounced like 'aching,' without the g, it is actually spelled e-a-k-i-n."

"That would actually be a surname probably handed down from some relative of Scottish descent. Rest assured, Garth. I will look after your friend, Eakin Lambert. Count on that."

They shook hands and confirmed their agreement in the unspoken and unheard terms with which they had learned they could communicate that unusual evening several months prior to this meeting. Later, Eakin would joke with Garth about his actions on her behalf, teasing him for thinking that she might need a protector. In many ways Texas is more American than the rest of America. Its people fought for its independence more recently than the rest of the country, and had more recently been a place of pioneers. It was partly this bold and autonomous Texan element in Eakin's nature that would permit her to immediately see the value in and accept the presence of an African-American man with the two facial scars and the Caucasian features and who had may have personally experienced his own death on more than one occasion. The other parts of her that were closely related to what made her different from other Texans would also play a role, since she had risen well above the position taken by Garth's classmate and friend from Texas, Preston Cobalt. He had not invited Earnest Dapple to join all his other friends in flying down on the Cobalt family's oil company's passenger jet to a graduation party on the family's private island on the Gulf of Mexico, saying that it was because the family's "servants would not understand." Eakin deeply valued individual worth and could see it behind skin of any hue.

Now Garth could begin to prepare for what was to be perhaps the most unreservedly fascinating phase of his entire life, law school. This was largely attributable to the fact that every single individual law student would prove herself or himself to be extremely and wholly fascinating in his or her own right. They were not only fascinating, they were fascinated. They were fascinated by every case they were required to read, by each of the law professors in every one of their first year classes and by those subjects, by the very heft of the law books they were required to carry, by the law itself, by the fact that they were at Yale, by the prospects of being vastly successful lawyers, by the briefs they would have to write and the legal arguments they would have to make, by the tests they would be taking, and mostly by the endless and eventful and involved discussions they would tirelessly conduct among themselves on each of these things just mentioned and on all the other details and minutiae relating to the law school. It was as if all of

Garth's humble and self-effacing doubts that he had, which caused him to question even the possibility that he was perhaps more worldly-wise than other people, could be obliterated simply by taking a look around him in the law school library.

Then again, there was something about being less of a striver than most of the other law students who were able to get into Yale Law School by having perfect records and getting perfect grades at their respective schools that made Garth slightly less than completely in awe of his own accomplishment. This was also the way in which any former Harvard undergraduate might come to view graduate school at Yale, a point of view which was fortified by the presence of Elliot Barker in Garth's first year law school class. Though Elliot had been born to finance, his path to it was going to be through law school. This was either a tactic of delay or it was an unorthodox approach in much the same that his having been suspended from private preparatory high school had been both. His presence was to make an important mark on Garth.

Garth had settled upon the idea of law school quite specifically as a delaying tactic, since he was yet unsure what it was he wanted to do with the rest of his life and he saw law school as the logical extension of a liberal arts education, which it was in a sense since it touched upon the subjects of commerce, crime, property, trade, taxes, public policy, government and many others. He would work as hard at it as such an approach demanded, knowing all along that he never felt that his future was intimately tied to his performance in law school. He was not sure what he wanted to do or to have as a career.

Elliot's approach to law school was different, reflecting his peculiar attitude. He had none of Garth's compunction but he had a bit more resolve. Garth always felt a little bit guilty and disappointed by his own feelings of seeming superiority. He was ashamed that he felt that he looked down upon the bulk of students who stood transfixed by the sublime nature of the legal education they were to receive, and by their own exalted state in relation to it. Garth wished those people pleased him more and he felt he was wrong that he did not like them better. His guilt about his feelings of disdain was the source of his compassion and his empathy. He felt much like what he thought he had read in Walt Whitman, that the strongest self and the most ardent lover of the self must be the most likely to embrace the other and to be the most compassionate toward the crowd. Elliot was quite at home in his disapproval. He lived in it and did so with a certain dramatic touch that allowed him to appear jaunty and ironical and out- wardly a part of the social structure, while he managed his elemental and essential disdain by seeing law school largely as another venue in which he could drink, do drugs, chase undergraduate women and generally and wildly succeed. This dichotomy had been apparent in college. There Elliot had been at every party, was already at the local tavern by the time the other students would repair there for a break in their studies, was more often seen to be drinking or dissipating or philandering, while at the same time he managed to obtain the very best grades and the top scores through a method which was apparent to no one, not even his closest friends.

Garth cared less about law school than his classmates, while Elliot appeared to care even less than Garth did, and perhaps quite literally did care less. Whatever he may or may not have felt at heart, it did not stop Elliot from secretly and directly applying himself to the academic tasks that would bear fruit. The result of this divided approach was the substance from which myths are fashioned and it was something of a shining cynosure for Garth, who was more sincere and more fully integrated in his distaste for the place but less confident about following up on those feelings. The Elliot legend started quietly enough on the first day of the Law of Contracts class, when the professor called upon Mr. Barker and Elliot simply said, "I pass." The idea that one could not consider genuflecting before the sacred professor and falling prostrate before the critical nature of a legal question would not have crossed the mind of any student in that class, with the exception of Garth who noted it and wondered about it and identified with it. Their fellow students were simply too quietly taken aback to consider it deeply at all. That class proceeded in a way that was natural, by which the professor was to teach the students the vagaries of the law and vicissitudes of the exercise of its authority. Individual students were questioned at random, and then one student, every so often, was questioned over and over again, and driven to painful distraction in a way that is not unlike what happens on an elementary school playground when one child is bullied. That child, or in this case that student, either endures to learn how to better face such adversity or does not survive at all. And the other students learn that the law can be a playground bully making them more prepared. In this process of aiming questions at students randomly and boring in on one or two students particularly as a demonstration, each of the students was called upon at least a few times. And each time the call came to Elliot, he would pass. Finally, about midway through the first semester, after about four or five passes the professor addressed this behavior.

"Mr. Barker, you simply cannot pass on every question as it is posed to you."

"Yes, I can," said Elliot.

Suddenly there was no sound of students shifting in their seats, pages being turned, notes being scribbled, quiet whispering, or even of breathing. It was as if it were a solemn mass being conducted in a cathedral, which is what it was for most of these parishioners, and the most significant and holy part of the high church liturgy had been reached.

Elliot continued, "Because the test in this class and in all others is anonymous. We take and sign the test by assigned number. Grades are allocated without knowing the student's identity. And there is no portion of the grade allotted to class participation."

Apostasy throughout history usually finds one of two ends, with a burning at the stake as had happened to Jan Hus, the great Czech dissenter of the very early fifteenth century, or with the beginning of a new movement as with Martin Luther who started the Protestant Reformation only a hundred years after the Hus barbecue. There were no stakes at which to burn Elliot because he had been correct in the same way that Luther had struck a very human and democratic chord in the music of faith. No great religious upheaval was to occur in this first year law class though. There would be no law-book-toting Electors of Saxony creating a Lutheran legal faith based on the seeds sown by Elliot Barker. The kernel had taken root in one heart. Garth Teller saw the cold calculation that was expressed in Elliot's remark and which was disregarded by the other students. Garth had always known Elliot to be a magnificent porcupine, an inverted version of that creature, curled up with the outside appearing to be points of casual disregard, easy-going indifference, carefree aloofness and even his apparent apostasy, while curled up on the inside was probably something other than all his vulnerable parts. If it were his underbelly, it was composed of the hard stone of economical ambition that would not be wasted on fawning, or weltering in the sublimity of the shared experience of preparing for the very best legal jobs that the country could offer. This economy of effort on the part of the hedgehog heretic is what Garth then explicitly saw and in which he then believed.

As is often the case with inexplicable faith, the rest of the students failed or refused to see any of this, so there was no reformation consisting of students suddenly now passing on questions. It was as if nothing had happened to their views of how they would go through law school. They still lavished each other with statements and showed each other actions consonant with

Gerald Weaver

being in awe of the institution and their role in it. It was this unchanged setting in which the legend was to be enhanced. The same students who were in that Law of Contracts class were in all the first year classes together as a cohort, and the setting for the next folkloric event was at the close of first semester of the class on the Law of Civil Procedure. In that class the entire grade was to be based upon a brief or a legal paper written by each student undertaking to support a supposed or hypothetical question of a new area of the law that lacked much legal precedent. The purpose was to teach each student the procedures of civil litigation at both the trial level and the appellate level. After the anonymous submission of the papers had occurred, there was to be an ungraded moot court session in which each student was to present his or her argument before a mock tribunal of three appellate court justices, consisting of the professor and two third-year law students. Garth's fellow classmates spent many dozens of hours in preparation for their moot court appearances. Garth and most of his classmates knew that they should be in the audience when Elliot was going to make his presentation.

About two minutes into his oral presentation, as often happens in appellate courts and which had certainly been happening in the sessions of this moot court, Elliot was interrupted by a question from one of the justices. His answer was, "I will get to that later in my presentation."

As in the Contracts class, the silence in the courtroom was deafening. It was all that Garth or anyone could hear. The fascinated faithful were gripped. Garth smiled because he had an accurate idea of where this was going. He also knew that these types of surprises would continue right on through the remaining years, up to the time when Elliot would inevitably be named editor of the law review, would collect the order of the coif, and would receive many other top honors.

The next time it took much less than two minutes for Elliot to be interrupted and again with the same question.

"As I said, that question is answered later in my argument."

"I would like to know your answer now," a third year student pressed.

"And I would like to be on a beach in Hawaii," Elliot said, without the slightest hint of sarcasm but as if he were making a legal argument, "and the answer you seek will only make sense after I have led up to it."

At this point, the professor decided to intervene.

"Mr. Barker, I have to say that I have not very impressed with you or your approach to this. For one thing, you are not wearing a suit and a tie. You are wearing a sport jacket over a polo shirt and a pair of khaki pants, which strongly suggest that you have gone to bed in them. You are now not answering questions. You have refused to pay this court the proper respect."

Elliot gently said, "This is an exercise and I understand that. And in this exercise I have to pretend that I am arguing before a court of appeals. If I have to pretend that, I do not see why you cannot just pretend I am Clarence Darrow."

The mention of this famous American legal luminary from a long past generation gave it the status of a precedent, which should not be foreign to any legal mind. Garth clearly heard in it strains of Shakespeare's Rosalind. Men have been dying from time to time, and worms have eaten them, but not for failing to be in awe of a first year ungraded moot court exercise in law school. This historical perspective may not have been lost on the professor and it certainly was felt by Garth, but the students were merely struck by the heresy. The Yale Law School was a cathedral, but a larger part of the grounds were a cemetery, the place where new ideas, individualism and defiance go to die and be interred. A low murmur of whispering and of the commotion of the departure of the handful of students who could no longer contain their surprise and had to repair to the hallway outside the room to express it could be heard. These hallway expressions then filled the supposed courtroom. In an effort to no longer prolong the proceedings, and as has certainly happened in hundreds of thousands of appellate court rooms since the dawn of the American republic, the justices had already quietly made their decisions while they then let the attorney make the remainder of and the bulk of his argument, tuning him or her out all the time.

Garth could no longer attempt to greatly succeed in law school with either the passionate religious conviction of the fascinated faithful or the cynicism of his friend Elliot. He reached the point where he saw it all rather clearly. He could quite easily do well enough to get by in law school and to continue his idea of a graduate school liberal arts education and delay a decision on his future. His view of law school, law books, law professors and indeed of the law itself settled into him in exactly the way that lower back pain will settle into a man in his sixth or seventh decade of life, painfully, unquestionably, resentfully and right along his spine. It was with this approach which had been inherent in him but had only been illuminated by his friend, that Garth met the next two developments of his early law school career, communicated to him by two other different college friends.

The first was a call from Earnest Dapple, now a fledgling reporter for the Associated Press news agency in Washington, DC.

"I hear you hate law school," Earnest said. Garth could normally hear a smirk in Earnest's voice, but he was sincere.

"What the hell gives you that idea, Earnest?"

"You know me, old pal. I have ways of finding things out. But it is also not that at all. It is mostly just paying attention. Elliot can manage that law school mess. He has a thick skin. He will just accomplish it with his standard approach of appearing to be dissipated while handling the place quite well. You are a bit more sensitive and more of a true believer. And, let's face it; there is not much to believe in up there in 'low school.' And you know it, dude. Those horrible law school strivers must be getting under your skin. None of them are going to question authority or sit down to smoke a joint and discuss Montaigne or go play pick-up basketball."

"I cannot say that you are wrong. It is not a bad place to spend time though. It is still a great educational institution. And I have two and half more years before I have to get a job."

"Yes, but think, Garth. You are a thinker. Look around you and consider what jobs will be available. Do you want to spend seventy hours a week working your butt off just so that you can make a six figure salary in order to allow some big company to pollute, or to underpay its workers? Or, do you want to go on the other side and get paid almost nothing to serve your clients and yourself up to the great American legal meat grinder. I can't think which would be worse for you, pal, working for the bad guys or consistently losing to them."

"I guess I have some time to think about it."

"That's the smartest thing I have heard you say yet. So think about this, old friend. You belong here, Garth, here in Washington, DC, and working on Capitol Hill. I know you have never thought of it, but I have. No sooner was I here and talking to these people than I realized that this is the place for you, absolutely. You would fit right in and not only that. You would excel. The place is about ideas and advocacy and flinging the bullshit and it is about caring. That is you and we both know it. And you would be such a star here."

"It is a little bit late for me to change the path I am on."

"I have thought of that too, friend. You do not have to change. You can take a look without changing. There are summer internships here. You have no plans for this coming summer and most first year law students do not look for law firm summer associates jobs. That is for second year students. And if you decide you don't like it here, a Capitol Hill internship will not look bad on your résumé. Listen, buddy, you can come down here over spring break and you can talk to some people about a summer internship.

I have just mailed you the directories for the House of Representatives and the Senate. You will get them in a day or two. Start with your own Congressman and Senators and look at some subcommittees that might like a bright Harvard grad who is at Yale Law School. Make the calls and set up interviews. Then when you come here you can stay at my apartment. You will have no trouble getting a summer internship. I am sure. And once you do, it is likely you will then be hired for real."

Garth may not have been able to hear a smirk in Earnest's voice at the beginning of the conversation but by this point he was hearing a great deal more. It came to Garth as clearly as if Earnest were in the same room with him and it came to him as clearly as he could sense what Elliot had been doing in class. Garth had been born with a sharp mind and an intuitive instinct and his experience had polished those two assets into a pair of lenses that allowed him to see things in them that others would miss. In a sense, later in life he would be able to see things in new people he would meet because his previous acquaintances had served as templates. But now he was looking directly at Earnest through what he could hear in his voice. Garth could see a loose and poised readiness to the slouching of Earnest's lanky and long frame and there was a singular expression hovering about the region of that gaunt face. There was a twinkle in his eyes and curve to his lips. He was not frowning or leering but a short glance might have seen his look as either one. Only the trained observer could really see it if he looked for a long time, but Garth could see it right through the phone. It could not be described in any more satisfactory terms than a look of bland cunning and cold calculation. Garth saw it immediately. Earnest may have been sincere about what he had said, but for him what he sincerely believed was that in Washington Garth could become another a tool in Earnest's box. He wanted Garth to work on Capitol Hill and to succeed so that Garth could become an asset to Earnest's own career. Now, this is where the sincerity truly lay. Garth normally took an ironic distance to what Earnest had to say but he knew that Earnest was also a true believer, one who had faith only in his own self-interest. So this was not a social or a friendly call. It was a carefully considered exercise dedicated to the only thing that mattered to Earnest.

"You know what, Earnest? I will give it a try. You can count on that. Thanks," Garth said. So, Garth did something that was fairly common for that time but is no longer done. He hitchhiked to Washington, DC. Staying at Earnest's apartment over the spring break, he made his rounds on Capitol Hill and was awarded an unpaid summer internship in the office of the Congressman who represented his home in Texas. Garth had frontloaded his student loan for his second year of law school and that is what he would spend to live for the summer. He would figure out the rest later. As it was, he now approached law school in the modified Elliot Barker manner. He would waste no time or energy on the supplicating and the genuflecting and the catechizing. He would focus only on what he had to do. There was still a visit from one more old college friend that was yet to frame the ending of his first year of law school. And it would be something special, what Garth's grandfather would have called a real doozy.

PINK AGAINST THE RISING TIDE

Melinda Sherman had long ago begun slowly to see that although the men in her family were not as strong as the women, there were certain advantages that accrued unfairly to being male. Much of the strength of the Sherman women seemed to spring from this very situation; a certain complacency seemed engendered by the benefits of being a boy, while a kind of power was usefully developed in their absence. Aside from the wonderful expediency of being able urinate standing up and anywhere out of doors, Melinda could see the vast bulk of these boyish advantages were not inherent but conferred. She decided she would set about seeking to attain as many of them as she could.

How this decision of hers seemed to have proceeded from the just and rightful judgment regarding the Sherman family passed down by the flawless apparatus of the Government Office to Repair Everything is not clear, except perhaps to consider that a void was created and into it Melinda had decided to step. Firstly, she would keep her hair short but with a better trim than she had been able to give herself with a knife and scissors prior to the trip to Dayton. And it was effectively the end of dance class for her.

A year before, William Sherman had decided to find after-school activities to provide physical exercise for each of his children. It was convenient that there was a two-story red brick building only a few miles away that housed a dance studio on the first floor and a karate school on the second floor. *Tiffany's Dance Studio for Young Ladies* had been started fifteen years earlier by a former dancer who had been the last dancer not to make the cut for the shows at the *Grand Old Opry*, in Nashville, Tennessee. She had returned to London and opened her studio. Fifteen years of relative prosperity and economic growth then had allowed for her business to flourish. Social turbulence had sprung up in much of the rest of the country then, relating to opposition to the war in Viet Nam and to the growing demands for expanded civil rights for women and minorities. It had settled down over that decade and a half leading up to the end of that war, and the ideas of this social change had already begun to settle into the American mainstream. They had not filtered out to the rural areas of the country, particularly in the southern United States. So, many little girls had been happily walked through Tiffany's doors in order to learn to dance and to get fit and to dream starry dreams, but mostly to please the women who were walking them through those doors, by virtue of wearing the pretty dance clothes.

Only a fantastical stretcher of the metaphor would even begin to try to draw a parallel between a dance school for little girls and a religious order or a cult, though such a metaphor might easily have been drawn like a cover over the frame of an Ivy League graduate school. It is clear even to the least exacting mind that the rituals and baptisms and rites and confirmations and catechisms of a dance class for young ladies are not in the least bit theological, but are in fact more simply tribal. They belong to the tribe of pink. Pink tights and shoes and dresses and ribbons abounded. A pink frame of mind was imposed from above upon this population of diminutive young ladies; almost exactly as some Congo tribe's adopted dictates are perceived as coming from its unseen forest and river gods, which in the case of this pink clan are their mothers. This pinksmanship will have been so durable and quaint that these girls would later grow up to read pink books, pink books about dolls and going to college and gardening and even pink books of a feminist bent.

For many years prior to this and for many years into the future there can be no doubt that mothers have and will continue to subject their daughters to the most beneficent and kind-hearted and well-meant pinking. Thankfully, the results of such a treatment were never thought through even to the nearby point of considering what might happen to a son who would be pinked in such a manner. The whole wonderfully picturesque practice might be brought to a precipitous stop. It doesn't stretch the imagination to see what might happen when the rather singular Melinda Sherman entered into this collective pink blush of girlhood. She had not been brought and prepared by a focused and attentive mother armed with ideas and plans and materials of a decidedly pink strain but by her sweetly inattentive father, a pinkless man who did not also kindly hover over the processes of the little tribe, but split his time between his daughter downstairs and his son in the karate school on the second floor.

Into her first dance class Melinda walked. Dressed in gray tights and black shorts and a brown top with black shoes, she had been inordinately proud her new dance outfit at the time of its purchase. Her father did not much like, or even know, pink and was unable to distinguish the difference between a hot pink and a ruby pink, or determine a bamboo pink from a baby kiss pink. Her mother had not participated in the endeavors surrounding the dance class and its clothes, and Angelina Sherman had little use for pink at all. It is perhaps Melinda's inner grasp of this latter fact that allowed that pride which she had originally felt to indomitably maintain itself even when it was diminished by what was apparent to all on that day of her first class. She appeared more than anything as if she were the black and gray and brown housefly that had just landed on the pink birthday cake. What Melinda had felt then was not unlike a sensation that has here elsewhere been described, a feeling of being separated and different. But in her case there was not a trace of superiority or of compassion. It was more largely a kind of tender defiance or a gentle pride, a dignity that can arise from human frailty. Melinda could let her blood struggle with the frosty glances of her classmates. She would reverence the hope that would never allow her to become a prisoner of this new place. She could live and breathe and perhaps even thrive there, just for herself. Her virtuous decency would keep the tribal brooms from sweeping her away. She would resist the barking and blasting and would as well not seek out or require any manner of charity, which was anyway unlikely to come to her in such a place.

The young chieftain of this pink tribe was a girl whom Melinda had known from kindergarten and who had ascended to her position, as is always the case, through virtue, hard work, heart, prudence and beauty. She had been the elected chief through the prudence of having been born into a prominent family, by the hard work she had shown to make herself popular in the elementary school, and by the virtue of wearing the nicest, most expensive, varied, coordinated and preternaturally pink outfits to every lesson. She was beautiful and young and fresh not so much from the hand of Mother Nature, but fresh and young and beautiful from the hand of her own mother. The compassionate, gracious and generous character she so expressly and patently exhibited with all the other girls was the current not so much of her heart but of her art, which precociously in one so young were the same thing. She extended to Melinda one charitable and kind-hearted sidelong glance, full of graceful and benevolent condescension. Her ladies in waiting also made the same generous gesture only in shorter duration and with less conscious exhibition. The remaining students just stared until their gazes wandered off one by one.

The girls were put through the dance moves and instructed with the greatest care and enthusiasm by Tiffany, the teacher. They were encouraged with varying degrees of tremendous success to attempt to remain in step with one another or at least with the rhythm of the music. Sunshine poured down upon them even in this interior space in the form of the appreciative and inspiring attentions of their mothers, who waited in the hall but who could watch through the windows installed as a product of the marketing virtuosity of the dance studio's proprietress. This was a hallway convocation that often inspired William Sherman to spend the larger half of his split time away from it and at the karate school upstairs. The synchronicity of the tribal dancing group and its movements were thought by the instructor to be enhanced by the constant physical interaction of the girls that occurred between dance sets and at the arrival and departure of the dancers, who would spend these times hugging one another and fawning over one another in a way that they had learned from the denizens of the hallway and in a mode that was distinctly pink as well, with as many squeals of happiness and compassion and fawning compliments and expressions of support as might be expected from the meeting of long separated sisters or of skilled diplomats from antagonizing nations.

Melinda found herself in these situations almost always to the side of them, with a book to her nose and alone. In such a way she began to become functionally invisible, which also suited her as well as her unusual outfit did. She liked reading. She also liked the movement and the music and the effort and the concentration of the dance. As well, she was fond of the way in which it took her to a place outside of herself or perhaps just deeper, which was a mysterious process itself and one that seemed to improve her efforts. Since the instructor was not a member of the tribe, she was able to notice this and to notice the natural athleticism of the girl in the brown and black and gray. One day, as she was trying to teach the tribe a new part of a dance routine, she had singled out Melinda to come to the front of the class and to imitate the teacher after she had demonstrated this particular set of moves. Melinda's considerations were rarely trained upon what was outside. Her concentration was usually of a more inward nature and this allowed her to watch, remember, and execute the maneuvers in such a way that the instructor noted to herself that while her dancing lacked most of the emotional and stylistic embellishment that could only come with years and experience, it surely possessed a skill and strength and athletic grace which was unusual in one so young who had so little experience. Proud of her observation and instinct and discovery, Tiffany took no time at all to announce her findings to the rest of the class, and to persist in such statements and to enhance them at the point at which it was noticed that the other young ladies failed to perform at a similarly high level. The approbation and accolades of the tribe that were to rise up to Melinda's ears after this were swift and sure in coming.

"You nasty little girl," extolled the first admiring lady in waiting to the chief, "why don't you go back to that cold crooked dark old house and stay there, where there is no sun and there are no birds?"

"Don't think you can push us around," a second admired. "You weirdo. Stick to playing with that strange brother of yours. And don't come back here."

"We all know you are cheating some way, you little witch," added another.

And then the chieftain's lieutenants repaired to their leader's side to succor her. The tribe's foremost member, it appeared, had happened to injure herself as well in attempting the same set of dance moves, and she focused the pain of this injury and of many other unrelated and sincere grievances unswervingly in Melinda's direction, with a hurt and sharp glance, whenever she was not gratefully rewarding her acolytes for their sympathy and comforting assistance. The rest of the clan just looked at Melinda as if she had again been that fly and had this time landed in each girl's glass of milk. The instructor was either unaware of this or had over the years become numb to this type of behavior. She continued to single out Melinda, to use her to instruct the other girls, and sustained her commendation of the athletically gifted little witch. Nor was that particular girlish appellation too sorely off the point, because in terms of this particular pink tribe Melinda could never rise to the rank of chieftain or even to that of one of the top understudies. What she could and did become was something along the lines of that pink tribe's shaman, its magician, and its witchdoctor. The appeal of such a thing to her was great, even if she could not fully understand or explain it or perhaps because she couldn't explain or understand it.

To the members of this clan she had become important, even though she was still excluded from the social intercourse of its associates. The idealistic untidiness of her independence and dignity would be forever lost on their young minds, but she would remain an ineluctably important part of their preparation for the end of the year show, which was the focus of the second half of the term of the class. She put more of herself into those preparations than she knew that she had, and certainly more than the other girls did. The joy of working on a project had appealed to her, as had her noteworthy role. In her mind, the particulars of what was to be the approaching show were coming quite well together in the practices. On the final day of preparations, the dress rehearsal, she even sought to wear a little makeup and to put on the dress she had been instructed to ask her father to buy. And she also prevailed upon him to watch the entire dress rehearsal from the hall with the adoring mothers. And much to Melinda's surprise and credit, the dress rehearsal went rather well.

Then came the day of the show itself. It was quite another matter, although that perception was apparently lost on every other person either performing or attending. It was an applauded and congratulated and highly praised disaster, at least in her eyes, and it tested every inner strength she possessed to maintain her honest and sincere opinion in the face of the almost overwhelming current of approbation. Many years later she would read of something called an *auto da fe*, in which innocent men and women were tried and condemned and executed in public by medieval courts of the Inquisition. Because of this dance show experience, she would be able to place herself figuratively into the front row seat of the one individual in the audience at such a feudal proceeding who knew the whole trial was just so terribly wrong, but could not speak out. The entire dance show was a festival of happy and supportive squealing that started the second the girls all took the stage. There was even a distinctly pink cast to these cries, since they emanated largely from the sisters and mothers and female friends of the performers. The dancers were out of step, and this was met with calls and shouts of positive reinforcement. Cheers and clapping accompanied the forgetting of entire sets of dance steps. Stumbling generated high-pitched verbal accolades. The names of the dancers were called out from the audience with whoops and hollers. And afterward the tribe merged with its audience and the atmosphere was one of unalloyed and happy approval.

Melinda ventured a single small comment to her father: "I thought we were much better yesterday, in the dress rehearsal."

Before he could either agree or disagree, the chief of the tribe, who had overheard her remark, interjected, "Oh, don't be silly, Melinda," she said, looking to Mr. Sherman to see that he took in all her graciousness, "we all looked very pretty. And that is what really mattered."

To part of this, at least, her father readily agreed. He told her she had been wonderful and had indeed looked very pretty. The reactions to this that Melinda may have had did not evidence themselves right away. Instead, they stood like horses at livery in the stable, waiting for the day when the coachman would take them out and hitch them to a four-in-hand or a dog cart or a landau or a hackney or a phaeton or a hansom or a cabriolet. Just such a day was to have been preceded and precipitated by the events surrounding the finding of suspected abuse by the Government Office of Repairing Everything. Melinda's second year of weekly dance class had already begun when that stately event occurred. At home she had then become more of a kind of parent, as she took over much of the care of her now unemployed father. Her relationship to her mother changed as well, since she was then to that gentle lady something more along the lines of a representative or an advocate for the damaged man who had even more time to spend in his chair. And he also spent less time at the dance class or even watching the karate lessons, choosing instead to sit in his car as he waited the one or two hours per week that the children shared in their respective classes.

There was a different set of circumstances entirely from those of the pink tribe that constituted the experiences of the students in the class with Melinda's brother, Porter, in the karate school up the stairs from the dance studio. For it to have been called a karate school was a creative misnomer and another example of a marketing device. At this time, it was shortly after the United States had left Viet Nam and it was roughly only twenty-some years after the end of America's Korean military misadventure. The owner of the karate school had been stationed in Korea with the United States Eighth Army, and following the end of that war had returned to Kentucky from that place with several years of training in a Korean martial art known as Tang Soo Do, and with a pregnant war bride. As no American at this point had heard of any martial arts other than judo and karate, both of Japanese derivation, this soldier allowed his establishment to be called a karate school so that it would be recognized and because its practice was much closer to karate than to judo. The owner of the karate school had a deep appreciation for the principals of this martial art, and he was moved to bring them to the boys of his hometown. He felt it would improve their lives if they were to learn the values of discipline, respect, faithful practice, self-control, rigorous training, humility and skillful competition. Nowhere was the significance of these values more in evidence than in the person of the young man who was to have emerged from the loving union of this soldier and his Korean bride to become the teacher at the school at this time. Young Steve Callahan was the picture of all that can be called upright.

This young man was as open as the look on his boyishly handsome, mixed race countenance, and in his light brown eyes. The posture of his solidly built frame of medium height, and its movements, illuminated the honest and forthright nature of his character in the same way that the buoyance of those movements and his gait reflected his tireless and guileless good nature. If the mothers at the dance studio were there to watch their daughters be pretty in pink, the mothers at the karate school, and there were always a few, were likely to be there to observe the young Mr. Callahan with what had to have been for any middle-aged married woman the equivalent of a school girl's swoon. He won their attention not with his masculine presence, which he had in some quantity even though it was callow and yet to be fully formed, but with his sterling and very accessible good nature and quiet strength, and his lack of any bravado or posturing. All of this was polished to a bright but respectable shine by the respect, discipline, and humility he had learned from his parents, and in the preparation he had himself received in this martial art, training that was mirrored in his close cropped cut of light brown hair. When he spoke, he did so without a trace of cunning or deceit but with an unsuspicious frankness that bore the impress of truth. So, these admiring mothers were functionally prevented from anything close to actually swooning, because it would have been an improper way for them to think of this young man who was prepossessing in the beauty of his uncomplicated goodness. What they really were feeling was that this was the kind of man to whom they would like to introduce their daughters. And that was what would actually happen at some point for someone else's daughter.

On the western edge of Normandy, there is a tide that arises in the Baie du Mont Saint-Michel, with the swiftness of many rising tides in the northern latitudes. But since the sand of that bay is very shallowly inclined, the tide moves forward, they say, at the speed of a galloping horse. In quite a similar and distinctly French manner, the tide of a woman's passion was once described by an odd poet of those people as, "*comme la mer, qui vers elle montait comme vers sa falaise.*" At roughly the same latitude as Mont Saint-Michel, but in the Western Hemisphere, the tide may rise as much as sixteen meters in the Bay of Fundy. On the North American coast of the mid-Atlantic and of the Gulf of Mexico, each only about five hundred miles from where Melinda stood at this particular moment just a few weeks into her second year of dance class, the tides rise much less poetically but with the same droll inevitability. Water rises too on the Laurel River near Melinda's home, and on the Great Father of Waters into which it eventually flows, and it does so often with greater effect. What arose within Melinda now shared with those floods of the continent's interior the quality that it was periodic but that its interval was not as regular a one as the sea tide. But it shared with those noted and more regularly timed lunar ocean tides their swiftness and precipitousness and their inescapable nature. And as earlier described by Charles Baudelaire, what arose in Melinda was something metaphysical and not unalloyed with love. It suddenly appeared to her that she was standing in very warm air, and it seemed that the heat was transferred to the air around her from some hidden place inside her, with warmth that extended happily and expansively toward her surroundings and even to the pink girls within those environs. This heat was also a strength that expanded all of her capabilities and which left her with no doubt that she could attempt and do things that the other girls would not think of doing, and in fact could not spiritually or even physically do, even if the notions had occurred to them. She felt tireless and slightly bored, and what came to her again was another vision, a prophecy of a man, perhaps the same one who had come to her over the Ohio River. She did not know for sure. She knew only he was male and he was significant. Within a minute, this rising tide had carried her up the stairs to the karate school.

She walked in, and as she had been seen to do before in the bathroom of her home, she began to swiftly and quietly remove all of her clothes. Before she could get too far and after she had resisted his verbal efforts to stop her, Steve Callahan had gently taken both her and her brother by the arms and had led them into his office, where the disrobing continued, after he ordered his senior karate student to take over the beginning exercises of the class, and while he assured Tiffany, who had briefly followed Melinda up the stairs before she had to return to her own class, that he would take care of everything and would inform her of the results. Melinda was in the state in which the world had first discovered her, when Steve had returned to the office. She was hugging her brother.

"I love Porter," she said, smiling, "and I love karate."

Steve was not so much good-natured as it actually was his nature. It was with this unreflective goodness that he maintained the same assured swiftness and unadorned quietness as he reached into his closet for a small karate outfit and had it on Melinda before she or her brother or even he had much time at all to think about what had just happened.

"Well, I guess you are in the right place, young lady," he said as he pulled up the white pants, tied them tight, wrapped her in the white top and fastened the white belt around her top.

"And I love you, Mr. Callahan," she said.

"Then you will do as I tell you, because I am your teacher now," he said.

And with that same unmediated simplicity the gender barrier at the karate school in London, Kentucky was forever broken. Whatever it had been that had troubled Melinda, or had made her feel different or that had pushed her outside the norm of the society and behavior of young girls, it had found its perfect settling place in the hands of young Mr. Callahan, whose spirits rose and enlivened at the prospect of what he knew his effect on this young girl could be. If there was ever a man born to be a father, and to be a father who incorporated all the best characteristics of both a father and a mother, and whose very nature set him outside of or ahead of the time in which he lived, it was this young man. She made him smile the kind of smile that had an inexplicable tear ready to fall from the face that countenanced it. Her unusual nature and circumstances made him exercise the greater expanses of his own nurturing character, and he found that she made him like himself better when she was around. This young man achieved what would have been at the very best an awkward or even impossible occurrence, with calm aplomb and moderate confidence, consequently with almost no outward notice or alarm on the part of each of the participants. Melinda, her father, her brother, Tiffany, the boys in the karate class, all accepted this change, which was really a small but noteworthy watershed event in the social development of London, as seamlessly as if it had been just another day at school. Watersheds do not come in the color pink however, so this particular change as it was seen in the tribe on the floor below was more along the lines of a blessed restoration of a traditional way of life that was something along the lines of what the entire white population of the South might have felt, had the Confederacy won the American Civil War.

This trope can be twisted to other effect as well, for if the female states on the floor below were tightly bound together by bonds of pink into a cohesive and hierarchical tribal structure, the entities on the second floor were a loosely formed confederacy of many different hues, to say the least. There was only any order there at all due to the effect of the smiling adjurations of the teacher, and by his example. In fact, during

the short interval by which Melinda was swiftly admitted into this confederacy, and while the oldest and most advanced student had taken over
the opening exercises of the class, the relative autonomy of the individual
states was beginning to express itself in various examples of wandering,
calling out, poking, joking, and laughing. The confederacy was in danger of
becoming so loosely confederated as to lose its definition as a single entity
by the time Mr. Callahan had re-entered the room with the two students
from the Sherman family, but he soon personified their stalwart Articles of
Confederacy and they fell into order quite quickly and happily.

The order into which they arranged themselves was according to the
shade of the belt that each wore, but the hue and type of each boy varied
within that arrangement as if it were an open-air market of boy makes and
models. At the front of the class were two boys in white karate outfits with
blue belts. One was lanky and lean and tall with an aquiline look of sharp
ferocity in his face and posture, while his counterpart was a stalwart young
man of obviously compact strength and earnest helpfulness. In the back of
the class were the white belts, which were behind the yellow belts, and then
it proceeded to the front of the class through the orange, green and red
belts. And within the echelons of each of belt colors there were stripes of
the more advanced color. So there were orange belts with green strips and
green belts with red stripes and red belts with blue stripes. All of these belts
were on boys who were tall and short and older and younger and slim and
hefty and blond and brunette. There was even a belt on one of the boys who
had picked up Porter and Melinda in the stolen car on the trip to Dayton,
and on several others of his wild ilk, for whom this martial art was largely
an opportunity to fight and to do it in a way that was accepted and even
encouraged. Other boys were there to immerse themselves in the joy of
achievement, boys who would relish the opportunity to work hard in order
to move up from each level to the next, as if they were Boy Scouts but a

brand of Boy Scouts which were philosophically less martial even where they were physically more so. Still others were there because they were made to be so, errant or lost boys, rebellious boys, or boys whose fathers had decided were not aggressive or disciplined enough.

Melinda found herself in a veritable liquor cabinet of young male spirits, and the air was filled with their vapors, while the eye was met with the colorful variety of each label and the promises of what was within each bottle. And among the markers and scents and spiritual contents, as well as on the belts that cinctured each waist, there was not even the slightest hint of pink.

Mr. Callahan led the class through warming up and exercising, and then the boys practiced their forms. A form was a set of martial arts moves, performed in a prescribed order for a period of a few minutes. Each level or step, each belt with stripe, was achieved by mastering the form for that respective level. So the boys broke down into groups for this practice and Mr. Callahan wandered from group to group in order to inspect, to encourage, to assist, and to direct them in their efforts. As he worked with each group he kept a watchful eye on the white belt group, or the least experienced students, and particularly upon the one new boy, the female boy who had come to his class, floating upon a peculiar rising tide that he neither understood nor judged, but which he deemed had deposited upon the shores of his class something important and new, something that attracted him and called from within him all the better strengths of his masculine and fatherly nature. When it came time for the closing exercise of the class, he felt the same pride in his own power of observation and discovery, and in his instinct that Tiffany had once felt with respect to Melinda, but his pride was infused with a disinterested and unselfish love. He chose Melinda to be one of the participants in the white belt sparring exercise.

Class closed with sparring, and members of each level practiced sparring with each other and not with boys from other levels. Sparring involved a Korean version of the Native American practice of taking *coup*. A point was scored by a hit to the front of the torso of the other combatant, and only by that. Practice sparring was not in earnest and no boy was ever permitted to hurt another. It was merely an exercise in defense and in using the moves that had been taught in each form. But the reward for the hour of hard practice came when two boys from each belt level were outfitted in the protective head gear and the small foam gloves, and were permitted to spar in earnest in front of the entire class in order to see which boy would win by scoring two hits first. Steve knew that students thrived on this actual competition, and that it was the possibility of being chosen for the watched event that kept them active and attentive during the practicing of the forms and the practice sparring. Since any boy could remember, the blue belt sparring match between the more accomplished two blue belts was always the last event of the practice, and at each level leading up to that it was never expected that the newer members at any level would be chosen. The surprise of this day was that the blue belts went first and the white belts went last. And the final bout was to include that one of the white belt contestants who was the newest student, who had been a student less than one hour, and who was the strangest boy of all, Melinda Sherman.

The vestiges of the internal tide that had arisen within Melinda were still present at that moment, or else she might have been overwhelmed by the prospect. She faced her opponent. As she had just learned in the practicing, she bowed to him. He bowed to her. Then he advanced and she tried to move and to dance and to keep away from him as best she could manage. But she did not stop him from moving in directly and shooting out a straight arm, and landing a flat hand to her chest. That was one point. The boy walked back to his side with a look on his face of qualified and mitigated triumph. The uniqueness of the situation prevented him from reacting as he might have done, if the boy he had struck had not been a girl. It was with this somewhat mixed look on his face that he approached the second time and executed the same move. Melinda simply knocked his expected blow aside and countered with a strike of her own, this time hitting her challenger on his chest. The score was now one to one. The next blow would be the deciding one, and decidedly the mixed emotions of the rival were no longer mixed. He sensed that the crowd of boys watching, who had been relatively indifferent to the girl in their midst, were now of a heightened emotional state at the prospect of seeing something actually happen that they had never dreamed could happen. This combatant now came at Melinda with a combination of reserve and coiled aggression. He feinted and danced and waited for her counter before he would attempt his scoring strike. This time she was not only in karate class, she was also in dance class, and the tidal warmth and confidence were also still in her. He pretended to strike and she made the same block, only this time as she swung her arm to the side and moved her upper body away, she kept her footing solidly on the ground and continued to move her top half away and down, as she spun on the leg on that side and executed a reverse kick directly into the stomach of her antagonist, who had charged into her after she had moved to block his feint. She struck the blow and won the sparring match and knocked him down all in the same instant.

There was silence and inaction. Everything stood still for several moments. The larger issues of this particular day would be resolved later in a way that Melinda or anyone else might easily understand. Her brother would be happy to have his younger sister in his class with him. Tiffany would remit to the karate school a portion of the fee she had received for Melinda's participation at the class at the dance studio, doing so out of her own sense of correct behavior, which then had been stimulated by that same sense as communicated to her by Steve Callahan, who although more than ten years her junior, was capable of affecting her in this or other ways. And although the financial circumstances would later dictate that the Sherman family could not afford to keep either Porter or Melinda in that karate class, each child would continue in it because its proprietor simply could not see it otherwise. William Sherman would be oblivious to most of this, only to weakly say to Melinda what he had said to her after the show at the dance class, which was that she was wonderful and he was proud of her. Angelina Sherman would have a more distinct reaction to all of it, and she would not let a single soul have any idea what that reaction might have been. So, these larger issues would quietly amount to nothing very much. What was yet to be seen would be how the class would react to what had just happened.

TERRA INCOGNITA

It has been said that absence and mystery are not essential to the development of love but that they are often its powerful auxiliaries. The character and quality of the absent person for whom love may develop are not on constant display, nor are they subject to the casual moments of disinterested examination that will occasionally occur to the mind of even the most ardent enthusiast. Faux diamonds and pearls may appear genuine at a distance, when closer scrutiny might reveal their flaws. To much the same effect, the attractive qualities of the far off and adored person are augmented, and the large gaps between the conscious attention to those features are filled by the fervent mind of the admirer. In such cases, the culprit, or the active instrument as it were, will be the warm and vibrant imagination of the doting party. Such a resourceful fancy has been known to survive and even to thrive on the barest sustenance, growing entire lush and resplendent gardens of tender and affectionate attachments where there has been little water or where there are few nutrients, or where the soil may actually be rocky and barren and the water supply brackish. This has happened normally and universally throughout the history of our species, where the primary agents of such romantic growth have been the spades and rakes of the gardeners who wielded them.

There was no electronic media or social network at the time Garth was in law school near the end of the nineteen seventies, but the development of such manners of instant communication has provided a current example that is illustrative of this very phenomenon of love and the imagination. In the world of instant electronic communication which has recently usurped much of what was the social function in the days of Garth's youth, it is not uncommon for the imaginative lover sitting at a computer screen to become so moved by the pictures and words of an individual he or she has never met, that he or she will then begin thinking of the unknown lady or gentleman from day to day, from hour to hour, until he or she has become very desperately in love. It was simpler in this previous time, the time of the story, because the scraps and fragments that would frame the gaps filled in by the lover's imagination would had to have arisen from the social context, in the form of sightings of dusky hair and dancing shapes and starry eyes, or actual contact with kisses, tears and smiles, or perhaps even a more involved contact with the loved one's temperate will or firm reasoning or emotional strength.

Garth had experienced all of these and more in his relationship with Tabitha, and now she was no longer on the same campus. She was in her almost singular way even farther away than that. Tabitha had a way of making Cambridge, Massachusetts seem like the *terra incognita*, which was as it had been depicted in the map which Martin Waldseemüller had drawn from the voyages of Amerigo Vespucci. This same map was the reason that America is not more commonly called Columbia, a fact which is all the more quaint or alarming since its depiction of North America bears little resemblance at all to the actual continent. Tabitha could simply disappear, or in a sense drop off of the map, in much the same way as had seemed to have actually happened to Massachusetts and Cape Cod in Waldseemüller's famous work. In this dramatic absence on her part there was no cruelty, no wily calculation toward effecting the earlier described phenomenon of the lover's imagination, no other romantic interest, and not even any carelessness with regard to her relationship with Garth. There was simply something in her neurophysiology, something that would not be diagnosed or understood until many years later, a physical condition of the brain that gave for her a startlingly deeper meaning to the tired old homily, "out of sight, out of mind." Her attention was not unlike that of those computer view screens onto which current day romantics project their imaginary loves. It was bright and vibrant and it was focused and she could not bring herself to think of anything that was not on it, such as a first year law student in far off New Haven, for whom she actually did have a great deal of devoted affection. It is just that letters to Garth or phone calls to him, even return phone calls, simply did not often cross her mind, while it was directly focused upon the bright events of her senior and remaining year at Harvard.

Garth had been left alone to putter around in his garden of Tabitha and what grew there was not on barren soil nor did it lack moisture. There were the memories of the way her keel hummed when she was dancing or at hull speed, of her willowy and lissome frame, of that feline way she had about her, of her insightful mind, of the way she responded wholly to all that was masculine in him, of her excess of vitality, of the direct and frank nature of her gaze when it was on him, of the way he felt when he was within her focused attention, and above all of the way in which her eyes contained a lambent green flame that hinted at more thought and feeling than a single soul should contain. These reminiscences meant that this garden of his loving imagination grew in rich soil, and was well watered and it received just the correct amount of sunlight. It was fecund and luxuriant and it was made to appear all that much more so to Garth, because there was in his heart another place that truly was a desert, and that was his entire surrounding life in law school. His Tabitha garden was also an oasis. This gave, for him this time, another instance in which another tired old bromide had taken on a fresh and profound meaning, that is, "absence makes the heart grow fonder." He had always been drawn to her powerfully and in ways that were new to him, but it was her singular brand of absence that had made him fall irretrievably in love with her.

Garth walked out of the Yale Law School on the afternoon before his final examination of the second semester of the first year of law school. It was not all that long after he had taken his spring break trip to Washington. That final examination was in the first year class on Criminal Law, and his approach to it was an excellent example of all that separated Elliot and him from their class-mates. Criminal procedure had been the topic in the first semester in that class. Procedure, or the province of the sort of thing that is known in popular lore as "a technicality," is nine tenths of criminal law, so the mid-term in this class was weighted at ninety percent of the grade, and this particular final examination was worth only ten percent. It was exactly the opposite of every other first year class, each of which weighed their final examinations at ninety percent and the mid-term at ten percent. Every single other student in that class still approached that ten percent value final examination as if he or she were preparing for the actual oral argument before the United States Supreme Court in *Brown v. the Board of Education*. They all were planning to go to their study groups and cram for hours that evening. Since Elliot had aced the Criminal Law mid-term and Garth had received a very strong B grade, it was almost impossible that either of them would change his respective grades no matter how they scored on the final. They were the only first year law students who were not going to study. They were planning to eat, play basketball and go out on the town, though gently, that night.

They left the law school and they turned right to walk up Wall Street with the intention of getting something to eat on York Street, on their way to go play pick-up basketball at the Payne Whitney Gymnasium. For some reason Garth turned to look back at the law school and perhaps this was because he knew that his summer sojourn to the nation's capital could mean that he might not return to it. On a campus of beautiful neo-Gothic buildings it was one of the most striking. He must have been feeling just a bit pre-nostalgic because he then convinced Elliot to go a little bit out of their way and walk across the undergraduate quadrangle known as the Cross Campus. He was walking while listening to his friend and absently staring at the residential colleges and the classroom buildings and dodging soccer balls and Frisbees and catching upon the breeze strains of rock and roll music and the hint of marijuana smoke. As before and always, he was struck by the lack of gloom and by the blonde aspect of everything, including the architecture and even his old Harvard friend beside him. There was one person there who was not Yale blonde.

"Hey, Garth, Garth Teller!" she shouted in lilting soprano tones. It was Tabitha Vivenda.

If she had stripped off all of her clothes and had run up to Garth and jumped on him and wrapped her naked and slender legs around him and started kissing him right there in the middle of Cross Campus, it would have had exactly the same effect. He was mesmerized, excited, lost to all that was not between them, enchanted, enlivened and transported. He was beyond embarrassment. Garth shot Elliot a look that combined his feeling of being helpless before this particular circumstance and being ecstatic about that fact, then he turned back to face Tabitha. Elliot stood to the side and wryly smiled. Tabitha might not have even seen him.

The smile of Elliot Barker itself could comprise a short and interesting book. It set within his handsome fair-skinned and prematurely matured face as a southerly counterpoint to his worldly eyes, which were slightly downturned at the edges and were a watery shade of light bluish gray. The dire coruscation of these liquid lights contained within them a combination of intermittent flashes representing the very slight possibility of extreme action or perhaps even violence, and the more steady background illumination of a profound melancholy, a sad acceptance of the idea that no action not even one that was extreme or violent had any hope of making any real difference. This combination and competition of radiances resolved themselves into a lively amalgamation that was always and simply going to be the ocular hint of the prospect of suicide.

His smile was more thoroughly life affirming and wicked, breaking out beneath those cool eyes like desert sunshine that would fill every available space with its blinding and fiery vivacity. It was the daring smile of a Hedda Gabler, as she tossed the sole copy of Løvborg's world-changing manuscript into the fire, or the knowing smile of Porfiry Petrovich, as he questioned Raskolnikov about the homicides he had committed. And if it can be possible at all to imagine Hamlet sincerely smiling and not merely acting it, then it was just such a comprehensively knowing smile. It was in these and in all other respects quite unquestionably Northern or even Gothic, though it was located to the south of his eyes. Elliot let his smile shine at three quarters strength on his friend and it spoke to Garth much of what it always seemed to state, that everything in life is very transitory and that permanence or meaning may only be loosely attached, as if it were a label with glue that would surely fail, to anything either through a kind of careless and childlike ignorance, as is surely the case with most of the people in the world, or through a kind of skeptical willfulness which was the way in which Elliot did it, and thus prevented himself from slipping into the abyss. This particular smile told Garth that Elliot was certain that the feelings Garth and Tabitha shared did not escape this essential transient nature of all things and that perhaps they were rather emblematic of it. Two other vapors poured into Garth through that smile, and the first one was that even though this smiling look was a kind of prediction or a prognostication it carried within it a feeling of certainty that flowed from a far more experienced consciousness, which also made it something more like a memory, as if Elliot were actually remembering forward to what he knew was going to have happened. There was also something very resigned but akin to affection in it, as if Elliot had wearily sized up the world but had pulled Garth out for a separate consideration.

"I leave you to the fate that is shared by all, old friend," is something along the lines of what that smile said. And then he left the two lovers alone together.

"Was that Elliot?" Tabitha asked, without taking her green eyes off of Garth.

Tabitha's almost unique facility for being absent was so pronounced and effective that the awareness of it did not go away when she was present. There were two dialectics at work, each of which promoted the feeling of her absence even when she was present, as now she was. The feeling of her absence was largely a memory, but it was always very much a living and growing one for Garth even while he was practically overwhelmed by the warmth and intensity of her affection. He was stunned by seeing and hearing her but this very circumstance reminded him of the moments when he had in fact been largely deprived of those joys entirely.

This awareness of absence was separate from memory as well. It was also suggested by the very heightened nature of her presence itself. There was simply something more to her than there was to other women, and this difference suggested that there was something else to consider in the prospect of being with her. The first such item at which Garth's mind then arrived was the way in which she could disappear. These two powerfully suggestive elements, the memory of a distinct opposite, and the evocative hint of a noticeable difference, were augmented by a third phenomenon, and that was that Tabitha was also in some way absent even in the process of being right there in front of Garth. This had been indicated by her failure to register that Elliot had also been there and by other examples of solipsism.

The first two syntheses of absence arising out of presence occurred in

Garth's mind but this third one was actually in the young lady herself, and it was in a constant blend that was ever shifting in balance. It was not then absence, since it was in her some way alloyed. It was mystery. And this was equally and separately as maddeningly alluring to Garth.

Tabitha was quite attached to Garth. This was a statement as incomplete and as misleading as it was central to her appeal. One may eschew the purchase of a new car because one is quite attached to the twelve-year-old vehicle one has been driving. Such a mild devotion greatly understates the character of attachment in question between these two young people. A data analyst may be attached to the United States Embassy in Prague and no such indirect association could remotely describe Tabitha's type of attachment. No, when the two of them were together she was attached to Garth in the way that the radio transmitter is attached to the Eiffel Tower. She was quite attached. There was nothing subservient or ancillary or pre-feminist about it. Tabitha kept up a stream of her own opinions, suggestions, statements and actions. She was lively and insightful and vibrant and intellectual and artistic. She just simply let him drive, in a manner of speaking. It gave her a quality almost unique among the women he knew, in that she was game for anything. Garth never really pushed this, but in his heart he knew that she would go along with him on almost any sortie or gallivant or daring exploration. It was exhilarating. He could be himself, do what he wanted and go wherever he chose, and do so with the vibrant company of a brilliant and passionate and beautiful sylph.

"I think we should go the top of Saybrook tower," he said.

"That sounds fun. What is that?"

"Saybrook is the residential college, or dorm, sort of like our Harvard houses, only better. It is where Eakin lived when she was here. And they have a seven-story high tower and we can get on top of it."

"How is your friend? And how did that elopement thing work out for her?"

"Actually, I think she is pregnant and still doing quite well at Harvard Business School. Her husband, Dick, is working at a bank in Boston and I think the plan is for him to take care of the baby when it is born."

"That is unusual."

"Yeah, but so is Eakin. And she will get a much better job when she graduates from business school than he ever would."

"She sounds so strange. Maybe I should meet her sometime."

"Hey," Garth said, "hadn't we planned that I would come visit you in Cambridge in two days?"

"I don't remember," she said. "All I know is that my exams ended and it suddenly occurred to me that I missed you terribly. It was all I could think of. So I took a train directly here."

They entered Saybrook College and went through the courtyard to the entryway that led to the tower, and they climbed seven flights of stairs to go through a door and emerge on the top of Saybrook tower, which had stone walls along two of its sides and a simple steel railing along the other two, making it more or less open on the side where it faced the freshman dormitories. The view was exceptionally pleasant, overlooking the tops of the many stone structures that had been built by highly skilled stonemasons that Yale had brought over from Italy. The much taller Harkness tower, which held a clock and a carillon loomed over them. It was late afternoon and the blond stone of the buildings seemed to glow in the ambient and slanted light. No one could see them from the street. There was somewhat of a viewing angle from the fifth, or top, floor of Wright Hall, the freshman dorm across High Street from them. Since physics makes windows function more like mirrors when looking through them from bright to dark, Garth and Tabitha could not see into those rooms and put them out of their thoughts.

Tabitha's striking animated face had a strange and stirring property that was always present. It was that no matter in what mood she seemed to be, her countenance exhibited a capacity for the possible expression of terror or abject fear, as if she had on regular occasions been fearfully surprised by events or persons which would suddenly appear to her from outside the tunnel of her attention. It was difficult to map out on the topography of her face and would sometime lurk in the corner of her mouth or in a flicker of her eyes or in the tension of her cheek. It was rarely right on the surface and lurked more like a pale shadow, something indistinctly seen and not for an instant absent. Sometimes Garth thought he was only imagining this and at other times he could clearly envision what he was certain was the way in which it would all coalesce into her stark expression of unqualified terror, even though he had never actually seen it. One such moment was at the instant they had emerged onto the platform of the tower top. It gave her face a greater degree of glowing allure than it usually expressed. It had too bright a shine for Garth to be able to tell if she were actually afraid, but he became certain that if she were scared it was also something that she liked, as seems to be the case with women who want to go to horror movies. It was an inescapably charged scene and Garth could not hinder Tabitha's determination to attach herself to him at that moment in a specific way which best remains between the two of them, and also only concerned whomever may have been obscured behind the light-reflecting windows of those fifth floor rooms in Wright Hall.

They climbed down the tower and went to get dinner at a local Chinese restaurant. Tabitha had already gone by his group house before she had met him on the Cross Campus and she had found one of his roommates who let her put her bags in the house. They were both so distracted by their affection and each other's attention that they could barely manage to eat some barbecued spareribs, fried pork dumplings, half a Peking duck, wonton soup, beef with broccoli, some salted and breaded fried shrimp in the shells and kung pao chicken, washing it all down with a few cold beers. The bill arrived at the table accompanied by sliced orange pieces and two fortune cookies. Tabitha opened her fortune cookie, smiled and showed it to Garth, "A man with brown eye surprise haste good luck for you."

"What does yours say, Garth? Mine seems to be about us."

Garth opened his and looked at it. He smiled and she started to fidget in her seat. He told her that his fortune was directly pertinent to hers and to their lives. Then he popped it in his mouth and ate it and told her he could never tell her what it said. It was a lark, a goofy joke. He had no idea how she might take it, which was not quite as well as he might have hoped.

"I can't believe you did that. You're just cruel."

"It's a joke."

"No it is not. It is mean."

"Okay, okay, I will tell you what it said."

"You can't very well do that now, can you?"

"Sure I can."

"Just forget about it."

When he told her what it had said, she ignored him. She was genuinely upset. And she stayed that way for several minutes. There was something about her mind that could become very focused on a particular thing, and when that concentration might become frustrated she would not like it very well. He was unsure what to think about it, or what it had to do with anything, or if the problem had stemmed from some inexcusable tone deafness of his or from one of her quirks. But he had one idea.

There were no real dance clubs nearby that he knew of, so he took her to the one local tavern that he knew had a jukebox and which occasionally had live music and dancing. Tabitha was naturally given to sporadic effusions of a very communicative and expressive comportment, and two things, strong drink and dancing, had the effect of animating the deeper currents and mysteries of her heart. After only two mixed drinks and listening to music on the jukebox, her inherent playfulness and passion and expressiveness were soon warming to life. Garth then heard about her family, her studies, her jokes, her social life and the furious fancies of her heart, all at great length and with colorful effect and all while she stood only a foot or two away from him, most of the time with both hands on his one forearm, the one that held his own drink. Had she been a fine English Pointer hunting hound, she might have been said to have once again been "on point." This suited Garth well, as the fortune cookie imbroglio was no longer on her view screen and he was again the object of her exquisite and heightened attentiveness.

It is a commonly overlooked verity that the abuses we suffer in childhood can become the stalwart pillars which keep upright the palace of our adulthood. Garth's two older sisters had been born six and eight years before he had, and were only nineteen months apart in age. This was a very natural setting by which it hardly has to be explained that the young boy was often the subject of much torturing at the hands of a tandem of teenage girls. Part of this unrelenting and cruel torment had been that Garth was often forced into the role of an indentured dance partner for one or the other. Through a syndrome that for some inexplicable reason bears the name of a Scandinavian capital city, he came to actually identify with the dance even though he would never allow his sisters to know of this change of heart, which was augmented and vindicated when he was later to attend his first middle school dance. All the middle school girls danced only with other girls, and the brave and stoic boys would gather at the edge of the dance floor to jointly scoff at the entire terpsichorean enterprise as a waste of energy. Garth did not stand on such a principle when one or another of the girls urged him onto the dance floor. Almost as if by two concomitant Pavlovian principles, that of being directed to dance and of simply being directed by females,

Garth found himself walking out onto the floor and dancing his way into the good graces of his feminine classmates. While he fully expected to find that he had also boogied his way into some trouble with his young buddies, he found that his actions actually led some of them to be less principled than they had originally appeared to be, and they would then attempt to join the young ladies and him, only without the benefit that Garth had from his training. At this point in this particular evening this scene from his adolescence was the subject of a reenactment and soon Garth and Tabitha were dancing to the jukebox music in their corner of the bar.

Elliot Barker in the meantime had been without any notice or consideration left to his own devices. In such a state he was far from impoverished. He had felt the need for some manner of diversion and he had considered the timing. Upon conclusion of the last final examination of the first year of law school the next day, almost all of the class would disband and head off to their respective summer habitats. Elliot saw this dispersal as an opportunity to temporarily abandon one of his cardinal rules of personal behavior, one which he had learned long before this, and one which in the popular vernacular went something along the lines of saying that one should not make a bathroom of one's kitchen, or one should not locate an important function at the site of another critical utility. In this case it was not a question of not relieving himself where he also ate, but it was his personal prohibition not to go hunting among the homes of his own neighborhood. He would abandon this particular rule for this evening alone, because his neighborhood in this instance was breaking up and the repercussions of whatever stalking and bagging he might do in it would be quickly be dissipated by the scattering of his classmates. He had long since marked his prey and at this point his task would be to locate her and flush her from cover.

Susan Stratton had arrived at Yale Law School from the Pennsylvania State University in a way that had been remarked upon earlier by Elliot, who had told Garth that it was his understanding that every over-achiever from Scranton or Erie, Pennsylvania gets into Penn State and is convinced that he or she got into Harvard. Apparently, Ms. Stratton had not been satisfied alone to mentally elevate the great state university of the keystone state to the status of an Ivy League school, but had set her sights on an actual Ivy League graduate school which she had reached in a similar manner, by working very hard to achieve something well above that which she might have reached, relying upon her natural gifts alone. She also had in fact been that sacrificial lamb whom the professor in the first year Contracts Law class had selected for a continuous barrage of questioning. He could not have chosen a more useful candidate than this earnest blonde woman who had actually gone to high school in York, Pennsylvania, and who was already intimidated by the setting to which she had successfully aspired. She visibly cringed at the fourth, tenth and seventeenth time she had heard the professor intone, "Miss Stratton?" And she had stumbled over her answers, which had been at best only half correct, as the professor had so kindly shown the class. She had done what she could to hide her tears in each of those cases and she did her best to bounce right back up each time, as if she had been one of those blow-up clowns that are given to children for a punching bag, meaning that at the bottom of her, Susan Stratton had a good deal of sand.

There was also more than sand and blonde hair to her as well. She had bright blue eyes and a very pleasantly attractive face. Her form was well proportioned with a hint of athleticism. Elliot had spotted her long before the Contracts professor had, as well before his classmates who had their attentions drawn to the more superficially attractive women, the ones who made themselves up and wore dress clothes to class. Elliot had also made note of Susan's emotional constitution, which was quite sensitive but also resilient. And there was something more. When he had his own small contretemps with the professor and had stated his intention to always pass on questions, Susan Stratton had stared at him with a direct and startled expression that was a mix of awe and disbelief and respect and a sense of an unalterable difference between herself and the object of her gaze. Her stare had lingered on him long beyond the time Elliot and the professor had concluded their discussion, and it had softened into something else which seemed, to Elliot at least, to reside somewhere along the meridian that runs between reverence and lust. Only his self-proscribed rule against philandering where he also studied had held him at bay. But now his friend Garth had left him with little alternative for entertaining himself, and now there was only one more night before his first year law school class would disband. As Oscar Wilde had once written about Hamlet, Elliot's aesthetic sense was his only moral guide. He was going to do something, which to him was interestingly beautiful. He was going to do Susan Stratton.

He needed to find out where her study group was meeting that evening, and he had to fly by the seat of his pants on this because he had been denied the opportunity to scout the terrain by the fact that he had only chosen this course of action when Tabitha had arrived to deprive him of Garth's company. The only person that he knew was in Susan's study group was Rick Phelps and Rick had also been a Yale undergraduate, so he had been given the job of being a counselor to a group of freshman. He was paid for this and he was given free housing in a freshman dormitory. This was Elliot's only chance, since he did not know the other members of the group other than Susan and could not have known where any of them lived. He would take this chance and he decided that he needed to dress the part, so he had gone by his apartment and had grabbed his Criminal Law book and went to Rick's room and knocked on the door. As luck would have it, he had found them. When the door was opened, there was a general look of disbelief upon the faces of the members of that study group. Elliot quickly charmed these away with his smile and by humbly asking if he could study with them this one time before their last examination. He sat down quietly and, after some awkward silence, Rick Phelps spoke.

"So the professor had once hinted that in Texas and only in Texas there are two additional legal precedents for the affirmative defense of justifiable homicide, beyond the one that exists in every other state, which is self defense. I have read all the Texas murder cases and I cannot accurately define what they are. Since he made specific mention of this, there is a likelihood that it will be on the test. Does anyone have a handle on it?"

There was some more awkward silence, and then Elliot spoke.

"I think you could say that these two affirmative defenses boil down to first, honor, and second, the son of a bitch needed killing."

They all looked at him. One or two looked at him blankly. One or two seemed to understand him. And at least one of them looked at him with a lusty veneration, or a reverential passion. It was Phelps again who spoke.

"Of course . . . I think I know what you mean. There are a few Texas cases of acquittal, which in other jurisdictions would have been second-degree murder convictions, where a husband escapes conviction for killing his wife's lover. I see that, and now I see that the other cases where homicides have been excused were when the victim had been a wife-beater or a head of a drug cartel or had otherwise escaped conviction for other crimes."

It was not long after this that Elliot had more or less commandeered the study group. After what he had convinced them was a successful conclusion of their efforts, he led them from the Rick Phelps' room on the top floor of Wright Hall to the local bar that had a juke box and from time to time had live music and dancing. Then they all settled into a large corner booth just in time to see Garth and Tabitha return, she from the ladies' room and he from the bar to get drinks, and resume their dancing. The men in the study group smiled knowingly and quietly elbowed each other, while the women simply blushed. Elliot was sitting next to the blushing Ms. Stratton. He put his hand on hers. He had distinct plans for testing her overachieving in very specific ways.

For Garth the rest of the evening was a whirlwind of Tabitha. She was warmly and passionately effusive on the dance floor. Dance was where and how they had first connected. This evening was in that way an anniversary celebration as well as a reunion. Every undulation of her willowy form was an expression of an unusual feeling that could only be called a combination of her joy and of her passion, and each such movement was focused with laser intensity at Garth. Though they were watched intently and were the subject of much discussion, she saw nothing but her boyfriend and heard nothing but the music. Others got up and danced alongside them, but for Tabitha they might as well have been in another room. Garth was the subject and object of her dance, and he would have given her anything for which she might ask, as if she were his personal Salome, more dangerous than Wilde's, more romantic than Strauss' and even more electric that Rita Hayworth's. But all she wanted was his attention and his dancing companionship, which he gave her unreservedly. Then at a certain point in time the evening swung on an invisible fulcrum, and he was again reminded of the wisdom and principles of the middle school boys. For two people in love, dancing is a beautiful and fulfilling expression of their affection for one another, and then it comes to a point when further dancing is a waste of valuable energy. So Garth took his stand on principle and led her to his residence.

He did not sleep a wink and it was a night he would remember fondly forever. The next morning he suddenly realized that he was going to be late for his final examination in Criminal Law. He bolted from the bed, grabbed a cold coffee off of the kitchen table, drank it and threw on the same clothes he had worn the evening before. He had a hangover and he felt sure that he was quite ripe, and as he dragged himself to the law school he half wondered if sea gulls might follow him, or cats. The test had only begun five minutes before he arrived, and his classmates were each hunched over it and looking at the question about homicide in his home state of Texas, when he walked into the room. He slinked as quietly as he could to the front of the room and picked up a test from the proctor. He was still in a haze and had thought he had been as discreet as possible, when suddenly Elliot Barker stood straight up from his chair and began to clap. In this, Rick Phelps followed him, as did the remainder of that study group. As a murmur spread through the room, each of the other students joined. It may or may not have been the first and only time a Yale law student received a standing ovation for showing up for a test, and it certainly was an amendment to the legend of Elliot Barker at law school, which then briefly become the legend of Garth and Elliot. By the end of law school two years later, it had again changed to the legend of Elliot and that other wild guy from Harvard, because Garth never returned to that law school. He had moved on to Capitol Hill and to politics and to a married life with a beautiful young woman whose vibrant presence contained within it the strains of an inescapable absence.

GOLDEN FRISBEE

Melinda stood next to her fallen foe, not really comprehending what she had just done. Porter appeared stricken and Mr. Callahan was smiling broadly. In the next moment, she was suddenly overwhelmed by another tide, this time a foaming surge of riotous boys, all disorderly, aggressive, territorial, independent creatures, and all of them charging right at her, grabbing her, pulling at her, smacking at her and shouting.

"Way to go, Melinda!" they seemed to roar in unison and then sequentially.

"Wow!"

"Did you see that? It was a reverse spin kick. And she is just a white belt."

They piled on her. She was their hero. She was their surprise, their special associate, the member of their hunting party who had brought down the mastodon, the legendary story they would tell their parents that night and their friends the next day in school. Then Mr. Callahan stepped in and said that there was something all of them had been forgetting. They quickly formed ranks around the two sparring partners. The boy whom she had defeated stood up and faced Melinda. She faced him. They bowed to one another.

Standing upon the grand eminence of twenty-first century wisdom and peering backwards into the darker space of a few decades earlier, the wise observer may decide that this merely was an anachronism (while the less thoughtful onlooker of today might see it as a brand of titanic and incalculable foolishness.) The parents of this boy had sadly failed to fully weigh the options before placing him in a situation in which they would actually be paying rock-solid American dollars, in order to give their son the opportunity to learn how to lose. The abject folly of their mistake may have been unfairly and more clearly illuminated in this case by the exaggerated and unique particulars of this situation, since their son was now actually bowing before the person who had vanquished him, and that individual was a karate neophyte. But it is perhaps too facile and lacks deeper consideration to feel that this family had been grossly wrong-headed in the arena of child development, when one has already been imbued with the more enlightened values of our current day. At this previous time, a blue ribbon for the first place finisher and a red ribbon for the second place finisher were being insensitively awarded in the "Field Day" events at the London Elementary School. The incorrectness of this barbarous practice springs too easily to the mind of a more modern parent for whose children that one blue and one red ribbon have long been replaced by white ribbons for each and every student which now say, "Everyone is a winner at London Elementary." The overt wisdom of shielding children from negative results, from losing, from bullying, from being the least bit disappointed, was not as accepted once as it is now to the more progressive mind. The imputed grace with which Melinda had then bowed and acknowledged the effort of her defeated foe, and the ostensible dignity with which he accepted his defeat, and her acknowledgement of it, were only universally to be realized by the turn of the twenty-first century as being hollow and dull. At this earlier point in time the only great minds with the prophetic astuteness to see ahead to this currently accepted wisdom were those dance studio mothers on the first floor. They had farsightedly grasped the correctness of placing children only in activities that are a form of a vanity press, where everyone is an applauded winner, and the fragile and developing identities of American children are allowed to be cultivated without anything negative ever happening at all. These mothers were prescient and in fact were path breakers in what more generally was to become the way in which children are now to be consistently and usefully rewarded, simply for trying, in which those generous prizes are to bear no relationship to the effort or skill that went into the rewarded enterprise, and in which children would be safely protected from what they actually would have to face in the adult world. It was the wise and accepted way of raising children that derived from what had earlier been so thoroughly pink.

Certainly, this more sensitive and positive approach would have more adequately prepared Melinda for what she was going face in the months to follow this particular day. The antiquated notion that there is a lesson for a child to learn, and in a game at that, from the idea that an individual might actually lose, or that not all enterprises end in applause, or that victory most often is achieved by the individual who earns it, probably did not serve her well as preparation for what was to come for her life at home. She clearly would have been better prepared had examples of loss never visited the precincts of her heart, because very soon that home life was about to devolve into poverty, illness, a parade of strange men, religious fanaticism, betrayal, recriminations, and utter bereavement.

And as often as not, such developments will take up their residence in the American game of baseball. The events of the day in which Melinda had been floated up to the karate school do not do justice to the monotonous dreariness and sorrow with which her days and evenings at that time had trudged painfully forward, nor did the memory of those events survive within her beyond the front door of Mr. Callahan's establishment, once Melinda had crossed that threshold in order to go to the parking lot and get into her father's car with her brother. That old man had shrunken beneath the pressure of some hidden grief, which marked the unsettled and despondent wandering of his troubled mind. There had been traces too in his maundering words and in his failing wit of what appeared to be a nascent madness. For anyone who might have cared for him it was a time of anxious watching and concerned attendance to any of the signs that might have been a confirmation of a more settled and permanent disquiet and despair. Such pithy apprehensions would have lain heavily upon the breast of an older or more experienced person. But to a child, to a compassionate and loving youth such as Melinda, they constantly surrounded her and they were ever present, the source of countless inclinations toward restless action. Melinda suggested to her father that, when they were to return home, they play a game of catch with a baseball.

William Sherman had loved baseball. He had learned it from his father and he had been teaching it to Porter. Porter had taken to it in the way that a turkey takes to flight, with great effort and noise and an ungainliness that took him some time to begin to overcome. But fly he did. He loved his father enough to work at it, and it had become for Porter the one thing at which he became consistently successful. His academic record was streaked with elements of disappointing failure, mixed liberally with outstanding results that stood in greater consonance with his considerable intellect. But those intermittent disasters did not occur in Porter's youth baseball career. There he had made slow and steady and good progress. Baseball was the place where the two Sherman males loved each other the most and with the least interference and dissonance.

It surprised and saddened Melinda to see that her father was no longer active or interested enough in life that he would suggest to her brother that they practice pitching a baseball, that he would no longer see it as a reason for which to rise up from his chair. And Porter would never be more than a passive element, one who responded but rarely initiated, even in what was the considerable way in which he loved his father. So Melinda struck upon this as a way to move the old man out of the chair and into playful interaction with his children. She did what might have occurred to her brother, if such things ever occurred to him. She essentially dragged both of the Sherman males out into the yard to toss around a baseball, and to get her father to resume his instruction of Porter in the development of that boy's pitching.

This was one of those subtle and gradual changes that had been occurring in Melinda but which had found greater expression after her first vision at the river and after the overland odyssey she had initiated. There was for the first time an element of self-persuasion to her efforts. They had not even been efforts before, but had simply been unmediated expressions of love and support and compassion. At those times she would hug her father or kiss him on the cheek or simply talk to him. Now there was an element of the imperative and of necessity that was somehow greater even than love, which was also subject to the kind of nascent intellectual consciousness of her own role and capability which had begun to form in the girl. It is not at all uncommon for men far more accomplished and well educated than this nine-year-old girl to make their inclinations into duties, and to take gratifying credit for the imputed self-denial seemingly inherent in this manufacture. For a certain element of calculation to have inserted itself into the process of loving her father was useful, and in this case even more loving, since his deterioration seemed to call for more than she might have been able to muster earlier.

A palpable fear and uncertainty were suppressed by this love and in this effort, and they would on occasion return to Melinda like a blast of cold air from a window flung open in the winter. She could and would quickly close that window. The chill of weakness would pass and she would then summon the resolution to persevere, by relying upon the inward fire which was the one idea that her father's survival depended solely upon her strength, and that no help would come from her mother's restrained deportment or from her brother's naïve inattention. She was sensible of a new confidence and energy within her, because, whatever way in which she had felt the responsibility had been divided before, she knew now that she must think and act out of necessity in order to shoulder the burden of his life entirely on her own. When Porter's efforts at learning better how to pitch had faded, and he returned no more than the effort that he sensed coming from his lethargic father, each of them weakly tossing the ball back and forth with little intent to teach on the one side and less effort to learn or to enliven the situation on the other, Melinda jumped in for the first time and demanded that for a change she be the one to receive the instruction in pitching.

No less of an American sports commentator than a ropey fellow named Henry James provided, in 1875, to all American sports enthusiasts of every subsequent age, a brilliant and accurate prognostication on what was much later to become the ascendance, in the American popular imagination, of football over baseball, and the reason for the same. He did that approximately one hundred years prior to it actually happening, when he said that Americans are the only people who judge things on the first impulse, when they do judge them at all. Football, the most commercially successful of all American sports, has in the greatest degree this appeal to the American first impulse. Basketball is the third grand American sport, and the essence of the charm of this great athletic contest is that it is the city game, and wherever there is a park with a basketball hoop, the sole and mere requirement for it to be played by any small group of individuals is for one of them to have brought the ball. Football requires a great deal of equipment and a specialized field, as does baseball, the now second great American game, but still the nation's pastime, or past time. Baseball arises from and speaks to that part of the American soul that comes, though now diminished, down to us from the past, the part that is pastoral, that respects a game that reduces nicely to a box score in what were once known as newspapers, that can be understood very well when heard on a radio, or that moves with enough pace that it can be enjoyed at the park in between other intentional distractions such as conversations and children, that is elegiac, that is susceptible to numbers and the musing thereof, that has found its current cultural and social place through a personal transition from millions of fathers to millions of sons during individual games of catch, that carries the echoes of Walt Whitman, and that opens up its nuances and subtleties to the observing student and presents a larger universe within its smaller text in a way not unlike what happens in the studious observance of the writings of that same poet, and that is completely unlike any other American sport. This segment of the American psychology that gives rise to and appreciates baseball is referred to by its more technical and scientific nomenclature by sociologists, psychologists and other noble scientists, who have labeled it the baseball part. With a toothpick between his teeth and the *Daily Racing Form* in his hand, Mr. James may not have opined upon baseball as he had upon the cause of the rise of that other sport's popularity, and the reason for that may be perhaps that he stands within that baseball part of us.

Into this long tradition Melinda inserted herself to become one of the rare daughters among the millions of sons. In a way she was serving two impulses, firstly the desire to energize her father in any way, and in particular in this case, to get him to become more engaged in the instruction of pitching, and additionally because she had long before this watched many of Porter's instructions and had wished and wondered if she could do the same as he. She took to it quickly and naturally. And she noticed a spark of interest in her father's expression and since he would still not speak, she addressed him.

"See, father, I know how to place my posting foot on the rubber and how to bring the ball down, back and up over the line behind the rubber that is on an axis directly toward the plate. I also know how to bring my landing foot straight down on the front part of that axis line, pointing directly at the plate," she said, glancing down at the lines her father had long ago chalked and re-chalked on the driveway.

"I see that, Melinda," her father said quietly.

"And, I think I am finishing my motion straight down that axis line with both my pitching hand and my follow-through leg."

"Yes, Melinda."

"Why do I have to do that, Father?"

"I think you already know, Melinda."

"Am I throwing strikes?"

"Yes, you are, dear."

Never had a pupil a more humble, docile and fretful teacher. And never had a master a more patient, tireless and considerate student. They stumbled forward in the lessons. She never really was able to elicit much more activity or commentary out of him, but at least when they were outside her father was faintly engaged. He was catching and returning the ball and he was answering questions. She, more often than Porter, was the one on the chalked pitching mound, since Porter's participation had sunk to exactly the weary level of instruction that was coming from his father, and Melinda saw that he was not much help. So she would jump into the pitching rotation and start asking her questions while throwing strikes. A brace of consequences flowed from this. She had dug a grand mine, and had extracted a sampling of ore of a method by which to get her father out of his chair and to engage with his children. And even though a number of girls who were slightly older than she had already recently broken the Little League Baseball gender barrier, very few had been as good as she, and none of them had been in Kentucky, where Melinda went on to play for several years, becoming one of the best pitchers for miles around, winning almost eighty percent of the games she pitched, and striking out an average of one and a half boys per inning. This too was a way to get her father out of his chair. He had to drive her to her games in order to answer her persistently lively questions, and to faintly and feebly accept or defect the frankly salty encomiums and overly colorful compliments of the other parents, many of whom were the fathers of the boys whom Melinda had struck out.

There is a point at which an attempt at verbal expression becomes like being a sculptor working in marble, where the teller of the tale must wrestle with his subject even less than he must struggle with his material. The words have their own stony grain and calcified veins and pockets of creamy softness that force the story into a shape that seems to arise from the stone as much or more than from the sculptor, and almost independently of the imprint that is meant or hoped to be formed. Saying that William Sherman remained in his chair is simply the way to express his condition with the greatest efficiency, and without letting the verbal marble take over to too great a degree, which is simply what would be the case with using words like depression or anxiety, which carry so much of their own flinty dispositions into the narrative. And it was the way Melinda saw it. He was just in that chair too much. And he was there as conditions around him in the home declined.

On this errand of elevating her father from his chair each day, she would hurry home from school to get to the house as quickly as she could and in this she was not always impeded too greatly by her brother. Normally, he would trudge along and he would present to her a flat affect as she would ask him repeatedly why he was not moving more quickly, or as she would ask him whether or not he loved their father enough not to pick up his pace. Further asking of questions, she soon learned, only served to slacken the look on his face even further, and to have the same effect on his plodding pace. At these times her brother was actually being very attentive, just not to his sister. His awareness was more intently focused on the bright houses and on the flights of birds that turned like waving hands and dipped in the sky. He watched the gamboling of local children or the way in which a slanted ray of light illuminated the gloom under the trees. What was particular to Porter in these instances was that these houses and birds and trees and children were actually to be found only in his mind. Sometimes when he would not just slog along slowly and attend to these fields of the daffodils of his soul, he would simply take a seat and do it, or walk backwards and do it. Or he would pose as a statue and do it. Melinda had hoped so fervently and for so many long months for a change in her brother's demeanor, that when the change did surprisingly manifest itself, she was not as suspicious of it as she might have been, had it sprung out of a blander foreground. It came to her as a gentle and needed shower in a drought, and not as an all-out storm.

Almost at once and almost two years into the period of Melinda's conscious effort to keep afloat the dwindling spirits William Sherman, the wild flowers dancing in the breezes and the butterflies in the inclined beams of sunlight, the florid scents and the watery pools, the blowing leaves and chirping birds to which Porter attended upon the road home from school, were to be seen on that actual path, and this time seen as well by his sister. It is known how her desire for this change prevented her from taking more notice of it, but she was even more greatly compelled to not seek beneath its surface by the impelling need she felt to get home.

It has been said that genius is capricious, that by its very nature it is not the product, but is the generator, of concerted human effort. But there are also extreme circumstances which give some dauntless souls the unmediated desire to act without regard to all the normal and cautious considerations that must be measured otherwise, such as when a ten-year-old child who has never driven an automobile drives a very sick sibling to the hospital emergency room, or when businessman's failing business is saved by a counterintuitive and dramatic change of operation that requires expending the few remaining corporate resources, or when a flight attendant lands a faltering airplane when neither the pilot or co-pilot is conscious. These are not adrenaline-fueled outbursts of strength that arise from perceiving threats to a loved one, but are kinds of a rare and mysterious bestowing of a superior knowledge upon an individual who chooses recklessness over inaction. Such fruitful visitations are quite outnumbered by the car crashes, the dramatic bankruptcies, and the plane wrecks caused by similar choices. This admittedly is the pesky element of caprice asserting itself into the process of attempting to force genius, an effort that it normally flatly denies at the beginning.

Such a rare bestowing is certainly of a manner of genius, though it is strictly a practical brand. Melinda's need, and her quick and unthinking reaction to Porter's change, quickly generated trips home from school which were accelerated not only over the pace of the recent trudging, but over what might be expected on a good day. Melinda simply urged him to some distraction over the forward horizon or near it, and he would flit and fly to it and all she needed to do was quickly follow him and continue to point out some new figurative carrot without ever picking up again the stick of questioning. They would proceed like bees over flowers only in a straight line to the crumbling Sherman home. That her brother had moved from appearing to be held in place by a deep and inner traction, to a deportment of a more naked senselessness and aggravated lack of all consideration, was either lost on Melinda or of little use to her in the job she saw as her foremost. She had the same inherent sense that all individuals have at any age and without thinking, that there is in all mad creatures some element that is seen to be of the divine. But she was not disposed or even able to discern until much later the way in which for her brother that element was coming from a direction just off of that source by only a few degrees.

Melinda's version of this brand of genius was to remain practical and sane while straining against the winds and the rains of their opposites. And the wind and the rain, well, they were to be every day, inside as well as outside the siblings' home. Walking into the Sherman home at this time was not entirely unlike what it might have been at any time in the last few centuries to travel to Italy, or more specifically to Rome. Every step was through the monuments of a burial ground of a life and of a time, each of which were more golden and larger than the present ones. In response to this the Italians adopt a lively and worldly devotion to the joys of the moment and they do so with *sprezzatura*, and it confers upon those monuments the moderated quality of appearing to be almost merely a setting for the buoyant and urbane carryings on of the those citizens that are lighter than those of the much earlier long periods of armed or spiritual empire, or of that era of the first spark and flowering of the rebirth of classical values. Melinda could not speak Italian and was only able to find that country on a map by virtue of its unique shape, and she unquestionably was not in a position to move in time with those relaxed and belated rhythms of the Mediterranean. She was more sharply conscious of the sense of loss; the understanding that what had been best was in the past and always would be. And she was also like a Roman Italian in that she was unlike most everyone in London or Kentucky or North America, all of whom are imbued with that sense that they are on a path toward, and not away from, a time and place that is larger and more golden.

There was very little that was good to eat in the Sherman home, and the plastic slip covers which the children's mother had at one point put on the furniture were cracked and broken, and the very furniture which she had sought to protect with them was sagging and breaking. Most of the food was of the variety that in many American homes can be found in the backs of the cupboards and pantries, and is only ever even seen at times near the end of long power outages and continuous snow storms. It was canned and boxed and bagged and had been gathered at bargains and going out of business sales. There was clutter, distorted lumpish figures of things that no longer resembled what they once might have been, old cartons the contents of which had been emptied and forgotten and many scattered articles of indefinite origin. The graying floral wallpaper was peeling at the seams and edges, and the children wore clothes that were too small for them by the measure of a few years of their natural growth. The dust motes that may be found in any home had convened to become dust groups, dust institutions, dust villages and towns. There were great dust metropolises that had been founded upon corners and moldings. Light bulbs were out and carpets had been soiled. There was a haggard and brigand aspect to the kitchen, which gave the appearance of having been used in the manner more of a scullery or a galley, only without the maintenance each such a place might require, such as if the stove had been used not to its original purpose but as the site of a campfire. Unseen to all who would not have investigated, was Melinda's well-ordered and very spare bedroom, the only such neat one in the house. In the center of all that was on the first floor was the easy chair and in it was William Sherman, who had developed a bad cough and a serious limp, who had not had work in years, and who had begun to seem more and more like a door that had come out of the jamb, making the worst kind of noise whenever there was a failed attempt to put him to use. Around him moved one purposeful young girl in her early adolescence, and she was always working to give him medicine, engage him, feed him and get him out of the chair. Recently out of his mouth there were occasional dispersals of blood, foul breath and histrionics. Also around him were the more shadowy movements of a kind of ludicrous sprite, a harlequin spirit of a teenage boy, seemingly removed two or three steps from the requirements of gravity. There was also the more shadowy passing of a phantom, compact, blonde woman, attractive in her middle age and moving swiftly and quietly, and only at the apogee of the orbit of her husband.

During one such transit, the father of the Sherman house blurted out to no one in particular, "Don't let her come near me. Is she still there?"

"Father, Father, please relax. It is only Mother," Melinda said, casting a glance at the older lady who only knit her brow as she looked at Melinda and the man.

"Keep her off me. Send her away. I can't bear her near me," he exclaimed, sinking deeper into the soft chair and casting harrowed glances at his life's partner, who was slinking along the wall past him in the living room.

"Please be calm now, Father," Melinda said. "Everything is all right."

"I am weak and helpless now, Melinda. She will murder me," he said, and the mother of the two children suddenly stopped in her progress and gave Melinda a look of sad surprise. "I have sorely disappointed her and she will extinguish me for it. I have not done well by you children, especially you, Melinda, and I will be punished for it. Look. Look at her eyes. They burn into me. See how they do. If you had known how she has shown how I have disappointed her, you would know what that look means. She is an evil spirit. I have seen her cry because of me. Keep her away."

Melinda looked at her mother, whose look of sad surprise grew into one that was more of a startled sadness, but now contained a glint of something else. There was also a question in that look, and an abdication to Melinda on the demands of dealing with the father of the Sherman family. Melinda made a tender and sympathetic face which clearly communicated its meaning to her mother, saying, "Perhaps you had better simply not be in his sight, and his health may be better if he does not see you." And the woman vanished. The appearances of Melinda's mother had already begun to become more infrequent. It was at first due to the fact that she began to work in the evenings as well as in the daytime. For some time she had held a secretarial job at the local federal prison, which had hours that allowed her to get home fairly early in the afternoon. After William had lost his job, she began to work evenings in real estate or as a waitress or at a retail sales store. Melinda was never sure. She only knew that her mother came and went in the evenings and often in the company of a different person, one with whom she was working at the time. At one time or another she had seen her mother picked up or dropped off in the evenings by a local labor official, an Irish man, a college student, a distant cousin of hers, an orthodontist, a very short fellow, some men in the business of sales, and a colleague or two from her day job. They had all been very nice and behaved even quite gentlemanly to Porter, Melinda and their father, who was civil with them as well, in his docile way. After a time though, Angelina Sherman had gradually undertaken in the evenings more often to simply go out to the person's waiting car, and to come into the house from the car that had carried her to or from her home, without making any introductions. Even before the Sherman father's outburst and certainly after it, sightings of Mrs. Sherman had begun to become less numerous, more fleeting, somehow less illuminated, and always more lacking in substance or activity. Melinda was not entirely sure she was still living in the house, which not all that alarmingly did not overly concern the girl whose responsible nature made greater dictates upon her, in order to deal with a more ominous situation. At least her mother was not an impediment.

Porter's alterations in comportment had not been limited to his walks home from school. They had immigrated into all the regions of his various endeavors, so that now it was as if all the locations of Melinda's own activities were at that point shared with a highly-strung nomad carnival youth who had a little too much to drink. The closest thing to an explanation that she could ever get from him was a phrase, occasionally tacked on as the caboose of a long train of excited and motley and often unrelated other expressions, ". . . you know, because we are orphans," or, " . . . because it seems we orphans are again without foster parents." He was agreeably sprung free then from all filial, fraternal or other familial restraints, and suddenly the entire world was for him more commodious and comfortable and his awareness of the wider and more outward curbs that were imposed upon by this broader world were hardly within his notice, or only jokingly so, such as the time not long before this when he had brought home his report card, the first one with some failing grades.

"It scarcely matters," he had said, "since I must soon embark on my life as if I were Robinson Crusoe. You may be my man, Friday, Melinda. We will go somewhere to be free of all spies and listeners, to a desolate and sequestered island sort of spot where children are in charge, and all they need be concerned about are the rats and mice. We will have no school and there will be no authority and we will be fine, secret and stealthy fellows together, slinking about where we may. Such is the life of orphans once they have been liberated from the corruptions of a government-sponsored system of foster care."

His mother had told him that if he were to continue on his current path he would be a failure. His father had mildly concurred. And Melinda, who had made use of Porter's changes in order to lose less valuable time with her father, now began to concern herself with the ways in which his alteration encumbered her efforts in other ways.

On the driveway one day, as Melinda sought further instruction in the art of pitching a baseball from her father, Porter had wandered off only to return at the head of a troop of neighborhood dogs, barking and howling. He crossed with his domestic pack back and forth across the imaginary axis line between her on the pitching rubber and her father behind the plate. One of the dogs leaped at a particular pitched ball and deflected it enough that it struck her catcher on the chest. Many young boys in the local Little League had been kindly and instructively reminded by their fathers numerous times of having been struck out at the hands of a girl, and this had been due to the fact that Melinda had regularly thrown strikes. But they were of the looping variety, and landed in the catcher's glove with little enough velocity and not sufficient to do much damage to a man, should he be struck by one of her pitches. Despite this, Mr. Sherman coughed and stood up as a trickle of blood came out of the corner of his mouth, and he fell over on his side because his one leg was not strong and well. Catchers play the most dangerous position in baseball and are often injured by runners barreling home, intent to break up the play of a catcher making a catch and a tag, on a ball thrown in from the outfield. They are also often struck and hurt by deflected pitches unlike this one only in velocity. This was perhaps the first time in the long history of the national pastime in which a catcher had sustained injuries from having been set upon by a pack of dogs. They had been so wired and made high-strung by the hopping and pirouetting that Porter had done, that they fell upon the older man, snapping and barking and bouncing. The catcher stumbled again in trying to rise and repeatedly fell, barking his elbows and knees on the pavement, while he was among the barking canines. It was a tableau that Melinda or anyone else could not fail to see with an inner eye, and draw from it some inescapable meaning that could also not be explained. Porter laughed and moved on with his pack. Melinda put down the glove and ball and helped her father into the house.

Then after another year had passed and as swiftly as he had first changed, her brother, the mercurial orphan, became again much more like he had always been since before he had fallen prey to the inward distractedness, or since he had become the font of the outwardly directed frenetic behavior. He became the brother Melinda had known growing up, sweet, funny, a bit feckless, distracted, expressive, smart and imaginative. He walked home with her from school without incident, quietly, as she directed him in helping her with their father. This was an all in all very good development and she welcomed it. But this time its foregrounding had given some cause for a more careful consideration of any change, no matter how salutary.

There are in the way of all thinking some very deep and profound elements that are only touched as if by a feather or a needle, or by accident. They will remain, as do many great truths, silent before the most strenuous efforts to render them sensible. Only the slightest and most casual strumming may play these most meaningful strings in the soul of a person. Gone were the Bacchic histrionics of her brother. And gone was the delving deeper down within himself. Here he now was as normal as he had ever been able to have possibly been. But there was something else about him, and it was perceptible to Melinda as a bit of a glow.

"So, Porter, what has happened to you this time?" she asked.

"You know, Mindy, how we saw those pictures in that book by that guy, Frangelico?"

"You mean that art book with the very old religious paintings?

"Yes, and in that one, in those Frangelico paintings you could tell the people were holy because the sacred people had these golden Frisbee plates behind their heads?"

"Those were their haloes."

"Well, that is what you see now. That is why you asked me that question. I have been waiting, because I knew you would see. I knew you would see the golden Frisbee I have behind my head."

"So, are you telling me . . ."

"Yes, I have found Jesus, and he has found me."

She eschewed telling him that she had indeed noticed the glow, because she did not want him to launch the identical twin monologue again and more importantly because she was moved beyond words by his admission. It would take some thought, a great deal more, before she could give it any expression.

The contagion of the world's slow stain had left its expected marks on

William Sherman. He had been a mild mannered and loving man of good, but not all that strong, character and he had allied himself in marriage to a bright, lovely, vibrant, woman from a foreign land, a region of ancient suffering and historic privation. It had been one of those strange and strong infatuations that occur daily all the time in the thoroughfares and market-places and parlors of the world. He had entered into this match with all his moderate strength and fullness, all his capacity for love, and all of his honest good will. And he had paid for it every day of his life. Each one had ended with the sun setting on some small part of him, which he had sloughed off. Now that measure of who he had been, whom he remembered from that old time, became like the late spouse of a person who had long been a widow or a widower. He felt a kind of pity for the youth of his former self, and a not too nostalgic remembrance of what had been the strength of his naïveté, and he knew that this young William had long been dead to him.

The old and current William had come back into the house after baseball one day several months later, and sank more deeply into his chair, perhaps so profoundly that he might not be able to rouse himself from it again.

"I feel very weak," he said. "And there is so much I have to someday begin."

"Yes, Father," Melinda said as Porter stood quietly by, "we will do so much more."

"We will win a few baseball games, Father," added Porter, for the first time in some while, actively assisting his sister in her ministrations.

"So I have been thinking too," the father answered. Then he clasped their hands and no one spoke, as then his grip relaxed as if he had begun to fall asleep. Melinda put his hands back on the arms of the chair and stroked the one of them. She wiped his forehead with a handkerchief.

"It is all going to be better now," he weakly added, coughing. "You two will help me, won't you?"

"We always will," they added in unison.

"Before I had a family I was truly ignorant and now I am merely one of the wicked. I know you will forgive me being a dreamer. I do not have to ask that. And you will forgive your mother. No, you know that there is nothing for which you will need to forgive her."

His children were silent, as he sought to raise himself a little bit. He slipped back down into the chair and into a recondite and ineffable weariness. Then he sat up and with a new and sudden clarity.

"There is something important, Melinda, that I need to tell you about yourself," he said.

He again slumped down and this time into that place where secrets are too easily and forever kept, where if he had been handed a thousand teacher commendations he would not have been able to grasp a one of them, to the place from which not even baseball nor the love of a devoted daughter could ever extricate him, and forever to that cold and empty place past which Melinda also began to hope he might pass. She hoped he might move beyond the void, to a brighter and higher world where he would finally be peacefully happy, and where perhaps he might personally be in a situation to be able to get to the bottom of what was, with Porter, this whole Jesus business. At least he might be in a position to do that, one better than the more grounded situation in which she was. She felt the loss of her father as if it had been a complete and utter draining, leaving behind a dread vacuum into which then rushed new responsibilities and cares and duties relating to her brother.

So she herself would try, that is, to get to the bottom of it.

IN LIFE AS WELL AS IN FICTION

"Tell Garth to get me some wordage on that thing there," Garth distinctly overheard Congressman Fitzkin say to his chief of staff, Genevieve Chester. Genevieve turned to go speak to Garth and was surprised to find him right in front of her.

"Is 'wordage' even a word?" he asked.

"How would I know?" she answered. "I didn't go to Harvard."

"Well I have heard of wording and verbiage. But I never heard of that word."

"But you know what he means."

"I sure do and I will get right on it."

Garth was just glad that the Congressmen knew his name. It was only two weeks into his unpaid summer internship and he seemed to be making fairly good progress. He had been given the unpaid internship because his parents lived in the Congressman's district. It was true that all the other interns were college students and Garth was a law student and that he had gone to Harvard, but he was happy to have risen above the position of just being a constituent who was allowed to hang around the office for the summer. He had immediately taken to the tasks that he had been handed, the first of which was answering letters. He quickly was given other tasks such as researching legislation that was coming to the floor of the House, and providing memoranda that the Congressman could read and by them better understand the issues. It helped that Ms. Chester liked him. That is, it was useful in the office, but it actually meant that she was far colder and more distant to him than she was with anyone else. She was only a year or two older than he, and apparently had been given her job despite the lack of any Capitol Hill experience. She was also quite attractive, so the insecurity of her position kept her from appearing to be too close to the good-looking young Harvard graduate who was at the bottom of the office food chain. But she was interested in moving him up, because she had hoped he might replace one or two of the legislative assistants, who were permanent staff and whom she knew were dead weight.

He returned to his desk and got to work on "that thing" for the Congressman, which it turned out was the second energy crisis of the decade, the one that had been precipitated by the fall of the Shah in Iran and a drastic cut in the production of Iranian oil, at that time the world's second largest producer of oil. (The first such crisis had been six years before this, in 1973, and had been the result of an embargo on shipping oil to the United States from Arab states in protest of the support that the United States had given to Israel, in defending itself against coordinated attacks by Egypt and Syria on what was the holiest day on the Jewish calendar.) Though Congressman Fitzkin was only a freshman Congressman and one from whom little was expected, Garth was excited at the prospect of having a small voice in such a pressing national and international issue. Earnest Dapple had been correct; this was a world that appealed to him much more than the law ever could.

"It is a word, brainiac boy," Genevieve Chester gloated as she stood over his desk with a copy of *Webster's Dictionary* opened in her hands. "It says right here that it means the same thing as verbiage."

"Okay," Garth smiled, "but who blankly asks for verbiage? What does he think should be done?"

"He is not paid to think. You are. So let us know what he should think on this matter," she smiled right back at him, closing the dictionary.

Garth thought she was attractive and he made it no secret to her. This made her nervous as much as she liked it. She was still a little out of place. He fit in on Capitol Hill a little better than she did. For one thing he already knew more people there, people from high school or college. His own style of dress was casual prep school. Even though it was not so much a fashion statement as it was an expression of his lack of interest in clothes, it also was practically the uniform. Genevieve went to greater lengths to dress up and have her hair done, but it was much too much in the manner of her hometown, apparently somewhere well outside the Washington Beltway. Still, Garth liked that he would see her on Pennsylvania Avenue outside the Cannon House Office Building and she would be the only woman not wearing a khaki skirt and a blue blazer over an oxford cloth blouse. Whether it was some Middle American version of high fashion or not, it was draped over a very fit and slender feminine form that could not be obscured by any article of what Garth had dubbed Terre Haute couture.

The possible solution to the energy crisis that Garth first considered was no different than what everyone else was talking about, deregulating the price of American crude oil which had been held down by regulations developed under the Nixon and Ford administrations. In 1973, the price of gasoline had gone from roughly thirty-five cents a gallon to about sixty cents a gallon, and in 1979 to about a dollar and twenty cents a gallon. Such high prices reflected the increase in the cost of oil produced outside of the United States, but the price of US produced oil had been held down by regulation to one third the price of foreign oil. Eventually, President Carter would deregulate oil production to spur domestic development, and he would tax the oil companies on their windfall profits. When Garth had summed up all of these options to the Congressman, he was summoned into the Congressman's office for the first time. He went in with Genevieve.

He explained that the immediate impact of deregulation would be an increase in production in the Alaskan oil fields and more oil would flow through the Alaska Pipeline that had been built in response to the first energy crisis.

"I supported that pipeline," the Congressman said, "even though they all said it would disrupt the migrations of the caliboo."

Garth shot a quizzical look at Genevieve.

"Those caliboo don't vote."

"I remember," Garth said, "that they had to build crossing stations for the caribou at regular intervals on the pipeline."

"What I care about, Garth, are the people. They vote," Congressman Fitzkin added, "and right now those people are waiting in gas lines. I need some big idea. Do you have anything that no one else has done, something to make people take notice?"

"We could draft a bill to create a national oil company," Garth suggested quietly.

"What do you mean?"

"Almost every major Western democracy has a national oil company. Holland has Royal Dutch Shell, the Shell stations. The British have British Petroleum, BP. The Italians have Eni and the Belgians have Fina. The Brazilians have Petrobras. In fact, Winston Churchill came up with the idea of British Petroleum because he realized a long time ago that oil was of global and strategic importance and he felt the government needed to have a stake."

"Do you mean to tell me that Shell is not an American company?"

"No, sir, it is not, and it is owned in whole or in part by the government of the Netherlands."

"And no one else has had this idea except me and Winston Churchill?"

"Since the biggest private oil companies are American, and since we have a history of seeing government ownership as socialism, it is not an idea that has caught on here yet."

"Let's run with it."

The idea of a national oil company was a little left of center for the United States, but it had some appeal to certain people for that same reason. A bill to create such a corporation was drafted and the Congressman introduced it, and it received a great deal more attention than anything the Honorable Mr. Fitzkin had done up to that point. The bill attracted co-sponsors. Reporters called. Ralph Nader endorsed it. It was even part of a hearing on the topic and the Congressman was asked to testify. Just as importantly, the lobbyists for the large American oil companies became concerned and they came to call on Congressman Fitzkin. The Congressman represented a rare district with very little oil, and these important companies had previously ignored him. Garth was immediately hired as a legislative assistant and was paid a salary. He replaced an older man, named Slupkey, who had been hired simply because he had been defeated in the Democratic primary against Congressman Fitzkin, and he had treated the job as a sinecure, which it was. Garth bought a motorcycle, moved out of the one room, month-to-month rental apartment that he shared, and moved into a two bedroom apartment with a Harvard buddy of his who was attending law school at Georgetown University. He also transferred from Yale Law School to go to night school at Georgetown. And, he proposed to Tabitha. She accepted.

Several months later in the early summer about four weeks before the date of their wedding, Garth received a phone call at work from Mr. Murray Goldstein, bandleader of Murray's Miracles, the band Garth had hired to play at the wedding reception.

"Mr. Teller," he asked, "is this a good time to talk?"

"I am kind of busy," Garth said, "but if it is important, please go ahead."

"I think it is important, Mr. Teller."

"Go ahead then, please."

"Is your future mother-in-law, Mr. Teller . . . Is she, well, is she a colorful kind of character?"

"That is an understatement," is what Garth thought to say about Gabrielle Barrett, the strikingly beautiful, alcoholic, brilliantly selfish woman who was Tabitha's mother and who was on her fourth husband, but what he said was, "You might say that, Mr. Goldstein."

"Well, Mr. Teller, you might want to call all your other wedding vendors, the florist, the reception hall and all the others."

"Can you give me some idea why?"

"Well, I don't want to make anybody angry, Mr. Teller, but I got a phone call from your future mother-in-law telling me that the wedding had been canceled. I told her that I was still going to show up as we agreed because I had not heard from you, Mr. Teller, and you are the one who wrote me the check and made the agreement with me. Then she said, 'But I am the mother of the bride,' and I told her that the name on the check I had was not hers. But, Mr. Teller, not everyone else is like me. You might want to make some calls."

"Thank you, Mr. Goldstein. I certainly will. Oh, and you are right. The wedding is still on, until you hear from me otherwise."

"That is what I thought, Mr. Teller. That is what I thought. I have been around long enough to have seen this kind of thing before and as I said, you and I had the agreement."

Garth's first call was to the florist, who had indeed taken the wedding off the calendar. This was the case with the caterer, the dressmaker, and even the church.

The wedding had been set for that summer. Tabitha's mother and father had long been divorced and were remarried, he to his third wife and she to her fourth husband. Her father had graciously agreed to pay for the entire wedding, if only Tabitha would just as graciously leave her mother entirely out of the ceremony. Tabitha would not do that and instead had decided to try to include both of her parents. Her mother could not pay for it, and her fourth husband, Tabitha's stepfather for the last dozen years, since she had been nine years old, had kind-heartedly refused to pay for anything at all. Garth was living modestly and could afford to pay for most of it and could borrow the money to pay the rest. It had been agreed that the reception would be held on the grounds at the large second, or summer, home of Tabitha's mother and stepfather on the Connecticut seacoast. In her effort to be inclusive, Tabitha had done the traditional thing and had the invitations printed up with her both her mother and her father's names on them, with her mother's summer home listed as the site of the reception.

The bones of contention had only come up once those invitations had been printed and only a few weeks prior to Mr. Goldstein's phone call. Tabitha's mother began to insist that the seating arrangements at the church place Tabitha's father somewhere near the back of the church and his wife somewhere outside of it. She also insisted on inviting seventy of her very most intimate friends and all of the neighbors in her vacation community, and their children.

"Cucumber sandwiches," had been her response when Tabitha reminded her that Garth was paying for everything himself and could not afford to have such a large crowd served catered meals.

When Tabitha told her that they wanted to give a decent meal to the three dozen friends and family who would be coming some distance, her mother pointed at the invitations and said, "Whose name is on this invitation?"

It was at that point that Garth and Tabitha decided to move the reception to the country club where her grandfather, her mother's father, was a member. And the old gentleman stepped in to make the arrangements. He was well aware of the issues surrounding his only daughter. Tabitha gently informed her mother of the change and had left it at that. Whatever leverage her mother may have had was removed. What has been described as tunnel vision, which Tabitha had with respect to the limits of her attention, was actually an impairment inherited from her mother. A long-term interest is by definition something that is not on such a person's view screen. And Tabitha's compassionate and caring nature was not something she had inherited from her mother. Mr. Goldstein's phone call alerted them to this difference between mother and daughter. And after Garth and Tabitha had made their phone calls and had patched the wedding arrangements back together, they again made the same mistake. They had left it at that.

"I just got a second wedding invitation in the mail," the mother of Tabitha's high school boyfriend told Tabitha on the phone. "It was like the first one, except it is only a photocopy, it lists the reception at your mother's house, and it has a big red magic marker X across it."

Garth would not be caught like that again. He called the country club to find they had canceled the reception because they had received a call from the mother of the bride, saying that she would not be responsible for all the drugs and public sex that would be going on among the guests. Garth had to remind them that their member, Tabitha's grandfather, had not called to cancel, and that the friends of Garth and Tabitha were overwhelmingly Ivy League college graduates and that Garth worked on Capitol Hill.

He then hired two plainclothes policemen to attend the wedding and reception in case any more mother-of-the-bride stunts might occur. Tabitha called everyone who had been sent the real invitations in order to awkwardly ask if they had received any others. Garth double-checked with all his vendors and with the church. He called the bridesmaids and the ushers and discovered that Tabitha's younger sister and brother, who still lived at home, had been told by their mother that they could not be in the wedding. Then he thought to call his own parents. He could hear his mother fingering her necklace over the phone line. She was on a second phone while he talked to his father.

"We are glad you called, Garth," his father said. "We received an interesting phone call from Tabitha's mother. She said that the reason the reception was no longer going to be in her seaside neighborhood was because too many neighbors had complained about you and her daughter . . ."

"I know. Let me guess, Dad, about drugs and public sex."

"Yes. This is her own daughter she is saying that about, mind you."

"Don't worry, Dad. The wedding will go off as planned. It will be all right."

"It is not the wedding I am worried about at this point, Garth."

"I know. I know, Dad."

Four weeks later and without incident, two plainclothes policemen were among the thirty or so guests who saw Tabitha Vivenda marry Garth Teller. Several invited guests, all on her mother's side, never showed up and never responded to the invitation. And since Tabitha's mother had effectively taken herself out of the whole event, Tabitha's father stepped in paid for the catering.

After the honeymoon, Garth returned to work in the office of Congressman Fitzkin. A new legislative assistant had been hired to replace another one of the original sinecures, and Genevieve Chester was a little bit more relaxed because her position had been solidified. As is so often the case in life as well as in fiction, this is exactly when the ax will fall. That November the Congressman won his reelection and replaced Ms. Chester with a man who also had no previous Capitol Hill experience but who had the resounding virtue of being the brother-in-law of the Congressman's mistress. The attractive Ms. Chester may or may not have known that she had been originally hired to assume the role of mistress. She had never taken that second job, choosing instead to play it straight, which is rarely if ever the way to play anything in politics. The new chief of staff cleaned out the office of original hires and kept only Garth and the other new legislative assistant. These two quickly conferred and began quietly to look for other jobs. And it was in that conference that Garth learned that this new friend of his, Barry Thomas, had once run a Congressional campaign. This was why he had been kept, in order to provide the political advice to the new chief of staff. Garth had been kept because he had been doing most of the legislative work, and maybe because the mistress approved of him.

Garth mined Barry for all the information and advice he could find on how to manage a Congressional campaign. He even took notes. Barry was his new best friend. He was brusque and highly intelligent, of Irish descent, and had grown up in New York City. They respected each other's intelligence and were regular guys together, drinking beers late nights at the local Capitol Hill watering holes. Tabitha had surprised Garth after her graduation and at the time he had first begun his internship by telling him that she was going to Duke University Law School. They had never really discussed her future, but the law did not seem to suit her any more than Garth, and probably less so. She had the temperament of an artist. She could do the research. But Garth could not see her arguing cases. So, that first year that he was actually paid in Congressman Fitzkin's office, Garth knew that Tabitha was going to be in Durham, North Carolina. This encouraged him even more to stay in Washington, DC. The memories of what it meant to be away from her and the way she had of being further away than mere geography also had encouraged him to ask her to marry him. He did not want her to fall off of the Waldseemüller map and into *terra incognita* again.

After the wedding, Tabitha went back to Duke and Garth went to campaign school after work in bars with Barry.

But Garth had another plan, one which he did not tell Tabitha. The following year was going to be a redistricting year. Texas was likely to gain between two and four new seats in the US House of Representatives. One of those new Democratic candidates was likely to consider hiring a bright young Harvard grad from Texas who knew both politics and Capitol Hill, as a campaign manager. Garth had seen that there were a few ways to be hired or to advance on Capitol Hill. One way was the patronage way, to be part of a politician's entourage or train. A second way was to be a policy expert, someone who could do the thinking for a Congressman or a Senator in a particular area. There was a third way that Garth had chosen to take. Every thought and every gut feeling that Garth had experienced on the subject told him that the life's blood of the place was the politics, that persons who had made their own way with political acumen were not as dependent as others. He also knew that everyone would expect him to take the policy path because of his education. But he wanted the nuts and bolts, the ballots and phone calls, the press releases and volunteers, the fundraising and polling. And he would become a double threat, an operative with policy ability.

The upcoming year was a redistricting year. The census finally determined that Texas would get three new House seats. But the state legislature was taking its time drawing the map for the new districts. And a federal lawsuit had been filed regarding the shortage of minority representation in the Texas delegation and it was a possibility that a federal court would draw one of the new districts. So the state legislature did not want to act before that was resolved. Garth had compiled a list of every state senator, state legislator, every mayor or county commissioner that he barely knew or with whom he had some connection and he prepared a letter for each one. The letter introduced him and in it he detailed how a Congressional campaign might be run on his or her behalf. It was long and detailed work. He mailed the letters, not waiting for the final lines to be drawn so he might know to which persons would reside in the new district. And in the middle of the night on most nights he would wake up, sometimes in a sweat and most times with his mind very actively addressing the possibility of his running a campaign. It was all a fever dream, one called ambition.

On weekends Garth would either ride his motorcycle to North Carolina to be with his wife or she would take the bus to Washington to be with him. It was on one such weekend that they received a visit in Washington from Eakin Lambert and Dick Trent and their son, Anthony Trent. Eakin had received her master's degree in business administration and the young family was on its way to Birmingham, Alabama, where Eakin would begin her career at the US Steel plant there, as an assistant plant manager. Tabitha, who like Eakin had also kept her family last name, was presented to Mr. Richard Trent. She found him to be bright and charming with a captivating gaiety. He had an easy manner, which worked very well with the baby boy. It struck Garth that he seemed unchanged since he had first met him, as if he had been untouched by the experiences of the last three years.

"Why have you chosen a job in manufacturing, Eakin?" Garth asked. "I thought all you Harvard Business School types went into finance."

"Those jerks, they spend their whole lives getting rich, but have they ever made anything? Have they created a single job, or created something new? They're just parasites." Tabitha found her attention focused on Eakin. The customary ease and confidence that Eakin shared with Tabitha's husband was noticeable, and for Tabitha that was something she more or less had to stare at until she had put her mind around it. Garth sensed this and attempted to put his wife at ease. And because there was a bond between Eakin and him that would survive undiminished whether he spoke with her or not, he began to engage Dick in conversation.

"Dick, did you just do that drawing right here and now for the baby?"

"Oh, yeah, give me a sketch pad and a pencil and I will forget appointments and business and how to add and subtract money. My wants are few. Anthony here and I are kindred spirits. We have no idea of time and we both are fond of things that are blue."

Garth found this entire conversation to be remarkable and troubling.

He knew that Dick was the only man Eakin would ever love and that she could not see anything related to him with even a trace of objectivity. So he was hoping that Tabitha would see and hear what he was seeing and hearing, so that he could talk to her about it later. But she was looking at Eakin and hearing very little.

"In a way," Dick continued, "I live for love. You are all such practical people. I wish I could set you to music. That would make a great song. The baby boy is like Eakin. He is such a little universe in himself. And she, oh my god, she is like the morning. Birds mistake her for the sunrise. I hope to spread bowers on the path before her for the rest of her life."

Garth could almost love him for that sentiment, but there was something awkward, something different. He wished his wife were paying attention. Eakin just smiled her wry smile.

"So, Teller, are you going to putter away on Capitol Hill or are going to finish law school and become a famous litigator?"

She knew him almost better than he knew himself. She knew that his ambition was not contained in his job as legislative assistant to Congressman Fitzkin and that he must be brewing some plan. He could also tell by her sarcasm that she knew that the plan did not include law school, even though she had mentioned it. He sensed that she knew the plan, and that he had not told his wife about it.

"I might do something soon," was all he said.

"So, Eakin," Tabitha interjected, "you and Garth grew up together, right?"

"Well, one of us did," Eakin answered.

"And you guys went to that camp together?"

"Until your husband got us kicked out, that is."

"But you never wanted to date Garth?

"No, I usually just wanted to smack him, you know, for being such a clueless dork."

"Oh. Oh, okay."

The next day, Dick and Eakin took Anthony and went on their way south. Garth asked his wife what she thought of Dick.

"Oh, him, he was nice."

And he asked her what she thought of Eakin.

"I don't know. I wish she wasn't so familiar."

Garth was at work some days after this when he got another call from Earnest Dapple. He would come to see these calls as milestones.

"Hey, Garth, old boy, you seem to have taken to Capitol Hill like a duck takes to duck sauce, just like I predicted."

"You were right about that. I have to give it to you. So what is the purpose behind this call?"

"I guess I mean to say that you should not get too comfortable."

"Why?

"You do know that the governor of Texas is a Republican and that he will have the biggest say in what happens with the redistricting for Congressional districts. And the federal court has created a heavily Democratic Hispanic district on the Gulf coast. The state legislature is going to have some demographic leeway to try to gerrymander districts to try to knock out some Democrats."

"Okay, so tell me something I don't know."

"Your boss is going to switch parties and become a Republican, to get help with redistricting."

Garth suddenly remembered some things that Congressman Fitzkin had once said to him, about a big idea, and something, "that no one else has done," and, "that would make people take notice." And he remembered that his mistress was a Republican and that the brother-in-law had been sequestered in long phone calls over the last couple of days.

"What makes you think I don't know that?" he said to Earnest.

"Thanks, Teller. I appreciate it."

Earnest broke the story the next day. On the following day Congressman Fitzkin made his announcement. Soon after that the new lines were drawn. Congressman Fitzkin was given a new district, one that included much of his old district and some new Republican areas. Barry Thomas and Garth resigned their positions in the Congressman's office, stating that their commitment to the Democratic Party prevented them from working for him. Garth again sent his letters out, but this time they were focused on Democratics living in the Fitzkin district. He met with some of them and talked to more of them, but none of the people he spoke to decided to run. Then the filing period closed. On the Democratic side, four of the candidates were private citizens with no name recognition, and the fifth candidate was a state legislator to whom Garth had never spoken. Garth knew that this man would win the Democratic primary and would face Congressman Fitzkin in the general election. Garth was despondent. He did not know this man and did not know anyone who knew him. Garth no longer woke up in the middle of the night in a cold sweat.

Then he got a call at home.

"Garth Teller," the state legislator said, after introducing himself, "every son of a bitch for miles around tells me I should hire you to run my campaign."

"How soon can you come to Washington?" Garth asked.

THE JESUS BUSINESS

The Jesus business, it seemed, had one of its local franchises at a storefront establishment known as the Christian Community of London, Kentucky. Melinda possessed a strong nurturing instinct, which had been energized by her need to develop her innate fierceness. She also had newly cultivated a faculty for detached calculation that educated it to a greater effectiveness. Importantly, this instinct had been informed by what may only be called her visions. If the Christian Community had been a giant Burmese python that had swallowed her brother whole, then it would have been her inclination to allow it to gobble up her, so that she might have a chance to fight their way out from within the belly of the beast. Before she would act, she would take the initiative to look over the place. There was little she could determine by viewing it from the outside. She was curious to see what specific branch of commerce was such a business, and at first she was convinced that it was more than anything else something like a single big box store belonging to a large retail chain, such as Wal-Mart or Sears. It looked like such a large retail establishment, and it seemed to draw the same large crowds, and from an identical demographic, which certainly should mean that it had somehow evinced a very broad appeal, selling a little something for everybody and at the lowest possible price.

Her impression that it was a Wal-Mart of the soul was not misleading. It gave her an excellent insight into the broad and robust appeal of the establishment, but it fell short of helping her to understand the depth and power and elusiveness of what it was she was about to confront. She might have been better served to understand it as a metaphysical abattoir.

She had just buried a father whom she deeply loved and there was little she would not do to keep something similar from happening to her brother.

When we cast our gaze toward the horizon our view is almost always restricted by the buildings in front of us and all around us, and by the trees and the hills that lie in the direction of our observation. We are not unlike the narrow philosophers who are content to examine what is in front of them and not give any thought to the truths that are hidden beyond their inspection. What is within the buildings or behind the hills is as far from our consideration as are the fields of Elysium or the markets of sunken Atlantis. The world is broad and complex and subtle and most of it is hidden to us. We are therefore and forever simply looking down the street.

Melinda's view even at a young age was never so restricted, or it may be more accurate to say that she never settled with what she could see merely looking down the street. This was mainly due to the regular occurrences of the particular manner of manifestation, one that visited her once again as she walked home from where she had stood to observe the Christian Community of London, Kentucky. If what had entered her at that time had simply been a dream, it might have been ascribed to the recent passing of her father, since it had many of the themes that could have identified as being in common with that loss. But Melinda had been awake when she felt what by this time had become a familiar tingling in her jaw and a gentle buzzing in the back of her head. There was a rhythm to these sensations and the cadence of them stayed the same as they increased in amplitude. Soon she was looking at another familiar mental image, one that was a harbinger of what could only be called her visions, as is certainly recognizable to the multitudes of others who share with her this common faculty. She could no longer see the road or the trees or her surroundings but could only see images of blocks, which were the colors and sizes of the wooden blocks in children's toy boxes, and each one of these blocks would stretch and in their centers they would become attenuated, as if they were taffy being pulled. No one has to be told what sort of thing followed this.

Melinda had stepped into a three-dimensional movie with sights and sounds and scents, and she was suddenly in a park full of Japanese cherry trees in full blossom in the early spring at the point where two rivers flow together. There were shadowy figures of many people moving about, taking in the view and the floral scents in the air. Three central figures in this vision were in stark contrast to the spectral crowd around them, as if they were the only figures that had been filled in by crayon in a coloring book. They were a man in his early middle age and his two children, a boy around thirteen or fourteen years of age and a girl about two years younger than the boy. Even though these envisioned children were roughly the age of Melinda and her brother they were different in significant ways. The boy was quiet and tall and blond and appeared thoughtful and the girl had round, full facial features and big, expressive brown eyes. The man was attractive, tall and fit, with deep-set and very dark brown eyes, with black eyebrows and a high forehead and brown, almost black hair. He and the girl had that look of being one-quarter part of an indistinct ethnic derivation that could have been Latin or Middle Eastern. The boy was lighter and looked clearly northern European, but his features too closely resembled that of the man and the girl for them to have been anything other than family. The children were running and playing with each other while the father watched them kindly and diligently without hovering over them or getting in the way of their playing. His deep-set eyes conveyed a sad intelligence and a gentle resignation, but with a spark of his own youthful playfulness.

"Dad, Dad," the girl shouted as she ran toward him, "Seth called me a bad name and said a dirty word to me."

"Oh did he?" the father said.

He immediately got down on one knee and put his head at the height of the girl's face and he smiled, "and what do you think of that?"

"I think you should punish him," she said, glancing at her brother, who was looking rather sheepish.

"And why do you think that, Hanna?"

"It makes me dirty and bad too when he does that."

"I want you to remember this," the father said to both of them. "Nothing from outside of you can ever make you bad or dirty. Only the things that come from inside can make you be those things. Who we are and what we are at heart is never truly in danger from the outside world. The only danger lies within."

And at this point, Seth began to look a little bit sheepish again. His father stood up and placed his hand gently on the boy's head.

"So, maybe you should think again about saying things that disconcert your little sister. Don't you think, sport?"

"Yeah, Dad," Seth said, as both he and his sister hugged the man around his waist.

"Now what do you two say about us going to get a cheeseburger and fries?"

It was a variation of a vision that would occur to Melinda many times over the coming years and she would subject it to various interpretations. When it had ended and she found herself again on the streets of her hometown, she needed to take a few moments to adjust and to acclimate herself to her surroundings. In order to do this she took deep breaths and surveyed all three hundred and sixty degrees of the landscape that surrounded her. Over and over again, she said the one thing that represented her strongest connection to the real word, which was the name of her brother. This same brother was then subject to her gentle interrogation when she returned home.

"Porter, what is it that makes you so sure about this Jesus business?"

"I don't know. I guess I don't like to be alone."

"You will never be alone. You always have me."

"That is kind of the true, Mindy, but only on the flip side. You always have had Dad and me in your heart, and always did what you could to take care of us. So you are not alone. But I always am and always will be. But I can be alone with Jesus and it is all right."

"That is awful, Porter," Melinda said sadly.

The theological landscape of the Sherman home had long been a damaged snapshot of the Protestant Reformation. William Sherman had been a Lutheran and the Sherman children had been baptized as such. They had also had attended services and Sunday school at the local Lutheran church until their father had begun his downward slide. Neither of them had been confirmed. Their mother, the former Aniolek Bol, and her entire family in Kalisz, Poland had been Catholic, even to the point that two of her aunts had been nuns. But Angelina Sherman had long since lost all faith in or understanding of a God whom she felt had permitted World War Two, the Holocaust, and the predations of the German and Soviet armies. This skepticism had found its way into the religious training of the children, and they approached church only as something they must do. William Sherman's fallback position had been to rely upon the foundation in faith of Luther's priesthood of believers. He often read Bible passages to the children and discussed their meanings. While the brother and sister may have approached the sacraments of the Lutheran Church with something less than faith, their father had hoped to inculcate them with a feeling for the Scriptures. In a curious irony, at the insistence of their mother they had also been baptized in the Catholic Church when each of them had been born. When William Sherman had questioned his wife, she said, "Well, I don't want them to spend eternity in Limbo." And when Porter had asked her why she kept a rosary in the car, she had told him, "I don't want us to get into an automobile accident." Some part of her clung to the outward elements of her native faith, and in this way she was not too different from a few of the more devout of the creed from which she had fallen.

"I don't understand, Porter," Mclinda asked. "When father read to us from the Bible you never showed any interest."

"That's the thing," he smiled, "I don't need the Bible. All I need is Jesus. And he can come to me when I am alone without the Bible and without going to church."

Melinda's understanding of Christian theology was limited, but this sounded strange. She was going to make a point to try to always accompany her brother on his sojourns to the Christian Community of London, Kentucky. The next such visit was the following Sunday. Porter, in his musing, had been correct in one respect; the children now were effectively orphans. Their mother was a ghostlike presence in the home and they largely were on their own. Decisions such as this one, where and how and whether or not the children would worship, were for them to make. Porter had decided to join this large non-denominational congregation, and Melinda decided to go along with him.

As they walked there on Sunday morning, the first thing that struck Melinda was the sheer number of cars in the large parking lot. There were well over one hundred vehicles, meaning that a few hundred people would be inside for the service. What she and Porter did not know was that their native Kentucky had been the genesis of exactly this sort of thing. In fact, some have said that the American nineteenth century began in Cane Ridge, Kentucky. At the very least, the vast social and religious phenomenon, of which Porter and Melinda were about to become a small part, had begun on August 6, 1801, only ninety miles north of where they stood.

Twenty-five thousand people, an astounding number given the population and modes of transportation then, had gathered for ten days for America's first great revivalist camp meeting. In the words of the primary minister to this great flock: it was reported that there had been spontaneous barking, dancing, laughing, speaking in tongues (the first record of such), jerking, singing, falling to the ground, and running, as the Holy Spirit had entered various of the participants. What came out of Cane Ridge were various religious groups but one large and syncretic and particularly American spiritual movement, the drive toward a religious experience that was Christian and not denominational, that had no creed, that sought to be the original apostolic experience of Christ, that focused on adult baptism or being born again, and that was based solely on the experience of faith and not on Bible study or on any catechism.

Here, almost one hundred and eighty years later, Melinda and Porter were at the beginning of another religious trend in America, which may be the tip of the long shadow of Cane Ridge. For the many years following their first visit to the Christian Community of London, Kentucky, more congregations of all Christian sects would break off from their denominations, more people would leave strictly organized religions, more congregations would engage in informal services (with coffee and doughnuts and music and without a liturgy), more churches would loosen the restrictions for entering the clergy, fewer people would seek to become ministers as a profession, or would attend regular service, and all of the old mainstream Protestant denominations would shrink in size while the Catholic Church would only be able to keep its membership levels stable through the immigration of people from the countries of Latin America. While the apologists of the large Protestant denominations would call this an emergence of a new manifestation of the spirit, it was a diffusion of American religion, even though the United States remained the most religious nation of the industrialized West, excluding only Ireland. Only one religious development would see an increase. More people would attend huge services at non-denominational mega-churches and upwards of ten percent of all worshippers could be found in the one percent of these largest churches.

Among this throng of people, Porter was energized. His own volatile demeanor began to show an increased possibility that he also might engage in spontaneous barking, dancing, laughing, speaking in tongues, jerking, singing, falling to the ground, and running. Melinda, on the other hand, felt fearful and overwhelmed. So she was glad to hear a familiar voice.

"Melinda, Melinda Sherman, it's me, Tommy Kitt," it said.

Before her stood the same lad whom she had defeated in her first day of karate lessons, in all his good-natured, red-headed, smiling glory. Tommy had figuratively been smitten by the girl who literally smote him. He had climbed up off of that floor only to find that he was in love with the young lady who had knocked him to it. It was not the first nor the last time that such a thing has happened in the world, and such happy circumstances are not alone confined to karate schools.

"Oh, Tommy," she said. "It was a lucky kick, you know. I had no idea where it was going. In fact I think I was falling down to the left as I swung my leg around."

"I stepped to the right, as I saw you spin. It was an accident or a coincidence. You became famous after that day."

It was not the only time such fame had been acquired so easily, nor are such situations limited to karate bouts.

"And here you are, coming to the Christian Community of London, Kentucky," added Tommy. "I don't believe that there's such a place in all the world for coincidences as London is!"

"I am beginning to think you are right, Tommy. I sure am."

"You have to come sit with us," Tommy said.

His parents gave the Sherman children that unique look which is only ever reserved for children who have lost a parent.

Melinda knew that Porter would not want to sit with the Kitt family but she also knew that he was suggestible and very attached to his sister. So with Tommy and his parents on one side and Porter on the other, Melinda entered the building. The huge meeting room was the shape of a half sphere and along the straight edge, in the middle, a stage stuck out into the rest of the room. On the stage were a few chairs and a speaker's stand. The rest of the half-round room was lined with rows of theater chairs in concentric semicircles. There were two aisles running to the stage from the back in such a way that the seats were divided into sections that each represented a third of the seating capacity. The ceiling was high, and gradually rose to be at the highest point just over the stage, so that the space resembled half of a round tent. The walls were blank. It looked like a great big camp meeting tent of a building. They sat down together, not in a pew, but in a section of seats near the rear of the building.

The minister, Reverend Seymour Barton, approached the speaker stand. He had a receding brow and a strong-featured face, once noble but somehow faded. His eyes were cunning and clever and showed a great deal of penetration. He was a large-framed man with dark eyes and graying dark hair and his flesh was a little loose about his face and hands. He rested his chin on his hand in deep thought. He smiled a smile that made Melinda tremble. There is a tone of voice that individuals use when they convey a secret which is also piece of particularly good news to someone else, a tenor that is happy and congratulatory and somewhat smug, as if the sharing of the good and previously undisclosed news put both the speaker and the hearer into an exclusive club. This was the tone of voice with which the minister addressed his flock of hundreds, with a leather copy of an unopened Bible in his left hand.

"It has often occurred to me that the Bible is not a textbook for outlining all the actions we should perform for God to secure our faith, such as prayer, service, witnessing, worship, fellowship with other believers and giving money. The good news is that God has acted first."

Melinda was surprised. There had been no invocation, no confession, no prayer, no hymn, nothing like what occurred at the beginning of the Lutheran services she had remembered attending. She also had the same anxious question in her mind, which had occurred to her when Porter had told her that Jesus could come to him without the Bible and without a shared creed, and not through some holy sacrament. Then she was concerned because all the notices had said that the service was to be an hour long, and from all appearances, this man was going to fill that entire hour with his sermon. Porter appeared to have delved down deep into himself, or perhaps he was alone with Jesus. But Tommy had noticed her concern.

"I will tell you my secret, Melinda," he whispered. "Just take the main words, like Jesus or God or the Spirit, and substitute other words for them. That is what I do. It is how I get through this thing."

She immediately accepted this remarkable wisdom and listened accordingly.

"McDonalds has secured our faith in McDonalds itself and for itself. It is not what we can do for McDonalds that saves us, but what McDonalds has done for us through the Big Mac that saves us. The Menu is a text that describes how McDonalds has redeemed man to itself and for the glory of McDonalds. The Menu is a text, which gives us reason to feel overwhelmed by the Big Mac's presence, its kindness, its greatness, and the personal sacrifice of McDonald's love for us. We should be overwhelmed with giving thanks, for the Big Mac is there for all of us, through the humility of the

Big Mac and by the medium of the Holy Ketchup. And the Menu becomes an inspiration by which we humbly accept the Big Mac, through the Holy Ketchup. The mind controlled by the Ketchup accepts that the Big Mac has atoned for our sins. The Ketchup will guide you to embrace what McDonalds wants for you through the Big Mac. The Menu is the good word, which says that the Ketchup may enter each of us and show us the sacrifice that the Big Mac has already made for us through the glory of McDonalds. McDonalds loves us, each and every one, through the Big Mac, and on a personal and intimate basis."

Melinda began to smile as she digested the remainder of the hour-long sermon, for which she had previously had little appetite. Her smile was that of one who possesses a tantalizing secret. Paired with that of her brother, it gave them each a rather beatific appearance. At first Melinda thought that she was imagining that the minister had occasionally settled his eyes upon the two of them, but as the hour progressed she could see that he indeed had spotted them, and had singled them out for some greater portion of his attention.

As the two of them exited the building after the sermon, Melinda was only half surprised to see that Reverend Barton had stationed himself at the one of the three exits through which the Kitt family and she and her brother were about to exit. He stopped the family to shake the hands with its male members, and to quietly exchange some words about the two Sherman children, which Melinda could not hear. She also noticed that her brother had the figurative golden Frisbee behind his head again in a very pronounced way, and it may have been that he had imbued too much of the Holy Ketchup. But his state was more likely due to the proximity and the attention of the Reverend, who placed his heavy hand on Porter's shoulder and asked him a question.

"And who is this young lady, Porter?

"This is my sister," Porter smiled.

"I assume she has a name."

"Her name is Melinda."

"We are happy to meet you, Melinda," the man said. "And we are very glad that you have chosen to come with your brother and to join us today." Then he turned away and spoke directly to Porter alone.

"Will you be able to come to my office in a minute so we can discuss your progress in our community?"

"I would love nothing better," Porter responded.

He stood behind the minister as that man greeted and dismissed the remainder of his congregation, including the Kitt family. Melinda turned to Tommy to thank him for being there and for helping her.

"Aw, you know there is not much I won't do for you, Melinda. It is my pleasure. You're the best," he said in a manner which, in addition to being very complimentary, was notable in such instances for the novelty of also being sincere.

She grabbed him by the shoulders and planted a kiss on his fore-head, and for Tommy it was more blessed than anything that could have happened to him in the service. There was not enough ketchup in the world to have made him feel any closer to divine than he felt from that kiss. She turned around just in time to see her brother disappearing back into the building with Reverend Barton's hand on his shoulder. They both had apparently forgotten her. This fact, and her considerable athleticism, allowed her to quickly slip inside the structure, get behind them and glide inside the office door just as it was about to close behind them. For all his spirituality, Reverend Barton was a worldly man, and worldly men do not have their eyes on the heavens but on the ground level around them, where they know that their sophistication works best quietly and when it is beyond notice. He did not show any surprise at the sudden arrival of the girl, and instead showed the open countenance of a gentleman who has neither done nor considered anything for which he feels the need to explain.

"Hello, young lady," he said. "Please have a seat. I trust you did not find the sermon too boring. You both seemed to be accepting the message clearly, with a blessed understanding."

"I felt the Spirit move within me," Porter said.

"Well, you know that the next step is for you to be born again," the reverend added.

"I am ready."

"I am not sure," Melinda interjected, "how my mother would feel about Porter being born again. And it seems to raise the question of who will nurse him once that happens."

"Well, isn't that an eccentric comment?" Reverend Barton said. "Of course, being born again is a deeply personal experience. I believe, Porter, that you are on the cusp," he added placing his hand on the boy's knee. "You just have to be baptized in the name of Christ."

"We have both been baptized already," said Melinda, "twice."

"And that was probably when you were infants, and too young to know what you were doing."

"Yes," Porter said, "and all of that does not count. What matters is my new life in Christ."

"Exactly, said the corpulent minister, "only by being born again can you attain the life everlasting."

"Well, sign me up too," added Melinda. "Let's begin the catechism so that we can be ready."

"No such thing will be needed, young lady. Each soul is competent to receive baptism as long as she does it willingly and with accepting Jesus as her personal savior. The Lord is already there for each of us and will be always."

"I have never been more willing," Porter said, in a transported state already.

Melinda was a bit confused by the discussion. The matter of faith to her had always been intellectual, and was indicated by the discussions she had with her father. There was to her mind a great deal of understanding that was necessarily involved. She did not see it as so direct or as so, and here she could not find the word, but the word might have been primitive, or perhaps shamanistic. She did not know of a way to see faith as an expression of enthusiasm arising from the mere experience of simply knowing that one has received the spirit. To the degree that she was attuned at all to a religious impulse, it was to what would surely have to be the study of the Scriptures and an understanding of the teachings of Jesus that might come from that. The idea that Jesus was not resurrected and sitting in heaven with God, but was simply walking among us and ready to be tailored to the personal acceptance of each person, was only beginning to dawn on her. But she did know that her brother had grasped the idea wholeheartedly. And she also knew that there was something going on with her brother in this place, to which she felt compelled to attend. During these last several moments, he and his shepherd had begun to huddle closely together.

Melinda had an instinct that for her was so compelling that it was almost something to which she responded automatically, as if it were an involuntary reaction of her nervous system. In this way it might have been like speaking in tongues for her. It may have been like her own private Pentecost, but it was more linked to her survival. She watched her brother and she felt it arise within her. At another time it might have taken over. But she had gained some detachment from the way in which she had learned that she had to try to manage her father, rather than simply respond to him lovingly. And if it had not been for this, her clothes again might have been in an instant in a pile upon the floor in the next few moments.

"I have visions," she blurted out.

The Reverend did not react. He only kept his hands on Porter's knees and continued to talk quietly to him. But Porter came a bit out of his trance, and sat back to look at her.

"That is right. She does," he said.

"We all have visions," the Reverend said.

"No, not like Melinda's. She sees things and they happen in the future. She either sees what will happen or her visions make them happen."

The sincerity of his comments caught the attention of Reverend Seymour Barton, and for the first time he stopped and turned to look at Melinda. He no longer was dismissive, and behind his penetrating eyes various calculations were occurring. And Melinda suddenly had faith. She had faith that her efforts to be in constant accompaniment of her brother would no longer meet resistance or be dismissed. Her instinct, educated as it had been, had again not failed her. Later her mind would move forward beyond this comprehension of having accomplished her mission. She would then understand that Porter would be forever seeking adoption, and that she could never fill that bill. Melinda would just have to be on the lookout for a better place in which Porter could land, a sort of foster home that would give her less cause for concern than the Christian Community of London, Kentucky and the right Reverend Seymour Barton.

CAVIAR VS. CHILI

"So, which one is that?"

"Which one, what?" Garth answered with a question.

"Which monument?" said Garth's potential Congressional candidate as Garth had turned his rental car out of the parking lot at Washington National Airport, having met the man for the first time upon the landing of his plane from Houston.

"Do you mean the tall pointy one, the one that is an obelisk?"

It was the first trip to Washington, DC for Texas State Representative Wilton Carlson. He had come as a result of the single phone conversation he and Garth had. Garth had been recommended to him by several of the men and women whom Garth had contacted regarding each one's possible candidacy for Congress, but who had for one reason or another decided not to run. Garth had invited Representative Carlson to Washington to decide if he would hire Garth to manage his campaign, and to make the rounds of the labor unions and other groups whose political action committees normally might contribute to a Democratic candidate in a Congressional election. It was Garth's idea that these meetings would generate enough political contribution commitments to convince the candidate to hire him, even though Garth was only twenty-five years old and had never run a political campaign previously. If the trip was ostensibly for the Mr. Carlson to decide if Garth and he could work together, Garth had already made his own decision about the matter.

In fact, Garth had done more or less what millions of Britons have been doing for hundreds of years every time they have bitten into a meat pie. Each man and woman of England, in millions of instances for generations, had expressed a laudable and honorable trust in his or her fellow countrymen each time he or she had taken an initial bite out of an individual pie, which had been advertised to have been a Shepherd's pie, a steak and kidney pie, a pork pie, a chicken and rabbit pie, a corned beef pie, a Cornish pasty, a chicken and mushroom pie, a Bedfordshire clanger, a game pie, a Scotch pie, or a squab pie. And each had quite properly accepted at face value whatever they had been told was under that pie's covering crust. Each had done so without suspiciously or dishonorably considering that what might lie in wait for them in that bite was what Sam Weller had once reported that a pie man, with whom he had once lodged, had been known to occasionally place within such a crust, in substitute for the named contents, which had been reported to have been, to wit, the savory and delectable meat of a prowling street feline. Garth felt himself no less upright, and worthy, or braver than any of the British gentlefolk who had gone before, when he had considered the meat pie that was Wilton Carlson. Garth had immediately decided that this candidate would fittingly serve his appetite, as well as his digestion and to no less a degree his health, without too much concern as to its actual contents.

Yet, the odd question regarding the most easily recognizable monument in the capital city had Garth wondering what cat meat might taste like.

"That one . . . is the Washington Monument," Garth said as he considered that even in an election district as small as a state representative's, a few thousand voters had bitten into this pie before, and at least some of them had not been so entirely a political gourmand as to be completely ignorant about what he had ingested.

"How much did you have to drink on the plane?" Garth ventured.

"I hate to fly, damn it," Mr. Carlson returned, "and I know of no other way to manage such a long flight. There were also some good-looking flight attendants on that plane, and my discourse is always more dazzling after I have had a few."

While the incidence of a politician being too indulgent of his own appetites is certainly an entirely rare one, there are indeed some uncommon instances of such behavior. What Garth had not known as he calculated the extreme odds that any politician, and a Texan at that, would be a drinker, was that in this case there was something unique. The singularity of this particular case was in fact stated to Garth in the following instant, and although his native skepticism and the man's squiffy state required him to not accept this proclamation at face value, he was later to learn the absolute truth of it.

"You know, Garth, politics is an emasculating profession. All these sons of bitches are afraid to say what they think, or to be who they really are. God damn it. I am going to keep my balls where they are, and functioning at their customarily high level."

"We will stop and get some coffee and a late breakfast," Garth said.

There were a couple of hours before their first appointment.

The political action committees of the labor unions and the liberal causes would normally fall in line to support any candidate who was obviously going to win the Democratic primary and oppose a Republican Congressman, but many of them at this point had expressed some hesitation to Garth when he had been calling around to make these appointments. Their reservations seemed to be based on two concerns and the first one was that the battle would be a difficult one to win, because this particular Republican Congressman would receive a great deal of support from his national party and from the White House because he had made himself a high profile cause when he had switched parties. The second issue was never fully expressed to Garth but, from what he could tell, many of these representatives of the political action committees had received some reports about this state legislator which had caused them to question him as a person, specifically they had some unstated worry about his ability to last out the campaign and to sustain scrutiny. The question about the Washington monument and the subsequent explanation perhaps began to supply Garth with some detail of what these people had left unsaid. Still, many of them are in the business of gambling and are also ideological. Garth had made appointments with the ones who had expressed a willingness to take a stand politically, and who were willing to take the risk in order to be the first Washington friends of a man who just might become a Democratic Congressman. Garth's own doubts were balanced by his commitment to make this campaign happen, no matter what was in that meat pie. And the scale was tipped in favor of that decision by the fact that Garth was beginning to like the candidate.

Garth had a good taste in his mouth and it did not seem to be cat meat.

At the first meeting, with the representative of the political action committee for the Unite Mine Workers, Garth laid out the targeting data and the results of previous elections to show that this Congressional District was still slightly Democratic, and that a well-known Democratic candidate ought to win it. All that was needed were the funds to do the advertising, which would raise Mr. Carlson's name recognition, and he would be in the race. And even though Ronald Reagan's vote totals in the nineteen eighty election in the precincts of this district were such that he would have "won" the district, it was now two years later and the area was in an economic recession. And the President would not be on the ballot in this mid-term election. The first question the Mine Worker official had asked had been about winning the primary, and he had been assured that Wilton Carlson would win when Garth explained that his candidate's state representative district comprised fifteen percent of the Congressional district and twenty percent of the Democratic vote and that none of the four other private individual primary candidates had any experience or name recognition whatsoever. Then the man asked about potential negatives that each general election candidate might have, and he discreetly cast a sidelong glance at the one candidate who was in front of him. Garth began to explain the primary negative for Congressman Fitzkin, which was that many Republican voters might not be ready to embrace the Republican Congressman who had so recently been a Democrat, and that his party switch would energize the Democratic voters, when he was interrupted by Mr. Carlson.

"What Garth here was trying to say in his Harvard way, is that he and I are Texans, and that we know those people in that Congressional district. And a Texan thinks that a girl ought to go home from the dance with the fellow that brung her," he said with more of a drawl than Garth had heard him use before.

The Mine Worker representative laughed and said, "I am from West Virginia, and we are exactly the same way. I can tell you that this organization will contribute the maximum to your campaign in the primary and in the general election. It is a pleasure to meet you both, and good luck."

Garth and Mr. Carlson were already a fortuitous pairing, and they improved their presentation with each subsequent meeting. Wilton Carlson was personally appealing to the individuals who met him for the same reasons that Garth had initially sensed. He was direct and confident and appeared uncomplicated, yet he was also crafty in his down home way. He let Garth talk about the numbers and the trends and the plans before he would get in his own comment about Garth's education, as if to say, "And I have a bright campaign manager, to boot."

By the end of the day, the campaign had received pledges for over forty thousand dollars.

Over dinner, Wilton told Garth that in his previous campaigns for state legislator he had never raised half of what Garth had helped him raise in one afternoon. He never acknowledged that he had decided to hire Garth; he just assumed that they were both already working together.

He said he was willing to accept Garth's decisions on what he was to pay himself as campaign manager, how many people he was to hire, what the campaign message would be, what the schedule would be, basically on every major political choice. It was more than just an agreement to hire Garth; it had been a ringing endorsement. Garth felt confident that the day's work had done well to advertise his abilities in at least one aspect of managing a campaign, but he also knew that in his own way he too was a bit of a meat pie, but Wilton Carlton was not going to question his contents, and for this he liked the older man even more.

That man was also an attractive package politically, as well as in person. He was tall and thin, and his strong-featured face had a craggy handsomeness to it that also made him seem older than a man in his late forties. There was a laconic and masculine Texas version of grace to him that meant that his gaunt face would accept praise and remonstrance with the same expression of mischief and wisdom. So much about him put Garth onto the memory of his late grandfather that Garth wondered if this was the way that old man perhaps had been when he had been younger. Wilton Carlson's brown hair was a kind of living museum exhibit of the time when he too had been a much younger man. It was a bit too long and was combed across his forehead in the same way that it certainly must have appeared in his high school yearbook. There was also a slouchy species of uprightness to him that showed that his four years at the United States Naval Academy, and his five years in the service had imparted something upon him that was otherwise not to be seen. The restless light that lay behind his brown eyes reflected what had been his tendency to move from one job to another following his service, until he had found the state legislature in much the same way the troubled sons of hereditary nobility in England once had found the House of Commons, as a place to settle for a man of some promise and no particular expertise.

His final suggestion over dinner was to go out on the town. This was an offer Garth could not refuse. He really wanted to go home to his young bride, but he could not pass on the opportunity to keep an eye on this twice-divorced man who was the key to Garth's future success and who had already demonstrated a proclivity for not taking that or himself all too seriously.

When Garth finally got home at around midnight after having safely tucked his charge in the hotel bed, he was hardly undressed and in bed when the phone rang. That woke his wife, whose slightly disquieted look turned to mild distaste when he covered the receiver.

"It's only Eakin," he said.

She had not ever gotten over her youthful tendency to call Garth at any hour, usually after she had been drinking and had some news.

"Teller, what's up?" she asked, and before he could answer she added, "I am moving back to the Houston area. I mean, we are moving."

"So am I," Garth chimed in, only to see Tabitha's face register alarm and anger, just before he turned to carry the conversation to another room.

"I got a job as a plant manager . . . a lot more money . . . and I really kicked ass here in Birmingham," Eakin said.

"What do you mean?"

"There were real productivity problems at this plant . . . and I turned them around . . . from like sixty percent . . . to ninety-five percent . . . productivity, that is. So I was hired away from US Steel by Inland Steel to run their oil country pipe and tube plant."

"That's great, Eakin. I always knew you would succeed at that Birmingham job. I have no doubt that you are much smarter than all the people at your work."

"No, Garth, not at all. All the good ideas I had . . . I stole them. Really, I did. Every day I would take off my jacket, and go down onto the plant floor and talk to the mill workers . . . really talk to them. They had never had a manager or an assistant manager do anything like that. They might have been suspicious, but since I am a woman they were not threatened by me, and they were interested in telling me what their problems were. So every change I suggested at the plant was something that I got from them. And when they saw that I was making the changes they had suggested they wanted to work harder for me, so it was positive in two ways."

"Well, that was one very good idea you had then," he countered.

"That one was not even my idea," she said.

"What do you mean?"

"That guy, Ben, your friend, the one from Boston, he suggested it."

"Wow. That is out of the blue. You are still in touch with him then?"

"Yes. He was helpful to us in Cambridge. I will tell you sometime. I owe you for that. And he is way too smart for me to not maintain his friendship. He is probably smarter than either one of us, or smarter than you at least."

Garth pondered this news, when Eakin interrupted.

"So, wait, you are going back home now too?"

"Nearby home, I am going to run a Congressional campaign fairly far outside of Houston," he said.

"You are going to win that campaign, Garth . . . because that is what you are. You're a winner."

"So, that was your friend, Eakin Lambert," Tabitha said accusingly after Garth returned to the bed. "And I have to learn from your conversation with her that you are going to Houston?"

"We talked about this before," he said, "several times. It was contingent on what happened today, with the campaign," he said, and reached toward her.

"Well, I don't remember," she rolled over and added, speaking to the wall opposite, "have fun in Texas. I have a good job at a law firm here in Washington."

It may or may not have been the first time that Tabitha did not remember something that was no longer in her focus of attention, and it would not happen too much more than several hundred times in the future. But this time, it had the power to startle and disappoint and hurt.

Garth flew home, visited his parents, bought a twenty-year-old rusty Chevrolet Impala and drove to the town where Wilton Carlson had his state representative office, and had already rented a commercial space to house the campaign headquarters. He was shown into a space that had once been *Bob and Bubba's Butcher Shop* (the sign was still over the door), and was confronted by one desk on which was one phone, in a room with nothing else other than three unemployed, and largely illiterate, young men who were convinced that Wilton Carlson was some hero out of legend, to whom they were fanatically dedicated. Garth immediately dispatched them on the highly critical task that would consume both time and geography, which was to scout the entire Congressional district for the best place to put up yard signs. Meanwhile Garth opened a bank account, deposited the campaign checks, got the phone company to install ten more phones, hired a sign company to put a proper sign over the door for the Carlson for Congress campaign, opened a Post Office Box, identified the local printer, and rented several desks, tables, a television, a telefacsimile machine and a photocopier.

Then he began the process of scouting for and interviewing for the paid campaign staff who would occupy the positions of volunteer coordinator, press secretary, researcher/writer, receptionist, and the person who would serve as liaison with the key people who might tend to get in Garth's way, such as the local elected officials, party committee members, union officials and people who had been important in the past state legislative races. He hired a volunteer coordinator, who was local Democratic committeeman of capable intelligence and a tireless worker himself, who did no more or less than Garth would tell him to do. The press secretary was a personable young woman who had just graduated from college, and who would never be able to tell the press anything other than what she had already been told by Garth. The researcher/writer was a very bright, but introspective recent college graduate, who knew the issues but would go unnoticed in his other role which was as "keeper of the body," the person who would accompany the candidate and take notes about all that happened. The receptionist was also attractive, and was the daughter of the president of the largest union in the district. The most all around capable staff person was Rich Sartory, a son of a local politician who held the liaison job, and who was Garth's sounding board and sort of an assistant campaign manager.

Rich was the scion of a local small time political family and a little younger than Garth. He had graduated from the University of Texas and had worked on some local campaigns. He was medium height, thickly built, with black hair and dark eyes, which advertised his Italian heritage and kept his intelligence hidden behind a hedge of reticence. His only expressiveness was in his appearance. He tended to wear cowboy boots when he wore a suit.

The Democratic primary went as expected. The campaign for the general election also went well based upon the precepts set forth by Garth. Most of the fundraising, and all of the fundraising by mail, requested only very small, single digit dollar amount, contributions because it is easy for a person to make such a small commitment, but a person once committed will most often protect and further her investment by doing and giving more. Five-dollar contributors later hosted good-sized gatherings in their homes and at their clubs. In visiting each town, the local newspaper reporter was invited to join the candidate in campaigning door-to-door because that sort of humble approach was to be made a part of the campaign's narrative even though it is not a fruitful way to campaign in a district in which tens of thousands of votes would be cast.

The opponent's party switch was portrayed as his having been swayed by the ways of Washington and having lost touch with local values and the local people. Most importantly, every article that appeared in each of the several local papers was photocopied and sent to every other reporter and to the list of national news outlets.

There is a silent fulcrum buried in the deep of the night upon which swings the perception of a long night out on the town turning into a painfully early morning. It may be ostensibly, and perhaps too easily, said that this tipping point is at 3:30 AM, but it is not always, and it is more dependent upon contingencies related to location and activity and personnel. This campaign had its own silent fulcrum, and was to be found not much subsequent to an event in which Garth had been greatly assisted by his distant friend, Ben, acting through his childhood friend, Eakin.

The news reported that Vice President Bush was going to appear at a Saturday lunch fundraiser for Congressman Fitzkin to be held at a local country club and which would exclude the press. Garth knew that he would have to devote a great deal of thought to this report before he could decide its significance to the campaign, when he was interrupted by one of the illiterate worshippers of the candidate who had returned from his sign-scouting detail, and was at that moment working for the campaign's volunteer coordinator as an envelope stuffer.

"Hey, I know that place," the young man said. "There is a little park near there. We could have our own event."

"This is Candy Lane of Channel Four News," is how one of the Houston television news reports of the event began, "and I am standing on the street outside of the one-thousand-dollar-a-plate country club fundraiser for Congressman Fitzkin. Vice President Bush is inside, but no members of the press are being allowed to cover the event. But you can tell by all of the out-of-state license plates on the Mercedes and other expensive cars driving into the country club lot what sort of event it is. Outside on the road with me are dozens of unemployed men and women who are protesting. Let's speak to one of them."

"That traitor Fitzkin don't stand for nothing but himself."

"I voted for him as a Democrat and then he betrayed us."

"He only cares about the rich people now."

"I am going to vote for Wilton Carlson."

"Speaking of Mr. Carlson, our Channel Four colleague, Penny Samuels, is with the candidate right now," Ms. Lane continued, "at an alternative three-dollar-a-plate fundraiser he is having just a half a mile down the road from here. Penny, take it away."

"I am here with Democratic candidate for Congress, Wilton Carlson," Penny chimed in. "As we can see from all of the families and picnic food and games here, this is an entirely different sort of event. Tell us, Mr. Carlson, what do you think of these two very different fundraisers?"

"It is a case of caviar versus chili, Penny. I intend to serve all of the people who cannot afford a thousand-dollar-a-plate fundraiser. I care about getting my unemployed neighbors back to work. I am not interested in feathering my own nest," Wilton drawled, smiling.

"And they may have the Vice President of the United States, but we have the Lions Club clowns."

Then he became quite serious and again drawled another thing he had been drilled to say.

"So every time you see or hear an advertisement for Congressman Fitzkin, just remember that this is where his money came from, from wealthy people who do not even live in this Congressional District," he finished. This statement would be part of every advertisement that the Carlson campaign would run up to the election. Garth had figured that the Fitzkin campaign would flood the district with advertising, so his goal had been to try to turn those numerous advertisements into reminders of the Carlson message.

All three of the Houston television network affiliates ran this same story as their lead-in on the six o'clock news, recapped it on the eleven o'clock news, and ran it again at noon on Sunday. Congressman Fitzkin had easily raised one hundred thousand dollars in campaign funds, while the Carlson campaign spent more money than it made on its little event. But Carlson had received television news time that would have cost two hundred thousand dollars, had it been purchased in advertising, which most viewers tune out anyway. Garth had recognized an idea worth stealing when he had heard the campaign volunteer express it. The local news people had felt that Bush's visit would be newsworthy, but they had no angle by which to cover it until they later had received the Carlson Campaign press release entitled, "Caviar versus Chili." The event and its coverage caught the attention of a lot of people, including Garth's old friend from the Owl Club, Earnest Dapple, who called Garth.

"Teller, old man, I am looking at your press release here, and I understand that you have caught the attention of the Houston media."

"What can I do for you, Earnest?" Garth replied.

"I think you mean what I can do for you, buddy. I just finished having a drink with Tim Brown of the *New York Times*, and he was looking for a political story from the hinterlands, so I told him about this thing and he liked the idea of coming to visit you. He will be calling you very soon."

So the phrase, "caviar versus chili," found its way onto a subheading of the *New York Times* story that described candidate Carlson beginning his day at 8:00 AM attending two coffee klatches held for him by past contributors, going door-to-door asking for votes, speaking to a union hall full of avid supporters, going to a Lions Club dinner, attending a high school football game between the two largest schools in the Congressional district and attended by several thousand people, and then going to both of the team supporter after-parties until past midnight. When the article in the *Times* was sent to all the local reporters, their newspapers assigned those reporters to follow candidate Carlson. It was a Congressional race of national significance, right in their own back yard.

Candidate Carlson's name recognition was close to one hundred percent and his message was reaching the entire district. The *Times* article also generated visits from other national news outlets including the national television network news. Garth had gone from Washington money people telling him they were unwilling to help because he was managing a campaign for David against Goliath, to the same people telling him that his campaign did not need their help because the entire district perceived the race as David versus Goliath, and to Americans and particularly Texans such a message was irresistible. This did not bother Garth because he knew they were right. He was going to win this campaign, or so he thought.

"Garth, I have this reporter on the line from the *Tribune*," the press secretary said, one afternoon only three weeks before the election. "She says that she will only talk to you or to Wilton. Her name is Mary Jade."

The *Tribune* was an organ of the Republican Party in a town that was not even in one of the six counties of the Congressional district, but was nearby. It was owned by Dexter Pott, who was a scion of an old line Republican family whose old money harkened back to the Gilded Age, when rich people felt no compunction to be mean, an atavistic characteristic that had survived through generations to the aforementioned gentleman. Mr. Pott's name, in an example of journalistic reserve and inhibiting objectivity worthy of Mark Twain's story of journalism in Tennessee, had appeared on the Federal Election Commission's reports as actually having contributed the maximum personal amount to the Fitzkin campaign. Garth picked up the phone.

"I will listen to you, Ms. Jade, but I will not tell you anything that you cannot get from our press secretary."

"I understand, Mr. Teller, that your candidate has a long-time girlfriend with whom he has been keeping house for well over a decade, including during the time of both of his previous marriages. She lives in Elgin, outside of Austin, and they have two illegitimate children together. Her name is Dorothy Sampson. He has this shadow family, and has had it for more than a dozen years. We will run this story in tomorrow's evening paper. Do you have a comment?"

"I know your evening paper won't be printed before noon. I will call you in the morning," was all Garth said.

He sent all the staff home early that evening. When the candidate came by the office shortly after that, only Rich Sartory and Garth were there to meet him. The three of them sat down. Garth spoke first.

"I have asked Rich to stay here because I may need his advice, and because I want there to be a witness to this," Garth said. Then he related what the reporter had said.

"I only need to know one thing," Garth concluded. "Is it true?"

Garth looked at Wilton and then at Rich. Rich looked at Wilton and then at Garth. Wilton only looked at Garth, blankly, stolidly, with a stare that was as enervated and as level as any Texas salt flat Garth had ever seen. It had lasted more than a minute and gave no hints of changing.

RUNNING, AND RUNNING

There had always been a runner inside of Melinda. Something within her was simply driving and kinetic. Equally, there may have been some indistinct hint of some object away from which she felt compelled to run, and there could have been a constituent element drawn from all of her visions toward which she was also compelled to swiftly move. There was no running in karate, but there was a bit in baseball, and she had loved the way the grass passed beneath her airborne feet when she was chasing a fly ball in the outfield. Melinda had progressed through the levels of the various color belts in her karate school, and she had even once won the countywide sparring tournament in one of the belt levels, and had come in second at another level, all against boys. She became a black belt, only two years after she had started. And when she had reached the age of thirteen, she had been put on a baseball team coached by a sage and deeply philosophical man, who had the kindness to direct her to sit on the bench because he had the wisdom and foresight to see that there was no future in the game of youth baseball for a girl.

Her place on the field was taken by boys whose own long and grand futures in the game were to be between a few months and a few years. Her place on the pitching mound was taken by the same coach's talentedly rotund son, who celebrated his inability to throw strikes by drooling onto the tops of his shoes and scratching himself, and who quit the sport in the middle of the following season to seek another venue in which to drool onto the tops of his shoes in greater earnest. Melinda's interest in each of these athletic endeavors had already been waning, one due to having largely mastered it, and the other due to the intervention of these benevolent forces. Then she discovered the joys of running, and in particular she discovered she could join the cross country and track teams of her high school. The pleasure of running was augmented by the magic of it. Her kinetic composition and her agitation at the physical level were expended by running, while these same forces, to the extent that they were mental, were self-contained and turned to great positive use while she ran. She had always been her own best company and she learned to appreciate this in the solitude of running. She also shared with all runners that heightened state that is reached at a certain level of training, where they find a euphoric result from the effort which is elegantly and simply physiological. And Melinda was very fast.

A nose may run and so may a political candidate or a river or a clock, and Melinda had run too in this other than literal fashion, when she and her brother had returned home from the time she had first joined him in the office of Reverend Barton. She had run to her father's Bible, and then performed the same figurative deed through it several times, with special attention to the Gospels because she sensed that to have done that would later prove useful. She took all that she had gathered from this, and had run it over and over in her mind most often while she was running. The trees and the fields of the cross country course would move past her, as she considered that the words of Jesus in the Gospels were riddles and aph- orisms and parables, that he concealed as much as he revealed and that most certainly this ambivalent, enigmatic and often shocking, wandering radical was not the same wholly regenerative Jesus to whom the people of the Christian Community of London, Kentucky referred when they said His name. They would also refer to God the Father as an august being who bore no resemblance to the irascible, often vengeful and capricious, vague, and all too human, eponymous character Melinda had found in the Old Testament. And the Holy Spirit seemed to her to be a bit player in the Bible but it was clear to her that there was a hugely Pentecostal element to the faith of the congregants at the Christian Community of London, Kentucky, so that it was the Spirit that was forever entering them though it was the spirit of an entity to which they referred as the Lord. To Melinda's observation this meant Jesus, sort of with God tucked under his arm.

Melinda's feet would hit the ground with an elemental rhythm which propelled the progress of her internal contemplations, and she knew that any thoughtful and reading individual could only reach faith through the Bible by means of metaphor and synthesis and the aesthetic appreciation of the beautiful poetry of the good book. Yet to her fellow congregants, the Bible was inerrant. Not only did she understand that the book was full of ambiguities and obfuscations and contradictions, there were parts of it that seemed to sanction slavery, killing and polygamy. The only way to have faith in its inerrancy was to not have read it, to arrive at a primitive belief in what the minister said about it as he waved it in the air.

She knew then, after many miles of running, what she might do, and that was that she could fabricate her visions before reporting them to the reverend. She would run with that idea.

In the course of the two and a half years between when Porter and Melinda had entered the Christian Community of London, Kentucky and this time when Melinda was in the ninth grade and beginning high school, the pair had been baptized and Melinda had related many of her home-made visions to the Reverend Barton. These variously included visions of hidden treasures and baking with yeast, revelations of injured travelers who were helped by benevolent non-believers, visualizations comparing those who are always prepared to those who are not, images of lost animals and children and valuables which are later found, terrible visions of the evils of acquiring wealth, stories of gracious forgiveness, revelations about the rewards of persistent prayer. Often the reverend would have Melinda speak of her visions before small groups, and sometimes these would contain newly converted congregants. In the search for material for his weekly hour-long sermons, he would often make use of her reported epiphanies to make various points, mostly about lessons from the Bible about grace and accepting the Holy Spirit. In a small way Melinda was responsible for a slight, but evident run-up in attendance and membership within the Christian Community of London, Kentucky. She always reported that her visions were preceded by the very same types of fits or seizures which came before her genuine visions. On occasion she would stage such a fit for the minister's benefit.

Of course, nothing like this had ever happened in any church or revivalist camp meeting or Christian community. No one in the long history of such events and institutions had ever fabricated these sorts of things or had acted them out. So Melinda was certain that she had committed a terrible sacrilege, and that God would single her out for a unique and terrible punishment if, that is, the reverend and his congregants were correct and their faith were true. About that Melinda had some small lingering doubts, and in fact she had fairly well determined from her consistent and thoughtful reading and considering, that one of the most difficult achievements in the world was to be a Christian, and to live an entirely Christian life. And never was such an enterprise as almost impossibly challenging as it was when one was surrounded by Christians. In a way, she was no different than the worshippers at the Christian Community of London, Kentucky. She knew her own heart, and she was certain that it was good. Her initial and primary motivation had been to protect her brother and she had successfully managed to keep Reverend Barton's focus and fat hands off of Porter. And at this point in their lives, Porter's attentions and yearnings had begun to move in another direction. For one thing, for two years he had been quite a successful pitcher on the high school baseball team and the acceptance and popularity that accrued from that had been fulfilling. And as always, he had appeared to begin to wander off into another fascination, one that his sister had yet to discover.

So during one sermon she began to have a visitation.

Her outburst of the afflicted did not rise nearly to the level of Abigail Williams or Betty Paris but it was noticeable to those around her and particularly to Reverend Barton. It was in the early spring of the nineteen hundred and eighty-third year of what at that time was still called the year of our lord. The high school baseball season and track season were soon to begin. The primal stirrings of the forests and the fields were gradually and inescapably on the increase, and so were the arising emanations of the creatures that inhabited them. The same vernal infusing was also to be found ascending in the souls of the creatures who for that Sunday morning hour inhabited the Christian Community of London, Kentucky. When Melinda had ceased being stricken by her visitation, or when that appeared to be the case, the man on the stage whose once strong-featured face of faded nobility enclosed the dark and cleverly penetrating eyes which looked at her and then out over the audience, reached out his plump hand, and spoke in that confidently happy and informative tone which conveyed that they were now members of the same exclusive club, and he actually invited her into that club by suggesting that she join him on the stage. She walked up to the stage and joined him there.

Upon that stage at that moment stood two individuals. Only one of them was about to assume the role of a false prophet, a mocker of religion, a person who dramatically expounds without caring for that religion's primary doctrines or its most basic principles. One of these two individuals was going play upon the weakness and ignorance of the listeners, and cast scorn and contempt upon what should be held most sacred, and lead onto the path of irreligious and faithless conduct a good number of otherwise decent people. Each one of the individuals on the stage at the Christian Community of London, Kentucky knew that one of them was about to do this. But the final part of this riddle is that both of them also knew which one of them was going to do it.

Melinda, given the cue, began to reveal what no one but she could have known. She told the congregation about her personal vision. She was just warming up as she told them that she had actually just seen Jesus standing on the stage, only a few minutes earlier. Reverend Barton brought his hands in front of his chest and placed his palms resting against one another with his fingers together and pointing toward the ceiling, which was also where he directed his beatific gaze.

She began to stretch as she said that Jesus had just stood exactly where their minister had been standing.

The reverend reached out a fleshy hand, and rested it on one of her shoulders. She started to jog as she said that she had heard Jesus preaching to all of them, just as the minister had been doing.

This time that pastor dropped his eyes to look piously at the tops of his shoes. Then Melinda was running at a good pace, and she told them that she had heard Jesus tell them all that He did not bring them peace, but that He came to them with a sword, which He would use to divide them from their loved ones because if they loved their family members they could not be worthy of Him. There was an inaudible and collective gasp from most of the audience. Seymour Barton alertly turned and looked at Melinda. By then, Melinda had hit her stride.

"Jesus," she told the congregants, "has said that the reason He spoke to them in parables was so that they could hear and read what He was saying, but not perceive or understand it, so that they would not be saved, and their sins could not be forgiven."

Most of the members of the congregation voiced their surprise and dis-agreement. Some simply were stunned. Perhaps one or two people nodded to themselves. Reverend Seymour Barton stepped between Melinda and the microphone, and he assured the congregation that this teenager was clearly mistaken, and that Jesus loved each one of them, and all they had to do was to accept him into their lives and they would be granted grace and ever-lasting life. Then Melinda slipped around in front of him and before she left the stage, she spoke one more time into the microphone.

"Matthew 10:34, and Mark 4:12," she said, crossing the finish line on a dead run.

Then she walked quietly through the even quieter congregation, and took her brother by the hand, and walked out of the church just in time to see Tommy Kitt, who had scampered out ahead of them.

"Hey, Melinda, you really caught them all by surprise, didn't you? Just like that first day in karate class," he smiled. "You're like some kind of a character out of a book or something. Jesus Christ, girl."

With those very words, the Sherman children's adventure with the Christian Community of London, Kentucky was ended. Melinda's self-imposed penitence after this would be to make herself go fairly regularly to the Lutheran church of her late father. Her reward for Tommy Kitt, who alone in that building had approved of her vision, was a kiss and this time it was on the lips.

"Did you know that the ancient Romans painted erect penises every-where?" Porter asked her as they were walking home. "And they had statues and paintings of guys with erect penises everywhere. They even had erect penis talismans and tokens."

"Oh, no Porter," Melinda groaned, "Please don't tell me that you're the one who is going all around town, and in the school, and putting erect penis graffiti on everything?"

"And, we are all really Romans, even now," he pointed out. "They invented Europe. Then they invented the church. Then they invented that thing that made the Dark Ages go away."

"Do you mean the Renaissance? And I suppose that you are also the one who drew the big red erect penis on the notice in the school, offering a reward for the apprehension of the person responsible for drawing erect penises everywhere?"

"The Romans thought that the erect penis was good luck, and that it promoted fertility."

"Well, it certainly can do that."

"No, I meant they believed that the representations of it also did those things."

Then he said one more thing that Melinda did not know how to take. She did not know if it was sad statement on the march of human history, or if were an even sadder statement on the male psychology, or if it might have been meant as a warning.

"The erect penis rules."

"I thought it had no rules. Isn't that sort of the point?"

"The point is that the Romans conquered the world, ruled it for hundreds of years and they invented roads, plumbing, courts of law, concrete and those numbers that come after the Super Bowl. And they did this with an abundance of erect penises. So that, or they, must be a good thing."

"And since we are all actually Romans, as you say, then this penis graffiti thing you are doing is sort of a renaissance in its own right?"

"Exactly."

"So if I incorporate all three of your latest wild philosophies, then you and I are Roman orphans who are alone with Jesus."

"Very funny, Mindy. But it does make sense to say that every Christian is an orphan of ancient Rome. So all I am doing is bringing them home to mama."

"Just don't get caught, please."

There is a recurring figure that appears in the movies, video games and stories of our current modern moment and that is the large mechanical warrior, human in shape, but possessed of fabulous strength and durability and size, and always armed with a large number of devastating futuristic weapons. An actual human, who sits in a cockpit, most often controls him. Why the imaginations of the creators of these characters do not simply remain satisfied with placing this cockpit and these weapons in a tank or in an airplane is perhaps related to the universality of the feeling that Melinda felt when she was running. To her then, her breathing, her pain, her effort and the things that she saw and heard and felt outside of her were one extra step removed from her, as if she were a tiny Melinda controlling everything from within the cockpit of the larger mech-warrior that was her own body. This feeling of really being the internal "one off" Melinda was not all that different from what she felt when navigating the tracks and courses of her life. But on the high school tracks and cross-country courses, this feeling was palpable, and it was compounded and she could sit in her cockpit and turn down the pain and expand the breathing and push the pace. By the end of her sophomore year, she was consistently running the two hundred meter dash in just above twenty-five seconds, and the four hundred meter dash in a little more than fifty-six seconds, which meant that she was threatening to break the state high school records in each event. College track coaches sent her letters.

Porter had been one of the best pitchers in the local high school baseball league when he has been a freshman. Since his father had been dead for some years and the love they shared through the game was no longer in his life, he spent the rest of his high school career not really getting any better, but still being pretty good. He had been recruited by some of the smaller colleges in the area and he had an opportunity after his graduation to attend Union College, nearby and which wanted him to play baseball, although it and the other small schools who had been interested could not offer him an athletic scholarship. Through a combination of state financial aid and a college job and some loans, it had been determined that he would be able to attend Union College. Some might say that the Lord had other plans for him. Others would say it was actually the devil. If not Satan, it was at least the Proctor and Gamble Corporation of Cincinnati, Ohio.

Melinda and Porter were flip sides of the same coin. Porter was good-looking in a very interesting way, particularly the one found in a man who has a feminine element to his appeal. Melinda had a bearing that was striking in a woman who bears a masculine force. The masculine elements of Melinda's makeup have already been made apparent by this point, and the feminine constituent part of Porter's charm was to be seen first most clearly by the founder and owner of a new small-time modeling and acting agency in nearby Louisville. She had been passing through London that summer on a family matter, when she had seen Melinda and Porter at the local McDonalds restaurant. She had been made aware of a large modeling contract that would be offered to a male model to be used for the advertising campaign of Scope mouthwash, and she had been trying to decide which of the models in the stable of her fledgling agency would be the one she would send to Cincinnati for the auditions.

Then she saw Porter.

She knew he was the person she wanted to send. She needed to get him under agreement with her agency first. She approached the two teenagers and discovered that Porter was still seventeen. She asked to meet their mother.

"Mom, this is Nancy Torrance. She is from Louisville. She runs a modeling agency," Porter said to his mother after Ms. Torrance had driven them home.

"I am pleased to meet you, Mrs. Sherman," Ms. Torrance said.

"So, what is this all about?" Angelina Sherman probed, looking at Melinda.

"Ms. Torrance says that Porter has the look," Melinda said.

"That would be news to me," Mrs. Sherman replied.

"He does," said the agent. "He really does. He is a uniquely beautiful young man. Women will find him attractive, and men will not be threatened by him, but will also find they like him. Older people will see him as the child they wish they had, and younger people will identify with him. He unaffectedly has the unique quality of being attractive to all people."

Several deep impressions crossed Angelina Sherman's normally resolute countenance. Then she asked, "So do you think he might make some money from his looks?

"Certainly," Nancy Torrance replied, "and that is why I want you to sign this contract as the mother of a minor. And I would like you to take him to the audition in Cincinnati next week."

"How will this all work out, if he is to be paid?"

"My agency will be paid by the advertising company, then we will take out our ten percent commission and also make the necessary withdrawals for taxes and other things like that and we will mail the check to you, here. When Porter turns eighteen, we will renegotiate the contract with him alone. All this is, of course, depends on whether or not he gets the job. It is a small chance but I believe he has what it takes."

"All right then. We will do it."

When it came time for the audition, Mrs. Sherman demurred, and she gave Porter the keys to the car and told Melinda to go with him. So

Porter drove his sister along the very same path over which they had taken their hitchhiking sojourn. The audition turned out to be more of a cattle call, and the Sherman siblings felt very much out of place among the dozens of other aspirants and their companions. There was a mixed component of complacent and superior aloofness that they noted in every other potential model, or in the case of the younger ones who came with a mother, in that person. Melinda took the role of the stage mother in Porter's case and she was not quite up to the level of sophistication of these mothers. They had dressed their sons in very nice clothes and had obtained for them the very best haircuts, and some of them had applied small traces of makeup to their child's face. Porter was wearing a pair of jeans and a tee shirt. Melinda felt terribly outgunned, and when Porter's audition approached it was all she could to do keep him from being glum. She did not want him to see that he clearly was the least prepared of the group. She did what she could to distract him, and in Porter's case this always meant she had to make him laugh, and get him to talk effusively about himself and his eccentric notions. In such a mood, Porter entered the audition room and very quickly returned.

"You were only in there for five minutes. What happened?" she asked him.

"I told them the story of how we had hitchhiked to Cincinnati. What was it, seven or eight years ago?"

"Oh, no, Porter, how did they take that?"

"They seemed to like it. They were laughing."

Melinda felt like being silent the entire way home. She felt that they surely that they must have been seen as the worst kind of country bumpkins. Instead of being quiet, she and Porter recalled to one another all of the incidents of the earlier trip, and pointed out to one another all of the landmarks. When they had arrived at the house, their mother told them that Nancy Torrance had called and that Porter had been asked to return in two days for the photography shoot.

She said she would take him. Porter objected. He told his mother that Melinda being with him had been good luck, and that respect for that good fortune required that they had to return for the shoot in the same way that they had attended the audition. The wisdom of this approach appealed to their parent, who agreed and who immediately replaced the old rosary in the car with a new one that had ostensibly been blessed by the Pope.

To their surprise, when the siblings arrived at the photography shoot, they realized that Porter was not the only model who had been asked to return. Melinda silently gasped when they were told that two of them had been invited, and that the final decision of which one would participate in the shoot would be made by the representative of the advertising company which had been hired by the Proctor and Gamble marketing department, who had not been present at the audition. Melinda looked at the other boy, and this little item of mortality was one of those very most polished young talents, dressed in a nice suit, every hair in place, rosy red cheeks, and with a very smug stage mother who smiled kindly at Melinda, with a firm idea that she was dispensing a charity. Melinda looked at Porter. He was wearing his denim overalls and a flannel shirt. His hair was a mess. She at least wanted to get him to smile. When he was about to be called in, she spoke to him.

"Remember, Porter, you have Jesus with you."

"That's funny, Mindy," he said and disappeared into the room.

When he emerged, the director of the shoot was with him. He was snarling orders to one of the assistants to measure Porter, and then go to the local department store and buy him several outfits. Then he called for the makeup person and the hairdresser to get Porter ready. Turning to the other model and his mother, he told them that the boy would be paid for the day, and that he was wanted to stick around in case anything might go wrong with photographing Porter.

Melinda could not tell whether or not this was something for which this stage mother devoutly wished, but only because the mother had turned away at that moment. The boy's sole reaction was to look at his mother as if he were blaming her for not dressing him in overalls. Porter then became the nexus of attention for the dozens of functionaries. There were various photographers, including one or two to take instant photographs, which could be reviewed by the principle photographer, the director, the artistic director, the advertising company representative, the man from Proctor and Gamble, the lighting and staging directors and several other people. There were any number of other assistants and many photographs were taken, but only after Porter had emerged from being dressed, and made up, and having his hair styled. Two people had been hired to blow bubbles that were to float in front of Porter while he was being photographed with the model that had been flown in from the New York agency to play his mother. The hairdresser and the makeup man had also been flown in from New York.

At lunch, the two dozen or so functionaries sat at one table while the second long table had been reserved for "talent," and at it sat only six people, the New York model and her assistant, the boy who did not get the job and his mother, and Porter and Melinda. At the side of the room was a huge groaning board of cheeses, meats, salad, pasta, vegetables, casseroles, sandwiches, fruit, desserts and drinks. The talent went to eat first, and the model playing the mother brought a small salad back to the table, and her assistant did likewise more out of solidarity than from preference. Porter and Melinda were too stunned and excited to eat much more than a sandwich. The stage mother ate nothing, while her son loaded his plates with everything he could and did eat.

"I told the story about what you did at the Christian Community," Porter told his sister, "and they all laughed. I did not embellish too much. And thank you for reminding me of it."

"Man, this is a nice life," his sister whispered.

She could see that Porter was well beyond being able to confirm that statement, so much beyond that he, like Macbeth, possessed the imagination to have already placed himself inside of that life. And this was never more apparent than it was when the shoot had ended, and everyone said their good-byes. The thin and well-dressed hairdresser held Porter by the shoulders and kissed the air beside each one of Porter's cheeks.

"What? What! What . . ." he exclaimed, ". . . do we have here, another simply enchanting young star? Porter, Porter, I will be so delighted to tell everyone that I knew you when. They will all be so jealous, the grousing ninnies, when I tell them that and they see your face on those massive billboards and see you in the commercials."

The sweet-natured makeup man repeated the air kissing routine and said, "I am so looking forward to working with you, young man, so looking forward to it, you Adonis."

While the representative of the advertising company was telling Melinda and her brother that Porter would be featured in every commercial and advertisement that Scope would be doing for the next two years, and also telling them that it would be best if Porter moved to the island of Manhattan, the assistant to the New York model handed them her card, and told them that their Manhattan modeling agency would like to work with Nancy Torrance to coordinate Porter's arrangements for working in Manhattan, and for moving and for obtaining other commercial work in New York City.

On the way home Porter could not stop talking about his big day, and his even bigger plans. Melinda was happy just to agree and to watch him.

That part of her which was the little person inside her inner cockpit was in deep thought, though. Melinda had remembered that she had known all along in some way or another, at first quite subconsciously but very acceptingly and then later quite explicitly, that her brother had always been gay. She knew that she had sought to protect him first from their mother, then from the man who gave them a ride and had made her sit in the back when he had picked them up from hitchhiking, and later from Reverend Barton, not because she rejected the fact that Porter was gay, but because she had not wanted him to suffer for it. She sensed now, mostly from the hairdresser and the makeup man, that Porter was about to be among a different kind of person and that he would not suffer for it, at least not suffer any more or less than anyone else might through the course of a romantic life in one's early adulthood. She could hear the happiness in his voice, and she could have heard that even if she had been deaf. She did not feel bad that her brother would be much farther away from her than nearby Union College and that the Union College baseball team would have one less pitcher in its bullpen.

Melinda did break the Kentucky high school track record for the two-hundred-meter dash in her senior year, and the record for the four-hundred-meter dash the year before that. She was offered several scholarships because she was that good, and because, in this era at the beginning of Title Nine, colleges were scrambling to balance the number of newly required scholarships for women with the many that had already been given to men. She chose to attend the University of Kentucky, in Lexington. She had spent all of her time in high school running in one fashion or another, and she realized she had also been running for much longer than that. She had long been scurrying to help her father, to help Porter, to keep things in order, and after he had left, to keep an eye on her mother. When she finally packed the very few things she was to take to college and she had put them on the bus to Lexington, she got on the bus. For the first time she was able to think about things that she had never felt she had the time to consider. She thought about her father and how she still missed him and what he might have thought about her going to college on a scholarship.

She wondered if Porter were still as happy as he seemed the last time she had spoken to him on the phone. She wondered about college. She thought about her father's words to her, how his last statement had been unfinished. But through all of this, one thing was running through her mind. She was wondering now about her own sexuality. She had literally not had the time to consider it. And she was puzzled about her inclinations. She knew that she liked boys but that the boy to whom she had been closest had been Tommy Kitt, her personal cheerleader in school but for whom she felt no more than a safe and kind affection. She did not feel that she had ever been attracted to other girls. She simply did not know. And that is what kept running through her mind.

THE CLOWN KEEPS JUMPING

In this atmosphere of silent staring, Garth simply picked up the phone and dialed a number. Both of the other men looked at him with a breed of intense interest that only inhabits criminal defendants who are watching the jury file into the courtroom with their verdict, or which ranges in the hearts of either party in civil cases that involve life-changing amounts of money. The candidate and the assistant campaign manager could only hear Garth's end of the phone conversation, and they had no idea whom he had called.

"Hello, Cindy, this is Garth, Garth Teller. I know that this might seem strange, me calling you like this. I apologize. I would never do it, if there were any other way. I just have to get a personal message to Congressman Fitzkin, and no one at his campaign office or his Congressional office would ever take a call from me. So I have to rely on you. I am sorry."

Wilton Carlson and Rich Sartory could not hear her answer.

"I just got a call from a reporter at the *Tribune*. You know that Dexter Pott owns it, and that Dexter Pott is one of the Congressman's best friends and major contributors. Well, this reporter is talking about writing some story that kind of hits way below the belt. You know, it's a dirty tricks kind of thing."

Garth had called the home of Cindy Stanfield, Congressman Fitzkin's Republican mistress and the sister-in-law to the Congressman's chief of staff, the one she had placed in his office and the one who had engineered the party switch and had fired most of his previous staff. Again, Wilton and

Rich could not hear her response, and this time it was because Garth could not hear it either. She was silent on the other end and it was the silence of a person who is being told nothing that she did not already know.

"You and I both know that Congressman Fitzkin is not that kind of person," Garth continued. "He is just not a dirty politician. He would never do that sort of thing and he would never sanction it. I am sure that he has no idea that Mr. Pott is about to do it either. And if he did know it, I am sure he would put a stop to it, as I said, because he is not a dirty politician."

The answer on the other end was again silence, only this time it was the silence of someone who was trying to figure out exactly what it was she was being told.

"And the problem is, Cindy, that since the Congressman and Dexter Pott are friends and can be linked together, then I can show that the Congressman was behind this low blow somehow. And I will have to respond as if this thing were his doing. I will have to ignore the story and fight it as a personal attack from a dirty politician."

"What are you really trying to say to me, Garth?" was her answer, and it was one that any thinking listener could have later assumed, based on what Garth said next.

"I am not saying anything other than what I just said. I simply need you to get this message to the Congressman, because I am sure he does not know what his friend is planning. And when he does know, I am sure he will stop it. We both know he does not want to be associated with this kind of dirty politics."

"I don't know why you think I can talk to him. I do not think I can convey your message. You are going to have to try some other way," she had finally countered.

"Oh, I understand, Cindy. I just had to give it my best shot. Have a good evening," he said and then hung up.

At a time when incumbent Congressmen normally won ninety-eight percent of the elections, Wilton Carlson would go on three weeks later to defeat Congressman Fitzkin by twenty-one percentage points, even though his campaign had been outspent by a factor of five to one. None of the three men ever spoke about that phone call that evening, although Garth would later believe that Rich had figured it all out. Rich had always been a bit deep. Garth would learn more about later. When Garth considered what he had done, and from where this impulse had arisen, he could only think of his grandfather. From the moment of that phone call, Rich Sartory would always be even more guarded around Garth. And Wilton Carlson would always look at him as not only the man who got him elected to the United States Congress, but as a possessor of secret stores of knowledge and skill. In the brand of wisdom that is possessed only by youth, Garth thought that this was an entirely good thing.

Garth returned to Capitol Hill in charge of Congressman Carlson's office, and was a hero to his young friends, having gone from intern to chief of staff in slightly less than four years, and having managed a campaign that had ousted a Republican turncoat. He was a particular hero to his friends who had been fired by Congressman Fitzkin. His parents were less anxious about him having postponed law school. For the first time ever, he was well paid. Tabitha was proud of him and enjoyed all the perquisites that came from being a wife to a prominent political operative on Capitol Hill. The evolution of Wilton Carlson was one of those rare instances of something quite the opposite of what normally happens. Some men seem to be born with a purpose. Others learn what theirs is on their own accord, later in life. And still a much smaller group of men and women seem to stumble upon one. While most individuals are promoted up the ranks until they reach a position for which they are not equipped, Wilton Carlson found himself only after he had been promoted.

He was a much better Congressman than he had been a state legislator or a lumberyard foreman, or an insurance salesman, or a marketing executive, or a naval officer. His intelligence and his native political instinct finally were fully engaged. He capitalized on the fact that he was in a position to rise within the ranks of his party in the House of Representatives because he was a solidly liberal vote in the Texas Congressional delegation, which gave him a rare usefulness to the Democratic leadership. His Navy background and his hawkish stance on military issues meant that he could combat the Democratic weakness of appearing to be soft on matters of national defense. And he was an inveterate dealmaker and vote trader.

A brilliant German philosopher once said that all memory must proceed from pain but perhaps this is truer of what is important in a story. Still, painless events do occur and are important. Garth would finish law school in the evenings at Georgetown Law School. Congressman Carlson would obtain a seat on the House Armed Services Committee, and he would within a few years parlay that to a seat on the powerful House Appropriations Committee. Garth would attain the wisdom to see what had long been apparent to Congressman Carlson, which was that no man who comes to power is comfortable with the threat that is implicit in the independence of the person who put him in that position. Garth did not fear that there was a Night of the Long Knives in his future, nor did he think so poorly of the man's character. He simply came to instinctively feel what Congressman Carlson had long understood about the problem of Garth's power and independence. What was of greater importance was that he knew that this independence in his current position could possibly have a stultifying effect on his own professional development. In much the same way the two men had once tacitly agreed to work with one another, they also agreed that both their interests would be better served if they would then work apart. They combined efforts to see that Garth was placed in a law firm, which would hire him to be a lobbyist.

Congressman Carlson then obtained a true friend in the K Street corridors of lobbying power, and Garth was all that more effective as a lobbyist for having a good friend on the House Appropriations Committee. Garth was hired at a salary roughly four times that of the average American family and even though he was again plunged into the unsavory and morally damaging atmosphere of law books, (former) law students, and endless discussions of the law, he was partially buffered from all of that because his work was on Capitol Hill concerned making the law, and not wrangling with it. He would clutch his gold American Express credit card in his hand and guiltily smile at the other legal associates slaving away in the firm's library, as he would walk past it to leave the office and take some member of the House or Senate or their staff to dinner.

Congressman Carlson no longer had a staff member to whom he was deeply obligated, and he was free to hire only those who would be obligated to him. Those individuals would invariably be very bright and talented and determined and honorable young women, who also happened to be beautiful. The process was not so much like that previously mentioned Night, in which the black shirts had displaced the brown shirts. It was more that shirts themselves had been replaced by blouses, and short skirts. And, as had been the case with Garth, after a while one or another of these very capable young staff members would be placed in an important position in downtown Washington.

Two personal occurrences in Garth's life, so painless as to have been positively enjoyable and wonderful, were the birth of a son and a daughter to Tabitha and Garth, but only after several years of a two-income marriage that permitted them to travel, and to live well, and to put aside some savings. Tabitha was also advancing up the ranks within her law firm. In perhaps what is a German philosophical fashion, Garth would only later tend to remember other incidences that had occurred at this time.

Tabitha had always been a beautiful dryad to Garth. She conferred upon him some form of sylphlike magic, and he never considered having been selected by such an amazing and almost mythical creature as anything less than what mortal Peleus must have felt when Proteus gave him the secret for ensnaring the goddess, Thetis, in marriage. Anyone who has had extensive or even fleeting experience with dryads and sylphs knows that they have some notoriously difficult-to-manage qualities. Garth loved Tabitha not in spite of them, but because of them. Her ability to go absent, or to be that way in his presence, was endearing to him and it was just another way that she was not of this world, but was from a better place. It simply made sense for her to be personally evanescent in this way and it made her love for him that much more precious. It was all part of the poetry of who she was.

But not even the most erudite scholar may know what it is that a sylph will eat for dinner, nor was it a subject of conversation between Garth and his friends. So he assumed that it was beyond his earthly ken when his wife would on occasion only talk through an entire meal he had cooked, or when she would forget to cook, if the matter of cooking might have been left to her, and given this proclivity, it rarely was. The enchanting Tabitha also engaged in the mystical practice of misplacing or forgetting or even losing things, small inconsequential and almost unnoticeable things, such as the keys to the car or to the house, or her wallet or purse, or on occasion, one of the children. And the sedate traffic patterns on Mount Olympus might have poorly prepared her for the more fractious, errant and derelict drivers attempting to navigate the tangled streets of Washington, DC and its environs, so the family car was proudly bedecked with the dings and dents and scratches that Garth saw as the badges and ensigns of her otherworldliness. Her vocabulary was similarly Olympian, and Garth had to go to the dictionary to discover what she meant when she would ask him to stop "worrying" her, so that he could discover the fourth meaning of that verb, which was that she was referring to the way he would lovingly stroke her leg or her arm when they would sit together. He accepted it that many times when he would speak directly to her she would be unable to hear him because she was responding inwardly to some divine message. And the strains and the chords of these orphic melodies, which only she could hear, would often distract her from taking notice of such earthbound events as Garth's birthday, or when he would get a haircut, or the minor necessity of one or another of them calling the other at some point during each workday in order to coordinate which one of them would be able to get home in time to relieve the children's nanny. The sublime impulse would sometimes move her to speak animatedly at length to one particular randomly selected individual at a party or at a dinner, as if she had been visited by the muse of late night heightened college discussions, and it would only take one glass of wine in order for her conversation to reach this point of transport.

The place upon which Garth then stood was made pleasant by the bounties of his life and love. From his youthful heart he could catch a glimpse of that Proteus who might have spoken to him, and he could barely hear but not fully discern the secrets that were whispered, which he believed and that made him the unique adherent to the creed of his wife's discreet divinity. Many years later, Garth would encounter men of the world, men who were out of tune with what Garth could see in Tabitha's nature. These men would turn Garth's love into something forlorn and clinical, when they would lay waste to his romantic vision of all these beautiful flights of her sylphlike spirit, and they would tell him they were merely the symptoms of her attention deficit disorder. This diagnosis of Tabitha would arise appurtenant to the same conclusion that these men of twenty-first century science would reach about their son, at a time not long subsequent to their divorce. Between poetry and prose, between faith and science, there is a necessary transition.

About ten years after Congressman Carlson's first election, and only a year after the birth of Garth's and Tabitha's second child, their daughter, Garth found himself once again in a room with Wilton Carlson and one other person, and they were again confronting the possible end of that politician's career, which by this time had been quite successful and perhaps even brilliant. They were in the Congressman's office and the third man this time was Chip Mathers, the chief of staff to the Speaker of the United States House of Representatives. It was not unusual for Garth to be called upon in this manner. He still remained Wilton's primary advisor on political matters. This was again the reason he had been called, but he could tell by Chip's presence and by the fact that his normally effusive personality was being held in check, that this was not going to be the normal call about what to do on some vote or how to manage a sticky situation with another member of Congress. Chip was an ebullient, smiling Irish political type, with an engaging and bearish charm. He was a large man in height and build. Though he was not fat, he had a wide boyish face that gave that first impression. He had a staccato delivery. And little of all of that was in evidence as he deliberately and seriously began to relate the story to Garth.

"Apparently, some young intern came into the Congressman's office while he was at a Committee meeting. She came in to put a memo on his desk. When she did this she inadvertently moved some other papers, and discovered a couple grams of cocaine in a paper wrapper on the desk. So she called the Capitol Police, without consulting anyone else on the staff," Chip told Garth directly.

"Well, that should not be the real problem, because the Capitol Police work for the Sergeant at Arms, and he works for the Speaker. This could be taken care of discreetly. I am guessing that the real issue is that the young lady told some people back in the district, perhaps her family, and now you have a political problem," Garth ventured.

"But no political problem that is local to a Congressional district . . ." Garth continued, and then paused, ". . . no local political issue would concern the Speaker's office. So that means the girl did not talk to anyone. One of the cops did. Did one of the cops call the United States Attorney or something like that?"

"Something like that, but not exactly like that," Chip said. "There is a pain in the ass reporter who knows everything. He probably has a contact inside the Capitol Police."

"That's no good," Garth said. "What do you think, Wilton?"

"Well, I guess I can't blame this one on too much drinking," the Congressman quipped, " since with alcohol, I could summon AA and Jesus."

"The simplest solution is for someone in this office to take the fall. Some staff person can claim the drug was hers, and then you can find some way to pension her off," Garth suggested.

"That is why I am here, Garth," Chip said. "I thought of that. And we have been going over it. First of all, the importance of damage control makes it impossible to even breach the subject to any of the lower level staff people. They might simply turn and repeat the story. There are only two people in the office trusted enough to even speak to, and we just talked to each one of them."

"Neither one of them could commit to the idea," Chip said, "and even if one of them could be convinced, she would not have the gumption to go through with it. There would always be the risk that the whole thing would blow up in our faces. And there is a lot at stake here. Wilton is very important to the Speaker, and we do not want to lose this seat."

Chip looked at Garth and then at Wilton. Garth looked at Chip and then at Wilton. Wilton only looked at Garth, directly and openly, with a steady gaze that was as plainly reminiscent as any Garth had ever seen. It had lasted more than a minute and gave no hints of ever changing.

"It is simple," Garth said. "I will take the blame."

Chip looked at Garth with a look that showed how Chip had been caught on the tides of admiration, surprise, respect, sympathy and had been unable to express anything other than the welling up of all those and other feelings, until he reached a point of a tear creeping out of the corner of one of his eyes. He shook Garth's hand.

"It is an honor to know you. You hold our obligation, and our loyalty."

Wilton was wearing the same expression he once used to have when he was indirectly bragging about his "bright campaign manager", only it was magnified tenfold. He turned to Chip.

"I told you we would not have to ask him."

Garth would have to resign his position at the law firm and negotiate his agreement with the criminal justice authorities. This would help Chip to keep it out of the newspapers. The criminal aspect of it would be agreed, and Garth would be on probation for two years, and would do some community service, and would agree not work on Capitol Hill for five years. In return his record would be expunged after that time. Garth had just collected two large political debts, which might have some value someday, even though Garth would no longer be in the business of politics.

What neither Wilton nor Chip could have known was that Garth had already had his fill of lobbying, and particularly of working in a law firm. He did not like going to his friends on Capitol Hill to kindly ask them if they would let his firm's timber company client clear cut every National Forest, or let their client which was a mining company drill in the National Parks for an extremely low permit fee. He was not convinced that his reputation was being enhanced by the cable television company which his law firm represented, and which wanted to maintain its monopoly power so that it could continue to charge exorbitant prices. But the bad guys whose interests Garth had been asked to protect and enhance on Capitol Hill were princes of the church compared to the lawyers in his firm.

In most cases, these clients were the clients of the attorneys who handled their significant federal litigation. These lawyers would never allow Garth to talk to the clients about legislative strategy, nor would he be allowed to direct the firm's general strategy on legislative issues. He would only be called in like a trained dog, and at the last moment would be directed to try to make some impossible thing happen in some legislative committee. And when it did not happen as hoped, the lawyers would undercut him. And these more accomplished lawyers who represented the clients were magnitudes kinder and gentler than the younger ones in the firm, who would stab Garth in the back, just because he was not suffering as much as they were. In the final analysis, the very worst politicians were saints compared to the lawyers. Politicians cared what other people thought of them.

Garth gave up less than either Chip or Wilton thought he had. As much as he had been motivated to help Wilton, he was more motivated by his antipathy toward lobbying and lawyers. He may have been even more motivated by what had been happening in his home life. In the long and gradual transition from poetry to prose, from Tabitha the dryad to a wife with attention deficit disorder, there had been an odyssey of loss and heartache that had been concluded not at Ithaca with a happy marital reunion, but in a crash on the rocks where Garth feared that his wife no longer loved him. If Garth had known the science of his wife's impairment at the beginning, he might not have loved her. If he had known it before the beginning of the end, he might have been able to save his marriage.

Just when Garth had saved Wilton Carlson's political career for a second time, his marriage to Tabitha had reached a point where it seemed he was living with a phantom. The lyrical and mystical qualities of her absence within her presence had been leveled and smoothed out by the flat part of time's scythe. All the magical promontories had been flattened, and much had been prepared for the point at which time would use the business edge of his device. In the four years since their son, and the two years since their daughter, had been born, Garth could count on the fingers of one hand the number of times that Tabitha had initiated the necessary phone call about which one of them would get home first to relieve the nanny for the evening. Garth had reveled in the moments when he was all that Tabitha could see in her tunnel vision. But at this point in time when they had been married for twelve years, after ten or twelve hours at work she would come home, and he would feel like the rock that lay all around that tunnel. Her attention would delve deeply down into herself where some other considerations commanded her, mostly about her work. The forgotten birthdays had taken their toll, and the absent-mindedness that had been so quaint and endearing became the barrier between them. Leaving his job would give Garth the time and energy to address these problems and to try to solve them. They would no longer be wealthy, but they could live quite comfortably on Tabitha's salary. So he relieved the nanny for the last time one evening, and he took over the raising of children while he thought about another line of work.

Some chord struck deep then. It may have been something inherently Jewish, something that touched upon the profound familial traditions of that ancient people. It most likely was far more elemental and universal than that, but it was very clearly related to the one most Jewish person in Garth's life. Every moment that he was taking care of his son and daughter, Garth understood instinctively why his mother fingered her necklace. The earth and all its bounties and calamities had been made for his children. Seas rose and fell and rivers ran; winds and rains crashed and stormed, and the sun came out to end the tempest; order was held and laws were obeyed, while cars would crash and criminals would lurk; the planets and the stars circled in their spheres to determine the fates of those at their centers; and all these things bore no relationship at all to anything, or to any person, who was not his children. They were his covenant. He learned that love was purest when it was most giving and it expected nothing in return. His children did not thank him, but the help that he gave them was its own reward. And more, he found this impossible love inside of him that knew no self-interest, and the only way to manage the overwhelming nature of it was to give it expression. Every time he changed a diaper or tied a shoe or did laundry, he was keeping this bright hot thing inside of him from becoming unbearable. He was adding to that love, and giving it color and shape with every small thing he did, with every worry he compensated, with every gift he gave.

Peculiarly, the ideal nature of this love for his children fired in him a new love for his wife that was as powerful, but which was symbiotically linked to his passion for her. He called her with every success of each child, and put his son or daughter on the phone. He prepared elaborate family dinners for them. He made the house as nice as it could be. He spent extra time teaching the children, playing with them, and preparing them for life and for school. And he shared this all with his wife. And he desired her more than he had as a much younger man and with a greater resonance.

She told him that she did not need him to bring about her relationship with her own children. She could not shift her attention to the food he put before her. And the most important part was what is most difficult for anyone to understand, if one has never known a person like Tabitha. Unlike her, for the typical person, to be wanted and to be missed is a wonderful thing. This same person will also be disconcerted when someone is bothering her while she has a task that she absolutely must be doing, no matter what the motivations of the other person are. For an individual with Tabitha's impairment, this latter condition was also the first. In her mind when she came home, her every instinct and thought and feeling was trained upon whatever it was that occupied or had occupied her attention. It was her focus. For her to be approached by her loving husband at that moment was the same thing as if she had been trying to repair a watch that had to be fixed within the next several minutes, while some man was touching her and kissing her. She could not stand it. For Garth, that was maddening. When they had both been working and had been largely preoccupied, they had been able to have a stable and relatively cool and unchangingly bland marriage. Now that he was more in love with her than he ever had been, she could not handle it.

There was a certain inevitability to what followed. It was like the old Vaudeville act in which the clown is performing in the one spotlight on a darkened stage. Then the spotlight begins to move as the clown tries to keep in the light. The light moves more intermittently again, jerking across the stage, and the clown's efforts become more strenuous. Eventually, the light stops seven feet up the wall, and the clown keeps jumping up, trying to get into it.

Garth eventually gave up. Their children went to elementary school, and he took a job teaching English at the local high school, so he could be at home when they came home, and he could still have a job. When he stopped trying to jump into the spotlight, when he held back, when he finally had allowed the marriage to become bloodless, Tabitha noticed it. It may have been ironic that she noticed his absence more than his love, but when he joined her in being absent, she did not like it. But what she could not ignore was that her son and daughter were developing a deep and lasting and loving relationship with their father, a relationship of which she did not seem to be a part. The phone calls that Garth arranged for her children to tell her what they had been doing had the opposite effect that Garth had intended. She saw them as his effort to place himself between them and her.

She filed for divorce and for sole custody of the children. This was in the eighth year after Garth had stepped in front of the figurative bullet that might have taken down Congressman Carlson, or eight years after he had taken over raising the children. It was the turning of the century and the beginning of a new millennium. Tabitha had taken her time to get to this point and she arrived at it with the same hyper-focus that she had once trained on Garth. She was not malicious. But what she had was a lawyer's heart and head. She filed a tactical nuclear attack of a divorce complaint and the point of it was to scare him into surrender. She dredged up the facts of the "crime" she knew he had not committed, and accused him of being psychologically manipulative of the children and of her. And from the severe limits of her perspective, she thought she could make the complaint stick. But Garth was observant and politically savvy, and these traits were enhanced by his intellect and his passion, which always seemed to strike her from the outside, by surprise. If she could have felt his passion for his children, she would not have made her next move. Her final tactic was to remove the children from him, by setting up an apartment near their house. One day he returned from teaching, and opened the door to let the children in when it had been their normal time to come home from elementary school, but he was met by the process server. His children were not coming home.

SHE WAS ARMED FOR BEAR

On the grass next to the University of Kentucky track, David Goodman performed his stretching exercises as he gazed over at the women's track team warming up for their joint meet against the University of Tennessee. He was unable to look long at them all because his attention would always return to Melinda Sherman. He had never been so struck by any woman in his young life.

He was a rare student at the University of Kentucky. He had taken Latin in high school, was majoring in literature at Kentucky, and could not help but feel that what he was doing at that moment reenacted the myth of Actaeon and Artemis. According to that myth, when Actaeon had accidentally stumbled upon the sylvan pond deep in the woods where this goddess of the moon and of the hunt did her bathing, he knew that he should move on, and that he should not watch her. But he could not help himself. David knew that the Greeks had got one thing right in their myths of Artemis or of Athena or of Demeter. There were few things as charismatically attractive as feminine strength, a female form that has elements of beauty, severity and power. Like most men, he did not find female body builders attractive. But there was nothing so striking or irresistible as a female athlete, and not any female athlete, perhaps just this one.

Melinda Sherman stood about five feet eight inches tall, and appeared to weigh about one hundred and twenty-five pounds. Her legs were strong and not at all thin and they showed a moderate amount of definition without the sharp edges or chiseled look of a man. Supple and smooth and in goodly size and strength, her thighs and calves were very appealing, as highlighted by the slenderness of her ankles and knees. She was a good runner because she was slightly narrower in the hips than most women, but in no way mannish or less like a woman. She had a very slender waist, casting her hips in proportion and preserving the waist to hip ratio that is key to feminine allure. Even though she was not broad in the hips she had a bit of a protruding posterior, in the shape of an upside down Valentine heart. In fact, David Goodman was certain and afraid that he was inordinately staring at the one posterior for which he was prepared to fight, kill, and die. She was as alluring from behind as she was from any angle. She was strong and trim through the ribs and her chest was a medium size but firm and high and her body was given more of that hourglass shape by the fact that she was slightly broad in the shoulder. This was a trait that was slightly on the side of being masculine, but it too was in no way mannish. He had once seen her in a swimsuit, and she looked as feminine as any model. She just looked stronger and faster, as Artemis must have looked.

Her face was all the more beautiful, for also being handsome. Because of this, she would still be beautiful when she was seventy years old. She had a prominent forehead, deep-set hazel eyes and sandy blonde hair that she kept in a style that was full and between short and medium. Her jaw line was long and her chin was solid. She had strong cheekbones, and her lips had enough luxury to keep her handsome face from ever being masculine. Her nose was quite straight and not at all small, but it had a little fillip at the tip, which was also distinctly feminine.

David Goodman would eventually catch up to Melinda, and not just on the track. He would ask her to go out with him, and she would accept the offer. She would like him because he was a bit more thoughtful than the other young men who approached her at college, and because his appreciation of her was more fully formed and respectful. David tried to make her laugh and he asked her about her home life and what she was studying. Above all, he listened to her. He liked her for what she had to say, and how she felt about things.

There was much about Melinda that he could not have known, such as that she was waiting for the right young man, and that she was eager to find out something about herself. He also could not have guessed at the complexity of her history, or that she was also literally a visionary, or that there was some deep part within her that even she did not fully understand. He could not also have known that after a few dates she would invite him back to her room, and as soon as he turned around after having closed the door behind them, that he would find that all of her clothes had miraculously and incredibly swiftly found their way to the floor.

She was very much the goddess. Actaeon was punished by the goddess for having the hubris to see her unclothed. For that offense, Artemis had turned him into a stag and he was run to ground and killed by his own hounds. David and Melinda would be in a relationship for the better part of a year. He would not be run to ground, but would very much still be in love with her when it ended, so much so that he would continue to occasionally contact her in one way or another, for most of the rest of his life. And there would be no hounds or even any clearly delineated end. He would simply feel that she had slowly become another person.

And it was not that she changed her personality. She simply, gradually became another person, but only in connection to him, slowly getting to the point of not really seeming to know him, or know that they were in a relationship. It was as if they conducted their love affair backward in time, from caring deeply about one another, to dating seriously, to going out, to just being friends or acquaintances. It would mystify David, just as it would bewilder the other two men and one woman with whom she would have an intimate relationship in college, all also liaisons lived backwards: Charles Davis, the English major and hockey player from Providence, Rhode Island, Caroline Collins, the softball player and drama student from Louisville, Kentucky, and Carlos Compton, the African-American Studies major and basketball player from Cleveland, Ohio.

There would be one person with whom she would maintain a constant and warmly affectionate relationship throughout college, albeit not an intimate one, Tommy Kitt, who would regularly visit her from London. Tommy did not go to college after he graduated high school, but took a job as an auto mechanic. He was also kind of an anachronism, like a character out of a Victorian era novel, in which a word is used that sounds differently to the modern ear: "disinterested." The modern ear tends to take it to mean indifferent, or not being interested in something. Its original meaning was unselfish, or without a self-interest. Tommy was just happy to see her, to be in her presence, as just her existence gave him great joy. All of that was more than enough for him. Tommy loved Melinda disinterestedly.

When she had been younger, Melinda sensed this and respected it. As she grew up and had gone to college and became involved in other relationships, her understanding did not grow. In that way peculiarly inherent to this time in the life of a young adult, her understanding did not evolve. She tolerated Tommy, and it is the character of such a feeling that it makes the person who feels it so very comfortable. It is so pleasant to tolerate someone who does not deserve it, and it is no less pleasant when the person does deserve it. Perhaps most agreeable is that there is never any reason or foundation for such a feeling, and it arrives within a person as if it were a providence. But Melinda's basically good character was solidly beneath the outgrowths of later adolescence, and this ornamental superstructure did not outlast its solid foundation. She effectively cared for him more, and better appreciated and honored his disinterested love, as she moved through the University of Kentucky, and never more so than when he was there one day when she had been struck by a vision.

Tommy and Melinda had been walking from campus into town in order to get something to eat. Tommy lost touch with her, but only in the sense that she suddenly forgot that he was there. All he could see as he looked around were things that suddenly had become invisible to her. It was as if she were looking beyond all that was around them. She had stopped walking and stared into the blank distance. After a few minutes, she began to look around again, slightly distressed. And he thought he heard her murmuring her brother's name, over and over. He waited a few more minutes.

"Are you all right, Melinda?"

"Oh, I am fine, Tommy. Don't worry about me," she tried.

"You did have me very worried there for a second."

"It's nothing really, Tommy. I was just having one of my visions."

"I knew it," he smiled, "I knew they were real. I knew you really had them."

"Oh, I have them all right."

"What was this one?"

"You're not going to believe this, but I saw Jesus."

"Again, just like that time?"

"No, Tommy, not like that time."

"You were making it up that time, weren't you?"

"I was trying to protect Porter. It is a long story."

"But this one was real. I knew it. I could tell. I was right here and it was weird. What did you see Jesus doing?"

"He was crucified to that telephone pole. And he said a lot of things that did not make much sense. I listened for what seemed like a long time and I never really put it all together. But from out of all of it I got the very clear impression that I am supposed to join the Navy."

"Wow! Jesus is a Navy recruiter. That is too much. I can't wait to get back to London and tell all those people at the church."

"They won't believe it."

"Who cares? You are still the best and most interesting thing that has ever happened in that town. I will have to tell them, I will tell everybody, and at the Christian Community because I really think they will all half believe it."

Once Tommy had returned to London, Melinda began to receive Navy recruiting material in the mail. She smiled every time she got such a letter, and she read the material with interest. She also began to question her qualifications, and specifically wondered if what it was that made her feel so different from everybody else was also something that might disqualify her for the Navy. She felt she was more driven and less risk averse than the women around her. She also became very attached to her goals and worked tirelessly toward them. She also had found in college that she approached sex in the same way she approached many other things; there were times when she was driven to it. But it opened up a part of her from which she would eventually recede. It created an intimacy from which she would equally and eventually be driven. The emotional high of loving was followed by a low. That frightened her. And then there were her visions.

As she had once approached the Christian Community of London, she decided to approach another religious institution, this time the low church of mental health science. As a student she was entitled to health care at the University of Kentucky Hospital, and as an athlete she was accustomed to being given priority treatment, so she found her way to the Psychiatric Health Services department and scheduled an appointment with a therapist. This turned into several appointments and tests and discussions, and finally, one day, the therapist pushed a piece of paper across her desk to

Melinda, who read on that paper some words. She took note and the words she always later remembered were, "hypomania, cyclothymia, and hyperthermic temperament."

"Am I crazy?" she asked the doctor.

"I don't much like that term. And, no, you're not crazy. In fact, many highly functioning and successful people could be diagnosed in the same way."

Melinda had always known many of the things that the doctor had called her "markers" or her "presentation," but she knew them in a way the doctor never could. They simply were who she was. After she graduated from the University of Kentucky in 1990, she entered the United States Navy.

Lieutenant Carl Furth had been uneasy about this mission from the get go. In his seven and a half years as a Navy SEAL (Sea, Air, and Land team), this was the first mission that seemed rushed to him. Normally, there would be weeks of preparation and specific training and there would be drills based on the detailed requirements of obtaining each objective. Often times a mission would be postponed because something about the intel had been uncertain, or there had been some change. These covert operations were supposed to remain covert, and no one wanted to see them go wrong. This one had been different. It was the nineteenth of March in 2003, and there had been a sense of urgency to this mission that Carl assumed meant that the United States invasion of Iraq was going to begin the next day. No one was talking. It just felt that way.

It was to be an abduction mission. There was a top al-Qaeda official thought to be hiding out in a village in Southern Iraq, and his purpose there was to direct infiltration by al-Qaeda operatives into the Iraqi civilian population, in anticipation of the US invasion. He was obviously in possession of information that the US would love to have. The village where he was hiding out was fairly isolated and small, consisting of only eight buildings, none more than two stories tall. He had been known to be in a particular building near the edge of the village, and the objective of this mission was to secure that building, eliminate his four or five guards and get him out. He had been assigned the code name "Discreet," but the guys on these two SEAL fire teams had been calling him "The Creep." Carl Furth was in command of both teams of four men each, and he was to lead the one team into the building, while the other team was to secure the perimeter and repel any responders. Lieutenant Junior Grade, Hamilton Thompson, whom everyone called Hambone, was commanding that second fire team. Anyone who called him Hamster would live to regret it.

There was the opposite of formality within these two teams, as within all SEAL units. To look at them, you would not know which ones were the officers, or even if they were all in the same service. The same was true to listen to them. The bond between them was too close to rely on formality. Their training had been too rigorous for them not to know what each man's duty was. They were closer than most brothers. The man with whom Carl Furth had served the longest was a burly six-foot two-inch former Gold Gloves boxing champion named Donny Bhutani and the funny rhyme that his name formed was an indicator of how different he was from what was expected of a guy of Indian descent. He was from Georgia and he was more of a cracker than anything, but the team members just called him Ghandi in order to point out that he was not all that non-violent, and other than by his last name, you would never know his parents had moved to America from Mumbai just before he had been born. Jeff Dimock was a stoical and imperturbable long-haired blond guy from Central Pennsylvania who was of medium build and very wiry. They all just called him Shooter, because he was their sniper and he had consistently outscored everyone on every firing range. Nobody knows why the nickname of Mr. Baseball was given to Max Lowry, an African American from the Bronx who had never played the game, but who was a talkative bearded guy with a small but very strong frame, and who seemed to have an answer for everything that ever came up. All anyone ever called Carl Furth was Furthy, and he had gone straight into the SEALs from the Naval Academy. He had worked extra hard at everything he did in order to keep his team from holding that against him, which they did. Furthy was from San Diego and was straight out of a Navy family, and had wanted to be a SEAL since he had been about ten years old. He was about six feet tall and had the strong build of a former lacrosse player, and he was always known for doing a lot of worrying. He thought he was just doing his job.

And he had been worrying about this mission, mainly because of what made him feel that it had been rushed. They had taken off in a Blackhawk helicopter from an Army base in Saudi Arabia about two hours after midnight, and were flying with no lights and under radio silence. There was a lot of empty desert to fly over, and then they were to basically fly downhill through a gulley cut out by a dried out river bed, almost straight to this village that was on the southern edge of the Euphrates River valley, where the desert just starts to get a little bit more hospitable. He kept his eyes on the ground ahead all the time and ignored the men in the helicopter. They sensed his uneasiness, and were quiet as well. No one had talked about it, but they also must have sensed that the United States Army, the United States Marine Corps and the remainder of the Coalition Forces were just now taking a deep breath and seeming to prepare for the first leap forward into Iraq. Just before the helicopter was about to cross the border into Iraq, the Iraqi army installations along the border were hit by US Air Force sorties. The Iraqis were rumored to be pretty well dug in, and would not come out until coalition ground forces would cross the border. They would not be looking for a single Blackhawk and they were not in a position to see it if they had tried. Pretty soon Carl could see the target village a few miles ahead, where the gulley opened out onto the plain. Wearing his night-vision goggles, he could see the eight dusty buildings. Once they got close, he might not need them. There was some cloud cover, but it was also only one day past a full moon. This had been another reason for his uneasiness.

The Blackhawk settled into the cover provided by the side of the gulley at its end, and Furth gave the men the signal to rappel down to the surface. They got onto the desert floor in record time, faster than they had ever trained. Carl Furth recognized that they were very keyed up by the danger of this mission. His own heart was beating pretty fast, and he had entered that zone where every second seems to be stretched out. So while his watch told them they had moved in record time, it had still seemed to him to take forever. They were scrambling out of the prop wash of the Blackhawk, and were heading down out of the end of the gulley and over the open ground toward their objective a little more than half a mile away as the helicopter turned to go back to the base, when suddenly there was gunfire from the ridge above them and beside the helicopter, as it was hit several times and started to rattle and whir as it lurched out of range of the shooting. Furth's misgivings about the mission had not been misplaced, but this problem had not been because of any faulty intel. What no one could have known was that on top of that ridge there was a unit of the Iraqi regular army that had deserted its post and was getting the hell out of the way of the US Army and Marines, which it too felt were soon to invade. Now these same deserters suddenly had been given a chance to cover all their bases, by getting off the front line, and still being able to try to take down a US helicopter. Carl Furth realized that it was time for Plan B.

In a situation such as this, Plan B was just to stay alive until another helicopter could come to take them out. And any minute now, whoever had shot that Blackhawk would figure out where they were. They could hunker down in the gulley and try to ride it out there, but sooner or later they would be sitting ducks for the Iraqis up top. There were various small rock outcroppings here and there between them and the village but the only real cover was the village itself. So Carl signaled that they were to make their way to the village as fast as possible, by making as much use of the existing cover as was available. They would complete the mission anyway. And until the bad guys in the village discovered their location, their main concern was the force on the ridge and the possibility that whoever it was would fire down on them with rocket propelled grenades. So they used the existing cover to shield their rears as they made their way to the village. About two hundred yards out they stopped and eyeballed the nearest buildings, just as two armed guards came out of the tallest building and were looking in their direction. Carl did not have to signal Shooter. He knew just what to do, and in less than five seconds, he had taken out both the guards.

By the time they got to that building and Hambone and his fire team posted a perimeter around it, there were some stirrings in the village. Mr. Baseball checked the front door, and it was unlocked. Just before they were going to open the door several shots were fired through it from the inside. Mr. Baseball and Ghandi opened fire into the house through the door, and Furth kicked it open. One of the guards was dead and the other one was moving for the stairs when Ghandi took him out. They two of them moved to clear the rooms on the lower floor, while Carl and Shooter moved up the steps. The second floor was empty and so was the roof. Shooter stationed himself up there and Carl looked at him.

"I know," Shooter said. "I will kill as many as I can, and I will let you know everything that I see."

Carl turned to go back downstairs, when he heard Mr. Baseball.

"Hey, Furthy, you're not going to believe this," he said, "but we found

The Creep. He was hiding in the cabinet under the sink in the kitchen. We already wrapped him up."

"They are heading this way," Shooter reported, "and there are about forty of them. I have taken out two, and it appears that they are now spread out into three groups. The main one is advancing this way using the same cover we did. The other two groups of ten men each are going to try to flank us."

The Iraqi Army guys were also firing at will into the village, which may have helped to suppress any problems that might have come from that side of the village itself. What was going on at the other end was out of their reach to discover. Ghandi was already on the horn. That Blackhawk would not be able to return. The pilot, co-pilot and crewman would be lucky if they did not have to ditch their wounded bird before they got back over the border. Ghandi said he believed that there was some confusion on the other end of the line, so he had to place a call over the Navy frequency as well. In a minute or two he was informed that it would be the Navy that would respond. They would have to hang on for as long as it would take. By now they had figured out that there must have been some other al-Qaeda in the village, because they were being fired on from some of the other buildings. One of Hambone's guys had been hit already but was still able to man his post. Furth and Mr. Baseball took cover from this other team, as they moved to clear each one of the two buildings closest to them.

"The main bad guy group is setting up shop in that same little rocky outcropping that we stopped at about two hundred yards out," Shooter reported. "And the flanking forces are staying out of range to the left and right."

"Seahawk, ten minutes out," Ghandi reported just as Carl and Mr. Baseball had cleared the second adjacent building. There were nothing but what appeared to be harmless civilians.

Now fire was coming very heavily from in front, from the main Iraqi force. Bullets were tearing into the building. Hambone had moved his men to behind the building to face the remainder of the village. Shooter reported that he had killed or injured two and three of the guys in each the flanking forces, but that they would soon reach the village buildings on each side. Furth positioned his men to the sides, and hoped like hell that help would get there in time. The problem was that the whole damn place was too hot for any helicopter to put down anywhere. It was developing into a real firefight. Carl went up top to help Shooter and to see what he could see. They were doing what they could when suddenly Shooter said, "Seahawk at ten o'clock." Furth knew that no pilot would risk his life, or risk losing the one way that they all had to get out. It looked like they would have to fight their way across open desert to a reasonable drop zone. That would be suicide.

Abruptly the Seahawk turned, but not to get away from the fight. It swiftly and unexpectedly bore down on the main Iraqi force, its one machine gun firing. And it fired its Hellfire missiles into the position, all the while it was taking fire head-on. The twenty Iraqi Army men began to scatter. Some were blown to bits. Some dug in. And some ran. There was an opening now on that side of the village, but only a brief one. The Navy helicopter hovered on that side of the tall building about fifty yards out, and began to set down.

"I don't know who that pilot is," Mr. Baseball said, "but he sure has brass balls."

"Let's do what we can to keep his balls intact," Furth ordered and signaled his team forward. Furth and Shooter stayed on the building, and Ghandi and Mr. Baseball covered the side facing the village. Hambone's team advanced into the desert to clean up the main force, or to keep them as pinned down as possible. There were only a handful left, and they were not feeling too frisky. But there was always the possibility that the ones who had run away would return. Shooter picked off two of the remainder, and he looked at Furth, and Carl gave him the signal to go. It was still a mess. They were doing what they could to stay cool and keep up a suppressing fire in both directions. But now the village was starting to be more of a problem. Furth ordered Hambone's team onto the chopper. Two of them were now injured, and they needed help. Furth's team kept firing at the Iraqi soldiers in the village, as they backed toward the Seahawk. A portion of one or both of the flanking groups had reached the nearer buildings, and were setting up fire when Furth and his team heard the Seahawk crew member yell, "Clear out!" They looked and realized that the pilot had landed the chopper facing the main building. The pilot fired the last Hellfire into that building and it blew, knocking a lot of the fight out of the Iraqis. Shooter helped Mr. Baseball, who had also been hit, onto the helicopter. Only Ghandi and Furth were left when they looked up just in time to see a woman about thirty yards away, and coming from the village.

They had either not seen her before, or they had seen her and could not bring themselves to shoot her. She was covered in black. She was shouting something and Furth looked at Ghandi, because he was the only one on either team who understood any Arabic.

"I don't know, Furth. She is saying that she wants to come with us," he said.

They stood there, frozen for a few seconds. Then they heard a shout from the chopper. They turned in time to see the pilot lean his shoulders out of the cockpit, and shoot the woman in the head, dropping her immediately. Furth shouted for Ghandi to get on the helicopter, and turned to get on it himself. Then Ghandi turned around and went back to the woman. He lifted up her cover, looked under it and ran back to the chopper just as Furth was getting on it, and as it was lifting up off the sand. Ghandi took a bullet in his arm, spun around, and staggered up to the chopper. Furth and Shooter pulled him on board. He ignored them.

"Some thanks," Furth said. "Next time we will just leave you dangling."

Ghandi still snubbed him, and looked only at the pilot, whom he addressed.

"It's all right, Ma'am. She was armed for bear. I didn't want you to think she might not have been. Her body was lined with explosives."

Then Ghandi looked at Furth with a smirk that said, "You idiot, only you would fail to see that the pilot is a woman."

Furth turned to look at the helmeted pilot. She looked familiar to him. He had seen her before, and he had actually met her. He could not place the name. She was a Lieutenant Commander though, and his senior officer. He stopped to look at the co-pilot, who was slumped against the side of the cockpit. He was conscious but his right upper arm was shattered. Whether they got back now was up to the pilot alone. Then Furth remembered. He had met her in Bahrain, on shore duty. And he had seen her briefly on board one of the helicopter assault ships. He realized why he remembered her. She was damn good looking. You might have thought she was a very pretty man when you first looked at her. But she was not. She was a handsome woman. And her butt was so amazing that you could tell that it was, even through a bulky flight suit, like the one she was wearing now, the one with the blood bloom on her left shoulder, and the larger one on the right side of her waist.

His team was quiet and they were dressing their wounds with the help of the helicopter crewman. The only words said were when Shooter told Carl that he had put two bullets into The Creep before they left the building. Furth could not keep his eyes off of the pilot and this time it was not because he knew she was attractive. He could see that her face was getting paler. The rotor blades on the Seahawk were whistling, which is what they will do when they have been perforated by bullets. The Seahawk power plant was laboring. It was a long and drawn out return, but not to the base. They were heading to the pilot's home, a ship off of Kuwait in the Persian Gulf. Furth knew a thing or two about wounds. He was certain that the pilot was not going to make it. She finally sensed him staring, and he knew that she knew that he was offering to do something about her wounds. But she looked back at him as if to say, "No time for that now, Mister."

It seemed like an hour, but soon the ship was in front of them, only about twenty minutes after they had left the village. They were about five feet off the deck when she dropped the bird hard on it, turned off the engine, and passed out. The medics ran out to grab the wounded men, when Furth gave them an order.

"These guys can wait a minute. They are tough old dogs. They can lick their wounds a little more. Grab the pilot. I am afraid she might be a goner."

WHAT ANYTHING
MIGHT ENTAIL

The first thing that Garth did, when he had read Tabitha's divorce complaint and when he realized that it meant that he would not be seeing his children that day, was to sit down and cry. The second thing he did, after an hour and a half, was to call Eakin.

Over the previous twenty years, they had stayed in touch by phone and on occasional visits, and it had been astonishing that their lives had taken separate but parallel paths. Garth's success at his first campaign had followed her success as an assistant plant manager. After she had taken the plant manager position in Houston, the oil exploration business collapsed because oil prices had collapsed due to the recession, so she was being paid under contract to be a plant manager of a plant that was not operating. She convinced the owners of a plastic bag plant nearby that she could run it as a replacement for the manager they had lost. She did this even though she knew nothing about plastic, and by teaching herself all that she needed to know. She then had figured out that this inert plastic could be used to line hazardous waste sites, and had convinced the Environmental Protection Agency. At roughly this time, Garth had gone to work for the law firm, and her company became his sole personal client. They worked together to make this plastic the material of choice not only for hazardous waste sites but for all municipal landfills. She took company public, somewhere along the path of taking it from five million dollars in sales to one hundred and fifty million dollars in sales.

Garth well remembered the conversation the two of them had when she had gone to New York for that initial public offering of the company's stock. She called him from Manhattan one night. She had been drinking.

"Where are you?" he had asked.

"I am hiding out from the big investors and the stock underwriters at some hotel other than the one they booked for me," she answered.

"Do you think that is wise?"

"Hell, yes. It is three days until the initial public offering, and they have refused to buy out my previous contract. They have been calling the other hotel, and complaining about how irresponsible I am, and threatening to cancel the whole deal."

"That sounds scary."

"Forget that. Tomorrow they will be calling, and they will simply be asking where I am. By the third day they will be begging me just to show up and they will have agreed to buy out my previous contract."

She had been correct about that. Later, when Garth told her that she had seemed to have mastered the business of manufacturing, and given her success in New York, that maybe she should consider trying her hand at finance, she simply refused the possibility on point of principle.

"Those Wall Street bastards don't make anything."

Then, just several months before Garth left his job at the law firm, she had also called him, and this time she was very sober. Having literally created the market for plastic lining in hazardous waste sites and municipal land-fills, and after her little company in Houston had cornered eighty percent of that market, some of the big plastics companies had decided to move into that part of the plastics business. Her response had been to cut her company's prices worldwide. This had been successful in maintaining their market share, but at the same time it had cut into the company's profits, and had driven down the stock price. The same small group of large investors, who had bridled at her personal negotiating technique, also represented a majority of her board of directors, and they convened a meeting and fired her as the President.

When Garth tried to console her, she just laughed it off and pointed out to Garth that by firing her and not negotiating her termination, they had not been able to obtain an agreement not to compete. That would have been the civilized thing to do, and it would have cost them some money. And it would have been crucial, since she was the one person in the world who could give them a real problem that would cost them more than it would have to paid her directly.

She quickly took a large consulting fee from a Canadian company to help them build a plant to compete with her former company. And she flew to Taiwan, and created a new company there to do the same thing. Taiwanese investors put up the money and she put up the expertise, and they each owned half of the new corporation. Once it was up and running, it would be poised to take the Asian and Pacific markets from the American company she had once managed, because the Taiwanese labor costs would be cheaper, and so would transportation to the Asian market. And Eakin knew all the customers for this product in the world, personally.

Only one year before the day that Garth was served with Tabitha's divorce complaint, Eakin's husband filed for divorce. He had made the calculations, or perhaps his father had. When Eakin had been removed from the job as president of the company she had essentially created, she was still quite wealthy. Much of that wealth was in stock. Her new and proposed venture in Taiwan would draw upon these financial resources. This would affect the prospect of living at the level to which the ever-youthful Dick Trent had become accustomed. His choice was to gamble on Eakin, and hope that she would succeed in her new venture, or he could divorce her right then and there, and get half of everything they owned at that moment, in addition to child support for their three sons. He took the bird in hand. He filed for divorce.

He received several million dollars, plus child support. Eakin agreed to pay to continue to send the three boys to private schools. He placed Eakin in a position in which she had no choice. If she had fought the divorce, she would have lost the opportunity to get started all over again with her new venture, killing her chance to rebuild her fortune. With the limited amount she had left, and with the time she would have saved from not contesting the divorce, she might have a chance to get back on her feet with her new venture in Taiwan.

Garth knew what Eakin's husband had not known, or did not have the ability to understand, or did not want to consider. He knew she was a winner. She would succeed.

What Tabitha did not know, or what her impairment prevented her from knowing, was that Garth loved his children in a way that would prevent him from ever giving them up. And she did not know or could not understand the depth of his relationship with Eakin. When Garth called Eakin and told her what had just happened, it was if she had expected it all along.

"If you were still a lobbyist, she would have never done this," Eakin said. "She would never have given up the glamor of those Washington parties and connections."

"Well, I have to fight this thing."

"Yes, you do," she said, "One of us has to win one of these god damn things. And I know what it means to have your kids taken away. I will not see that happen to you. This Taiwanese thing I have going is about to start to turn a profit, and I am not entirely out of money yet. I will lend you the money to get the best lawyer. Don't worry about that. You can pay me back when you get the chance. And if you win, which you should, you will get some settlement from Tabitha."

They spent another hour on the phone, and Garth got from Eakin more than just a loan. They each had a way of holding up a mirror to one another and giving each the opportunity to see themselves in the light of the other friend's affection and respect and confidence. It was one of those moments, for Garth, that he would never forget. He then hired the best lawyer he could and he filed an emergency motion to get the children back, or at least to get them on a joint custody arrangement.

The judge at the hearing was particularly sensitive to the argument that while they had been married, Tabitha had never taken a single step to indicate her supposed fears and dissatisfaction with Garth as a parent. The judge decided that these claims were a ploy. The kids were sent back to Garth, pending the final action on the divorce. It had been an immediate and overall victory for him. Tabitha had gambled that he would surrender before all that she had lined up against him. Once he had not done that, she had to go back to work. She could not pretend that she could take care of the children during the day. Garth was working as a teacher, had the summers off, and he finished at school every afternoon when the children did. During the custody evaluation process of the divorce, the evaluator found that he children relied more upon their father than on their mother.

The custody evaluator may not have accurately diagnosed Tabitha's attention deficit disorder, but her issues as problems which made her less nurturing than Garth was. In the end, the process was going so much in Garth's favor that a settlement was reached, which was almost entirely a reversal of the complaint that Tabitha had filed. He received custody, child support, half of their savings, and partial alimony to be paid for two years. Tabitha would have the children on alternative weekends and on Wednesday evenings. Garth would have them the rest of the time.

He had won, but only in a manner of speaking. He was a single parent living on a teacher's salary and, using what he owned and what he made, began to pay his loan back to Eakin. And Tabitha's hyper-focus was not changed. She resented the custody arrangement. She was bent on making his life miserable, and using the children in order to do it. She also had the funds, and the energy, and the time. Her tunnel vision did not permit her to have friends, or to go out on dates and meet men, or to even have much of a relationship with her own family. Garth had been responsible with the care and maintenance of their relationship to her family and friends. He would think to do those things when they had been married. She would not. Garth was still very much a social creature and felt that he might be able to provide the semblance of a stable home life for his children if he could possibly find someone. He was mistaken on two counts. No children of divorce ever want either parent to remarry, at least not when they are young. And finding someone was going to be almost impossible.

Tabitha made it a point to provide cookies and ice cream where Garth provided discipline. Her house became a no homework zone. And she aggressively challenged him on every parenting decision, always taking the more popular position with these two adolescents. Garth did what he could to fulfill the parental role, even against this opposition. And he felt that it would be easier and better if he could provide for the children a more stable home life. So, he did what few men or women in their forties ever enjoy doing, even if they thought they enjoyed it when they were younger. He began to date.

One day, Garth was finally quite taken by one of the women he had met. She was a few years younger than he was and at forty years of age she had never married. Her name was Monica Burgess and she had once been a dancer. She was tall and fit and slender and very beautiful, with black hair and fair skin and blue eyes, a very stunning color combination. She had a job at a trade association in Washington. She was also quite smitten with

Garth. She enjoyed listening to Garth talk to her about art and literature and politics. She had a quick mind. She had a facility for the small things in life that make it quite comfortable. She enjoyed going with Garth to the children's games and to their plays. She understood basketball and baseball, both of which Garth had started to coach at the high school. She had good taste in music. And she was passionate. She made Garth feel attractive.

One Saturday evening when it was Tabitha's weekend to have the children, Garth and Monica were in bed when the phone rang. It was his daughter.

"Dad, I am at school and the dance has ended. Mom was supposed to pick me up ten minutes ago, but she has not shown up. I tried to call her on her cell phone, but I do not get an answer. Most everyone has left, and I am standing in front. It is getting a little scary."

"I will be right there to get you, honey. Just stay put. It will only take five or ten minutes," he already was dressing.

"You're not leaving?" Monica asked.

"I have to go."

"But it is your ex-wife's weekend. Why can't you just teach her a lesson?"

Garth picked up his twelve-year-old daughter and drove her to his ex-wife's house and waited for Tabitha to come home. She arrived half an hour later and was surprised to see him. She had forgotten the time at which the middle school dance had been scheduled to end.

Garth drove home and sat in the car outside, before he went back in to Monica. The only lesson that had been taught that night was the one that he had just learned. The most important trait for him in any woman he might date, or in whom he might have an interest, would have to be that she understood that he would never really be there for her, that he would be there for his children first. Women willing to take second place are rarer than one might think. Garth suddenly knew that his chances were very limited. He knew that he would not be seeing Monica again.

He focused on his teaching and coaching and found that it was far more fulfilling than anything he had done as a lobbyist or as a political operative. It was second only to being a parent, and similar. It was getting to the point when his son would enter the high school soon and he would be able to see him every day and maybe even coach him. Teaching young people awakened the dedicated autodidact in Garth. He had once taught himself how to run a political campaign. He found that teaching English in high school stirred his own need to know all he could. Every moment he was in school and did not have a class to teach, which was three periods out of eight, he had his head buried in a great book. He also read after he put his children to bed. He read all of Shakespeare and *The Essays* of Montaigne and *Don Quixote* and *The Divine Comedy*. Much of this for him was re-reading what he had already read in college, but at the level of an adult's understanding and experience he approached Ibsen, Dickens, Austen, Hardy, Wordsworth, Dickenson, Whitman, Dostoyevsky, Milton, Tolstoy, Proust, Joyce, Kafka, Moliere and all the other books he felt had stood the test of time. At his middle age, he overheard himself teaching his students, and he had taken his own teaching to heart.

Garth also held a special social place in the school social structure, and in the views of the students. He had gone to Harvard and had a law degree, and had been a lobbyist, and always had his nose in a great book. The students thought he was very cool in the approach he took in his classes. He was rarely dogmatic about the lesson structure and did what he could to make every class different and he engaged his students. He felt the need to make them find it interesting. And his day was made during the many times a parent would tell him that one of his students had caught the reading bug from him. The other teachers took a different kind of special interest in him and were always trying to match him with their single female friends. He was always a bit wary about that. Then one evening when he had gone to a party one of his colleagues was having, he met one of her friends, Renelle Jourdan.

Ms. Jourdan had many attractive qualities, the primary of which was that she began the conversation by asking Garth about his children. She seemed to understand that he was a father first and a man second. In fact, he was a father and a mother first, and then a man. She also complimented him upon making that observation. She got his attention when she said that she could tell that he not only did *"les ordures travaillent,"* but that he enjoyed doing it. That she was French also did not hurt, especially since she had been correct in her assessment, and that he liked to do "the garbage work" of raising children. She came to these understandings by being a single parent herself. She had gone to college in America, at Columbia, in New York and had settled in Washington with her husband. They had one child, Remy, who was of the roughly the same age as Garth's children. She had been divorced for four years, and her husband had gone back to France. She worked at the Washington office of France Telecom.

She reminded him of the good things about Tabitha. Renelle had her own strong opinions, and she was not afraid to express. She had an arch and roguish sense of humor, and laughed heartily when he had said that he supported the idea of marriage between gay men and marriage between lesbian women, but that he was more concerned about what might be the pyrotechnics of gay divorce. There was music in her voice, and the dance in all her movements. She was very slight of build, European in her looks and dress. Her hair was brown and her eyes were green and she had a high and intelligent forehead, with strong high cheekbones that traced an elegant slope down to a very strong jaw line. She had a devilish smile and deep set eyes, and above all, or more accurately in front of all, she had a strong nose with clean lines. It was prominent and straight and perfect for looking down at the world, which she never appeared to do. She had too much appreciation for the world to disparage it. And she had seen so much of it; she had traveled extensively. Garth was guardedly optimistic, because she was highly attractive, and she saw him first as a parent.

Their schedules would be difficult to coordinate but they both expressed a desire to try to make it work. The first opportunity came when Garth's ex-wife would have the children for the weekend. He went to her house and he met Remy, who was a very bright and very sweet boy of about twelve. It was there that he learned that Remy generally slept in his mother's bed, and often with their two dogs. He also saw that there were very few other barriers in place within the home. Renelle lived with her son in a way that expressed her dependence upon him as the sole emotional connection in her life, and this as well had created in Remy a type of separation anxiety that was painful to witness. This twelve-year-old boy could barely part with his mother for even a few hours in the evening. He cried, and kicked, and yelled at the baby sitter.

Garth was caught between two very difficult choices. On the one hand, there were single women of a certain age who were attracted to him for all the reasons that single women are attracted to single men. These women most often had little or no idea of the adjustment required when such a man was a single father. Garth realized that many divorced fathers were able to remarry single and often times younger women, because they had been willing to sacrifice their relationships with their children. He had seen such marriages.

Divorced women who were also mothers were much more likely to understand who Garth was and what his priorities were, but then that raised the possibility of having to blend two families. Garth was wise enough to know that marriage required compromise. There were many things about which he could compromise. He might marry a woman who did not drink wine or any alcohol at all. Or he might marry one who did not eat cheese.

He could see living with a woman who did not dance or did not like base-ball, or who did not like to travel or to read. He was guarded about possibly marrying a woman who was overtly religious, or who voted Republican. But he could not see changing anything about the way he raised his children. It was too important. They were too important. Garth's children to him were a matter of faith, so blending them with another family began to seem like attempting an inter-faith marriage.

He kept to himself again, and focused on the children, and on teaching and coaching. He would keep an eye out for a single or divorced mother who shared his values in the area of raising children. He would also keep his antennae up for any very rare single woman who understood the meaning of parenthood, who might love him because he was a father, and not in spite of it, and who in all likelihood did not want children of her own. Finding either of those types of women was unlikely, and finding one whom he then might like, and who might then like him seemed impossible.

Eventually, he did drift into a casual relationship with a woman who had children in middle school with his children. Her children did not really know his, nor did his know hers. He would have to see how these two families might fit together. There were also some other issues that would have to be worked out, although this woman did seem to share most of his values when it came to raising children. He was certainly not going to rush into anything. And he did not feel the need to rush. She had not romantically struck him in the same way that Monica or Renelle had. She was pleasant and bright. Her name was Melody McGrath, or more truthfully that was her stage name. She ran her own small, but successful, public relations firm and before that, she had been a newscaster on one of the local Washington network affiliate station's nightly news. Her name had previously been Shoshana Moscowitz. And that was another slight question. Marrying her would be a return to Garth's roots after a fashion, and he was not certain he was ready for that. But the best thing about Melody was that she was sensible, and the fact that he did not feel like he was in a rush was something that she understood and seemed to welcome.

She was a short, attractive woman with bleached blonde hair, and a lively and vibrant face. She even looked a little bit like Garth's female cousins or one of his sisters, except they were all taller and thinner and they were not blonde. She and Garth talked on the phone, and saw each other privately on the rare occasions when they each were free. It was casual and comfortable. Then, one day, she invited him to one of her business parties that she was having for all of the clients of her public relations firm. It was the typically low-key way in which they had gone about seeing one another. She would be busy moving around among her guests at the party, and he would not get to spend much time alone with her, but that was not so terrible. And it was on the Wednesday evening before Thanksgiving, and since it was one of the alternate years when his children would spend that holiday with their mother, he would be free that evening. So he decided he would go to that party and see if he might enjoy himself. He would also help Melody, if she needed any help. He was up for anything, he thought. He had no idea what anything might entail.

REASSIGNED

The wars in the Persian Gulf had been a watershed in the evolution of the role of women in the military service of the United States. In all previous wars only small numbers of women ever served outside of the roles of nurses or administrative personnel, unless of course they entered the service pretending to be men, as has happened since the beginning of warfare. In Operation Desert Storm, in 1990, thousands of women had been deployed in forward positions and by the time of the invasion of Iraq in 2003, there were so many women deployed, more than thirty thousand, that the lines between combat positions and non-combat positions had been fairly well blurred. Women had died, and had been taken prisoner, in each of those wars. In 1988, the Navy had allowed the first woman combat jet pilot. By 1994, hundreds of women had been deployed to combat ships and several of them had been helicopter pilots. They were used for anti-submarine warfare, sea rescue, vertical replenishment, sea insertion and a host of other non-combat actions. One of these women had been Melinda Sherman.

Carl Furth went to the hospital deck to find out how she was doing and he discovered that she was in surgery. He and his two fire teams were to stay on board for a while, since some of his men were also being treated. After a couple of days he went back to the ship's hospital, only to find that she was still unconscious and in a coma. Her co-pilot had been moved to a hospital on land in an effort to try to save his arm. Her situation was still too risky for her to be moved. Carl went in search of the crew chief from her Seahawk. He found the man in the mess hall and he sat down to talk to him.

"So what do you hear about Lieutenant Commander Sherman?" he asked.

"Sir, do you mean General Sherman? That's what we call her, 'General Sherman.' Did you know she is a direct descendant of William Tecumseh Sherman? She'll pull through. I have never seen anyone like her, man or woman," the seaman said.

"How is that?"

"Oh, too many ways to say, really. She's a triathlete. Was a runner in college, and just kept running in the Navy, plus swimming and biking. She beats most of the men. Like she thrives on the pain. Never seen anyone fly like her. A helicopter is controlled by the cyclic, the pedals and the collective. They interact with one another. Not like a car. If you do something with one thing, you have to do another thing with another to compensate. But it is more than that. It is organic. She is a natural. Becomes part of the damn thing. One time, returning from a supply run she took us on a detour through a canyon, just to see how fast and close she could fly to the walls and floor. Insane."

"She's kind of young to be a Lieutenant Commander."

"Not really. She has been in for a little over twelve years. She just gets promoted first chance every time. No one works as hard as she does, flies as well, or knows so much. There was no question she would be sent on the rescue mission for your teams. Most of the combat helicopter guys were tied up taking SEAL teams to attack and hold seacoast oil installations just before the invasion. She is a better and a braver pilot than any of them anyway."

"So, wait a minute. You're telling me she has never fired the weapons on that Seahawk?"

"Hell, it is the first time she ever flew that chopper. The one she normally flies is not armed like that."

"And she shot that woman?"

"That was a hell of a pistol shot, wasn't it? Even I did not know she could do that."

"And she is awful damn good looking."

"I don't even see it any more, especially after what happened at the end of last year. I just know she is the best pilot I have ever seen and is a leader. I would follow her sooner than I would follow the men around here."

"What happened at the end of last year?"

"We had a new co-pilot, a Lieutenant J.G. They rotate co-pilots as part of their training to be pilots. We had to fly some civilian officials to some big social event at Naval Air Station Bahrain. She was also invited to the event. After the civilians had left, she just dropped her flight suit and her under shirt and pants on the hangar floor, and stepped into her dress uniform. This co-pilot must have popped a boner. He could not get over it. He later filed a sexual harassment claim."

"What happened?"

"You can guess that. Same as happens when the subordinate is a woman. The claim went up the chain of command, and rank trumps everything. In fact, most of the brass was eager to help their hardest-working helicopter pilot. The co-pilot got shipped out."

"You were there?"

"I don't even see it any more. She's just General Sherman to me. Know what I mean?"

"I suppose I understand you, sailor. But I cannot know exactly what you mean."

"Well, other than that one thing, she is absolutely totally buttoned down around here and everywhere else. By the way, you are not the first one to fall for her. They all do. And don't worry, Sir. She will pull through. She's just like that."

Carl Furth and his fire teams were patched up, and were flown back to their base and base hospital a few days later. Melinda Sherman then lay in a coma for two weeks and recovered, having lost her spleen, some of her liver, and the ability to have children. She also lost her clearance to fly helicopters. While she had been in that coma and before she came out of it, her condition had stabilized, and she was flown to a Naval Hospital, where she eventually came out of her coma.

When her body lay unconscious, wounded and recovering on board ship and in a Navy Hospital, she had been in another place mentally.

In her vision, she was naked in the water, surrounded by bright sunlight and mirrors. She took some time to get used to the brightness, and even longer to become accustomed to seeing herself everywhere she turned. It was only then that she decided to find what lay in the deepest depths of the mirrors. For many hours she would concentrate beyond and behind her own image, to a place where she found herself surrounded by an audience, as if she were the professor in a class. She would stand in the forefront of what was clearly a lecture hall, and she would not speak but would wait for her students to speak to her. She focused on them, and implored them with her eyes and her spirit to tell her something more of where she was. They merely sat there and looked back. She began to concentrate on them, one at a time.

Her first subject was an old man with a gray beard and a bent posture. The more she focused her thoughts on him the younger he became, only then to become a tiger, and then a dragon, and then a woman, and then to become a being in which the properties of all three resided. She managed several transformations with each of the other students. And she found that when she did this she could hear her own voice addressing the assembly, even though she never actually spoke. In all of this she felt that her spirit was no longer a captive within her, but was a kind of fullness that extended beyond her into all other beings. The speech of hers that she heard addressing the pupils spoke of essential unities, of death with life, of light in darkness, eternity within time. And she felt that the speech, the presence of the class and her own efforts were all making her stronger. She came out of her coma, and she knew then that she had always had the power to dream anything into existence. And she knew that she had a purpose that was larger than she was.

Reassigned to the Pentagon, she was put in the Navy public relations office. She was attractive, a war hero, well spoken and a woman. She fit the bill for what the Navy wanted to show the world at that time. She went to work on the Navy news show that was part of the military television network. She coordinated Navy oversight on television shows and movies that sought to depict the Navy. She appeared at press conferences, and worked on the logistics of the "Mission Accomplished" speech that President Bush gave on the aircraft carrier, USS Lincoln. She bought a small house in the Del Ray neighborhood in Alexandria Virginia. She hired a small public relations firm to train the sailors-turned-newscasters at the Navy television news program. She continued to run in triathlons. She still had her visions.

Soon after she arrived back stateside, she went to visit her brother in New York City. He was still a successful model, and he had moved into the field of acting, and was getting some decent parts in shows on Broadway and a few roles in New York-based television shows, and even in some movies. He had a large and very beautiful apartment in the So Ho neighborhood of Manhattan, occupying an entire floor of what had once apparently been a warehouse. Two locked doors secured the front of the building. There was no doorman. There was a lock on the door to the elevator, which opened right into Porter's apartment. There was modern art everywhere, and the plan of the apartment was very open. He was very happy to see her.

"You are looking great, girlfriend, and I am so glad that you are out of that nasty war now."

"I miss flying," she said. "And I miss the atmosphere of being on board ship, of being within a chain of command, of having respect."

"But you are in the Pentagon now, big wig."

"Yes, I work there, along with twenty-eight thousand other 'big wigs.' And it is totally different from anything I have ever done. There are a lot of politics."

"Yeah, but people just love you, Mindy. Politics will be a snap for you."

"I don't know, Porter. I have some rough edges, and I am rather weird."

"That may be the best thing about you. We're both weird. And that is not surprising, given where we came from."

"So, how is Mom? Have you seen her lately? I guess I have to make a trip to London to see her."

"She will never get over the fact that her only son is a daffodil."

"Oh, is that what you are?"

"You know what I mean. I send her flowers on her birthday and Mother's Day and on Valentine's Day, and she gets a present from me on Christmas and her birthday. I call her every few months just to talk. But she rarely, if ever, makes the effort to reach out to me. I swear, one day I am going to get a complex."

"What has she said about me?"

"She asks me about you. She complains that you never write or call. I tried to explain to her that it is all done by email now, and that you were stationed overseas, so she should have learned how to use email, so she could have stayed in touch with you the way I have done. I don't think she wants to reach out to you either."

"Well, how is she doing? How is her health?"

"She seems to get more spectral every time I talk to her. I see her every couple of years. When I fly to some location, I will occasionally make a stopover in Louisville or Cincinnati, just so I can drive down there to see her. The house is still falling apart. She stumbles around in it, most of the time talking to herself. She keeps speaking to me about Texas for some reason. She and Dad used to go on camping vacations there, and I went with them when I was a baby. I think we stopped going when you were born. She keeps mumbling about taking another vacation there, that is, when she is not talking to me about women. She weakly attempts to interest me in some woman she knows or has seen in London. As if."

"Just stay away from the bathroom."

"Yeah. I know. Right?"

"Do you always have to talk like one of the *Mean Girls*, Porter?"

"I am one of the mean girls. You know that, Mindy. Right now, I am trying to make George Bush blow up."

"What the hell are you talking about? And you do know that if you say that too much or too loud or to too many people, you will eventually get a visit from the Secret Service."

"I know he is your boss, little sister. And I do not mean I am trying to blow him up with explosives or anything like that. It is just that I am studying on the ancient art of meditating on someone until they spontaneously combust."

"That's a crazy myth."

"No. I read about it in a book once. And I believe I can do it. I can make a man burst into flames, leaving nothing but a dark greasy coating on the walls of his room and a burnt patch on the floor, and leaving him so that people cannot tell if he is charred piece of wood or some burnt coal. And I am not just talking about your commander-in-chief. I have a few other people in mind."

"At least you are not alone with Jesus, anymore."

"Oh, but I am, Mindy. I am. And here he is right now."

Porter said that just as the elevator door opened, and in walked a very young Puerto Rican man with light brown skin and black hair and dark brown eyes. He was about five feet five inches tall, shorter than Melinda by a good three inches. But he stood at her height because he was wearing high heels, as well as a neat summer sundress.

"Melinda, this is Jesus Torres."

"Nice to meet you, Jesus," Melinda said. "That is not quite the same, Porter. His name is not pronounced the same."

"It is the same to me. Trust me, Melinda," Porter remarked.

"I think we may have a connection, Melinda," Jesus said. "My brother, Esteban, was at Pensacola when you were there, I think."

"Steve Torres is your brother? Wow. I guess that is just another one of life's coincidences. He is a good sailor and a brave man, your brother, and a hell of a pilot."

"He seems to think so," Jesus smiled.

"Well, you know us pilots, I mean, those pilots," Melinda corrected herself.

"He sounds delicious," Porter chimed in, "just like my sister, only a boy."

"Watch yourself, Porter," Melinda and Jesus found themselves saying accidentally in unison.

They laughed. Then they got ready to go out to eat. Jesus changed into a shirt and a pair of pants and sneakers and out of his work clothes; he was an actor in a drag queen review. The three of them went to eat somewhere in the West Village, a place on Christopher Street called the Stonewall Inn. Porter and Jesus were practically beside themselves with a kind of knowing secret when they asked Melinda if she knew where she was.

"I don't have a clue," she said.

"Okay, so one night in June of 1969 the New York City Police moved in to bust up the place and roust the gay men," Jesus said. "It had been standard police practice for years. But that one night the gay community fought back. Over two thousand gay men surrounded the police and there were riots deep into the early morning hours. The men returned the next night and the following night, not to riot but to protest. This place is the birthplace of the national gay rights movement."

Melinda had always loved her brother and had always more or less known he was gay, and in her mind this story and his situation could not be separated from what she had to face as a woman breaking ground in the military.

She was overwhelmed and began to cry. Jesus smiled at her, and put his hand on hers.

"Don't get carried away, Jesus. I think my little sister is crying because she would rather be at the Henrietta Hudson," Porter said. "That's the lesbian hangout in these parts."

"Don't joke like that, Porter," Jesus said. "We would not be all that welcome there."

"Not if we had my sister Melinda with us, especially if she was wearing her Navy uniform."

"Besides," Jesus added, "I am pretty sure your sister is straight."

"Well, you are the only one then. I think my little sister is not sure what team she is playing for."

Melinda just smiled, and said, "I am not ready for any relationship right now."

Porter just beamed. It was very good for Melinda to see her big brother and to see him happy. For a good part of her life he had been her project, just as their father had been before that. Now, it was Melinda's turn to beam. She was happy for her Ceylonese twin brother.

She took the train from New York to Washington after she had said farewell to her brother and to Jesus. She spent the time on the train as almost everyone does, looking out the window and thinking of her own life. For almost two hundred years train travel has had this effect on men and women. The train was the first device to move men and women faster than their horses could take them. It became the first spiritual transition mechanism. A person would be in one place, and very soon, would be in a completely different place, without having done anything more than sit down. Such a thing cannot help but spawn contemplation. And scenery passes by as if they were scenes from a life, while the wheels describe the progress of thought.

Melinda had always been on a train, in manner of speaking. She had always been getting away from one thing or place, and she had always seemed to be moving toward something. For her the train had stopped. At least that is what she had figured out by the time she pulled into Union Station in Washington, and the actual train came to a stop.

She walked the short distance underground to the Washington Metro and got on a Blue Line train to King Street station in Alexandria, got off and began the ten block walk north to her house in Del Ray. It was a cool brisk late fall Sunday afternoon in November. She consulted the calendar in her head. Thanksgiving was coming up in four days. She thought she might schedule a trip to see her mother in Kentucky. She was not looking forward to that possibility at all. She loved her mother, and when she had been a child that was all that mattered. But at the time she had left for college and then for Officer Candidate School and Flight Training in Pensacola, Florida, it had slowly begun to dawn on her that in her mother's mind there had always been some opposition to her. She never knew what it was or why it was. She only knew that it was palpable, perhaps more so now that she had been away for over twelve years.

She walked to the local delicatessen, and purchased some prosciutto and some dried Italian sausage, along with a bottle of cabernet sauvignon, a baguette and some provolone cheese. She laid these out for herself, and ate while taking her time around the house. She watched a little television and she read a bit. Soon, in the flush of the wine, she dozed off. She began to have one of her dreams again.

It was the same one, or at least it had the same man she had seen for almost thirty years, the tall dark man who was associated with water and children. She saw him clearly.

Then she awoke, cleaned up the foodstuffs, and went for a good long run. It was dark and the clear, cold air braced her and woke her up. She pushed herself until it hurt her in the way she liked so much. She returned home, took a shower and got ready for bed. She stared at the phone for a while. She convinced herself that she would call her mother the next day, or the one after that. Or maybe she would just surprise her mother with a visit. She decided on that plan. It was the kind of lone wolf thing that appealed to her, just to pick up and travel. She would make the drive to London and drop in on her mother. And if her mother was not there, she would stop in and say hello to Tommy Kitt and his wife, and she would see his children for the first time. Or she could just turn around and drive home. She would leave first thing in the morning on Thursday, because she had to go to a party on Wednesday night. She liked the idea of a party that was not all Navy or Pentagon people. She was looking forward to seeing some of the regular Washington social life. And she had to go.

She had given her word to Melody McGrath, who owned the public relations firm that trained the Navy television station newscasters, and was throwing the party.

A PARTY OF TWO

Garth had begun to be apprehensive about going to Melody's party. She was nice and felt the same way that he did about children, and there was no real impediment to moving forward with her. He knew that Melody was formidable enough to form a partnership, one that would calm down his home life and his ex-wife. Perhaps just as importantly, Melody's two daughters seemed likely get along well with his children, to form a reasonably blended family. But he did not feel something that he knew he should feel about Melody. She did not awaken his feelings as had Monica or Renelle.

He had begun to form the opinion that he should talk to Melody about it. It was not fair to do otherwise. They did get along reasonably well. He was unsure.

It had been a while since he had been to a real Washington party. Since the divorce and teaching and being a single father, his social life had diminished. And it certainly had fallen off from the times when he had been a lobbyist or a chief of staff, when fundraisers and receptions with Congressmen and Senators, and captains of industry and finance, and the occasional Hollywood personality, had been the order of the evenings. This party would not be at that level, but it would still be several magnitudes greater than the small gatherings he had occasionally attended at the homes of his fellow teachers. Many of the classic Washington types would be in attendance. On reflection, Garth was not much looking forward to that either. He hadn't really missed it. He was ambivalent as he walked into the front door of the hall that Melody had rented. Such a feeling does not often admit to an extreme.

Hamlet, in lecturing his mother, speaks to her of how passion had mutinied in her matron's breast, and he condemns her for her feelings for his uncle and stepfather, Claudius. He tells her that she cannot call it love, and that in middle age the great power of passion is tame and humble and waits upon the individual's judgment. Hamlet speaks in this case more in speculation than from experience. In youth, passion is a flame that melts all that stands before it; judgment, consideration, and inhibition. With maturity, these virtues, or perhaps they are forms of lassitude, settle into the bottom of a soul and form a more phlegmatic constitution. They create a weighty and solid foundation. In almost all cases these substantial encumbrances prevent the more seasoned personality from being blown about lightly in the strong winds of desire. But when the great loving gale blows, it picks up the entire structure at its foundation. It then projects the experienced, and seemingly settled individual forward with all the greater momentum and force that is available to the grander mass that is the matured soul.

After he had been at the party for about half an hour, something happened, and it was not as if he had fallen in love at first sight. It was more as if someone whom he had loved all his life, and whom he had thought gone, had suddenly returned to him. She looked more than anything like home, a home he had never really had, except in the innermost chamber of his heart. It was something that had happened to him only once before. But this time he had a much greater psychological mass and spiritual density. The entire experience flooded into him like a symphony. There were too many instruments and tones and progressions and harmonies for him to effectively track or understand all of them. And they reached him with the immediacy and the power which only great music can. All his years and all his experiences and all that he had ever been were bound into that larger structure. And the gale was blowing it straight at Melinda. There was nothing he could understand about it. He could only be it.

He tried to regain some footing, and began to attempt to apply his reason to his will. But, at his age and with his experience, this greater mass that was moved by passion contained within it the tools and road maps and insights that would better assist his desire, than ever a young man could be thoughtful in his callow concupiscence. His life, travels and his reading, and his success and his loss and the sacrifices he had made, had all taken his native instinct and his innate intellect, and had polished them into a lens through which he could see a larger picture from smaller fragments. He began to pay attention, and to see what others could not. He saw in all her movements and expressions, and in the way that she managed the party, that this was a woman who was always alone, even in a crowd. He felt such an ineluctable kinship with that. It was clear to him that they were each well off of the path that most others take through the woods. It only remained to be seen whether they were off of it in the same place, whether or not throughout his whole life he had wandered alone and were to suddenly look up and see this other person, also alone but in exactly the same spot.

He knew that he would talk to her, and that he would know it all within a few minutes of the start of the conversation. He was bursting with things to say to her, and he wanted to start the conversation with a little something different. He was well out of practice, so he decided to rely upon a stratagem of his youth. When he had been in college and saw a young woman whom he wanted to meet, he would discreetly inquire from someone else to obtain her name. For the sake of discussion here, the name could be Susan. Then he would approach the young woman and with a look of hurt he would ask her why she only ever pretended to ignore him when they were "out in public."

The woman would inevitably then say that she indeed did not really know who he was. And then he would say, "See, Susan. That is exactly what I am talking about."

He had once learned that to get a spark was better than nothing, and that from slight antagonisms the strongest affinities may grow.

There was little need to wait to find this particular woman alone; it was her general state. The greater concern would be to obtain her name. He felt for some reason he hadn't considered yet that he could not ask Melody. He had to wait almost another half hour before he was certain that this person had introduced herself to some people, and after she had left them, he asked them her name and discovered that it was Melinda Sherman.

"Hello," he said, "I am wondering why it is that whenever we are out in public and only then, you pretend that you do not know who I am."

"I know perfectly well who you are, Garth. And I have not been ignoring you either. I have been waiting for you to stop bumbling around and come up to speak to me. It has only taken you an hour."

He was stopped in his tracks, but only for an instant. Some part of him had been frustrated but the larger part of him, the experienced part, told him that a door had just opened, and to a better world than he had ever known.

"Why don't the two of us just get out of here? I know a nice tavern just around the corner where we can talk."

"That would not be fair to Melody, would it? And I believe you have not even spoken to her yet."

Again he was stunned, but his imagination had run well ahead of the conversation. And even this comment propelled him to the other side of the stream. He was, as had Macbeth, imagining himself the king. And what was to be done to get to that point was almost irrelevant. So he began to raise objection, to test these far deeper waters, to see if there was some impediment to what suddenly seemed so inevitable.

"I am a father," he blurted out, "and a single parent."

"I know," she said. "It is the sexiest thing about you. And you have a few sexy things going."

Now he did not know what to say. She continued.

"And yet I wish but for the thing I have: My bounty is as boundless as the sea, my love as deep; the more I give to thee, the more I have, for both are infinite."

"Oh, my God," he said, "that is Shakespeare, from *Romeo and Juliet.*"

"And it is a way of loving that most men never learn, unless a man has been a father and not just a father, but one who loves also as a mother loves, as you love your children, Garth."

"There is only one way to find out if I am imagining all of this. I will be at Haines Point tomorrow at noon. If you are also there, I will know that all of this is for real and not imagined. Do you know where Haines Point is?"

"It is where the Anacostia River flows into the Potomac River. There is a park there where you sometimes take your children."

"I sure do," he said, no longer surprised at anything she said.

"Seth and Hanna; I am sure I will like them."

He just smiled and shook his head, and then he said, "I will see you tomorrow, Melinda Sherman. I am leaving here. There is only one other thing that I have to do before I go."

"I know," she said. "See you tomorrow, Garth Teller."

Nothing had prepared him for any of this, except that everything he had ever done had prepared him. He smiled at Melinda and she smiled back, and he turned to find Melody. She was busy talking to some of her many clients. He noticed that her drink glass was empty, so he went to the bar and ordered a gin and tonic, and brought it back and handed it to her. He took the empty glass and started to take it back to the bar, when she reached out and touched his arm as if to tell him to stay. Her guests moved away and she turned to speak to him.

"What is up? You have been scarce tonight."

"Melody, there is something I have to tell you," he quietly told her. "I don't think it is going to work out between us."

"That is bullshit, Garth Teller. What you really mean to say is that you have just fallen in love with Melinda Sherman," she said with obvious hurt.

Garth remembered his three sisters, and his mother, and his ex-wife, and he also remembered that they too always seemed to know things he did not. And given what had already happened tonight, he was quite accustomed to his state of ignorance, relative to women.

"That is not right, Melody. I just met the woman. I am talking about us. I just have to be honest."

"I suppose that is a brand of honesty. But I saw you with Melinda. I know, Garth. But I guess that it could not have happened if everything had really been in place for you and me. And to tell you the truth, I half suspected that this would happen when I invited the two of you. Something else tells me that you two fit together, something I simply feel."

"Thanks, Melody. Thanks," he said, as he regarded her with new admiration.

"She is thirteen years younger than you," she said. "And she seems a little bit crazy, you know."

"Oh yeah, that reminds me. Did you happen to talk to her about me?"

"That is a shitty thing to do, Garth. You have not broken up with me for ten seconds, and now you are asking me for help with your new girlfriend. Well, I guess we are both grown-ups. No. I never said a word to her about you. As I said, I had sensed there might be something between the two of you. The last thing I wanted to do was aid and abet that, although it seems now that this has been my hidden purpose all along. Go along, Garth. Good-bye. I will console myself with the fact that you are only half Jewish."

"Thanks, again, Melody," he said, and kissed her good-bye on the cheek.

It was a cold and blustery Thanksgiving morning. Garth could only think of his meeting Melinda, but every once in while another thought would filter in, and it was an unusual one.

He would think about how he had once loved Tabitha. And when he was no longer confronted by the overwhelming stimulus of Melinda, he was able to think more clearly and he knew that one of the things, or more accurately two of the things, which were so overwhelming about Melinda were her eyes and what lay behind them, the lambent green flame that hinted at more thought and feeling than a single soul should contain. He did not know when he met Tabitha, or even at this point, a little more than a decade after their divorce, that a more clinical and less romantic observer would see attention deficit disorder where he saw the flame. He only knew that it had eventually been a problem, had been the problem. He also could not have known at this point in time, that the same type of unromantic and clinical observer had observed hypomania, cyclothymia, and hyperthermic temperament, where he now saw only something lambent and green, or in this case more of a hazel. But he sensed the possibility of problems in Melinda, and he knew he would be more understanding this time.

There was something in his nature that could only be drawn to what some might see as psychological impairment, which he saw as a shine, and which is mother would come to call "crazy eyes." His love once failed to overcome that impairment, but perhaps it would this time.

He pulled up to Haines Point exactly twenty minutes early. His idea had been to have a chance to watch her unseen as she arrived. This woman so clearly had got the drop on him he was hoping to eke out some small advantage to counter it. But there she was already. The wind was strong on the point and it was cold. She had once been one man's Artemis, but this harsher climate seemed to suit her better, as if she were something more northern. In the wind, wearing only a jacket, and with that wind whipping her hatless, sandy blonde hair, she did appear to be a Valkyrie, for she was certainly in her element. The discomfort of the wind meant nothing to her. She was focused on nothing but him. His own more southern temperament became impervious to the wind as he got out of the car and locked it, and strode across the grass to her.

They said nothing to one another as he took her in his arms. They stood entwined in the cold wind, alone in a large public park on a family holiday, flanked by water on three sides of them, and the Washington Monument in the distance, and he did not kiss her. He wept. And so did she.

Countless explanations could be offered, but none would fit. She had dreamed of him all her life. He was the father she never had. He was already behind the barriers that she had raised to all other men and women. He was someone who would take care of her for a change. He was all the things she had never had the time to be, and which she respected and craved: he was well read, well traveled, well educated, well spoken. He would open new worlds for her. He was the mother she never had. He loved her as no man ever could. He would love her for the things that drove other men away. He had been her vision all her life, the man she knew she would love.

She was his second chance. She respected his fatherhood, and loved him for it. She would be his redemption. She was sturdy enough to be the shore upon which the storm of his idiosyncratic passion would crash. Her otherworldliness was mesmerizing. She was the promise of yet more life, into a time without boundaries. She was the woman for whom his life, his marriage, his children, and even his career, had prepared him. She was the next child for whom he could care, and whom he could nurture. She was as strong as he, and would be like his best male friends, only much more. She would keep him young.

These were all horrible and crass reductions. They are the damage that words do to real feelings and real life. The two of them simply had found one another, and had been on that path since before either had been born.

Tears turned to kisses, and kisses turned more passionate, yet neither knew how to move from that spot. He had wanted to ask her how she had known so much about him, but he knew he would never ask. She knew he would never ask, and she loved him all the more for it. He felt how strong she was and she felt his desire. New goals popped into her mind, with new risks. He was overwhelmed not only by her, but by his plans for them. And above all, he knew he could finally be completely honest with someone, and that it would not get in the way of their love, nor would their love impede their honesty. He knew that he was not the same person he had been only eighteen hours before this. All of this passed unsaid between two people who had yet to speak three hundred words between themselves. And then she spoke.

"Follow me to my house."

They had not been that far from her home. It was just across the Potomac, and down the George Washington Parkway, a ten-minute drive. She parked in front of her house, got out of the car, and waited for him on the porch. She held her keys in her hand, and she knew exactly how many inches inside of that front door would be the spot where her clothes would land.

She looked at this man as if he were still of her visions, as if it were a dream. She knew that he would never hurt her, that he would never abandon her, that he would love her as a man, as a father, as a brother, as a woman loves. She summoned what she had felt, leaning over the bridge railing on the Ohio River all those years ago. She was that small girl again. And she was also the wounded pilot, saving the lives of her fellow servicemen. She felt that all the love she had poured into her father, into her brother, and into her career would be returned with compounded interest. She watched Garth's handsome and kindly face as he got out of his car, locked it, and headed to the porch. He bounded up the steps and stood behind her. He did not hug her again, but she could sense he was taking in her scent, feeling what it meant to be behind her, and savoring her tantalizing closeness. She felt his looming presence and she loved it.

She opened the door and was about to disrobe, as he would have turned to close it. But he did not close it. He was on her immediately and pinioned her against the wall. If someone she had known a long time had done this, she still would have felt a small shred of fear, or worse, of disappointment. As it was, she was more excited than she had ever been with a man. He was six inches taller than she, and seventy pounds heavier. He held her wrists against the wall, and kissed her on the neck. Then, her wrists were behind her back, and were suddenly and mysteriously restrained. He then stopped and kissed her gently, closed the door and he spoke.

"You are so overwhelming, that I am completely at a disadvantage. I am just trying to even the odds."

She was too excited to say anything, and she did not know what moved her more, his precipitous passion, or the gentle way he smiled and led her into the bedroom. He took his time with her. She had never known anything like it. He was a *cordon bleu* chef, and she was the seven-course meal he was preparing. She was in a warm bath at a spa. He loved her as Caroline Collins once had, but with more passion, more skill and almost as much of a feminine understanding of her body. He loved her as a man would, or as several men would, or as no other man could. And only then did he free her wrists, and remove the remainder of her clothes.

Then the strangest thing of all happened, eclipsing all that had come before.

There are two major types of fisherman who fish inshore on the North American continent. There are fly fishermen, and there are the rest. There are those who fish with bait and lures and cast and retrieve and sit on the bank or in a boat. Then there are the artists who seek the most remote places and stalk the spookiest fish and try to fool them with the most elaborate presentation of the most artificial flies. Garth had just shown her two hours of bass fishing. Now he was going to show her the subtle joys of fly-fishing. He kissed her scars, the ones on her left shoulder and on her waist and above the right front side of her pelvis. Then he rolled her over and began to give her the longest and deepest and most loving massage. She was a flexible and strong woman, and he was able to pull her shoulder blades up from her back and go to work underneath them. He kneaded the sore spots at the base of her back. He drove the stiffness out of every muscle and filled her with warmth. All the running, training, flying and nurturing she had ever done were being relieved and released. It took another two hours.

Melinda smiled to herself because none of this had ever been in any of her visions and she knew then that his reality would exceed all else. When it was finally over, she rolled over on him and spoke.

"Okay, this time without the wrist restraints."

"I worship you."

"I am starting to get that idea," she laughed.

It was later when the prosciutto, the dried sausage, the baguette, the provolone and the cabernet sauvignon had been taken, that the words began to flow. It was a flood of honesty and tears and laughter and understanding.

Almost everything that had ever happened to each passed between them in the next few days they spent together. They then knew each other's histories, and began to see how they had been engineered to fit together. They professed their love to one another. She reminded him to call Seth and Hanna. She asked him everything about them, and loved him more for all that he said. She told him she would never be able to have children, and that she would be honored to know his, and hoped that one day that they would accept her love.

Garth and Melinda touched hurt and lost parts within one another with a magic spell that had taken all the bad things that had happened to each, and had in a moment made them into good things, by virtue of how these things had made them fit perfectly with one another.

At some point, the talk began to be about careers. Garth insisted that Melinda was entitled to several more military honors than she had received.

"What I have done was part of a covert mission, and the services do not advertise their covert missions," she said.

"I know a couple of very important people who owe me a large favor."

She smiled and hugged him. She sensed reserves of skill and strength that had lain dormant in him. She began to understand what she might come to mean for him. She already knew what he meant to her.

"And after that," he said, "I believe you should run for Congress. It has been a long while since I have done anything like that, but I am pretty sure I could run a campaign to get you elected."

"I had a vision when I was in my coma. And now I realize that this is what it had been about."

"Yes, and more. There is really no limit on what we can do, with love."

"And let there be no limits between us, Garth," she kissed him.

"Hell, yeah, Melinda, you already let me tie you up. I think we have established the no limits part already, President Sherman."

BOOK TWO

UNCLE ELLIOTT SURE KNOWS A LOT OF STUFF

The triumph of hope over experience is how Samuel Johnson once described second marriages. This is often misquoted as the triumph of hope over reason. In either case it is only accurate by half. In many second unions the decision to remarry is made after that same internal contest has concluded with exactly the opposite outcome on the field. The taking of yet another spouse in either case, be it when sad experience is sacrificed to brighter hope or when experience and reason conspire to overthrow a gadget as slim or as hope, is reminiscent of the family who builds their fashionable home on the banks of the River Thames. When the sun is shining and there are picturesque rowing boats navigating on the famed river the home is one of the most desirable residences in the world. But then there is the possibility that the river will make an uninvited appearance in the living room.

Experience may lead the way when a person will select a new mate for reasons of comfort or compatibility or stability, but there might be an occasion when an equally uninvited guest will arrive with the ineffable force of inspiration or of some other rash cousin of hope. And as well, into the stronghold of love and hope, the smallest drops and rivulets of experienced reason may penetrate and weaken the bonds that hold the building together and may erode the structure at its foundation, with the same relentless inevitability the power of water left to do its will.

Garth was in love and in such a case hope is the ascendant. While his experience told him that Melinda was an almost perfect match for him and there might be issues, such as their age difference and his children, he reasoned that his experienced love would help him to overcome it. Melinda had never been disillusioned by marriage and Garth had come to her from her visions. She was in love and if she consciously thought about it at all, she only saw his intellect and wisdom and masculinity and the way in which he would open new worlds for her. There were parts of Melinda of which she was not conscious and which could arise startlingly on occasion. And yet, she felt she could rely upon Garth to manage. This was why he had been sent to her, to be the man to love and to guide that unseen part of her. It had been that unknowable element within her that had seen him in the first place.

For him, the long dormant sword was finally out of the scabbard and there were many engagements to mount. The first would have to be accommodating his children. So he invited Melinda to the home for dinner and she arrived from work in her uniform, bearing gifts. As she handed a Navy pilot tee shirt to fourteen-year-old Seth Teller, Garth could see that he was struck by Melinda in much the same way that Garth or any man might have been. Although his loyalties to his mother would put up a wall around his affections, her physical appeal already amounted to a significant breach. What remained to be seen was whether or not Melinda would plunge into the gap. It was her own heart, the heart of the gentle girl who had once taken care of a father and a brother, which gave her understanding of the damage to be done by such precipitous action and she left the wall and the fissure alone and kept her distance. It would be for Seth to make the move, to sally forth at his own bidding. He was certainly watching her attentively and admiringly through the opening. And he liked the shirt.

Around Hanna Teller there was a double redoubt with moats and tall casements and towers. Her loyalty to her mother was reinforced by her understanding of the special relationship she herself now had to her father. There had been one female in her father's life, her mother, and now her mother had been somewhat replaced by Hanna. Two is company, it has been said, and Hanna felt joy and pride at being the lady of the Teller house to the extent that her mother was no longer there. She would not be too quick to give that up. And as with every child of divorce, Hanna felt that her mother was welcome to return and reassert her role as the primary woman in her father's life at any time. Hanna saw herself as temporarily holding her mother's spot as the lady of the house. This female number three definitely made it a crowd, a threat not only to herself but also to her mother's chance at reuniting with her father. And nothing stiffened Hanna's resistance more than her own apprehension of the palpable romantic spark between Melinda and her father. This as well was reinforced by Hanna's dual perception of what appeared to be both her brother's capitulation and also the alluring power that had effected it.

Melinda's experience in college and high school athletics, which had been strengthened by her service in the Navy, had educated her as to how to get along with someone who was on her team and who appeared to hate her with a passion. She would simply put the team first and would hold it as the only value. She would counter antagonism by not countering it at all. She would not place absolute trust in the influence of the love she and Garth shared but she would hope it might gradually bring Hanna along. She refused to see Hanna's attitude at all. She would focus only on seeing the beautiful and talented and brilliant twelve-year-old girl whom she already loved for being a part of this amazing man. She also knew it would be a long siege and one at which she could not and did not want to be totally successful. She only hoped that the two parties might come to some point of mutual respect and understanding. The wall would have to remain intact for some time. Her gift to Hanna was *Silas Marner*, by George Eliot. She saw it as an expression of her understanding of the process by which Hanna might reconcile Melinda's role in the family, which would likely take the several years until the time Hanna would actually be able to understand the book.

Melinda sat at the dinner table and she felt sure that she could see something that Garth probably was not able to see clearly, perhaps because he was a man and perhaps because it would make him feel guilty. These two very wonderful children were damaged and were in pain. This woman who had once been known as the "little mother" could tell that he did not see it for all that it was, because he had not been reluctant to show that he had great affection for Melinda. When he got up once to go to the kitchen, she followed him.

"You know, Garth, I am going to have to appear in front of the children to be much cooler to you than either you or I would like. You will have to be the same with me, for their sake," she said.

In every man and woman there is a startling capacity for self-delusion. Carnival people in the past would refer to the members of the public as marks. William Burroughs once warned his readers to be wary of the mark within. Each person is never more of a mark than he or she is with him or her. We fool ourselves daily. It is the mark of the enlightened person to know when he has turned himself into a mark. Garth had once thought he could make himself invisible and he quickly discovered his folly. His accusatory self-consciousness had marked his mistake. His reason had caught up with his will. It was to his credit that he could call himself out in these instances. And in this case he was no less guilty.

He had wanted his children to be able to move on in the same way that he wanted to make progress, to build a family life again. But it would be much more difficult for them. It would take more time for them to be able to accept another woman being loved by their father.

"I guess that means that you should not sleep here tonight."

"I can't," she said. "I am pretty sure that you do not want them to hear the racket you and I will make. Let us take it slowly. You must be as sure of me as I am of you and we both have to know that we will show our love best by not exhibiting it in front of Hanna and Seth."

"I love you, Melinda."

"I certainly hope so."

She went back to the table and focused on Seth and Hanna, but in a gentle and unassuming way. She did not force conversation upon them. She began to see in them things that she could love. She noticed that Seth had a charismatic presence. He was a very tall and thin boy for his age and was also very gentle. He was a northern blond version of his dark and handsome father and resembled him most around his dark eyes. He had a species of placid absent-mindedness that Garth did not have. This quality is what must have made him more gentle and innocent, as if his inattention had made the world appear as big and confusing to him as it would appear to a younger child. She was not surprised to learn at dinner that the younger children in the neighborhood considered him a friend and would often come to the door to ask him to come out to play, and that he would. Seth brought little mother out in her and she began to feel very protective of him.

Hanna looked more like her father, with dark hair, eyes and eyebrows, but there was also a feminine fullness to her lips and cheeks and she had a wider facial structure. Her skin was not as fair as her brother and she had that hint of the Mediterranean that her father also had. She was stunningly beautiful. There was a childlike fierceness to her that Melinda found alluring and with which she identified. Hanna shared her father's acute awareness of all that was going on around her and the things she said belied an understanding of motivations and unseen causes that was positively adult. This was a young lady around whom Melinda would have to be very careful and with whom she knew she could never be false. Hanna would peg her for a phony if she tried to manipulate her or condescend to her. She found herself feeling a powerful kinship to this girl who wanted no parts of Melinda in her family's life. It was this kinship and empathy that led her to suggest that she and Garth play it cool.

She saw both children in such a way that recalled her childhood and her brother to her in a way that was almost overwhelming.

When the dinner had finished, Seth suggested that they all play a board game and Hanna looked at him. Melinda looked directly at Hanna and said, "I think that is a great idea, Seth, but it is time for me to be going. I have a busy day tomorrow."

The small flash of approval from Garth's daughter showed that Hanna saw her leaving not as an accident, but as Melinda yielding the field to her and to the family. They all helped to clean up and to put the dishes in the dishwasher. Melinda kissed Garth on the cheek and there passed only between them a secret spark of yearning of the kind that normally exists only between the adults within an intact family, one that is the way in which the bond of romance is strengthened and brightened by domesticity. Garth wanted Melinda to be a part of that family with an atavistic power. She was beginning to love him all that much more for seeing in person the ways in which he was a father.

She left. The three Tellers sat down and played their board game without her as Seth continued to talk about how cool it was that Melinda had been a pilot and how nice she had been. Hanna said little but was a bit more attentive to her father, who returned her attentions.

After he put them to bed, he called Melinda on the phone and she thanked him for letting her come to dinner and he thanked her for opening his eyes. He drank a glass of wine or two during this conversation and then after it concluded he was still alert. It was late, almost midnight. So he called Eakin.

"How are you doing, old friend?" he asked.

"Oh, no, please don't tell me you are in love again. I know that tone of voice."

"That's very funny," he tried to say through a smile. "How the hell did you know that?"

"With you, Garth, it was always only a matter of time. I have been expecting this call."

"What about you? When are you going to find someone? I hate to think of you being alone?"

"I am never alone. You know that," she said. "I have you. I have the boys. And I have my work."

"How is that going?"

"Well, it is going well, too well."

"What do you mean by that?"

"I have been able to make a success of the company in Taiwan. With low labor costs and less transportation, I have been able to take all the Pacific Rim business away from my old company. We are making good money, and I am able to put some away and still pay my property settlement and alimony and private school tuition," she said.

"I am proud of you. I knew you would make it. So, what can be wrong?"

"Do you remember Ben Dessous?"

"How could I ever forget him?"

"He has been working for me for a while. And he pointed out something."

"He is working for you? Wow. So what did he point out?"

"Racism, he told me that it was an issue for a white person to own half of a company in Taiwan. And as soon as he said it, I saw the truth of it. They have a homogenous society and see difference as being alien. To put it directly, they hate us round eyes, Garth. And the fact that I am a woman does not make it any easier on them. So, I have talked them into letting me open a distribution company in Houston to compete directly against my old company for the North American business. I own this American distribution company outright and I have put Ben in charge of it. We are installing a production line, so that one day it won't just a distribution company. That way, when the Taiwanese run this current company out from under us, and they will, we will be ready. In fact, I believe I will be able to install a second production line within a couple of years."

"And Ben told you that? How long has he been working for you?"

"He really works more with me than for me. I rely on him for advice in a way I never have before with anyone. I had remained in contact with him over the years, since you sent him to me during graduate school. But when the divorce hit and I was really struggling, he sort of just showed up, as if he knew I could use him. I also think it is funny that you and he have not been in contact and that he was your friend first. He is now like my other best friend."

"Please give him my regards."

"Oh, I will. So tell me about this new woman."

And that is what Garth did and as he spoke to Eakin it became clearer to him that much of what he had always loved in Eakin was what he now loved in Melinda. He loved that he could be open and honest with her and that he felt no need to play any of the games that are so often imperative between men and women. For instance, he had always had to be careful with Tabitha when he expressed his feelings about Eakin. Tabitha could never understand or fully accept that his best and longest held friendship was with a woman. Melinda understood this completely. She viewed friends and family as part of a military unit or part of an athletic team. If one had a person upon whom one could rely then that person was like money in a bank account, and Melinda wanted to see Garth as well off as he could be. Melinda was as much a pal or a buddy to Garth as any man could have been, and as much as Eakin had always been. She was also strong and athletic and assertive and independent. Through all of his explanation, Eakin had been silent.

"Whoa," she finally said, "You really do love her. But you have not told me yet about her shine. I know you. You are not one to have your head turned by any woman who does not have some weird extra dimension."

"Well," Garth laughed into the phone, "if I could tell you about that I would not be in love with her. But you are right. There is something extra to her. I hope I have the rest of my life to find out about that."

"At least she isn't a lawyer. I'll give her that," Eakin said. "She won't drop some nuclear warfare divorce complaint on you, like the last one did. She may shoot you instead. Who knows? That might be an improvement. So, you are going to marry her?"

"I have certainly decided that and I believe she has too."

"You know, Garth, you can always come here if any real problem crops up, and you can bring the kids."

"I have always known that, Eakin. Hold on a second. Someone is at the door."

"At midnight? Who the hell could that be?"

Whoever it was had not rung the doorbell, perhaps as a way to keep from waking the children. Garth answered the door. It was raining outside. The man at the door was dripping wet, as if he had been walking in the rain for some time. His blond hair was flattened on his head. He looked ragged and tired as if he had not been walking in the rain but had been deposited on the doorstep by a storm tide.

"Jesus Christ, it's Elliot," Garth said into the phone.

"Barker? Tell him I said, 'hello,' Garth. And call me again when you get the chance." Then she hung up.

"That was Eakin. She says, 'hello.' What they hell happened to you?" Garth asked.

"You mean your friend, the tomboy? I always liked her. Do you have a drink?" Elliot asked as Garth let him in the door.

Garth went to the kitchen and poured Elliot a scotch, then he went to the bedroom and got his large terrycloth robe and handed it to Elliott, who took off his shirt and jacket and put on the robe, then removed his pants, socks and shoes. Garth ran these down to the washing machine and returned to the living room and to his old friend from law school and college. Garth looked closely enough to see that Elliott's eyes were blood-shot and that his skin was pallid. He was also shaking quite a bit.

"I need a place to hang out for a little while, a good while," Elliott said.

"What the hell has happened?" Garth asked.

"Not a lot really. It is all sort of run of the mill, you know. I just owe some people some money," he said.

He had not put the accent on the "some people" part that Garth fully expected that anyone less worldly than Elliott would have put it, since Garth knew that the mortgage company or the credit card companies did not drive their debtors to flee to the house of a friend.

"How much do you owe?"

"Not much. Just forty thousand dollars. I can get it together, no problem."

"Are you still working at the private equity firm?"

"They have given me time to take an administrative leave. They are flexible like that, with their people who bring in money and make it grow. I have been able to do that, so they have not asked me to leave. But I think they want me to dry out or whatever, before they will let me return."

"So, you can easily get your hands on the money then. You can sell some stock or raid your savings."

"That stuff is long gone. I have been living hand to mouth for the last several months."

"You mean, hand to nose."

"You are a funny man, always have been. A man has to have his hobbies."

"Only you would call a drug habit a hobby, Elliott."

"And only you would take me in like this, Garth. You know he hates you for that, for that virtue of yours."

"Who?"

"Earnest Dapple. You do know he was behind that whole threat to publish the incident with your old Congressman?"

"I am not surprised. I always expected that it might have been his doing. But he does not hate. He is just a selfish guy. He has also helped me, you know. And I always saw that as his way of viewing everyone else as pieces on a chessboard, to advance or to take as he sees fit. He had a use for me on my way up. And he had a use for me in trying to take down my friend."

"It is more than that. But, you are right. That is what is at the core of Earnest. He will advance himself by helping or hurting anyone. It does not matter to him. He has no love and he has no enmity. But he does have a special little dislike for you. And it is for the same reason that I am here. It is because you are basically loyal. It is what he saw in you at that old incident at the Owl Club, when you thwarted his big play. It is also what he saw in you when you sacrificed yourself for your Congressman and you kept him from breaking the big story of drugs on Capitol Hill. Your loyalty offends him at the core of who he is."

"That is all very interesting, but we have to see what we can do to help you right now."

"I am just telling you to beware of him."

"I always have been. What is your plan, about the money?"

"I still have a partial bonus coming at the end of the year. I have that in writing. I just have to get someone to invest in that, someone to give me current cash value for it. And then I will hand it over. I also could use a place to dry out. But I cannot let these people find me. They will not listen to me about my prospects. They have done too much of that. I don't care much at all what happens. That is sort of the real reason I am here. I know you will care. And you will do something."

"I have an idea, but let me sleep on it. You look like you could use some sleep too. You take my room. I will sleep on the couch. I get up early, you know. I have to get the kids up and get them breakfast and then I take them to school. I will be home in the afternoon before they will get off the bus. Then we can talk."

"It all sounds so domestic," Elliot said. "You're a better mother than your ex-wife."

"Thanks, Elliot. That is the nicest thing you have ever said to me, to anybody really."

The next afternoon Garth came home from school, greeted Elliott and made a phone call. It was a long call and it was private so Garth made it from his bedroom. When he came out of the room and went into the living room he saw that the children had come home from school and that they were on the floor with Elliott.

"Uncle Elliott is teaching us how to play craps," Seth said. "Come on, seven," he exhorted as he rolled a set of dice.

"How come you never taught us this game, Dad?" Hanna asked. "We have already won two dollars off of Uncle Elliott."

"You don't always win that game, guys. I hope 'Uncle' Elliott has explained that to you," Garth said. "Your after school snack's on the table. Why don't you go eat and then start on your homework."

"That's right, kids," Elliott intoned, "you have to make sure you do the things you must do first, before you take time to do the things you want to do."

"That has sort of been your saving grace," Garth said to Elliott as Seth and Hanna went into the kitchen.

"And what have you devised, Garth, to save me this time?"

"I have made a phone call. I will put you on a plane this evening. You are going to go visit a friend of mine. Well, actually, you will be seeing two friends of mine; one of them will take you in and will help you to dry out. The other one is sort of a specialist. He will be able to smooth over the problems you are having with your special creditors until such time as you will be able to pay them back."

"It sounds only a little bit mysterious. The only thing I can surmise with any degree of certainty is that I will be seeing the tomboy once again. I am grateful to you, Garth. That will be good. She will be a breath of fresh air."

That evening after dinner, the family drove Elliott to the airport. In the car Elliot told the children all about Bohemian atmosphere of the Schwabing district of Munich, why not to ever draw to an inside straight in draw poker, what the safe neighborhoods were in Rio de Janeiro, how to take apart an air rifle pellet gun without springing the parts and preventing you from putting it together again, where to find the best ice cream on the *Ile de la Cite* in Paris, how one of the healthiest things you can do is to drink a glass of red wine every day, that unless your name is Artur Rimbaud you should never try to write anything until you are thirty, how their father had once taken a Criminal Law exam without studying the night before, that one should always use both plumber's putty and plumber's tape when repairing a leaking pipe joint, that there was actually a Chinatown in Hong Kong, how to get into the Louvre without standing in the long lines, what the basics are for understanding *The Daily Racing Form*, that Australian women see American men in the same way that American women see French or Italian men, how very beautiful their mother had been when she was in college, the name of the best restaurant in New Orleans and the best nightclub, that the Czechs make the best beer, that there were books that could tell you how to see if someone was lying, how to make a silencer out of a potato, that Hemingway's great strength was as a prose poet and not as a novelist, that no matter how long they lived or what bad things they did that they could always count on their dad. And why that was a far rarer thing than they could imagine.

"Man, Uncle Elliott sure knows a lot of stuff," Seth said after they had watched him walk through the gate to the plane.

"And that, son, has always been his problem," was Garth's rejoinder.

Later that night, after the children had been put to bed, Garth called Melinda and related the events of the previous twenty-four hours.

"I am taking off from teaching tomorrow. It's a Friday before the alternate weekend I do not have the children. Seth and Hanna would go to their mother's house after school, all so that I can take you in to see Congressman Carlson. I will be able to stay at your house over the weekend."

"I know," she said, "I have been thinking of little else but that."

"I will give you a short briefing about the Congressman when we are on the way to see him. And don't worry. He is a very down to earth guy."

"I have met those political types in my public relations job for the Navy. I know them. But I have been staying away from you, for the sake of the kids. And the fact that you understand and appreciate that makes me want you more. So, I have something special planned for us."

TEARDROPS IN
THE FALLING WATER

The ancient Greeks excelled at many things, the greatest of which was perhaps the extent to which they were noteworthy fools. Only a society of ridiculous boobs could stumble upon the invention of something about which they understood almost nothing. They certainly understood epic and tragedy and comedy and sculpture and architecture, each of which they invented. But their understanding of one of their inventions, democracy, was so limited as to actually be ludicrous. In 401 BC, the great Greek general, Clearchus, commanded a troop of ten thousand Greek mercenaries in the employ of Cyrus of Persia to assist him in fighting a civil war against his brother, Artaxerxes, in order to see which would then become the king of Persia. When Cyrus perished in battle, the ten thousand Greeks in the midst of the Persian territory of Asia Minor became a minor nuisance to Artaxerxes. Clearchus also had a lack of understanding of the very high standards of oriental integrity, which matched or exceeded the ignorance that he and fellow Greeks also had with regard to democracy.

Therefore, in response to a very sincere Persian offer to discuss terms by which he and his men might peacefully remove themselves back to Greece, he and his top generals into a rode to the meeting with the Persians at which the Greek military command was removed from any meaningful connection with their own heads. In beheading the Greek generals, the Persians' idea was also to remove the head from the Greek army and thereby render it a useless rabble and easy prey for the Persian forces. Having been raised in a democratic society where each individual must be responsible to one another, Clearchus not only had become inured to the notion that society may only function when persons may rely upon each other's representations, he probably had an inkling of what was to happen in the event that Artaxerxes was not so reliable, or in other words what was to happen next. As Xenophon reports in his *Anabasis*, the foolish Greeks, lacking our modern and more complete understanding of democracy, merely elected new generals, turned their formidable phalanxes north and cut a terrible swath through the Persians until they had taken their "marching republic" to the sea, where there were Greek colonies and boats to take them home.

This same misunderstanding of democratic processes was also the mechanism by which the Spartans rather carelessly lost one of their great elected kings, Leonidas, when he marched his three hundred hand-picked soldiers to hold "the hot gates" against these same Persians, in 480 BC; the Spartans unwisely had figured they could simply elect a new king, which they did.

As Garth drove Melinda that next day past the cordon of barriers and heavily armed police surrounding the Capitol, it was clear to Garth that the great American democratic republic no longer operated under any principle associated with the discredited notions of the benighted ancient Greeks. A decade earlier, when Garth had worked on Capitol Hill, an individual constituent could park next to a House or Senate office building and walk into it in order to meet with his or her Senators or Congressman, in much the same spirit that President Abraham Lincoln would hold public days at the White House at which he would meet with citizens. Currently, Garth would have to park his car well outside the defensive cordon and would have to verify his appointment before he and Melinda could then pass through the metal detectors and then pat downs on their way to the office of Congressman Carlson.

The leaders of the United States had decided that they would be better served if the ancient democratic principles of the foolhardy Greeks were set aside for those more stalwart and sensible democratic doctrines derived from a place much closer in time and in place, namely in Latin America, by a Generalissimo here and there who had rightly and bravely seen the value of preempting anything so undemocratic as an election to replace a fallen leader, and had decided to surround himself with a fortress. There would be no Leonidas to be found in any of these exceptionally well-defended US government buildings. But there would be a Wilton Carlson.

Through the mind of Congressman Carlson there marched a phalanx of several Greek notions as well as one or two Italian and French ones, when he first saw Melinda Sherman walking into his office with Garth.

"I would say, Garth, old friend, that it appears that you had fallen into the outhouse but have climbed up out of it with a new designer suit. I had been concerned when I had heard about your divorce. But I see it has worked out quite well for you," the Congressman said.

"You Naval Academy guys are always so buttoned down and by the book. It is refreshing, the way you are always so in control of your egos and appetites," Garth heard Melinda say.

"Well, excuse me, Commander," Wilton said, "I should have adhered to Navy protocol, at least at the start. But you will understand if I have been a bit overwhelmed."

"That's perfectly understandable, Mister," Melinda said. "It has been a while since you served. And you only got as far as to be, what, a Lieutenant?"

"Garth, if you do not marry this woman, you are a fool."

"What might be foolish," Melinda said, "is to think that such a matter was to be determined by only one of us."

"I surrender," Wilton finally said.

"That makes perfect sense to me, Congressman," Garth answered. "It is very good to see you, Wilton."

The Congressman shook hands with each of them.

"Please sit down. It is good to see you both. It is particularly great to see you, Garth. I mean that sincerely. I really do. And it is also a pleasure to meet a true American hero. I have been looking over Commander Sherman's record here and I want to tell you that I am certain that she will be getting the Congressional Medal of Honor."

There was a compounded stillness in the room, lasting for a few moments, punctuated by the arch smile on the face of the Congressman, an infectious smile. Garth began to smile too. The playful love and shared respect between his candidate and Garth always made him happy. He felt a bit self-conscious about this in front of Melinda, so he looked down and tried to appear restrained. She just blandly stared at the Congressman and then at Garth. Finally, she spoke.

"Well, I am flattered, I guess, or honored may be the better word. But I hardly deserve that. And the door has closed on all that by now. It was a covert operation anyway. And as I am sure you know, Congressman, the military service branches are intractable bureaucracies. Once something is said and done, they close the book."

Congressman Carlson would not shake his Cheshire Cat grin. It was at once playful and knowing and engaging; a viral grin. Soon Melinda began to smile too, but in a quizzical way, almost against her will. It was one of those awkward and attractively embarrassed smiles that simply ask the question, "What?" Then she too joined Garth in looking down. But by this time Garth was no longer looking down. His experience had too well informed him. He knew not only of the capacity of his playful former candidate to be very earnest in the midst of his joking but Garth also understood the effectiveness of this crafty politician. Garth turned to Melinda. He put his hand on hers. He smiled again this time, but it was a loving smile and a warm one and he spoke to her, earnestly and warmly.

"Melinda, Wilton did not say he was *going* to work on obtaining the Congressional Medal of Honor for you. He said you would be getting it."

Melinda's questioning smile was replaced by a wide-eyed look of wonder and confusion. She slowly shook her head. The Congressman laughed now, quietly.

"Where did that cocky chopper jock go?" he asked. "You came in here, Commander Sherman, ready to fly by the seat of your pants and to shoot whatever got in the way. Now, I see that you are really quite humble. I admire the hell out of you for that. I needed nothing more than these last few minutes to be convinced that I was correct in my first assessment, that you are a hero and that you deserve the highest military honor this country can bestow. Every Congressional Medal of Honor winner I have ever met was quite humble. I was originally convinced of all that because there are a handful of Navy SEALs who would swear on their lives that you also deserve that medal."

Melinda looked up at him, with that same question, this time in her eyes and not on her mouth.

"And I know," the Congressman said, "that the military bureaucracy is inflexible and obdurate, except of course when they are not. When the proper incentive is offered, they can act with the utmost alacrity."

"The Congressman sits on the Defense Appropriations Subcommittee and on the Intelligence Committee," Garth said to Melinda, and turning to Wilton, he just said, "Thank you."

"Forget about it Garth," Wilton said. "She deserves it. And so do you, old friend. So do you. I may have been joking before, and I do agree with Commander Sherman that it takes two to make a decision about marriage, but I think the two of you make a magnificent couple. I believe that you will bring out the best in each other and that your bests are far superior to those of most other people. I am proud to know the both of you and I am looking forward to what the two of you will do."

"Thank you, Sir," Melinda said.

"No, Ma'am. Don't call me Sir. I am honored to know you. I preferred it when you call me Mister. And trust me, Ma'am, I would follow anywhere that you might lead me."

"There he goes again, Melinda," Garth said. "I am not entirely sure any of this is unrelated to the fact that he finds you attractive."

"It never hurts, Garth," the Congressman said. "You know what I always say. You can teach a woman to do every single job that any man can be taught to do. But you can't teach her to be beautiful. That is just there or it is not. Melinda is striking. That is always a good start. It is where I like to start, but I move on from there."

Melinda had relaxed now but her now smaller smile and her more comfortable demeanor had an undertone of her being preoccupied or distant, as part of her was still contemplating what had just happened. She still had something to say to the Congressman.

"I can see that you are sincere in what you say, simply by looking around your office. I also have no doubt that all these attractive women who work for you are also quite capable."

"You're damn right they are. And now I have another surprise for you. I have a visitor coming in to see me. He is outside right now. You know him, Garth, and you folks have something to talk about. So, I am going to step outside for a few minutes right now and have him come in here so you can use my office for your conversation. I will be back to hear how it went."

With this, he got up and walked to the door, stepped outside for a few moments and just like that the door opened and in walked someone Garth had not seen for twenty-five years.

"Preston! Jesus! Preston Cobalt! How the hell are you? Wait a minute, hold on. I am sorry. Preston, this is Melinda Sherman. She is my, I guess, she is my girlfriend. Melinda, this is Preston. We went to college together."

"Pleased to meet you, Ms. Sherman. The Congressman has told me a great deal about you. It is an honor to meet you," Preston said. Then he turned and shook Garth's hand and in the middle of the handshake he gave him a Texas swat on the shoulder. "You are looking pretty well yourself, Garth. You just win the lottery or something?"

"You mean like you did, the day you were born?" Garth laughed.

"Hell, yeah, cowboy. But you do have the luster of a newborn baby, right down to the drooling and all. It really is good to see you. You were always one of the good ones. And it does a body good to see you up off the canvas and back in the game."

"What brings you to Washington and to Congressman Carlson?"

"It's a family matter, really. My father passed away and my three brothers and I have a little matter of confiscatory taxes that could force us to sell the oil company my grandfather started."

"I see," Garth said. "The only way to pay the estate tax would be to sell the company. Because it is privately held, you just can't sell some stock. Wilton Carlson is from Texas and is a dealmaker and he is wired into the Speaker's office . . ."

"All we need is one little rider on that tax bill. And you should know that I used your name when I first introduced myself to your Congressman here. He has been nothing but very helpful."

"I am glad to have been of some assistance."

"Then Wilton and I got to talking about you, Garth, and about you, Ms. Sherman, and we both became convinced of the brightness of your futures. The Congressman believes that you are one of the best political operatives around, pal, and that you have been out of the game for too long.

He also recognizes that the political horizons are unlimited for you and . . . May I call you Melinda, ma'am?"

"Oh, please call me Melinda. The only person I want to call me ma'am is that randy old Congressman. And any old friend of Garth's is a friend of mine," Melinda said. "But please go on. I am fascinated by this."

"Well, part of what the Congressman and I have agreed upon is that the two of you should be well provided for, in the event you might move to Kentucky, where Melinda here might see fit to run for Congress. Cobalt Industries has many business partners in Kentucky and also has relationships with a herd of charitable institutions. In other words, each one of you will be guaranteed jobs in Kentucky, ones that would pay you well and which would give you the flexibility to mount a campaign for Congress. And I can also tell you personally that any such campaign would receive strong initial funding."

"And all this is in exchange for a 'small' rider on the tax bill that will be worth about a billion dollars to you and your brothers?" Garth asked.

"More like one point four billion, Garth. And I would have done all this for you two anyway," Preston said. "That is how shrewd our friend Wilton is. He never really asks anyone to do anything that is not already in their interest. He knows the way interests can align. He helps me and I help you and in the end your success is also in the interest of all of us. It is also in the interest of these United States of America."

"Wait a minute," Melinda interjected, "do you mean to tell me that some guys from some club they were both in at Harvard can meet in secret in some Congressman's office and determine some part of the political future of the country? Does it really work that way?"

"Some of the time," Garth said.

"When it is working right," Preston added. "The rest of the time it just gets all messed up by the amateurs."

At that moment, the lanky and loose-limbed Wilton Carlson strode back into the room, with his customary smile, the one that gave the impression that behind its gleaming teeth was something that he had been forbidden to eat, the same grin that gave the permanent impression that he had gotten away with something. He walked to the desk and stopped next to it, and rested one long thigh on the top of the desk, half sitting and half standing. He looked at Preston and Garth and he then took a long look at Melinda, who looked right back at him.

"Well," he said, "if we have all concluded our business here, then Preston and I have an appointment at the Speaker's office. It is an honor to meet you, Commander Sherman, Ma'am, it really is. And if that decision you rightly told me is one that requires two people, then I hope you know that Teller here, he is already on board. I also hope you do the right thing and give his life some new meaning, I mean, beyond being a father. I think he is the man for you. And that is saying quite a bit, because I already think the world of you."

Melinda had flown many a harrowing mission, including the one that had been the subject of this day's discussion. In those situations she always knew what to do and she had kept her cool. This was different. There were so many things to consider. This had been Garth's world, one to which her own life had never exposed her. It was a realm that had seemed at a distance even from him, from the dedicated father and teacher with whom she had fallen in love. She was now adjusting to learning these things about him, things she had only surmised before from the facts of his Harvard education and his previous work in politics. She had just been plunged into that world and it was a daunting occurrence on one hand and a heady experience on the other. The things that had been said about her possible future had been things that had been pillow talk, whispered late at night while lying in one another's arms. Things said in such an intimate and comfortable setting were one thing. Pronouncements made by billionaires and Congressmen were an entirely different matter. And although each had their own hues of unreality, the illusory nature of subjects whispered across a pillow was sweet and touching while the utter strangeness of these latter discussions was like waking up, having your coffee and seeing your name in a headline in the newspaper. It was exhilarating and terrifying all at the same time.

This time Melinda's clothes hit the floor just inside her home's front door in record time. Her skin was aglow with a luminous passion. Every fiber of her being ached for Garth. Her spirit was transported some-where else, some place very far away but actually deep inside of her, one that opened to a another deep where there was housed something in her that was very ancient, very bold, something elemental and perhaps simply better. She stepped in front of him, took his shoulders in his hands and looked into his dark brown eyes.

"In the bounty of my body lies a heart that gives itself to you freely and openly. I am your vessel. All of me is yours to touch, to taste, to violate and to command. I will do anything for you," she said.

For Garth it was an elemental call to all in him that was masculine, and not by any conventional definition of the word. In Garth the standard masculine traits were infused with and instructed by his strong paternal instincts. He had a passion to explore, to command, to acquire, to attack and to take risks, but these were only a smaller part of his larger need to nurture and to teach and to protect. Melinda's plea reached all these parts of him. He would attend to her, lovingly watch her responses, feel her and worship her. He accepted the license she gave him and saw it as a duty and a responsibility for him to undertake. And he would take her in any way that occurred to him at the moment or which he had harbored in his imagina-tion for years, but carefully and attentively. Nothing could have been more alluring to him or closer to the center of his being. To Garth it was a curious inversion. Melinda had surrendered herself to his command yet it was he who felt controlled by this surrender. To anyone in that neighborhood who may have heard the clamorous whisperings, the fierce chanting, the mystical shouts, and the enchanted weeping emanating from her home, it may have been all that was needed to convince them that there was a Pentecostal church service being conducted in her bedroom.

Several hours later they showered and dressed and emerged from their particular transports of religious ecstasy and settled into one of the secular requirements of spiritual enthusiasts everywhere since the dawn of such rituals. They ate dinner. It was after this dinner and over the remnants of a bottle of wine that Garth slipped a small black box out of his pocket and slid it across the table to Melinda, who opened it as he got down on one knee and asked, "Melinda Sherman, would you do me the honor of becoming my wife?"

"I love you, Garth Teller. I have loved you since before either one of us was born. My love for you has been determined by the stars. I want to be your wife more than anything else in the world."

There is a resolutely retroactive element to love of which Garth was particularly aware. It this sense, it was an expiation and a redemption. All that Garth had been and had done, including all the mistakes he had made and all the losses he had suffered, each most significantly leading up to his divorce, had all accumulated to make him exactly the person who would love and could love Melinda. It was instantaneously as if all those difficult and painful events were suddenly made into blessed and constructive proceedings because they gave him the understandings and the capabilities and the requirements for being the husband to this remarkable woman. Perhaps most of all, the thankless and sacrificing harvesting and sowing and maintenance he had done in the demanding fields of fatherhood, and of motherhood for that matter, had given him the need to love Melinda and the tools with which to do it. It was as if the healing hand of some prophet or messiah had passed over his past pain and made it all an unalloyed perfection, for having delivered him to this woman.

It had been a beatific, life-changing day and he would carry the memory to his grave. And it was not over.

Garth took a few moments later in the evening to go over his lessons and to read some critical essays he had asked his students to write. Then he called his children at their mother's home. Such calls were always awkward. With him alone, his children were normally frank and forthcoming as he had taught them to be by simply being the same way with them, openly sharing with them the events of his own life. He met their own statements without judgment and with understanding and affection.

One day in later years his daughter would come to him and say, "Dad, there is blood on my sheets. I think I just had my first period."

The first thing he would do then would be to strip the bed and wash the sheets and mattress cover. The second thing he would do was to call an obstetrician-gynecologist and make an appointment, to which he would accompany Hanna. Sitting in that waiting room he would be proud to note that he was the only male there not accompanying a pregnant wife.

But whenever he called his children at their mother's, they would speak to him guardedly and with an unmasked desire to end the conversations quickly and get off the phone. They loved their mother easily as much as they loved their father. When they were with him they happily would speak with Tabitha. But when they were with their mother they felt that to talk to him was to betray her. They felt the need to be more protective of her than they would ever feel that they had to be of him.

People who love one another are connected in ways that are evident even when they are apart. It therefore occurred to Garth that Melinda was missing. Normally, even when they were separately occupied but in the same home, there would be intervals of reconnecting, of checking in with one another. The time for such an interval had passed and Garth had noticed this. And something else told him that she was not there, not in that connected way. So he went in search of her. She was not in the dining room, where he had spread out his work and had been reading. She was not in the bedroom or living room. He looked for her in the kitchen where he found something disconcerting. It was the engagement ring, the one she had been wearing only for an hour or two. It was sitting on the kitchen counter. He went to the bathroom door, stopped and listened. He heard the shower running but he felt compelled to knock on the door and ask her to let him into the bathroom. He heard no answer. But since he heard the shower running and he was convinced that she was in it and not on the toilet, he opened the door.

The shower was indeed running and Melinda was in the shower. But she was sitting on the shower floor fully clothed and she was crying. At an earlier point in his life he might not have known what to do. But it seemed that all his previous experience had prepared him for this moment. He opened the door, and still fully clothed, he stepped in, sat down next to her and put his arms around her and held her. She looked at him as if he were a stranger or more pointedly as if she were someone else, someone who did not know him. Then he too began to cry. Teardrops in the falling water are indiscernible. They are evanescent as so much in life can be, including love, sanity, or even life itself. He was finally meeting that person all his instincts had told him he might expect to meet. He was holding onto and weeping with the other Melinda.

EARNESTLY HUNTING

In certain old moneyed families for which a definite level of education has been expected from one generation to the next, when a respected position cannot be obtained either through family connections, merit, inheritance, hard work or plain wild luck, for a young family member, it is more or less a custom that such an individual become a journalist. This is not unlike that manner in which third or fourth sons in well-to-do English families of the not too distant past would be sent to sea, the clergy, or to India. This suggested itself to the family of Earnest Dapple when he was at a very young age, not that he be sent to sea but that he find his way into the trade craft of reporting the news, it being the very best thing that could be done for a boy so talented at the skill of maintaining an exceptional level of disrespect for the well-being of his fellow mortals and possessing an even more laudable level of contempt for the truth or for English grammar and syntax.

This general thinking was reinforced specifically in the mind of the young individual himself by a flash of recognition he felt once upon a family trip to London, England, when he came across a bit of British journalism in that city called *Tatler*, the name ringing a bell for the boy as being a homonym for the exact nickname all his school chums had given him and had maintained for him ever since kindergarten.

In many such cases, the entry point for these aspiring young journalists is to work for a trade paper or a magazine. There are literally thousands of such publications, dedicated to almost every commercial endeavor or hobby, which invariably find it difficult to attract experienced employees from the highest levels of the journalistic vocation. It is not every aspiring Hemingway or Winchell or Woodward who wants to go to work for *The American Machinist* or the *Bioprocessing Journal* or *Cabling Business Magazine* or the *Defense News* or the *Electronic Engineering Times* or *Federal Computer Week* or *GPS World* or *Health Care Informatics* or *Industrial Engineer Magazine* or any other such technical or niche publication that might fill out the rest of the alphabet and beyond. Earnest had fortunately attended Harvard so he was able to start his career at the Associated Press office in Washington, DC. Earnest was curiously the reverse of what might be expected for other beginning journalists in that it was his highest aspiration to actually and eventually attain a position at a niche trade publication and to there crown and finish his career. And in fact by this point in this story he had done just that. After toiling at the Associated Press and other publications, he had finally achieved his dream and had become employed at "the journal of politics and government," the niche trade newspaper that is otherwise known as *The Washington Post*.

Some part of Mr. Dapple's success was attributable to an accident, the same accident that has occurred from time to time in our species since its beginning and which plays a prominent role this narrative, that being the accident of falling in love. The senior Mr. Dapple, Earnest's father, stood at the end of a long family line of just the sort of educated and moneyed ancestors as have here been described. Theirs was a family descended from one of the original passengers on *The Mayflower* who had later settled in Rhode Island and whose family fortunes had then been built and accumulated on shipping and the import export trade. Dapple boys had for generations haunted the halls of the prestigious private schools and colleges and had married within the closed ranks of this society. Earnest's father had taken the same path as most of the other men in his patrilineal line but had wound up in a slightly different spot. In college his route had crossed that of a young woman whose own family, though African American, had also long been educated and successful, a woman whose great grandfather had become a doctor in New England and who had passed that profession on to each of the men in his direct line of descendants. In almost every social, intellectual, and economic way, this young woman was little different from every other well-educated and well-to-do female in the elder Dapple's life. Since accidents have little regard for skin color, Earnest's father and this young woman fell in love peradventure. And against the strictures of life in America in the nineteen fifties, this love gave them the courage to defy convention and to marry. The end result of all this was an accident of an entirely different kind and one which is considerably less uncommon than a mixed race marriage was.

Earnest Dapple, though he descended from generations of privilege, may have been admitted to Harvard and may similarly have advanced in his career accidentally due to phenomenon with the poetically redundant name of affirmative action. Earnest saw this as neither and irony nor an injustice and in a smaller regard considered just compensation for the way in which some people genuinely looked at him differently, even though many of those looks occurred at his parents' country club or in the halls of Choate and Harvard. Much more largely, he saw it in the same way he saw each individual who made those same looks and the ones who did not, as a tool. His toolbox was assembled for the project of advancing the one thing to which he was entirely dedicated. And in that he was very earnest.

There is in the mind of most individuals a mechanism, which will not allow one to rest, once an unanswered but simple question has been posed, such as, "What was the name of that guy in that movie?" The mind will restlessly seek the answer, no matter how meaningless, simply because it is certain that it already has the solution somewhere in memory and that all that it must merely do is to find it. That is no less true than when we are on a city street and we hear the cry, "Stop! Thief!" and we make no small effort to join in the search or at least to find out what is going on and if the perpetrator has been apprehended. Far too many jokes have been told about the man who, hopelessly lost in town, refuses to ask for directions because he is far too enamored of his own ability to find that place for which he seeks. And no amount of science has yet to determine which of the two instincts is really the preeminent at work when a man meets a fascinating and sultry brunette and then he sets out to pursue her; the glamor and magnetism of the lady or the allure of the pursuit. This recondite human intellectual circuitry resides not in the mind at all but in some place more to the south, in the environs of the instinct.

It is a predisposition we all have, to be on the hunt and to revel in it. Earnest was no less possessed of this instinct than any man poring over a map and eschewing his wife's plaintive appeal that he simply ask for directions, but for him it was both more and less elemental. It was both his nature and his ethics, which is to say for anyone who may not grasp that, while modern and regulated hunting is replete with rules and concerns for the environment and other hunters and anyone or anything else that might be affected in the process, the more elemental hunter is only concerned with bagging his prey.

One of items in Earnest's toolbox had long been, to his way of thinking, Garth Teller of Texas and of the Harvard Owl Club. He had been put to use in the past at least once, in much the manner of an electric screwdriver, when Earnest had inserted him into the apparatus of Capitol Hill and he had provided Earnest with a scoop on an important national story. Earnest had come close to another story later but fell short of screwing it to its sticking point when the battery on the screwdriver had been surreptitiously removed.

The Wilton Carlson story had not been fastened into the body of the journalist's work and the screwdriver had drifted to the bottom of the toolbox for the time being. But when he caught a whiff of what had just at this point happened in that same Congressman's office with Garth and Melinda, there came to Earnest the cause of what can only be called an unfortunately mixed metaphor. The hunter delved into his toolbox once again.

The reaction to this same bit of news was somewhat different in the area of Houston, Texas, where the redoubtable Eakin Lambert was applying all of her business boldness and acumen in order to promote the sales and growth of the plastics company she owned in partnership with her Taiwanese associates, while also preparing herself for that future which Ben Dessous had advised her would eventually come, when they would run that company out from under her, and also where she was providing a landing pad for the erratically and hastily flung Elliott Barker, who at this point was in the early stages of his recuperation. He was standing in her office, his lank blond hair hanging a little too long to one side as he ran his hand through it, and was wandering around and generally taking in the scenery, while Eakin was being gently entertained by his peripatetic presence as she conducted business on her phone and at her computer.

"So, Elliot, have you wandered into my office today because you want to see if you can make yourself useful while you are here?" she asked.

"Why do the people in these photographs all the time look so sleepy?" he asked, and not quite in return.

"They are not sleepy. They are Chinese. And they are the furthest thing from sleepy that you can imagine. They are industrious. You can look up the meaning of that word in that dictionary on the shelf there."

"Yes, I guess I could help you with your finances or something."

"The root of that same word I just mentioned is industry. This is an industry. We make things. We are not parasites like you and your buddies on Wall Street. Besides, our finances are straightforward. We have costs and we get paid and with luck the second figure is higher than the first."

"Speaking of Chinese dictionaries, have you been informed of what Garth is doing lately? It seems he has a new girlfriend and she is some kind of tomboy, like you."

"Not all women who outperform men in the historically male realms are tomboys. And I have heard about the new love of Garth's life. She really seems like she might be someone special. I know he certainly has fallen for her hook, line and sinker, which is his way."

"No, I meant your financials. You must have some cash on hand at any given moment and it is a waste just to let it sit in some account until it gets spent. There are some creative ways in which you can put that cash to work even in the short term and even if it is not all that much."

"That is exactly what I am talking about, Buffalo. We are not an investment bank. We work for our money. We do not play with it," Eakin said.

"Apparently this Melinda is some kind of war hero and a triathlete and former college track star. That is certainly not the profile for Garth. He normally goes for the willowy intellectuals that have a touch of crazy, except for that whole thing he has got going on with you."

"Garth and I have no thing, or whatever. We grew up together, pulled the wings off the same flies, tossed the same craft projects out the kindergarten window, were thrown out of the same summer camp, and sneaked into the same bars. We were and are like brother and sister."

"So, you heard that old 'buffalo' story then?" Elliot said as his eyes smiled.

"Yes, I heard about the time you ran through a wall, or tried to run through a wall in order to get the attention of some girl. Your friends who were there still call you by that name. I think you said that is how you were going to crash through the wall, like a buffalo. It is a wonder to me that any woman ever found you attractive."

"I think you mean to say that you and Garth are like brother and brother, or boy and tomboy. The two of you may not have a thing, but if that is so that is because Teller has his eyes closed two thirds of the time, at least with women. You're kind of cute, in your way. He should have been attracted to you. And, hell, maybe this affair with this new jock tomboy is some kind of psychological transference of his unrecognized passion for you."

"Psychology is like religion. Whenever you make an assertion like that, it cannot be argued, because the doctrine presupposes and explains away any response."

"What do you mean women don't find me attractive? Do you think I don't see the way you are leering at me?"

At that moment Ben Dessous walked into the room. He was dressed in a blue pair of casual pants and a gray jersey, an outfit that showed he had not quite adapted full business dress but that was demonstrating that he was no longer on the street. His gait and his posture were similar. He might have seemed as at ease walking the new production line with the workers, as he would be at a meeting of the company's customers. Elliott looked at him and under normal circumstances might not have been able to hide his reaction to the scars on Ben's face or to the very dark hue of his skin. But Elliott was somewhere in between being distracted by Eakin and in that sluggish state that is a hallmark of recovery, which was why he had been addressing her comments one statement later than when they had been uttered. Ben noted that Elliott took his entrance in stride and was well aware of the reasons for it.

"Thank goodness you are here," Eakin said. "You have just rescued me from a maddening conversation, as out of time as it was out of reason. What do you have for us? Oh, I am sorry. This is Elliot Barker, the patient Garth sent us. Elliot, this is Ben Dessous."

"Pleased to meet you, Ben. And thank you in advance for taking this on for me," Elliot said.

"I am interested to meet you, as well, Mr. Barker. And technically I am doing this for Garth and Eakin, although I accept your gratitude for my effort," Ben said, as Eakin shot a sidelong glance, with an accompanying knowing smile, at Elliott. "I have made contact with some of the organization people on the street in New York. Although your creditor, Mr. Barker, is not specifically part their association, he operates in the same subculture and is amenable to their persuasion. The 'heat' will be off of you for the several months that it will take for you to dry out and to obtain your bonus."

"Thank you," said Elliot, "I mean, I am truly grateful."

"The fortunate or unfortunate consequence of this is that your indebtedness has now been assumed by that organization and is due them, rather than to the individual with whom you originally contracted."

"I assume that the unfortunate part is that I will have to pay some kind of interest. What is the fortunate part?"

"The fortunate part is that a specific question has effectively been removed from the equation. And in its place there is now a certainty. And that is that you may be assured; you will pay the debt. And you are welcome to think of the interest as your rent for staying here."

By this time Eakin was beaming. Elliot was shaking his head and smiling. Ben was moving on to another matter. He was already thinking about Garth, the man who had been his first contact in this world of money and connections and social mobility. The news about Garth and his new love and their possible plans had struck him in a different way. He had a way of seeing events that was more or less the flip side of the coin from the way in which Earnest Dapple saw people and things. Ben too had an eye for relationships and interests and the way in which those things fit together, but his instinct was to help and to put interests and people together in a way that might be beneficial, and not to himself but to them.

Garth had been the catalyst of more than one person's change of life.

The individuals whom he had once hired to work for him on that original campaign for Wilton Carlson had all learned something from him and had all in some measure been touched by the success of that campaign. The personable young woman who had just graduated from college and who had never be able to tell the press anything more than she had already been told by Garth had gone with the Congressman to Washington and had served as his press secretary there for a while, before she had been hired to read the news for a local Texas station and was at this point in the story a news anchor for a network affiliate in Houston. The volunteer coordinator who was local Democratic committeeman of capable intelligence and a tireless worker himself, who did no more or less than Garth would tell him to do, ran the local Congressional office for the Congressman, until such time as the many constituents he had helped had urged him to run for the local state legislative seat and he was now a State Representative and a strong political supporter of the Congressman. He was also happily married to the former receptionist for the campaign whose father's labor union connections had been useful in his own campaigns. Garth's researcher who had also been the keeper of the body had gone to law school at the University of Texas and now was a successful lawyer.

But none of these individuals had been more inspired by what they learned from Garth and by the success of the campaign than Rich Sartory, the reticent scion of a local political family who had been privileged to most of Garth's campaign thinking and who had been the other sole witness to the late night phone call that Garth had made to preserve the political future of then-candidate Wilton Carlson. Rich had never said anything about any of this to Garth or to anyone else. In fact, of all the people Garth had hired he was the only one who had never said a word to Garth once the campaign had ended. He had taken it all literally and truly to heart.

He had also run for State Representative, as had the coordinator of volunteers. Only Rich had not waited as the volunteer coordinator had done, building his support among the people whom he would later help as the Congressman's employee in the local office. Rich ran immediately and he ran for the state legislative seat that had necessarily been vacated by Wilton Carlson as he had moved into the United States Congress.

What Rich had garnered mostly from that fateful call Garth had made to the mistress of former Congressman Fitzkin had been a sense of its boldness. The courage of that call reached some part of him that had been fumbling for an outlet for his ambition. Rich had seen the local campaigns of his father and other family members for school board and local offices and had long been bitten by the political bug. His University of Texas education had raised his sights and had broadened his horizons. But in his youth he had not been sure of how to go about pursuing his own political dreams or even if he were going to be capable of it. The slightly older man from Harvard and from a more well-to-do suburban family had shown him that night that it was all just a matter of fortune favoring the bold. Garth had hired Rich in the campaign to do the necessary work of serving as liaison to the people who might tend to get in Garth's way, the local elected officials, party committee members, union officials and people who had been important in the past state legislative races. These contacts could not have been ignored but they would have bogged down Garth and kept him from managing the overall campaign. What Rich had learned from Garth was that he could make the bold move on his own part and that it would be for Rich to parlay his position in the Carlson campaign into garnering support from these same individuals for when he would run for the vacated state legislative seat. This is exactly what he did and when that seat had to be filled by special election, the local Democratic Committee had already been sewed up in support of a certain Rich Sartory.

Of course it was Garth's way to have applauded all this, had he been given the chance. Garth saw the success of the people he had once helped or hired as him having done something good and it made him feel better about having helped them. Only secondarily was he pleased that it also meant that people whom he knew might be in a better position to perhaps return his favor one day. So it had always bothered him slightly that Rich had not confided in him or relied on him in any way, as if Rich had not only disavowed Garth's role in putting Rich in the position to advance himself, but was also eschewing any further relationship. Garth had originally seen the slightly younger man as a protégé. This view had fairly rapidly changed and he came to see Rich as an utterly independent operator, which upon reflection Garth realized he should have seen all along. And at that point, Garth began to see him as someone who might one day be a potential threat to the career of Congressman Carlson. This had all vanished from Garth's considerations after he had left his career on Capitol Hill. Whether or not Rich Sartory had ever forgotten anything about Garth was an entirely different matter and it is just as likely that his reticence had always been about what may or may not have been his true feelings all along.

It may or may not have been that he had always seen Garth in the way that some men will see a progenitor or a predecessor, as someone to emulate and then to destroy.

As it was, Rich had a particular way of interpreting the things he had heard Garth say. Garth had once said that Texas was more like America than the rest of America. And by that he had meant that the characteristics that most Americans claimed to value were more evident in Texas, and perhaps this was because it had fought successfully to be an independent nation more recently than had the United States, and perhaps because it retained wide expanses and its freedom from authority for a longer period and more recently. As America may be the evening land of Europe, Texas was the evening land of America. These things may have also made Texans react perhaps a bit defensively to the changes that would settle into the eastern United States so that they were more stubbornly independent and outspoken. Rich Sartory's view of that was slightly askew and he saw it to mean that anything that he noticed in Texas was applicable to the soul of most Americans and that Texas was a very good place to start, if one had designs on America. In the time between the birth of each of these men, Garth Teller and Rich Sartory, and the current time in this narrative at which Garth had met and fallen in love with Melinda Sherman, three Texans had become President of the United States. Rich Sartory had not been idle since his first election as a Texas State Representative, roughly twenty years before this time in this story. He had taken to heart another tale he had once heard Garth tell and he had acted upon it.

Garth had once told Rich, "Everything I ever learned about politics I learned on a date to New York City with Tabitha." Garth related the story of the China Club, which at the time he and Tabitha had been dating was the one club in Manhattan to which everyone wanted to go, so as a result there was always a line outside the door and very few of those people in that line ever got into the club. The gatekeepers of the China Club admitted the celebrities and wealthy people of New York, and kept the aspiring public on the other side of the velvet rope at the door to the club. Garth had impressed Tabitha by telling her that he could get them into the China Club and he had taken her shopping to buy just the right dress in order to enjoy their evening inside of this club that was so in demand. This dress was both expensive and revealing and it almost required its wearer to not have on anything underneath and as such it was a delicate and alluring sheath over all the lithe and sensual joys that were her magnificent form. He even paid to have her get a fashionable Manhattan hairdo. He also put on his best suit. And through all this she was impressed with his confidence, that he was so connected and so worldly wise to be able to get them into this club that so many of their friends and other people had failed to enter. Upon leaving their hotel at around midnight that evening Garth avoided taking a cab and instead accepted a ride from one of the many black livery cars that often stop to pick up people who are hailing taxis on the Manhattan streets. The line outside the China Club was long and unruly at the time this car pulled up. Garth let Tabitha lead the way, getting out of the car. As he had predicted, they were waved past the lines. The velvet rope was lifted and they entered the club, where they drank and danced and saw celebrities. Tabitha was never more in love with Garth than on that night and she was never less aware that the reason they had been admitted had little to do with Garth and everything to do with her. Garth knew that it was in the interest of the doormen to admit her and all other beautiful women. Garth was then admitted as a necessity. And he did not explain it to Tabitha as he later explained it to Rich, that politics was not persuasion so much as it was recognizing other people's self-interests and aligning yourself with them.

The equivalent beautiful girl of Texas was, to the political mind of Rich Sartory, the burgeoning political, social and religious organization known as the Southern Baptists of Texas Convention, the group of Baptists who had wrested the control of the Southern Baptist Convention from the moderates in 1979 and had put it on the fundamentalist path. State Representative Sartory also felt that this most Texan of religious impulses was also something that was in its way more American than the rest of America. He understood that it was something that was at the core of most American social and political and religious beliefs, even if they did not know it. He was not unsophisticated in his understanding. He figured that the idea that an individual who had not read the Bible and who had no other Christian training could simply experience the spirit of the Lord and then would know that he or she was then permanently saved was simply about as American as any idea could get. There was no liturgy and no catechism and the grace of God was granted by the self and from within the self and without the mediation of any minister or creed or even by the Bible. This type of an inward looking revelation, he realized, was equally available to any Baptist, Lutheran, Episcopalian, Catholic, Presbyterian, Jew, Muslim, agnostic or atheist, and was in fact even at the core of any religion that had a creed and an organized episcopacy. He believed that coming to faith, in America at least, had to always start out as personal, individual and in a sense selfishly.

Rich Sartory accordingly dressed himself in the alluring political attire of intense opposition to abortion of all kinds, of male primacy in all family matters and in holding leadership positions within the church, of the defense of the traditional view of marriage as being between only a godly man and his supportive wife, of adult baptism, of the competence of the individual to actually know God and His will, and of the Bible's inerrancy in upholding that each one of these political positions were actually God's word. He understood that American society was changing, that it was becoming globalized, homogenized, diversified and modernized, and that the best method for the many Americans who resisted these changes to succeed would be the same technique that worked for the despots of Yemen or Iran or Gaza. They could assert with an inerrant certainty that God did not want these changes. And with this understanding, Rich Sartory rose from Texas State Representative to Texas State Senator and eventually, by this time in the story, to Lieutenant Governor of the State of Texas. He had however made one simple and elegant change in his approach. Along the way he had joined the political arm of the Southern Baptist organization. He had also become a Republican.

The possibility that Garth might marry a woman who would be awarded the Congressional Medal of Honor and who might be just the candidate for whom Garth would once again enter the political arena was only a delicate hint at this point, but it was met very distinctly and very particularly differently by three specific individuals. For Earnest Dapple it was the scent that put the hairs up on the back of his hunter neck. Ben Dessous saw in it the possibility of secretly putting together confluent interests in order to do something beneficial and helpful, and as something he needed to protect. For Rich Sartory it was the possible and uninvited return of the big brother whom he had happily presumed to be politically dead.

THE FIRST ELEMENT FELL INTO PLACE

Running Melinda for Congress at this point was the furthest thing from Garth's mind. He was thinking more of the running water that was drenching both of them and their clothes as he sat holding her on the floor of her shower. That water was gradually getting colder. They had been there long enough that the capacity of the building's hot water heater was reaching its limit. He knew that in a minute they would be quite cold so he reached up to the handles and he turned off the water. By such mundane considerations and artless actions are spiritual milestones sometimes reached.

"What are you doing here?" Melinda asked.

"I am holding you."

"Oh, but who are you?"

"I am the man who loves you more than anything in the world."

"I can't marry you."

"I know that," he said.

And he held onto her as firmly as he could, or as tightly as she would allow. He was reminded of the time his daughter, Hanna, had pneumonia as an infant and he had sat by her bed, monitoring her temperature throughout the night as it went down in response to the antibiotics he had quickly convinced her doctor to prescribe. It was also like the night Seth had lain awake crying for an inexplicable reason and would only stop crying and go to sleep if Garth held him while he walked around and sang to him. When he had stopped either one of those things, the child resumed crying. Garth had tried many times to put the sleeping boy back into bed, but instead spent the entire night walking and holding and going through his entire personal song book. It had been one of the best nights of Garth's life, he realized later.

He was also mindful at this moment in the shower of the many times he had failed to understand it when Tabitha had forgotten his birthday, or had not noticed he had a new haircut, or the fact that he could count on the fingers of one hand the times she had been the one to initiate the necessary phone call during the work day to coordinate which of them would get home first to relieve the nanny. He had taken most of those incidents personally and had been hurt by them. Such was not the case in the shower with Melinda, proving forever the truth of the well-known and quite celebrated maxim that a man should have children and essentially be their mother before he is ever allowed to enter a relationship with a woman.

For Melinda this odd situation was a circumstance that was utterly and specifically surprising except to the extent that the general outlines were eerily familiar. She had once again simply found herself in a situation that had no antecedent. This time she had discovered herself in her home with a man thirteen years her senior who apparently felt quite comfortable being there and who seemed to assume an intimate relationship between the two of them. This was not exactly the first time such a thing had happened, but it was specifically different. There was something gentle and fatherly about this man. He did not seem to have the deeply mystified and mildly angry countenance that was common to others whom she had abruptly discovered in her presence during this type of episode. He was surely older and a bit out of shape, as is common with men of his apparent age. He was not fit and young, like the others. His hairline was slightly receding and he appeared to be in his mid-forties. And this time there had been an engagement ring. It had been on her finger.

But perhaps the most noteworthy thing was that the mental or psychological process, which had removed her to this distant place, was acting in direct proportion to the depth and strength of her attachment to this man. Even at this distance she sensed that the love between them was unique, was singularly strong and that it was exactly what her mechanism had been fleeing or breaking or whatever it was it was doing. Her fresh perspective on the floor of the shower, being held by this gentle and loving man, was not so altered that she was totally unaware of that love. She still felt it. That too was different. And it was there in his eyes when she looked at them.

Someone less of a feminist than is common in this enlightened day once said that there is something about a distracted and unstable woman, especially considering the strong undercurrents that lie not far beneath her surface, which few young men are wise enough to know not to provoke. Many older men even lack the wisdom or perhaps the will to step lightly upon the thin ice, below which run these deeper tides of the reckless impulses of despair and destruction. Garth had read *Medea*, and more importantly the lessons of his life with Tabitha had been brought fully home to him when the recent diagnosis of Seth's attention deficit disorder had informed him of all the things he had done incorrectly or wrong in his marriage because he had been uninformed of her own form of the same impairment. Sitting in the shower, wet with Melinda, it was not difficult for him now to lose himself in sympathy for this beautiful and disturbed creature for whom his love was practically foremost. They stayed silently together like this for some long minutes, he holding onto her.

In movies and books and on stage the most tragic occurrences are often followed by a dramatic shift to outlandish humor. The valiant knight will fall to the most vile betrayers and highwaymen and will receive a beating of mythic proportions and following that he will be regaled by the droll and ironic ramblings of his squire, as if the beating and the joking were woven together like the stripes in a shirt. The ancient and angry king will make the most grave and violent mistakes in the most intimate setting, destroying the very fabric of his family and setting the worst fates upon those he loves most, and then he will soon find the wise and clever humor of a fool to chide and to comfort him at the same moment. These changes in fiction are well nigh unbelievable and strain the credulity of the audience, which then reassures itself with the calming realization that it is only a play, a movie, or a book. These overly dramatic and incredible transitions appear absurd but they are no more or less uncommon or implausible when they appear in real life. Only then we are the participants and are up to our elbows in the sudden deaths and reversals of fortune and passionate upheavals and their subsequent comedic episodes. This makes an inestimable difference. We generally live through the ferocious disruptions of our own lives, which we would see on the stage and assume are preposterous.

In this case as in many others the catalyst was sleep. And the humor to which the scene had shifted was flashing splendidly in a pair of clown pajamas. Her friends on the Kentucky women's track team had given them to Melinda as a joke on her birthday many years ago. She had held onto them for sentimental reasons and had long ago tucked them into the very back of one of the drawers of her dresser. Dancing, grinning and, well, clowning all over the surface of these pajamas were various versions of Bozo, Buffo, the Rastellis, Coco, Tarantino, Blinko, Frosty and other exaggerated looking versions of the comic pranksters. Melinda awoke the next morning and found that she was now wearing the long forgotten and largely symbolic nightclothes which were so clownishly loud they could frighten an entire elementary school full of clown-wary children or make the full comple-ment of a women's collegiate track team howl with laughter. Melinda had never worn these particular pajamas nor would she put on any pajamas. She always slept in the nude. So she knew something was up. She also had another feeling, one that was also vaguely familiar and something along the lines of a hangover; only it was psychological and could best be described as a lingering blank. She knew what she had to do, as always, in these situations. She lay awake for several minutes trying to put together the previous day and evening.

In this case it was particularly difficult because much of what she remembered strained credulity. She remembered visiting the Congressman's office and being told she would receive the nation's highest military honor. She remembered one of Garth's powerful friends from Harvard promising them both jobs and help in what might be a Congressional campaign. All of it seemed as if it could not have happened. More plausible was her memory of making love to Garth and of eating dinner with him. And then she remembered getting engaged to him. It was the last thing she could remember. While this perhaps was the most inconceivable circumstance of an otherwise already incredible day, it also explained that lingering blank, and the clown pajamas. Melinda did not know and could not have known that Garth had taken her out of the shower and had undressed her and dried her off and had put her in the only sleepwear he could find in her bureau, before tucking her into bed and kissing her on the forehead and then going into the living room to sleep on the couch. What Melinda did know for certain that morning was that somewhere in that house were Garth and an engagement ring. She went on the hunt for both, although she already had an idea where to find Garth. She found the ring on the kitchen counter and put it on her finger. She found Garth asleep on her living room sofa.

She stood and stared at him for several long moments. He was a man in his mid-forties, with a slightly receding hairline and he was indeed a little bit thick around the middle. He was dressed in casual clothes that showed some wear and were fitting with his position as a teacher. He looked unlike any of the other younger men she had ever dated. But he was still very handsome, with his dark eyes and hair and his strong features and sensitive mouth. She could not see the sparkle in his now closed eyes but she could remember it and she could sense what it meant. She could feel that warmth and intelligence and vitality and passion as if he were looking at her at that moment, and there was something new that she remembered and now recognized as well, something that she had previously only intuitively sensed, and that was a kind of worldly wisdom. And this was all unmistakable now, because he was in fact looking at her at that moment. A man who had served the role of both parents to his children could not remain asleep long when someone he loved was in the room looking at him. It was just an instinct.

"Good morning, Melinda," he ventured.

"Good morning, Garth," she answered. "I guess I owe you an apology."

Even before he noticed the glint of a diamond on her left hand, he said, "You never owe me anything, my love. I owe you, always, for the way you make me feel, for the way you redeem all I have ever done, wrong or right, in my life."

Then saw the ring and smiled.

"It doesn't always happen this way."

"What? Were you having one of your visions last night? Is that what it was?"

"Not exactly, yes, no, maybe, not really at all, no, it was something different. It usually happens more slowly, but not always. Sometimes it sneaks up on me like it did last night. But when it happens either way it is in response to the feeling that I am losing myself, that someone is getting too close. Normally I kind of live my relationships backwards in time, starting out close and then moving toward a friendship. By the end I am talking to my boyfriend in a way that sounds like I am making a presentation to a committee. None of them liked it. In fact they all hated it and reacted poorly. When it happens all of a sudden their reaction can be quite rash. And my response to that can be equally swift and precipitous. I often just find the signs of a struggle and that some of my things are missing, including the man."

"It will take more than that to lose me."

"Apparently."

"But where are the clowns? Quick, send in the clowns. Don't bother, they're here."

And before he could even finish singing that song the clowns were on the floor and he found himself set upon by a voracious woman of more than a dozen years his junior who was in many respects still a marvelous athlete. In the nude there was something about her that was more than alluring, more than feminine, more than attractive. There was something magnificent, something that spoke the word "creature," as if she were a superlative specimen of some grander species. This magnificent creature could always have overwhelmed Garth were it not for his own strength and passion being alloyed by his years of experience. He knew that the only chance he had with her on that couch or in bed was to subdue his own excitement by taking control of her as much as he could, by being a director more than an actor. This was not difficult for him because his feelings for her were entirely masculine but in a very seasoned sense. The night before in the shower he had protected and nurtured and loved her in a way that had no ego involvement and expressed no personal impulse beyond sympathy and love and support. This morning, relieved at what could only be called her return to him, he needed to assail her physique and to slake his lust for her and to plunder all of her physical riches. At one point he had been like her father and at a later point he was her ravisher. And while many a philosopher or prelate or psychologist or preacher or essayist or pedant would say that never should those two aspects of a personality ever meet, in Garth they were the same element, but only with Melinda. In his actual role as a father, this other part of him was shut down. But in this love affair it was the same thing for him to be both manly and maternal.

The need that Melinda had for him was even more elemental and direct. He was the first man who had stuck around in the face of her difference. He was also the only one with whom she had also maintained a vestigial attachment even from her distance. And he was the man from her many visions; she had known him in that way all her life. Whether this was the cause of his singularity or the result of it, she could not know. And it did not matter. To say that she desired him would have been to fall short in the describing. She was compelled to incorporate him into her very being, to bring him into her, to become him.

Later, lying on his back on the living room floor and looking at the ceiling, Garth asked, "So does this mean we are back on track to get married?"

"Yes," she said, as she propped herself on an elbow and looked down on his face, "and we can do it tomorrow if you like, only you have to promise to stop trying to sing old show tunes with that terrible voice. And I do want to run for Congress, in part because I want to see you get back in the game and I want to share this with you, and in part because I have this fire, this uneasiness. I don't know, I guess it has something to do with my visions. But it is intense and I think that I can serve it better by serving others. It is also a part of the way I need you, Garth Teller. I need you to do this with me, so together I may be more of who I really am. When I actually consider the visions, I think this is what was meant to be. It is difficult to explain. I used to think that I was being given occasional glimpses into the future, but now I think I sort of dream things into existence."

"I am naturally skeptical," Garth said, "and if anyone else had said this sort of thing I might not have believed it. In fact, I would probably run away. But here and now it all fits. It makes sense, even the revelations. I could not have imagined in the past that politics and love could mix. In fact I would say that politics would kill a love affair or that a campaign manager who is in love with his candidate would do poorly in each situation. But in this case it strikes me as perfect. It is almost as if everything that has happened in my life has led to this moment."

"I want to know everything you know, Garth Teller."

"Okay, now that really is a little bit creepy," he said, as he smiled and hugged her, "but I also know exactly what you mean. I will tell you this much now. If you want to know what I know, it means that you will have to read, and read a lot."

She was still perched over him on her elbow. His hair was a little too long and he was in need of a haircut and he knew this because it was now tousled and matted on his forehead. He felt he looked a wreck. But she on the other hand, though in her early thirties, was cast in so handsome and striking a mold that she seemed not far removed from her days as a college athlete. So smooth and supple, so vibrant and dynamic, she seemed less modern and real and human and more in manner of an Artemis or Athena. The worldly intelligence that was imprinted on her physiognomy and that shone in her green eyes also seemed to hint that the rough creatures of this world could not really be her companions. A thousand illuminations played about her eyes and face and smile and were complemented by an occasional fleeting shadow that was no less alluring or sympathetic than her brightness. She reached down with her free hand and, looking directly into his eyes, she brushed the hair from his forehead upon which then fell a tear, and then another.

Melinda's home was in Alexandria, Virginia, and it was very much the standard issue bungalow to be found in that town and in neighboring Arlington. It was a one-story wood home with two bedrooms and an unfinished basement in the Del Ray section of Alexandria. It had a front porch and a single windowed gable in the center of the front roof. The line of the roof ran parallel to the road so that the single gable stared out at the street. It was not unlike the thousands of other bungalows that had been built in these towns and neighborhoods in the twenty years following World War Two in order to house the workers of the growing government. For the months following the evening of the shower incident, this unprepossessing home became the nexus of Garth's love life and what could be called the postgraduate education of Melinda Sherman. The majority of Garth's time was spent at his own modest rental home in Bethesda, Maryland, where he generally slept, raised his children and went to work in the local high school. Only on the alternate weekends, when his children stayed with their mother, did Garth stay with Melinda. The rest of the time she came to his home every evening but only for dinner. And then she would go to her home and she would call him after she knew that the children had gone to bed. Much of their relationship was courtly and old fashioned. They rarely showed their affection in front of his children. And they spent a great deal of their time and their love in conversation.

"I am not exactly sure what all this reading has to do with politics," she said to him over the phone one evening, "but I instinctively understand that it has a great deal to do with knowing what you know and with thinking the way you think. I certainly feel it is making me smarter and a better person and is bringing me closer to you."

"I am glad you see it that way," he said, "but I am sure that nothing could improve your native intelligence or your innate good character. You have led a life few of us will ever comprehend and it has given your strong native intellect and your instinctive insight a great deal of context and perspective. What reading, particularly deep reading, can give you is a better way to be with yourself. It can enhance your interior life in a way that allows you to relate what you read to what you have experienced. In a sense, reading is listening to yourself think. And you can gain a more complicated and nuanced understanding of life and of yourself from reading, but only from reading books that challenge you. I saw an article in the *New York Times* the other day. It said that people who read for the sake of reading are no different than people who do not read, but people who read great books and challenging literature actually become more thoughtful and intelligent."

"You're a bit of snob. Do you know that?"

"Only when it comes to reading and to literature."

"I know," she said. "You really are quite down to earth otherwise, for a snob, that is. But I am happy and proud to tell you tonight that I have finally read all of those Jane Austen books. I know that we have been talking about them, but you have been quite reticent. You only talk about the plot points and the characterizations. That has been helpful, I guess. She really is amazing at characterizations. Those people in those books, they seem like real people, like you know people like them."

"That is certainly one of her strong suits," he said. "She is like Shakespeare or Tolstoy in that way. And that is saying a great deal."

"But now that I am finished with all of them I want to know what you think."

"Tell me what you think, first. And I will let you know."

"Okay, Mr. Harvard man, but you are making me feel like I am taking a test?"

"No, my love, I am the one taking the test. I hope I measure up to the task that is set before me by your confidence, your love, your compassion and your potential."

"Jesus, where did you come from? Who are you? You really are something," she almost sighed into the phone. "I guess I know why they make so many movies from the Jane Austen novels. They are such great romances."

"Do you mean that the movies are great romances, or the books?" he asked.

"I know you well enough to know that is a trick question. So, I guess I have to say that it is the movies that are really the romances. Right?"

"Well, those movies certainly do play up the romance aspect. And there is no doubt that the movies play to the vast numbers of Austen fans who only see the romance. In fact, a huge army of women who do not read her very closely or very well supports the entire Austen industry. They only see that the heroine gets the man in the end. They do not pay attention to who the heroine really is or what she does."

"Well, she does get the man."

"But she never goes after him. And a romance would be about getting the man, or about the circumstances surrounding that. There is so much more to that in all of her novels, more about the character of the woman. The heroine does not really care only about getting the man or completing the romance. She is about something else."

"I guess," she said, "that in *Pride and Prejudice*, she certainly rejects him at first."

"Exactly, she not only rejects him, she does it with finality. She does not tell him that if he improves himself that she will change her mind. She tells him to hit the road, forever. The story could end there. And she does this even though her family, her friends, and society would tell her to go ahead and marry the rich and handsome Mr. Darcy. In fact, every convention of a romance would have her just marry him then and there."

"But she does not think it would be right."

"Now you have got it," he said. "Austen heroines always only do what only they think is right, and always against the grain. Those novels are about having character, doing the right thing in the face of everyone and everything pushing the heroines to do the easy or romantic thing."

"I see that," she said, "and in *Persuasion*, her own heart is also telling her to tell Captain Wentworth that she loves him. But that would not be right, because she had rejected him earlier. So she does not do it."

"See, you do understand the truth beneath the surface. They are not romances. They are guides to having the strength to do what you alone think is right."

"But the girl always gets the guy in the end."

"That is what makes it fiction, I think. I don't know, but I think Austen has each book end that way to show that there is a reward for doing the right thing."

"Yeah," she said, "but I have to tell you, it is not always that you get the guy."

"No, doing the right thing is pretty much its own reward. But the implication here for life and even for politics is to look, and to think, more deeply. It is the only way to really understand something."

"You know something Garth?"

"What?"

He was waiting for her to compliment him, to express her love for his mind.

"I am wearing those clown pajamas. I always wear them now when I sleep alone at my own house. They remind me of how special you are."

"Oh, God, what an image. So it is me . . . and the entire women's track team at Kentucky, all rolled into one clownish symbol."

"That is fitting," she said, "although I am not sure exactly why it is, but it just fits. Maybe I should think more deeply about it and talk to you about it, tomorrow at dinner."

"I love you," he said.

"Of course you do," she answered.

The conversation from there is not one that may be accurately nor tastefully depicted. But it is one about which most adults may accurately speculate, based upon their own experiences. Garth hung up the phone and not more than a minute after that it rang again. He smiled as he picked it up.

"Hey, 'Send in the Clowns,' I love you," he said.

"I love you too, Teller. I always have. You're one of a god damn kind. You know that?" a decidedly masculine voice said. "But let's not get carried away."

It was Chip Mathers, who was no longer working at the office of the Speaker of the US House of Representatives, but who was still very much connected to the upper echelons of Democratic politics, as a consultant.

"Oh, Chip, sorry, I was . . ."

"Forget about it. It's late. I just wanted to be the first to tell you. That Congressional Medal of Honor ceremony will be next week in the White House. You can call 'Sentient Clowns' and tell her about it. Or you can wait until she gets the call herself from the President tomorrow."

"Oh, I would not intrude on that for anything. But I thought it would take . . ."

"About a year and a half," said Chip. "That's right. But shit happens fast in this town when it needs to. So all of it, the Member of Congress, the chain of command, the Secretary of the Navy, the Joint Chiefs, Human Resources, the Decoration Board, the President, the whole shebang, was pulled together in six months. Our friend, the Gentleman from Texas, your old Congressman, was working overtime. Deals were made. People want her to succeed."

"Holy hell," Garth said, "I guess it is all going to happen now."

"The rest is up to you, Teller, to the two of you, that is. You make quite a pair, you with both feet on the ground, her in mid-air. Or is it the other way around? Have a good evening."

And so, it did happen. That is, the first element fell into place. That next week, Melinda was recognized for the hero that she was, in a widely reported White House ceremony. Of course, it changed many things in very many important and significant ways that play a major role in all that was to follow. But it had one other small but significant effect and that was one in the Teller household. It happened at breakfast one day before the ceremony but after the announcement of the ceremony.

"I think that Melinda can move in with us now, Dad," Hanna said.

"Oh, we are not sure you guys are ready for that," Garth answered.

Hanna had a look on her face that can only be described as playfully or lovingly offended. Seth was simply smiling.

"You are either stupid or you think we are stupid, if you think that we do not know that the two of you are already married," she said.

"How do you know that?"

"Well, I think that the wedding ring and the engagement ring she always wears might have been a good clue," Hanna said.

"And it was in the papers, Dad," Seth added. "We are not little kids anymore. We are eleven and thirteen. We can read."

"Oh," Garth said.

ONLY THE INNOCENT
MAY FEEL INJUSTICE

The tall, lanky man got into rental car at the Louisville airport and started his drive to London. Along the highways and back roads he passed through the dreary rolling hills and tedious sylvan landscapes that darken that part of southeastern Kentucky. Melancholy horse farms with their sad white fences and miserable stallions and suspicious mares and rank colts menaced him from the roadsides wherever the gloom of the forests would temporarily withdraw. Crude and unruly wildflowers straggled along the roadside under the bright oppression of the rudely staring sun. An occasional farmer would scowl at the car and its driver from behind her sharp and threatening tools. Bleak and unwelcoming fields yawned at him from both sides of the roads. Low slung houses hunkered under the crests of the dark hills and the cruel wisps of summer clouds, as if they were beaten into submission. The town of London glowered before him on the dull plain between two rough ridges. The air seemed sour and the rustling of the leaves sounded like recriminations. And so it is that the subtle influence of our own demeanor and nature stimulates the very conditions and appearances of external objects to appear as spectral reflections of our own thoughts. The traveler who looked upon that natural environment and the creatures that peopled it was struck by how disconsolate and shadowy they appeared. He was seeing it all correctly and clearly, but the shades and the desolation were the products of his own jaded and distrustful soul. To have seen the authentic colors of this honest place would have taken a much more unblemished perspective, one that Earnest Dapple simply could not conjure.

He was not at all surprised by the bleak and foreboding effect that this place had on his heart. It was where Melinda Sherman had been born and had grown up. There were traces of her here and there, from the schools he knew she had attended to the places he knew she had visited. On some of the walls and telephone poles were the written and graphic vestiges of notices that had proclaimed the recent ceremony for a visiting hometown hero that London had for her. These also curdled his spirit. Earnest had a proclivity toward revulsion and he regularly disparaged any individual's personal success. He even despaired of simple human contact. The things that others liked about Melinda, her strength and forthrightness and her handsome beauty and her courage, exercised a kind of cruel taunting on his sensibilities. The love that she and his former classmate shared struck him as forced and false. This is to say that Mr. Dapple was a misanthrope and a malcontent at the core. He hated a great deal more than most men, which is a statement that is true in at least two ways. This is not a criticism of his personality and character but it is something more along the lines of a professional requirement. Any numbers of respected and famous journalists are the possessors of exactly these same first-rate qualities, though they humbly mask them from their ardent admirers.

He was onto the track of something. He believed that the shiniest and freshest appearing fruit tended to disguise worms and rot. He had an optimistic and affirmative faith in the hidden motives of the best people and in the skeletons that he was certain were in the closets of the finest and most upright homes. This particular scent trail brought him to London, even before Garth and Melinda had been able to fully complete their move there. He knew that Garth had once been a skilled professional at putting up smoke screens and dragging a red herring across the trail, as well as he knew that the presence of Melinda in town would make the inhabitants whom he might question think first to speak to her before answering. He had already been to Lexington, where he had searched the records at the University of Kentucky and had found some information that he found to be quite interesting, relating to Caroline Collins. He had retraced his steps to Louisville and had interviewed Ms. Collins. His supposed cover story changed depending on his interview subject and in this instance he had told that lady he was doing a feature story on Melinda. Normally, he found that his personal attractions were effective in getting less sophisticated folks to open up to him and he felt he was particularly charming to the yokel women. But in this case, Ms. Collins was resistant and rather taciturn. He was just as interested in what she had not told him as he was in what he was able to get her to say.

This part of North America is known for its farms and horses but it is also sits atop tens of billions of tons of bituminous coal. The mines of London's Laurel County alone had yielded several dozen millions of tons of valuable low sulfur coal and had provided jobs for thousands of miners. One such miner today was not digging for coal. He was seeking a deep vein of information about Melinda Sherman, one that no other reporter might even know existed. He had dug exploratory holes and had done geological surveys among the former parishioners and students who had known Melinda when she had grown up in London and he had become convinced that the discreet mineral he sought could be extracted in great volumes from Reverend Seymour Barton. Pick and shovel in hand, Earnest made his way to the offices of the Christian Community of London, Kentucky.

He found the Reverend waiting for him in his office. Barton still possessed a sharp-featured face and dark, penetrating eyes, surrounded by a nimbus of aging flesh. He was almost bald, with a few strands of gray hair behaving like standing-room-only customers at the theater of his head; that is, they were scattered mainly at the sides and back. A ponderous man, the Reverend was unlikely to ever move from his chair behind his desk and had in fact not risen to shake Earnest's hand. Earnest looked blankly at this bulk sitting before him and he saw only what he considered to be the mother lode. He had told the Reverend that he was researching the role of faith in the lives of members of the military services.

"So Melinda Sherman was sort of in your church for several years, right?"

"Well," the Reverend began, "yes, Melinda was a blessed member of our Christian Community. In fact, she first came to the word of the Lord here with us. And she found her calling here as well."

The substance of this response was more positive than Earnest had expected. The tone in which it was cloaked sounded completely unlike a mining instrument striking a deep and rich vein of secret information. On the surface it appeared to Earnest as if the Reverend were congratulating him upon being admitted into a club. The reporter was worldly enough that his own defensive ironies were fully engaged by this routine and he was aware that, rather than an admission or an opening being before him, his pick and shovel had struck an adamantine barrier. Earnest would swing his pick one more time before he would resort to explosives.

"I understand that this is where she had several of her so-called 'visions' of Christ," Earnest said.

"The Spirit of the Lord comes to all of us in different manners," the Reverend said, "even as it came to Melinda."

"Well, isn't it actually the case that Melinda Sherman fabricated one of these visions to embarrass you in front of your congregation and that she did this all to protect her homosexual brother from your unwelcome advances?"

"Have you accepted the Lord Jesus Christ into your life as your Lord and Savior, Mr. Dapple?"

"If you mean am I a Christian, yes. I was raised in the Episcopal Church."

"I do not think that infant baptism counts, Mr. Dapple. The Lord is a mystery far too deep for a child to understand. That is part of what Ms. Sherman saw that day in our Community service, when she cited Matthew 10:34 and Mark 2:12. She was saying that not all of us can find our way to Christ's truth. We here at the Christian Community of London, Kentucky are proud of the contribution we have made to the faith and life of Melinda Sherman. And that is about it, all in a nutshell. So if there is nothing else, we are happy to have helped you," the Reverend said.

"Just one more question," Earnest said as he stood to leave. "How much have your attendance and contribution levels increased since it has been reported that Melinda Sherman attended this church?"

"Community, Mr. Dapple, we call it a Christian community, and the Lord works in mysterious ways, Mr. Dapple, as I think I have already said."

Earnest considered for a moment that the history of religion and spirituality are more a matter of the holy profits than some people imagine.

There were many scenes in London, Kentucky that looked like an auction of Norman Rockwell paintings at Christie's. There were pretty clapboard houses and white picket fences, freckle-faced boys and friendly postmen, people fishing and shopkeepers greeting patrons, young couples embracing and small black girls in white dresses going to church, boys playing baseball and girls plaiting each other's braids, old-fashioned churches and one story schoolhouses, young couples in convertibles and women carrying bags of groceries.

These scenes repulsed Earnest Dapple.

There were even Boy Scouts and kindly old men. But there were other scenes, seemingly taken out of a documentary on Rust Belt decay. His particular aesthetic more or less embraced these. There were closed shops and faded signs, abandoned motels and old cars held together with duct tape, boarded up homes and untended junk yards, overgrown cemeteries and long unemployment lines. His heart practically soared on lofty spiritual winds to see the home where Melinda had grown up and where her mother still lived. Slanting into disorder, it looked as if it were about to concede defeat to the unkempt ground on which it stood. No birds or light or joy or flowers seemed to exist within its dour orbit. It was a damper on all affection and good spirits. To Earnest, it was exactly where he wanted to dig.

He made no subtle maneuvers. He told Angelina Bol Sherman that he was writing a story about her, that all the stories about her daughter had been written and he was focusing on the more interesting and important tale, that of her mother, the truly heroic one who had survived Nazi occupation and Communist rule.

"I actually escaped the Communists," she said.

He was to spend many long hours laboring in the information mines at this sorrowful home, the inside of which was even more despairing than the exterior. He would sit upon the cracked plastic slipcovers and pretend to drink tea out of a filth-stained cup as he also would pretend not to notice that the cat seemed to have the run of the countertops and tabletops in the kitchen. The older Sherman woman was slovenly dressed and he had to avoid looking at the various and alarming parts of her which would occasionally be revealed by the sloppy application of her worn out attire. She was in her way a human version of the exterior and interior of the dilapidated home. What had once been her diminutive figure was now merely lank and bony and stooped. Her youthful delicate features had become pinched and distorted and where her eyes had once reflected a vibrant luster they were now the twin lights of a distorted and unnatural aversion. Her fair skin was simply pale. Her blonde hair had thinned and grayed. Where her countenance had been alive with a deceptive cheer, its beauty gone, it now was worn into a scowl of near helplessness under a reign of dogged suffering, the horrid endurance of cruelty real and imagined, historical and current. She cast her leaden eye on Earnest as he asked his questions.

"Had the Germans actually come into your home?"

"It was all such a long time ago," she answered.

"What do you remember of the Russian occupation?"

"They replaced the Germans."

He asked if she were lonely, living in London by herself. He asked her how she and her husband had met, when Porter and Melinda had been born, whether she worked while they were growing up, what had the town been like then, had she and her husband given the children a religious upbringing, how old had she been when she came to America, whether she remembered her brothers and sisters in Poland and if she was still in touch with them. She treated each question as if she were drunk or half asleep and he was a police interrogator. Her answers were slow and halting and not to the point. He possessed a certain classic and sophisticated journalistic skill, which was to return to the same questions over and over when confronted with incomplete answers. He had found that many people would become exasperated and would simply blurt out what he had wanted to hear, or they would forget to be evasive. But the former Aniolek Bol could not forget that she was the one who was always exasperated. Her young life had been disfigured by an unimaginable oppression and it had sharpened her senses to the point that when she was older she was perfectly able to imagine it even where it did not exist.

Though the word "spite" is very simple and short, as is often the case with such Anglo-Teutonic root words, it has an effect and power that are as long and as complicated as any Latinate polysyllabic word in the language. It gave Melinda's mother that particular brand of persuasion that is most effective upon the self. She felt she had been martyred long past the time of her original sacrifice. So the presence of this attractive and very insistent younger man was almost not within her notice. The first day continued and ended in much this manner. He was sparring with phantoms. She was barely seeing or hearing him.

On the second day of his interview he began in much the same mode, questioning her about her past and her feelings then and now. He was met with much the same response. He had been convinced that he would only succeed if he maintained the fiction that he was only writing a story about Angelina Sherman. He had simply known that to question her about Melinda would be to engage her defensiveness and her protective maternal instincts. But he was getting nowhere with this woman. In what was either a capitulation or a spasm of anger, he abandoned what he knew was his only chance at mining the information gold he sought and he recklessly tossed his mining tools into the air. He knew he could never directly approach the particular topic about which he actually wanted know. But it was a lost cause anyway, or so he thought.

"Have you seen your daughter lately?"

"Her? I haven't seen her in years. She has never deigned to visit here, at least not since she moved away. She was always too busy with school or sports or with the Navy. I only hear about her from her brother. She did not even come here to my home to visit when she was in town briefly for her big hero ceremony. But I am supposed to meet her soon, her and her husband, when they move here. Porter says she has promised that much. Porter says her husband wants to meet me."

"Please don't tell any of them that you and I have talked," Earnest said. "I want this story to only be about you. I don't want any of their input. And besides, your daughter may be a little jealous of you."

"Oh, that one was always jealous of me. I don't mind telling you that. She was after my husband most of the time, trying to cut me out."

"I see."

"Do you want something to drink?"

"Only if you do."

She went to the kitchen and returned with a bottle of vodka and two unmatched and unwashed glasses. At least, Earnest thought, the vodka will disinfect whatever was in that glass. He took a sip and it burned his tongue and mouth and throat. He was not used to drinking any liquor straight. Angelina Sherman stretched her legs and arms as she downed the first glass. Some of her old color and vitality returned to her skin and face. She stood up and walked around the room in order to facilitate more leg stretching and she began to hold forth on the neighborhood, the children were all thieves. She commented on television, everything on it was a lie. Other topics she breached were the government, which was run by minorities, and love, which was a fiction. She looked at Earnest more as she stretched her thin legs walking about the room, as if she were seeing him for the first time. She smiled and began to ask him questions about himself. He answered her only to keep her talking and ended each answer with some reference to Melinda or to Garth. But these were not themes upon which she ever expounded. At some point her legs had stretched too much so she sat on the floor with her legs tucked under her.

She had a desolate and inattentive look on her face, except when she turned toward him. She continued to speak, saying very little of interest to him. Even though he had not even finished his first glass, his attention began to wander. And then at one point he unexpectedly found that she had crawled across the floor to him and was suddenly between his knees.

"I love you, Earnest."

He quickly lifted her up to the couch and wiped her forehead. She sat quietly for a while. Earnest knew that from such squalid depths were great discoveries often made in this business of mining. He believed that he was perched only a shovel thrust above the Comstock Lode or that he was at Sutter's Mill late in the evening of January twenty-third, 1848. Then she spoke and with a stunning lucidity and sober expressiveness, as if she were not merely recalling some past event but as if she were repeating a long remembered litany that recounted an experience she had extensively considered worth remembering.

"The sky was blue and the air was hot and dry, but the water was cold," she said. "It was also high for that time of year, late summer. We were unprepared. We hit the rapids at around noon and we made it through them, bouncing off of submerged rocks and sluicing through the swift channels between them. The water flattened and we relaxed and even celebrated. The next thing I knew I was in the river, struggling to keep my head up in the swirling, foaming water. I watched William paddle to the shore before I was trapped in a hydraulic."

"This was in the Laurel River, nearby here?"

"No, it was the Guadalupe River, in Texas. The force of the water pushed me under the surface and held me there. I knew enough not to fight against it. I swam downward and downstream. I came to the surface quite far downstream and in the middle of the swiftly moving current. The banks were undercut and there was no place to climb out. I was also being knocked and bruised by tree trunks and branches floating in the current. Then river had narrowed and the banks were like cliffs. The water moved even more swiftly. Before I knew it another set of rapids was upon me. I bounced off the rocks and debris. I struggled to keep my head up and my feet down and toward downstream. I had to struggle each time to get a clear breath of air."

"The Guadalupe River must be more than a thousand miles from here," Earnest said.

"We used to go there every summer," she said. "I was inhaling water, choking on it. I felt myself getting weaker. My will power was fading. I had a vague sense of the river widening and the water flattening and slowing down, but I was mainly aware that I was drowning. Then I was barely conscious of being pulled from the water. It was a man. That was all I could tell. He pulled me to the bank and left me there to go get a blanket, which he then laid on the bank. He moved me onto the blanket and dragged me up to his campsite. I could tell he was bandaging my head. He wrapped the blanket around me and put some logs on the fire. I did not wake up until the next day."

"Was this a long time ago?"

"It was the summer before Melinda was born. It was the last time we vacationed there. When I woke up the next morning I was confused. I did not know how I had come to be there, in a rustic camp cabin with an unfamiliar man. I was wearing his clothes. It was his fishing camp. He was a much older man, in his late sixties but still virile and good looking in a gaunt way, like an old cowboy. He gave me coffee and some biscuits and gravy. I began to remember pieces of the previous day. I knew I had to get back to my husband. This man had saved me, I remembered, at the exact moment when I would have drowned. He took my clothes down from a line where they had dried and he began to help me take off his clothes, which I was wearing. At some point I think he began to force himself on me or I just let him take me. I do not remember which. I do know I was grateful. And the entire thing was like a dream. I felt that he had been placed there for a reason. I either let him take me or I barely resisted. It just felt to me like the most pure and elemental connection I had ever had to any man. He had saved my life and I redeemed his effort. We did not speak after that. We did not talk about what had happened or about the day before. It was like he was reading my thoughts. He just dressed me and took me in his car to my husband."

"Have you ever talked to anyone else about this?"

"No, not even to my husband. We never spoke about it even for the years afterward. He died without us ever discussing it. You are the first. I don't know why I am telling you. Maybe it is because you are writing a story about me for the *Washington Post*. Maybe there is another reason. Maybe it is because I like you. Maybe it is just time for it to be told."

Earnest gave Mrs. Sherman his telephone number and asked her to call him anytime and to particularly call him after she saw her daughter. And he reminded her to keep their conversation between the two of them.

Tommy Kitt was not all that familiar with the ways of the world. As in this case, such a phrase is customarily used not to refer merely to the globe but to the rascals and rogues who comprise much of its population. This was not the problem one might imagine it to be for the unsophisticated Tommy. He had long been in the habit of acting merely upon his impulses without recourse to the complicated weighing and measuring of those things that might not be readily apparent. Fortunately for him and for those in his life and surroundings, those impulses were largely of a compassionate nature and were protective and honest and generous to a remarkable degree, so his lack of sophistication rarely had any adverse impact. Naturally, he was inclined to be kind and open to the affable and attractive and well-dressed man who now stood in his doorway, who was also in all respects quite worldly. Tommy's inherent liberality extended itself an additional notch for those who were young or poor or lost or mentally challenged or whom he saw as otherwise disadvantaged, such as in this case. The man before him was apparently African-American. That Earnest Dapple, who had knocked on the door to the Kitt family home which Tommy had answered, was a man of color was the first thing Tommy noticed. The remaining details of Earnest's appearance only occurred to him later, after Earnest had begun to speak.

"Mr. Kitt, I am a reporter from the *Washington Post*. My name is Earnest Dapple. I would like to ask you a few questions. May I come in? I am here to research a story on your friend, Melinda Sherman."

Later, as Earnest gradually picked himself up from the Kitt front porch, being careful with the hip he had injured in the fall, and nursing his sore mid-section, he could have had no idea what Tommy Kitt had been thinking during that introduction and explanation he had just given to Melinda's friend from childhood. Earnest actually tried to contemplate what might have crossed Tommy's mind and in this consideration he was well north of the locus of Tommy's decision, if it could be called that. Tommy moved from the heart and it was a stout organ as much as it was an empathetic one. It had taken Tommy the few moments which had been required for Earnest to speak his first three sentences to observe the way that reporter's clothes hung so perfectly on him, to notice the self-satisfied look on his face, and to compare what he knew of Melinda's character with what his instinct told him about this tall and urbane man in front of him. So by the time the name of his friend from childhood had passed from the lips of this worldly man, Tommy's fist had pounded itself honestly and generously into Earnest's gut. Earnest may have been confused but he was not completely surprised and he did not react vengefully. Only the innocent may feel injustice.

And in what was to be a very remarkable week for Mr. Kitt, Earnest Dapple was only the first stranger to show up at his door, asking questions.

A PERSONAL GUARANTEE

"Why the hell would you ever call her? We both know nothing good can ever come from it," Eakin said.

"But I have to talk to Tabitha about the kids. Melinda and I will be moving to Kentucky temporarily. Hanna and Seth will have to come with me for the spring. But it may be better for them to spend the summer with her. It will give me more time to focus on running the campaign over the summer and it will recompense her for missing her alternate weekends of visitation during the spring and the following fall."

"Repeat after me: Nothing good can ever come from you talking to your ex-wife. Why are you Harvard men so stupid?"

"You went there too."

"We both know that graduate school does not count."

These last three sentences were an oft-repeated litany in many of their discussions, including this particular long phone conversation.

"I think you might be a little bit jaded, Eakin, by your own experience."

"What happened when you talked to her the first time about the fact that she was not paying her share of the children's joint expenses?"

"She sued me, to claim that the coaching and singing lessons were not valid expenses."

"What happened when you talked to her about Hanna's summer camp?"

"She sued me, to make me send Hanna to horse camp instead of math camp."

"And what happened when you spoke to her the second time about her not paying her share of the joint expenses?"

"She sued me, claiming that Seth did not need a science tutor."

"Are you even beginning to see a pattern here? So just take the kids to Kentucky. She is going to sue you anyway. Why make yourself suffer? And why let her get the jump on you?

"I just feel that I have to be the one to try to normalize the relationship between the two parents of our children."

"Are you even listening to me? Have you been paying attention to your own life? Nothing good can ever come from it, nothing good."

Garth remembered that Dick Trent had used nine lawyers to sue Eakin thirteen times over the previous ten years, so he figured she was cynical for that reason. And he preferred to err on the side of doing the right thing, especially in matters relating to Hanna and Seth. So, he would choose to discuss his plans with Tabitha, against Eakin's advice. And his lawyer ex-wife would sue him. But the judge would allow him to do as he suggested. He would take the kids to Kentucky with him. They would spend the summer in Washington with their mom, or more accurately, spend their summer days with their mom's nanny. And they would return to be with him for the fall school semester. Tabitha would also again then stop paying her share of the expenses. Melinda and he would set up house in London, Kentucky, where they would begin her campaign for Congress. Hanna would embrace the change and would thrive, as she always reacted to any change. Seth would be a bit lost, more so than he usually was, and Garth would not really notice, much to his regret later.

"So, Eakin," he said, changing the subject, "how are you doing down there with my friend Elliott?"

"That guy is a profligate wastrel, which is another Harvard prototype. Give him ten dollars and he will spend twelve. Take him to a tavern and he will close it down, but not before becoming the owner's good friend, buying everyone there at least one drink, and making at least one waitress fall in love with him. He has more appetites than all the starving souls in India. He has the energy of a nuclear reactor but only for diversions and detours and altercations."

"Elliott was never one to get involved in altercations."

"You are right. But they always seem to spring up around him. He is like Odysseus. He is magnificent and heroic when you see him sailing across the horizon. But if you happen to be in the boat with him you are the one to pay the price."

"Still there are plenty of people more than willing to get into that boat, perhaps you for instance. Has my 'magnificent and heroic' friend 'made' you fall in love with him yet, Eakin?"

"Jesus Christ, Garth, his definition of money is 'something you throw off the back of trains.' If he ever wins the lottery, he will buy all his friends a house."

"First of all and again, that is not a denial on your part, Eakin. And secondly, that sounds like you think he is pretty generous."

"It is not exactly generous; it is lavish. And I had only one love in me. And that has already been spent."

"Perhaps that is better. It would be the thing to protect you in a relationship with him."

"I am not interested in being a mother to another male. I already have three sons. And there is always you, Garth. How the hell could I look after you, if I had some other waif in my life?"

"That is another non-denial denial."

"I'll tell you what, though. I let your friend, Elliott, have some of my company's cash to manage and he made some damn gamble on some Wall Street derivative or whatever and he doubled it in two weeks. It was good, I guess, but it scared the hell out of me."

"He knows how to make money, you know, before he throws it off the back of a train."

"I will give him that much. But even that is a problem. It was easy for him, the whole money thing. There is money in his smile, money in his gait, money in his posture. There is even money in his voice. Who the hell has money in their voice?"

"Daisy Buchanan," Garth answered.

"Whatever, but I will be damned if I will let him turn this manufacturing company of mine into some kind of a parasite financial institution."

"It sounds as though he gets your blood up, Eakin. That may be either good or bad, but it is not a neutral thing. Hey, wait a minute. My doorbell is ringing. I have to go answer it. I will call you later."

"That will be your other friend, the other one you sent to me, Ben Dessous. He left here this morning to come to visit you. Now, he is nothing but a net positive and a bit of a savant. He said he had to go up there to help you. Don't tie him up too long. Even though I know you always need some kind of help, he is far too productive down here."

"Thanks for the timely heads-up, old friend."

As he walked to the front door Garth realized that one of the indications of Eakin's potent and persistent love for him was the fact that she had never once shown him the slightest ounce of sympathy. When he lost his job, she did not console him. When Tabitha filed for divorce, she did not comfort him. She had never offered him solace at any of his professional or personal setbacks. It was a window into her self-image. She knew life ahead presented too many difficulties to ever waste time looking back. And she always treated Garth in the way he knew he should consistently see himself, as a winner, as a person for whom the greatest apparent impediments were simply bumps in the road. It was perhaps her greatest gift to him.

He was a little gray around the temples and wore more expensive clothes but he was still tall and thin and he still bore his trademark scars, across an eyebrow and the other on his cheek. There remained a mysterious hardness to his appearance. And his eyes had direct intensity and purpose. Garth himself had changed enough to realize that there had always been wisdom in that gaze.

Ben and Garth had not seen one another for almost twenty years. Garth had been getting periodic reports from Eakin about how instrumental he and his advice had been in developing her business after the original company that had made her its president had released her. After she had seemed to land on her feet with a Taiwanese joint venture, he had convinced her to start her own American production line and had helped to manage it. He had helped Elliott avoid his personal version of a collection agency. And he had done innumerable other useful and expedient things for Eakin professionally. For this reason and due to the heightened circumstances of Ben's and Garth's earlier involvement, those twenty years could have been twenty days. Ben looked and felt familiar to Garth.

For Ben, Garth was even more memorable. Ben had come to the United States from St. Croix with younger siblings and his mother, who had brought them to America to escape her violent and abusive husband. They made the significant jump from Latin American poverty to North American poverty. From the beginning, even in St. Croix, it had been Ben's role to try to protect his mother and his little sisters and brother. When they settled without their father within the small Crucian community within the Dorchester section of Boston, his instinct to protect and to help had grown stronger. It had dominated his life throughout the youth of his younger siblings and right up to the moment he had met Garth, who may not have been the first well-off white man Ben ever knew. But in that one night Garth and Ben had established a deep channel of nonverbal communication and they had probably saved one another's lives. Garth never saw him as anything but a comrade. And then Garth had trusted him to the care of Eakin and she had given him entrée into the world of business and commerce and safe neighborhoods. Garth had assumed Ben was not at all separate from all that the respectable world is.

Eakin had been a revelation, one that was derived from Garth, a white woman who did what powerful men did and who saw him only as a friend and an associate and who expected him to see her in the same way. Garth had been the opening to a new path. These people, Eakin, Garth, Elliott and their friends certainly did not need Ben's help, but for some reason they had still ignited that deepest instinct within him. There was something about each of them that was a little too blithe. He was moved to protect them from their own lack of fear for what the world could do. This urge was no more powerful than it was with respect to Garth.

Ben had arrived at Garth's door at the end of an eventful journey, which had begun with a conversation with Elliott and Eakin in her office. From there, he traveled to Garth's hometown in Texas and to London, Kentucky, then to Boston and eventually to New York. He made a few other stops before he ended his odyssey in Washington and Bethesda, at Garth's home. When Garth had opened the front door it was apparent that the slightly younger white man felt the urge to hug Ben, but a short communication sent over the silent wavelength to which they alone were tuned told Garth to belay that impulse. Standing behind Garth was a handsome and striking younger woman, one who would have stood out to Ben even in a large crowd.

Melinda's initial impressions of African American men had been limited by the experience common among attractive middle-class white girls in the South. One night when she was sixteen and her car had run out of gas on a deserted country road and she saw a truck full of boys coming down the road, she had been relieved to see that they had been black. A gang of white boys might have flirted with her, or worse. But these young men of color treated her with the deference they knew was required to place their behavior well beyond the disapproval of any of the old bigots who were still in great number. The black men she met at the University of Kentucky were mostly athletes. Her college classmates were gentleman, which were understatements in describing the African American men she came into contact with in the Navy. It was only in her later personal life and only the neighborhoods at some distance from those in which she lived that she had come into contact with urban African American men from the northern United States. This particular man was unique among all of her understandings.

Separate experiences had conspired to give this mundane meeting between three people a heightened and memorable aspect for each one of them, but even they could not know how critical this moment would later become. One of them already had a good idea that it would.

"It is great to see you, Ben. This is Melinda Sherman, my wife," Garth said.

"I consider it an honor to meet you, ma'am. You look very well, Garth, I am contented to see you so thriving," Ben said.

"I am happy to meet you, Ben," she answered, "Garth has told me a lot about you. He holds you in high esteem. Please, call me Melinda. And come inside. We can sit in the living room here. Would you like something to drink?"

"Yes, ma'am, I will call you Melinda. And just some water, please. Your brother, by the way, sends his regards. And so does Tommy Kitt."

"I guess you have been busy lately," Garth said. "Eakin tells me you had a conversation with her and Elliott and that it made you decide to do some legwork."

"I had already decided to embark on a research journey. Talking with your two friends was merely the initial stage. I want to do all that is within my power to assist both you and your wife. Eakin has helped with some preliminary information and has been astute enough to assess that my assistance will be worthwhile, so she has given me leave to do what I can. It is as much her effort as it is my own."

"I really appreciate your concern and helpfulness, Ben. But I am pretty sure that we do not need any help," Garth said.

Melinda returned to the living room with a glass of water for Ben.

"Garth, your oldest and best friend has disagreed with that statement in advance and also had predicted you would say it. And thank you, Melinda, for the water. I have just arrived from meeting your brother in New York because I knew he would be the optimal source of information regarding your mother. Apparently, she has received a visit from our old friend, the reporter, Earnest Dapple. The indomitable Mr. Kitt and several of Melinda's other friends from college and her childhood have been visited too."

"What?" Garth said. "That makes no sense. What interest could a major national newspaper have in the background of one candidate for Congress? Even if he were to make some kind of story out of it, it would not be big enough for *The Washington Post*."

"Earnest discerns what you and I also recognize, which is also understood by a small handful individuals, including your Congressman friend and Chip Mathers. The political horizons are unlimited for Melinda. Mr. Dapple is planning for the future. Your wife will become a story much larger than a Congressional district in Kentucky."

"That Medal of Honor story was only a few paragraphs on page three of the national newspapers," Melinda said.

"Yeah," Garth said, turning to her, "but it will make you special at every level to which you move."

"Women have run for high office already," Ben said, looking at Melinda.

"One or more have had military service. Many have been young. Some have been good-looking. But you are all of that and more, Melinda. You are strikingly attractive. You have depth. You will represent part of a conservative southern border state. You have strong Christian credentials. And you are a Medal of Honor winner. Women will want to be you. Men will want to know you. There has never been a candidate like you. You represent a sea change, and change is what many people want. But you will not seem to threaten the values of the older establishment, as so many candidates of change can do."

"If Earnest is onto the scent of something, it is not a good thing," Garth said.

"I am here to promise both of you of two things with regard to that. The first one is that you can be assured that I will monitor him. The second one is that I personally guarantee that he will never hurt you. Now, I am afraid that I must take my leave of you soon. Melinda, would you allow me several moments alone with your husband?"

"Certainly, Ben," she said as she walked over and shook his hand warmly, "I hope to see you again sometime soon."

"Perhaps not soon, but again, Melinda, I am sure," he said.

Ben turned to Garth and looked at him gravely.

"You who are quite accustomed to exquisite things do not often recognize the pitfalls and iniquities that lurk upon the byways of the world. This is a singularly significant endeavor upon which you are about to embark, Garth. It is one well beyond my own reach, but some of the potential problems of it are well within my grasp. Your friend, Eakin, has put it this way: 'Tell Garth not to blow it.' I think that may be just a bit too succinct for you, and coming from her, too familiar for you to take as seriously as you should. But you and I have a different history. So I must tell you. What you are about to undertake is far more dangerous and important than what you had done for me that night so long ago. This is the most solemn and sublime task you could ever undertake. It is an opportunity to change everything. I would not be applying myself to your assistance, were it not so. Approach it accordingly, with the utmost gravity."

"I really don't know what to say," Garth said.

"There really is nothing to say, or that you could be able to say without diminishing it."

"No kidding."

"There is one other thing," Ben said. "I am going to give you something to help you, something unusual and incredible. It is a drug."

"I don't do drugs anymore."

"I know. This is not like that. I am not talking about recreation. It does not affect you like any drug. And it is not illegal. In fact, it is not even really known and it will never be declassified."

"Declassified? What do you mean? How would you have come into contact with anything related to national security?"

"I am not exactly certain, myself," Ben said, "except that shortly after you graduated I was approached. I can only speculate as to how they became acquainted with me. My best guess is that our mutual friend, Earnest, must have said something to someone. I know you did not. Perhaps it was innocuous. I don't know. But I was specifically approached because they believed that I was intelligent and reliable and that I could serve as a liaison with the inner city."

"Wait. When you say 'they,' you mean the government. Can you be more specific? And why would any government agency want a liaison to the poor neighborhood, I mean, any agency concerned with national security?"

As Garth was asking this question, Ben looked at him steadily and sincerely in such a way that Garth understood that none of what Ben had said or was about to say was ironic or unconsidered or light-hearted.

"Elements of the National Security Agency established a laboratory and office complex in Boston at that time, to be near to Harvard and its researchers. They were developing highly specialized chemical warfare programs, but not the kind of which you might normally think. They were working on various discreet drugs and diseases that could be used covertly. Whenever they needed to do large-scale experiments, they did them in remote sections of Africa. But when they needed to fine-tune something or tweak it, they did their experiments in impoverished urban neighborhoods here, in this country. That is why they approached me."

"I don't see you testing diseases in your own neighborhood, Ben."

"I never did and I was given to understand that almost all the disease testing was done in Africa. I only worked with them on fine-tuning drugs."

"Wait a minute . . ."

"Yes, you are right. You have put two and two together. You were about to say, that is why the human immunodeficiency virus started in Africa and why it is only prevalent there. It is a disease that was created in an American lab."

"Still, that is hard to believe."

"Look at me, Garth. You have worked on Capitol Hill and you have an exceptional understanding of how the government works. Can you honestly tell me that such a thing is impossible?"

"I have learned not to dismiss any conspiracy off hand. That is for sure. I still can't see you giving experimental drugs to your neighbors."

"I never did that. I was given money to pay addicts and users to try what I was telling them were designer drugs. Anyone who participated did so voluntarily and all of the drugs were mild in their effect."

"What does this have to do with me? What drug are you thinking of giving to me now, and why?"

"They were working on a version of synthetic opiates that were combined with elements of sodium pentothal and amphetamines. The idea was to create a drug that was powerfully addictive but would discreetly encourage subjects to speak the truth. Introduce it into a Middle Eastern town and soon people are telling you where the terrorists are. But it did not work. They scrapped the program for that drug, based partly on my information, that is. All of the people who tried the drug reported to me that they felt nothing. And in fact they were right. It had no effect whatsoever on the users at all, at least not one that he or she could detect. I reported that and then they ran some of their own tests and came to the same conclusion. But they were doing their tests in a laboratory. My own tests were done in the neighborhood. And while my subjects reported that they had no reactions to the drug, a couple of them told me some interesting stories."

"I am certainly interested," Garth said.

"I knew you would be. And I also know that by telling you this I put both our lives in danger. But you and I can trust one another. What I did then was I tested the drug on myself and I found out its true effect. I had a hundred doses and then I put them away for the reason that they might have a use later. You and your wife and your political futures have turned out to be the reason."

"What do you call the drug and what does it do?"

"I call in Boz. Do you remember that old singer, songwriter, guitarist whose name was Boz Skaggs?"

"Yes. I am curious to see where this is going."

"Well, the gentlemen at NSA were trying to develop a version of skag, which is what the slang word for heroin was then. But they came up with something that was a seriously diluted upscale Caucasian version that was too mellow for anything and it certainly was not like heroin. So I called it Boz Skaggs, or just Boz, in the diminutive form."

"So you do have a sense of humor, after all."

"I fail to see what is so funny about that."

"Please, ignore me and just go on."

"What it really does is difficult to explain. It does not affect the user, but it affects everyone else who comes into contact with the user. It makes the user likeable, very likeable. It gives everyone who sees or hears the user a contact high; it makes them feel better just to be in contact. You can easily imagine the political uses of such a drug. I figure that you use twenty doses for the Congressional campaign, thirty for the Senatorial campaign and fifty to run Melinda for President."

"That is about the most insane thing I could have ever imagined," Garth said, "and I am not talking about the NSA developing HIV and testing it in Africa, or the story about the drugs they are trying to develop. I actually believe all that. I am talking about what you propose I do with this particular drug."

"I considered that, as well, before I determined to come here. You are just a little insane, on your own part. And both you and your wife have faced death. That gives one a perspective that some might consider extreme. There is nothing you cannot face. But I have to leave now. There are many things to which I must attend," Ben said. "You and I communicate the most important things we have to say to one another without speaking. We both know what you will do when I leave. Please take care of her, and yourself."

Garth said his farewell. He took Ben to the front door. And Ben was correct. They both knew exactly what Garth would do next.

ANY THIRTEEN-YEAR-OLD

The Porter Sherman Travelling Road Show was about to roll into Washington. His shots at big screen major movie stardom had fallen slightly short, and with a similar result he was also still shooting for his youth. He had continued to be cast in major roles in television shows that were filmed in New York. He was an important actor in Broadway comedies and dramas. He was given small roles in major motion pictures. But the longest running show was his daily life and he was taking it to visit his sister and to accompany her husband and Melinda on their move to London.

Prior to meeting his sister and her new husband for their journey from Washington to London, Porter made a side trip to the Washington National Zoo. He wanted to observe some of the Washington public or perhaps more accurately to be seen by the part of the public which might recognize him, and to delay his visit to his sister to the point where it would necessarily be thought of as "an entrance". He also wanted to use his own tardiness as a stimulus, to see and to judge the reaction to it by his new brother-in-law, to do something even at this late point in the game that might allow him to feel some independence from the merely chronologically younger sibling upon whom he once looked as his "little mother", and perhaps most importantly because both he and Jesus had an almost childlike interest in panda bears.

Porter persisted in denoting them as panda bears, while Jesus would insist that in scientific fact were really more closely related to raccoons. Jesus did know that in 1989 the giant panda had been officially named a member of the *Ursidae* family, but he did not allow that circumstance to impede his mocking spirit. He was relying on his lover's disregard for taxonomic science in order to poke at Porter's blind insistence upon the bear distinction, based solely on remembered affections from his childhood. Jesus was a very special member of Porter's public, one that was permitted to heckle the performer.

And on that topic of the public, Porter's own and the other more generally, which had perhaps been the first reason for his zoo detour, when he entered Melinda's home Porter had been so desperately holding back his commanding impulse to oration that he permitted himself only a couple of observations before launching his arguments into the empty spaces of the room, at the expense of making or receiving any proper introductions or greetings. His entrance being hurriedly made, he first quickly noticed that Garth was smiling at him in a bemused fashion, and that Melinda's disapproval was of the kind to be found only on a stage. She recognized him as her childlike older brother all grown up, and as an individual wholly distinct from herself, which is to say that she had received him far more satisfactorily than had the public at the zoo.

"God damn crazy panda ladies," he shouted, "they ought to be flown by rendition to some black operations site overseas and tortured. They are spies for the Chinese government, making recordings of encoded messages so they may act against our commercial and political interests."

"Hello, Melinda," Jesus said. "Hi, Garth. I am Jesus Torres, Porter's partner. I am pleased to meet you. And by way of explanation, we have just come from the zoo. Porter knows the crazy panda ladies must be spies because all failed to recognize him."

Garth smiled and nodded recognition. His spoken greeting to Porter, as well as Melinda's, was lost in the next verbal assault on the insane panda dames.

"Most of them stay there in front of the panda enclosures all day, every day. They make no secret of it. They all refer to the pandas as if they were their own cousins or close friends, calling them Wing Wang and Mew Mew, in the most embarrassingly familiar and anthropomorphic tones. One would get the impression that the pandas were their regular dinner guests. Most of the crazy panda ladies brag about having thousands of photos of their beloved Mew Mew and Wing Wang, and many of them take hundreds of pictures every day. Oh my God! Paparazzi for pandas! 'Oh, look, Mew Mew has turned her head an inch.' Click, click, click. 'Wing Wang has fallen asleep.' Click, click, click. I am not even mentioning the professions of undying love. 'Oh my God, if anything happened to Wing Wang I would simply die.' Click, Click, click. There are dozens of these crazy panda ladies who claim that they return every day. When do they eat? It is extreme. It is not as if the pandas are stars of stage and screen."

"Now we are getting to the crux of it," Jesus said, "and none of this is overstated. Those women are positively bent."

"I think, Porter," Garth said, "that they are just groupies. There are groupies for almost everything, for cops, for musicians, for soldiers, for sailors and Marines, for television stars, for politicians, for athletes, even for convicted felons and video game whiz kids. You certainly have your own groupies."

"That is my point. I do. But pandas aren't human beings. And my groupies and those other ones you mentioned are not nearly that *intense*, not like the crazy panda ladies. And our groupies are not all only women and no men. Even the few crazy panda ladies who recognized me from my television show, 'Zombie Housewife Forensics', or from my last Broadway show, 'Pac Man, the Musical', only wanted to relate to me in terms of talking about the pandas. 'Don't you think Mew Mew is being such a card today?'

So I have figured it all out. The pandas are not real. They certainly don't look real. They are communist animatronics, from some kind of Stalinist Disney World, only they were sent from China to communicate to terrorist sleeper cells in America."

"So they are not bears anymore?" Jesus asked.

"Are you even listening to me? They are only bears like Yogi or Smokey are, or like that corny Country Bear Jamboree at Disney World. I will make it my cause to expose them. Mindy, when you are a congressman you will have to tell the world the truth about them."

"That sounds like a good plan," she said. "And come here, Porter, let me hug you."

"So you are going to marry my sister?" he asked Garth. "You do know she is crazy, don't you?"

"So is love, when you really think about it," Garth said.

"That's what I am talking about," added Jesus.

"We are already married. And I am not really crazy, Porter," Melinda said. "I am totally freaking bonkers. We both know that. But you are not too far behind me, my clairvoyant Ceylonese sibling. You are apparently sane enough to arrive here just after the packing was finished."

This trip to London would be the first time Melinda had seen her mother since she had gone to college. Garth's children were gathered up. Hanna and Seth rode with Porter and Jesus in his Mercedes coupe and Melinda and Garth rode in the rented truck. Garth spent much of the drive reassuring her of his love and suggesting that the meeting could not be so terrible. Melinda spent much of the ride retelling Garth many stories about growing up in her mother's home. In the car with Jesus and with their new and somewhat famous uncle, Garth's children were enjoying the entertaining tales of television and movies and Broadway shows. Seth was particularly charmed. Hanna was having fun but at one point she leaned over to Seth and whispered to him what the expression on the face of Jesus also was sometimes saying.

"I don't think all of these stories are exactly true."

One story Seth and Hanna would long remember was about human spontaneous combustion, which Porter had claimed was not only possible, but that he could induce it by concentrating and visualizing the person he wanted see bursting into flames.

"I have done it already once," he said, "to an old homeless man with a terminal illness. He used to beg on the street outside our co-op building and he told me of his diagnosis and of his desire for a quick and painless end. He even asked me to help him, but I could not do so legally. My only option was to assist him by inducing spontaneous human combustion. When I last saw him he took off his cap, took out a bundle of old letters from his threadbare coat and wrapped that coat more tightly around himself while he turned the letters over in his hand."

"What happened then?" asked Hanna.

"The next morning when I stepped out of the building there was a trace of a smoldering suffocating vapor that had been in the air. There was something on the ground by the sewer grate, a blackened mass with a small glowing fire slowly expiring on it. There was a dark greasy coating on the sidewalk and the wall. And still burning next to the blackened mass were the remnants of the old man's coat and the letters."

When they arrived at London, Uncle Porter continued to tell his stories as Jesus, Garth, Melinda and the children moved belongings from the rental truck into the newly rented home. After a few hours, they had pretty well settled in with all their furniture and belongings having been unpacked, with the exception of those few boxes that all people who move do not immediately open and which invariably remain unopened for years in almost every case. Many people have moved such unopened boxes from home to home, and it is their increasing mystery that adds to the other reasons they remain unopened. The plan was for Jesus to take the kids to dinner, while Porter and Melinda took Garth to meet their mother.

Porter had remained in contact with their mother, although he had never introduced her to Jesus nor had he told her of his sexual orientation. She couldn't hold his head under water to force him to like boys less, and he was not ashamed at all; in fact he was well out of the closet in all respects but this one. But Porter had decided that it would all be a lot simpler if he just kept quiet about it with her. Melinda had far less to fear, but some part of her changed when she grew into womanhood and she inexplicably felt that by no longer being a girl she was somehow increasing her mother's antipathy. This change in the mother daughter dynamic that occurs upon the maturing of the daughter is not at all unknown to many daughters, but in this case Melinda felt there was more of an edge to it. In any event she was glad that her brother was with her. He would be an excellent smoke screen.

Porter bounced into the worn out old living room, having opened the door to his mother's home without ringing the bell or knocking. Porter himself was a large pair of floor to ceiling double doors with southern exposure on a mild and breezy day. The effect of his entrance was to fill the long closed-in place with light and air. His bright light filled the corners where the wind broke down the cobwebs and blew the dust up and around in rising eddies. The darkness and the musky air yielded quickly to a buoyant luster. Long dormant hues and tones emerged from the walls and furniture. For eyes accustomed to the light the change was barely to be noticed. But to the vision of Angelina Sherman, so long tenured to the pallor of a neglected and unkempt interior world, the effect of Porter's presence was not so much illuminating as it was blinding. The library of her accustomed thoughts, feelings and expressions was temporarily unavailable. She knew little other than that Porter could make her smile, and she passed through all the possibly awkward greetings and introductions just happy to watch her son. Melinda was glad of this. Porter did most of the talking and Garth remained quiet and watchful. The older woman gradually recovered and made small talk and she made ordinary comments upon all that Porter was saying about the newly married couple coming to town to begin new jobs and soon even she and Melinda were having a conversation. This lasted only a short while, which suited Melinda well.

Two Polish tourists in Barcelona will address their bartender in English. A German businessman in Bangkok will speak English to his potential customers. This ascendance of the English language to be the second language of most non-English speaking individuals, to indeed being the first language of international business, has been driven by any number of factors. The precedent external factor was the duration and extent of the British Empire, which flung English far into all the pink bits on the map. Then came the dominance of the American military, music and movies, economic power, and technological advances, which among other things made the internet a predominantly English speaking phenomenon. The primary internal engine of the language's success has been its adaptability. The Saxons of Britain once spoke a version of German, but then there were French-speaking Norman overlords, their priests, magistrates and nobles. Everyone adapted a new language synthesized from both French and German. This adaptability permitted Shakespeare and his Renaissance contemporaries to infuse the language with thousands of new coinages, mostly drawn from their Latin lessons.

The facility with which English evolves has led to the abandonment of archaic words and phrases and to the adoption of nuanced neologisms such as "lol", a subtle word the irony of which is unavoidable. We also have "selfie", which encompasses the spirit of the age. The language has jettisoned "betimes" and "fain", both words the form of which camouflages their adverbial nature, and one of which that is so awkward as to have both one meaning and its opposite. One can no longer be confused in hearing an English speaker say, "He would fain awake betimes and command the start of his day," or, "He was fain to awake betimes and grumble through the start of his day."

But somewhere in the back of Garth Teller's mind there was an archaic phrase and only this outdated phrase could describe to him what had happened and was happening to bring to a close this short conversation between Melinda and her mother. Angelina Sherman was staring him out of countenance.

Garth was mystified. Angelina was transfixed. And no one knew what might have caused the old woman to stare at him so long, not even she. Perhaps there is only one antidote for any breach in decorum or manners, that is, quick reflexes. A swift reaction had often saved Porter from his own bad manners and in this case he was the one to rapidly draw the meeting to a polite close. And the three of them left the home where Porter and Melinda had grown up. But it was not until long after that only one of them came to any understanding of what had just happened, and even then it was only the siblings' mother, and none of the younger people. At the time, it had simply been as if she had seen a ghost.

"Well, that was typically weird," Porter said.

"I am just glad we did it and it is done," his sister said.

Garth did not know what to say. He was still out of countenance.

Melinda and Garth settled into their new home and their routine. It was early summer and one of the tasks was to make sure the kids had plenty to do, so they were enrolled in some camps and the newly blended family joined a local swimming pool. Soon after that, Garth's lawyer would call and report having responded to the sixth, and counting, lawsuit filed by his lawyer ex-wife. A summer visitation schedule would be negotiated in court in a way Garth could never have arranged with Tabitha. Then Garth had to get down to the business of laying the groundwork for a Congressional campaign. He had not done this sort of thing in fifteen years, but he knew what to do. There was only one problem. In that time a great deal had happened, and most of it had changed the nature of campaigns. Garth was trying to figure it all out, when he had a visitor.

Leonard Rock just showed up at the campaign office one day. He was the anxious genius from among that group of whatever the collective noun for owls is. Though he had been a Harvard Owl Club member, Garth could never remember it.

"We are called a parliament of owls, or a stare of owls, or a wisdom of owls," Leonard said.

"Thanks," Garth said, "and why are you here?"

"You mean to ask how I knew to come here," he said. "It was suggested that I come here by our old friend, Elliott Barker, to whom it was suggested by an employee of your friend, Eakin Lambert. I am here to bring you into the twenty-first century. All of this or most of what you used to do in campaigns is now done electronically. And it is rapidly moving to handheld devices."

Garth watched Leonard's shaking fingers unpacking one of the several computers and monitors he had with him in his car. After he set it up and had called up whatever programs he had in mind to discuss, he simply stared at the monitor for a while with one hand on the mouse. With his other hand he probed his fingers through what was still a dark, tightly wound, curly and unruly mass of hair in order to scratch his head, which housed that anxious brain of similar description, which allowed him to simply see mathematical products, dividends, sums, and equations. Garth remained as amazed at his old friend as he had been in college. It was clear that Leonard's expansive genius had extended beyond finance and into computers and cyberspace.

Shortly after the time Garth had last managed a political campaign, digital supremacy was poised to traverse the country. But at this point in the first few years of new millennium, it was about to shoot like a meteor over the wide nightscape of the analog and paper-dependent world, making

society broader yet paler. As of yet, the lines were being laid under obso-
lescent graphic design firms and print shops, plans were being by hatched
by pallid boy and girl geniuses still huddling inside of antiquated brick and
mortar structures, equations were being devised and shared in calls made
over outdated phone lines, there were rumors passing that were designed to
eliminate the wire machines which transported them.

"You see," Leonard said, "all the polling and the targeting and outreach
and involvement and hand-shaking and mailing that you used to do in
campaigns can now be managed by algorithms. It is far more precise now
and it can be accomplished more easily, simply by sitting at a computer. Of
course, you must still use old media along with new media and you still do
the old style campaigning, but in many cases it is just to create content for
what you do online. Or it is dictated by what you learn online and is tailored
to each specific niche audience. Think of what was the science of direct mail
marketing back when you were doing politics. Now, figure that squared, or
taken to the third or fourth power."

"I see," Garth lied.

"Targeted messages for specific audiences can be reached via different
social media platforms. We will develop some specific digital media strat-
egies designed for voter outreach. Additionally, our websites, blogs, chat
rooms and the like will be socially connected, engaging voters before,
during, and after elections. Email and text messages will also be regularly
sent to supporters encouraging them to donate and get involved."

"I think I am beginning to understand," Garth said.

"You will do television narrowcasting, direct and mediated websites,
email, intranets, those chat rooms, or online discussion groups. We will
establish a constant presence, a permanent campaign, in social media and
cyber culture, one that you simply evolve as each campaign changes from
Congressional to Senatorial to Presidential. People will have on-demand

access to content anytime, anywhere, on any digital device, as well as inter-active user feedback, and creative participation."

"This, of course, will only be for people who are connected to the internet, young people. It will not have much use for the people who actu-ally vote, the middle-aged people and retirees," Garth said.

"Yes and no," Leonard answered. "More and more, older people are moving to the online world and many young people are moved to activism by their online lives. And this includes being moved to vote in larger numbers than has been customary for younger people. Additionally, yours is a long-term strategy. As we build the Melinda Sherman political brand among the youth, they will grow into being her supporters in later campaigns. And your wife is already a national figure. That is why there will be a video game. See, this local Congressional campaign has the capacity to begin to establish itself nationally right now. Her national support and involvement among teenagers will become part of her base for a Presidential election in however many years that will happen. It will also serve to broaden your fundraising base. And even when it comes to older people who are now not currently online, what you learn online will educate how you speak to them with old media. And it will streamline and expedite the way you use old media. You have mailed or faxed your last press release, my friend."

"Excuse me, did you say video game?"

"I have already made it, Garth. Don't worry. It is not fancy or expen-sive or anything. It can be downloaded onto any kid's computer and he can play it with his keyboard for free. It is roughly based on her experiences in the Gulf War as a helicopter pilot war hero. In fact, 'Melinda Sherman, War Hero' is the name of the game. We are rapidly becoming a nation that is less literate and more visually oriented. Trust me on this. Some guys I know at PayPal are working on an internet video sharing platform that will blow up someday soon. Videos will become viral and will rocket around the world.

Intranets that companies use internally right now will become templates for worldwide cyber-communities that are based on visual content."

"So, will a viral video will be like a funny or interesting story or picture that people will pass around to each other?"

"Yes and no. They will pass it around but they also will post it for many people to see. It will spread exponentially. One idea I have for your campaign is that I will create a character called 'The Zany Mullah,' which will be comical, an obvious parody. The Zany Mullah will attack your campaign in his own loopy style. Perhaps he will urge believers to burn your campaign material. It will work because America will love whatever the ZM hates and because he will be humorous."

Garth took a breath. He needed to take a break for a second.

"So, tell me about you," he said. "What are you using to get away from it all? How are you giving your brain a break these days?"

"I just told you the answer. It is what I have been talking about. The internet is my work, but it is also my escape from work and from life. It is better than drugs. You have no idea how it will evolve into a universe of escapism."

"Oh, now that is heartening news. This is the wave of the future, I suppose. I have one more question. How in the heck is an old Stone Age political operative like me going to manage all of this?"

"Man, Teller, any thirteen-year-old can do it."

"I am directly related to a twelve-year-old and a fourteen-year-old."

"That's perfect. We will double the output. They have an instinctive understanding for this. They simply see it all as a video game. I will be here for a few days. Just bring them over whenever it makes sense and we will get started."

"Well, I guess that helps answer the question about what they might find to do in this new place during the summer," Garth thought.

FREE FOOD AT A CHINESE RESTAURANT

Melinda had expected to spend her entire career in the Navy. She had hoped she might marry some handsome Navy man, perhaps a fighter pilot, and that they would have two ship-shape children. She had certainly figured that she would at least marry a man her own age. Politics had been the furthest thing from her mind since she had found that it could only confuse her purpose and her commitment to her individual missions. She had always believed her life would be like the recruiting posters had said, "Join up and see the world." The portrait of her life that she had painted in her mind had various background settings, and never included London, Kentucky.

She was also not a person, despite her mental complexities, who was prone to building castles in the air. Hers were all buttoned down expectations, very spic and span. No amount of aerial architecture could have given her the vision of her life as it was right now. Melinda retired from the Navy just after her twenty-year limit, drawing her half salary retirement income, and no longer able to fly or bear children, but now found herself caring for two kids anyway and still rather soaring through the sky. She was living a few miles from her childhood home and was married to a considerably older man with whom she had agreed to launch her political career.

Her combat experience kept her from being overwhelmed. Her strong love for Garth mostly prevented her visions, those lost times from which she would slowly return only to have seen those who had been with her looking concerned. Garth was the man from her lifelong visions. He was also like the father she had never had, strong, smart, independent, giving, insightful, brave, kind, compassionate, and patient. Something else in him, something sad and wounded, also appealed to her in part in exactly the way in which her own father had. She felt that only she could take care of that part of him, that she had to be the little mother to his injured fragments and gloomy strains. She was informed enough on her psychological irregularities that she had long quietly dreaded what she might do when she might have had her own infants and toddlers. But she had come to love Seth and Hanna and they were fairly resilient and were old enough to not really resent her. Perhaps she loved them more because of that. The two of them also called to her inwardly. These things were really all she needed to accept this life and to thrive in it.

This was merely a foundation, an excellent underpinning, but on this was built a magnificent structure. Garth had seen qualities and virtues in her that she had not known she had. He not only knew they were there, he was the timber and brick and mortar by which they would build upon this groundwork. She was hungry to incorporate his encyclopedia of worldly and academic understanding into her own being. She looked into the mirror of his and could see that she had an expansive mind she had underutilized, and that her need to nurture could be successfully and usefully exercised upon the larger world. She was learning to think deeply and to trust that thinking. She had begun to have the idea that being different and not fitting into the world was in fact a kind of leadership.

This entire new way of thinking was anchored to their fundamental love. It was as if their love affair and her political future as well as his were all one and the same. They were married and it was also a marriage of superior capability and outstanding capacity. They would do nothing apart. They were two people in one. They were a couple who ran a store and lived in the apartment above it, each pitching in, the work being part of the love affair, only their family store was her seemingly unlimited political future.

She knew she was the junior partner in this endeavor, but knew they were always equal, a feeling she always got from Garth. And she also understood that part of their life would be like their intimate life, where she would do anything for him. Just as it was and would be in their love life, she would be an equal partner by yielding. And through this relationship she would grow, and his nurturing would feed that growth. More importantly, her willingness and openness would help him become more who he really had been all along. He had been one of the best political operatives of his generation. He had been a father. He had been a teacher. Now Melinda's love and deference would help him become all of these at once, and more. The interaction between them would be their synthesis. They would be more than the sum of their parts.

There were two Chinese restaurants in London and Melinda did not know that Garth was in one of them, dining alone. She only knew he was late for dinner at home. He ordered a beer and some fried pork dumplings. He had another beer with his beef with broccoli. And he ordered shrimp with garlic. When the bill came with his fortune cookie and a sliced orange, he turned to the waiter and told him that he had left his wallet and his money at home and would come back to pay later. The waiter smiled and nodded and left. The owner returned to the table and told Garth not to worry about it. He could bring the money whenever he had the chance. Several attractive young women had approached his table, to talk to him and flirt. When he pulled up to the self-serve gas station, the owner came out and poured his gas and washed his windows. He would have checked the oil, but Garth had told him not. And a couple of teenage skater boys had also asked him if he wanted their help carrying his groceries to his car.

It had happened exactly as Ben had told Garth it would. Ben knew that Garth would take one dose of the Boz and he would see for himself whether or not it worked. To Garth, this one experiment was the only proof he needed.

"You missed dinner," Melinda said. "The kids were hungry so we all ate without you."

"I am sorry. I got carried away with my experiment."

He related to her what had happened.

"You are too precious, Garth Teller, and naive. I could have told you that skater boys and the gas station man are simply Kentucky friendly and helpful, unlike what you find up north. I am not surprised women might flirt with you. Many women find men in their forties to be more attractive than younger men. Don't I sort of prove that? But this whole Chinese restaurant thing is just too much! How many times have I heard you say, 'That is about as likely as getting free food in a Chinese restaurant'?"

"We both know I am not prejudiced."

"No. You're just hilarious."

"I think we should try it. I mean, you should try it when we announce your candidacy."

"I am yours to command, Garth Teller, once you figure out what your command is."

"You know I can't think straight when you say that. But really, I think that the Boz will help. It certainly can't hurt," he said.

"Okay. Just tell me, damn it, the next time you won't be home for dinner."

It was determined that matters would be so arranged. Melinda had once dropped an armed killer with an improbable left-handed pistol shot and had flown a helicopter seventy miles, wounded and bleeding. This sort of thing was a jog in the park for her.

For Melinda, every new and weird thing he did simply compounded her love for him. At this moment, she just wanted to get Garth into bed. Some hour or so after that, she fell quietly asleep. He then lay awake, ruminating on the vast number of possibilities which had arisen out of the conversation that they just had.

Passion seemingly arises from some depth or it falls from some starry height or the unsuspecting person falls into it. For many, he or she will consciously and deliberately take extraordinary pains to force themselves into a passion, and will fall to raving, by regulated and conscious stages. Historically this has been considered one of the feminine wiles, while even in that historical context this stratagem was always more of the province of males, specifically of the political variety. In these more politically correct times such passion is gender blind, an equal opportunity subterfuge, although it is still almost entirely political. Melinda had no need to force her passion in politics. Her passion was her husband and her new family and these feelings infused every fiber of her.

She walked with purpose to the lectern. She could never have imagined such a thing in her earlier life, being about to announce her candidacy for the United States House of Representatives for her district in the state of Kentucky. Typically, an announcement by a candidate for an office for a district not amounting to more than half a million rural souls would be done by press release. But an attractive wounded female recent Congressional Medal of Honor winner whose husband had Washington connections generated state-wide and national interest, which in turn intensified the local interest. There were two dozen reporters in that room and more than a few cameras. The reporters were very warm to her presence and her intentions. Many of her positions had already been outlined to the press.

Most of the questions were not really questions, so she did as politicians do when they address actual questions that seek substantive answers. She took them as opportunities to say what she had planned to say anyway. Then a young reporter from one of the small local conservative newspapers asked a question. The rest of the journalists swung to attention.

"Ms. Sherman," the young man asked, "do you plan to be a feminist candidate or a feminist Congresswoman? Or, I could just ask: Are you a feminist?"

Melinda smiled.

"There has never been any such thing as a feminist."

A hush came over the room, punctuated only by the almost silent sound of people pushing their microphones closer to the podium.

"Please excuse me if that statement seems overly blunt. I do not demean the great sacrifices and the brave struggles that the suffragettes and the feminists have made in order to give women the vote or equal protection under the law. I stand on the shoulders of those giants. Perhaps what I mean is that I hope to redefine feminism. Take a look at what has happened. Only one fifth of all Americans consider themselves to be feminists, while almost double that amount or thirty-seven percent consider feminism a negative term."

"What do you mean by 'redefine' feminism?" asked the reporter from *The New York Times*.

"Most candidates look at the poll numbers and they would balk at being associated with that term. I hope never to campaign that fearfully or to serve in the Congress like that. I prefer to speak the truth. And I would like to lead. Many in the American public think of feminists as whiners. It has always been the case, and more so now in 2004, that there is only one truly feminist argument."

"So, what is that single argument?" asked the journalist from the *The New Republic*.

"Every single woman in this country should have the right and the honor of being able to fight and die for her country."

In the back of the room she saw Garth's children and she saw Hanna as no different from Seth. In her mind she saw those sailors she had rescued. Then she continued in a way the ease of which astounded her. She spoke the way she would speak to her husband in private.

"Some people will say that women need to be protected from combat and becoming prisoners of war, or that they are not fit for it, or that they will cause men in combat to perform less effectively. These same people will tell you that it is an honor to fight and to die for your country. They are lying in one of those statements. It is either not an honor but is really a burden that we do not want women to have to bear. Or it is an honor and we are being damned unfair to prevent half our population from having the opportunity to attain it."

The room remained silent, so she continued.

"I will not lie to you. It is an honor to put your life on the line for your country and fellow citizens. I am living proof of that. I came upon my opportunity by accident. I was not in a combat position. Combat happened to me. Look around you. Would all of you even be at this event, if that had not happened? It is most decidedly an honor. And it is one that is being denied to your sisters and nieces and daughters, and has been denied them for too long."

She paused again. She had never planned to say any of this. She looked at Garth. He was beaming at her, tears in his eyes.

"It was, is and always will be the only real feminist argument. Everything will flow from that. For one thing, it will sure curtail sexual harassment in the military. It will change the way we see women. The workplace cannot be more exclusive than the battlefield. Besides, we have a volunteer military. The women who will serve in every combat role next to men will be the ones who want to serve."

Some intermittent and scattered scribbling could be heard. Then there was the sound of a small feminine voice. And it was moving from the back of the room to the front.

"I love you, Melinda." It was Hanna. "Now you are a hero. You are my hero."

She ran to the podium and leapt into Melinda's arms and hugged her. One of them was crying and the other was very close to it.

"I think that went well," Seth said.

It was much later, when the family was at home and had eaten dinner and Seth was bent over his computer screen.

"What makes you say that?" Melinda asked.

"I mean to say," Seth said, "that our server is crashing."

"That is not a good thing, Seth," Garth said.

"Dad! I bet if it is crashing it is because too many people are making contributions to the campaign from all over the country. The conservative websites are saying that Melinda wants to kill our daughters and that everyone knows women are unfit to serve next to men. Whoops! Some liberal websites are bashing her for pooping on the heads of Betty Friedan and Gloria Steinem. Double whoops! Get this! The news coverage is overwhelmingly positive, portraying her as new and fresh, someone who is not afraid to speak the truth. And people from all over are making donations of five, ten, twenty, even a hundred dollars. The tracker is reading that most of those contributing are under twenty-five."

Just then the phone rang. Garth answered.

"Don't worry. I got it. I am rerouting some of the traffic and signing you up for a larger and faster server," it was Leonard Rock. "You won't crash. If Melinda were a stock, I would buy futures. Her contributions are coming from within conservative and liberal neighborhoods on our demographic maps. The network news clips your son uploaded onto the site already have a couple of million hits. Her support is skewing very young. The future is hers, Garth. Congratulations. Oh, you have almost forty thousand contributors, nationwide, and have raised about three hundred thousand dollars in an evening. From what I am reading, the feminists seem to be pissed at you, though."

"She is a rock star woman political candidate," Garth said, "and she is a symbol of all that a woman can and should be allowed to do. The more they whine, the more she, well, the more she redefines feminism."

"That was a great line you coined there, Garth."

"I wish I could take credit for it. It was all her," Garth said.

"That is a hell of a partnership you have there. Tell her I said so. And tell your kids they are doing a great job on the digital front. Damn, Garth. Bye."

Garth conveyed those messages. Then Seth complained that Hanna should not get credit, because she was not helping him as he tried to manage the current online deluge. Garth glanced at Hanna, still mostly beaming at Melinda. She turned to the girl.

"Hanna, how would you like to call your mom? I bet she would love to hear from you."

Hanna made the call, had a nice long conversation with her mother, told Tabitha she loved her and then handed the phone to Garth.

"Who the hell do you think you are? Do you think that I need you to foster my relationship to my own children? Don't you ever condescend to me like that," Tabitha snarled and then hung up. Garth had little time to think about that. He only remembered Eakin's admonition, before the phone rang again. It was his father.

"Garth," his dad said. "How are you doing? How is everyone? I hope your announcement went well today. It was even on the news here."

"I'm fine, Dad. We're all doing well," Garth said.

Garth knew these infrequent calls from his dad rarely came without some impetus. His father was not expressive and almost never called just to ask how everyone was doing. Garth was not a clairvoyant or a visionary but he could see the impetus of this call. And she was fingering her necklace and looking impatiently at his father.

"Son, I am supposed to tell you something. I am not sure what it means but I guess it is important. So you should be told."

"Okay, Dad, I am listening."

"That guy from *The Washington Post*, Earnest Dapple, was here today. He talked to your mother and me."

"That is not all that unusual, Dad," Garth. "Earnest is an old friend. He was in that club with me at Harvard."

"I know, Garth. I know. He said as much, but . . ." and here he was interrupted.

"Garth? Garth, this is your mother." She was on the phone.

"Hi, Mom, how are you doing?

"I am fine, Garth. Thank you for asking. But I am concerned about Hanna and Seth, and you, and that new wife of yours."

"Everyone is doing well, Mom."

"But this Earnest Dapple character, I don't like him, Garth. There is something about him that just makes me nervous."

"A lot of things make you nervous, Mom," Garth attempted.

"It is not funny. I would hate to see him stir up some kind of trouble, especially with Hanna and Seth being there. I would not want to see them suffer because of something that scoundrel is trying to dig up about your new wife."

"There is nothing to worry about on that score, Mom. Everything has been covered and researched. We will all be fine. And Earnest is an old friend."

"Your father may believe that. But you and I are smarter than that, Garth Teller. We understand people better. That man is no real friend of anyone."

"I guess I am not going to argue with you on that point, Mom. You may be correct. He is a reporter after all. And my training is to treat them like spies of a foreign power, with respect and the appearance of openness but without giving away any real intelligence. Do you have anything specific to tell me?"

"Garth, he was asking questions about your grandfather."

"You mean, your dad?"

"Don't be silly, Garth. My father was beyond suspicion. He was part of the fabric of his family, his society, and his faith. I am talking about that wild man you loved so much when you were a kid, the one who married a Gentile, just like you did, twice. I never felt comfortable with that man. And he was never much help to your father. He was some kind of Texas cowboy and the worst Jew I ever knew."

"He was not the worst Jew, Mom. He was just secular."

"You are parsing words with me now. We both know what I mean. Your father, whose mother was that woman, is technically less of a Jew than his father. But he is a better Jew. But don't let's get sidetracked. If there is anything in this family that some malicious reporter thinks can be of use to him, it is that old man. I know you loved him. But even you have to know that there is something suspicious about your journalist friend asking about him. And it is not just me."

"I can't argue with that, Mom," Garth said.

Later, when they were alone in bed and talking, Melinda asked him about all of his phone calls. He told her what Leonard had said about the campaign. He lied about what Tabitha had said. Melinda smiled at this. He told her about the call from his parents. Melinda thought about the possible political implications for a moment, but her real interest was why Garth's late grandfather was such a figure, a man of such mystery and of a great deal of interest. She was fascinated. So the rest of their waking evening she lay in bed by her husband's side, his arm around her and her arm on his chest, while he told her all the childhood stories, some of which he had told before. Finally, before they dropped to sleep, she spoke.

"You are a lot like him, I can tell, Garth, even without ever having known him, which tells me that I would have loved him."

"He would have loved you Melinda, very much."

MAKE THEM PAY

Melinda awoke very early the next morning even more convinced that what she must do was devour Garth. This was a conclusion she had reached several times on prior occasions, but there was a new and pressing sense of urgency to her sublime hunger. Her first instinct was to consume him whole, from brisket to shank. Her more educated appetites informed her that the process would cause less indigestion and would be more orderly performed if she might consume him one small snack at a time. He was more than one repast, she accurately assessed, even if she could not calculate at how many sittings she would be required to dine on him before there was nothing left but the scraps, and with those she could make quite a soup. Even though she had arrived at this more sensible dietary approach of degustation, she still had to decide upon which dishes would be the first courses, second courses, side dishes, third courses, antipasti, desserts and most importantly at this moment, the appetizer. So she decided to take up fork and knife and begin with the particular hunger that her announcement the day before had given her.

She was certain that in this respect she was not unlike the runner she had been in college; the more she ran the more fuel she needed. She gently nudged him awake. He stirred and looked lovingly at her through a half-sleeping haze.

"Baby, do you remember when we had that discussion about feminism and *Hedda Gabler*?" she asked.

"Wait, are you waking me up with that troll, Ibsen? Are you trying to put me off my breakfast?"

"You said that *Hedda Gabler* was not a feminist book. I think I had that at the back of my mind yesterday. Every time I speak now, my thoughts and words are sort of an echo of our discussions."

"It is hard not to be totally in love with you. Do you know that?"

"I love you too. So, Hedda burns that manuscript of the greatest book ever written or whatever, and then encourages the author, who loves her, to commit suicide, and then commits suicide herself because her choices are limited as a woman. But it is not really that, is it?"

"Well, since Hedda is probably Ibsen himself and since anyone, male or female, can easily identify with her, I would say she is hardly limited to a merely feminine view or motive. She would have done the same, even if she had been a man. And if those circumstances had not been available to her, she would have found some other way to destroy everything around her. She is a negative aesthete. She hates what she sees around her. To her the world is ugly and oppressive. Everyone can relate to her because at one point or another, the world or certain circumstances have struck each of us in the same way. And one of our instincts then is to burn the whole damn thing to the ground, just like Hedda. She is more misanthropic than feminist."

"I guess that is what I was thinking yesterday, that the problem with feminism is that it ignores the universal aspects of humanity. Once you start to grind an ax, some people will react negatively. The only people who will care will be the ones who have a reason to grind the ax with you. The tendency then is to divide people. I think it makes the most sense to speak in universal terms. What! What? Why are you looking at me like that?"

"I only think I love you, Melinda. But I have yet to even see all of what you are. I guess I can say that I love your limitlessness. Or maybe I hope to learn to love the vast inner landscapes of you even though I cannot see them beyond my own horizons."

"Sometimes, Garth, I just want to gobble you up."

Melinda knew that her new venture into the political world would be like flying a helicopter over enemy territory. She would essentially be alone and there would be shots, intermittently trying to bring her down, except for those times when the fire would become more concentrated. To explain where her love for Garth might fit, it would be her commander, the mission itself, her fuel and her communications line, her avionics and weapons and her radar. It would even be the helicopter itself. The only thing she would do alone would be the flying and even then her training would be this love.

Saying that there had never been a real feminist until she had advocated opening up all military combat missions to women struck a chord. She understood it in human terms, which was to recognize the greatest sacrifice that a man can make for his country, for his neighbors, and to state that many women are willing to make the same sacrifice. It was offering to shoulder the load, not crying out for equal treatment. It took the status she had as a Medal of Honor winner and multiplied it. When Gloria Steinem attacked her, Melinda said that if an enemy combatant had ever shot Ms. Steinem she might have a more informed opinion. Melinda was a hot topic. People from disparate groups, liberal to conservative, began to support her candidacy and many were exceptionally supportive.

Due to her celebrity, she seemed immunized from the problems often faced by Congressional candidates. She was not drawn into local disputes or subjected to petty requests. Individual voters had little expectation of obtaining a real connection with her even after they met her. She did not have to work hard just to become known. She did not have to beg for financial contributions. Her campaign did not have to scramble for volunteers, invitations or endorsements. There was a general feeling of pride that she had grown up among the people who were her voters but also a sense that she was bound for greatness, as if she were the one among them who had the best chance to do something truly significant. They flocked to her but were not demanding. The district had a slightly larger Republican registration and the incumbent Congressman was a Republican, but Melinda's Democratic support was far more energized. To the independent or undecided voters, she had the appeal of appearing to shake up the old order of things and of being someone entirely new.

When she went to most of her dinners, appearances and rallies it felt like the arrival of a music or movie celebrity. Any other Democrat would lose this district because there were more Republicans and because that party tends to turn out on election days in higher percentages. They simply understand and advocate their personal interests more effectively. This advantage was slightly outbalanced by the level of excitement about Melinda among Democrats, her appeal to the middle group of voters, and the fact that her candidacy was bringing large numbers of new, mostly young, voters into the equation.

In order to dull the already limited ardor of her opponent's support, she went wherever more than a handful of a certain type of his likely voters would gather. That type was *men*. Melinda started to visit many veterans groups and sportsmen's groups. She smiled, slapped men on the backs, compared a few scars, demonstrated her skill with a gun, traded war stories, and basically revealed herself to be one of the good old boys, a patriot, and every much the man any one of them was in his own right. And they liked her as a woman, whether they were consciously aware of it or not. Many of them would eventually vote for her. None of them would be excited to vote for her opponent. She never mentioned or attacked this same opponent. She campaigned according to her own acclaim. Each time he attacked her, it cost him support.

He launched one such volley on the field of social issues. It occurred during the one televised debate they were to have, carried on one of the television stations out of Lexington, not in the district, but the nearest town with television stations. It was four weeks before the election and Melinda was tired and strained from the emotions of campaigning. The Congressmen pressed her at this moment on the issue of abortion.

"Are you for or against legalized abortion? We have yet to hear your stance," he said.

She had avoided answering many questions; had not addressed the issue. His direct insistence caught Melinda a bit by surprise.

"I have always been unable to approach that broader question," she drew her breath, "because I will never be able to personally confront the issue. Among the other wounds I sustained in my military service was the loss of my ability to conceive or bear children."

There were no tears and no trembling. Passion had been stripped from her words and her face, hidden in the flat, somber tone of her words.

"Since I will never know the power and the depth of what it means to confront such a personal question, I feel that I am not in the position to judge what any other woman should do. I can never be that woman, one facing a choice."

"Wait," her opponent uttered, "we can never know if that is true."

Somewhere in the audience, Seth Teller whispered to his father.

"Triple oops."

"It is in my service record," she said, "the record of my wounding, and was in some of the news reports. I will never be able to know or to feel what means to be pregnant. Not only am I unable to make a judgment, I should not even attempt to make one. And neither should any man."

By now Seth Teller knew what these missteps by others meant when they were directed at Melinda. They meant he had to get back to his computer and get to work, and wait for the phone call from his dad's friend, Leonard Rock. This time he would have Hanna's help. She was already putting the video of this debate exchange up on the campaign website, and was emailing the link to all the news outlets and to their supporters. She would also be the one to handle the phone calls while Seth coordinated the work that would be required to manage the increase in numbers of people accessing the website and making contributions. As it played out, the pro-choice forces recognized that this statement placed Melinda in their ranks, at the forefront of their positions. Feminist opposition to her campaign evaporated. The personal sympathy she generated even appealed even to many members of the anti-abortion organizations, and it made the organizations themselves reluctant to work against her. The polling numbers and the contribution levels were tilting largely in her favor.

For Melinda these facts took on an unreal quality. She felt she would win the election, but the knowledge of that would not quickly heal the pain. She needed Garth to hold her. A very deep and personal wound had been opened up, and had created a political gain.

"I am sorry, Garth," she said later. "I am sorry I can't have children with you. I am sorry the world knows that. I am sorry that they will look on our marriage as something less."

There are certain feelings for which the more seasoned of men know that there can be no possible verbal expression of sympathy. Garth couldn't engage his wife's feelings without making them worse or sounding like he was reducing the power of those emotions. He merely responded with gentleness and attentiveness.

So it was that Melinda Sherma, descendant of William Tecumseh Sherman, she who had nurtured a brother and a father, whom Jesus had urged from his telephone pole crucifix to join the Navy, who married a man primarily because she had seen him in her visions since childhood, who had been a great runner and an even better pilot, who had laid her life on the line for her fellow sailors, who had been motivated to enter the world of politics by love and not ambition, who had won the affection of her stepchildren, and who had just re-opened her deepest wound in public, passed through her first election and entered the United States House of Representatives . . . seemingly in the arms of her husband.

"You do know that this will be the hard part now, more difficult than the election," he said.

"I know," she said, "and I would know it instinctively, even if I had not heard your stories several times. The greatest test of character is not hardship. It is success. I will now enter a world in which everyone will want something from me, most people will flatter me for no reason, and no one will care to see me for who I am. It only appeals to me as something you and I will share, and that we can retreat into the safety and sanity of our marriage."

"Did you just say the 'sanity of our marriage,' or did I just imagine that?"

"I sure did. Almost everyone might consider our marriage totally weird. And that is how I am certain that it is sane."

"That is a very sane judgment, which also would sound unreasonable to most people."

"Just promise me one thing."

"What?"

"That now that I am the Gentlewoman from Kentucky, you won't stop tying me up in our bedroom."

"I prefer to think of it as tying you down. And I do prefer to think of it."

It was once very much the norm in the United States House of Representatives for new Members to be seen and not heard. They would leave discussion of the all the issues to the Member who had experience and would focus on learning, which a quaint old-fashioned way would have been simply called listening. Then at some point, later in their careers, the

Congressman's first speech would be scheduled and by long-standing tradition and out of respect every other Member of the House of Representatives would turn out. In the current time, America's elected representatives are not so parsimonious with their pronouncements. A more accurate and significant value is placed upon Congressional speech and Members of Congress actually begin speaking from the very first moment and continue until long past the last possible instant.

The press was interested in what Melinda might have to say. She spoke to them humbly about her respect for the people who elected her and for the institution to which they had elected her. But she said nothing on the floor of the House for several months. She and Congressman Wilton Carlson had bargained astutely and ruthlessly to prevent the Democratic leadership from assigning her to Veterans Affairs committee as a reflex to her being a veteran. They made sure she was assigned to the Defense Committee, a much more important and substantive assignment normally reserved for Members with some seniority. At those committee hearings and meetings, she chose to listen, and passed on her scheduled turn to ask questions. When these silences came to be noticed, she mentioned the lost tradition of the House. When it became known that she would finally speak, a year and a half into her term, there was a buzz of interest. The floor of the House was not at full attendance, but many Members were there. C-Span, the House of Representatives cable television channel even mentioned it and promoted it for weeks beforehand.

"Make them pay," she began. "Make them pay their fair share. That is all I am saying, or asking. I am talking about American foreign aid, and not the way we all think of it, but the way it really works. The polls show that most people in the United States oppose American aid to other countries. But actual direct aid is a miniscule part of the federal budget and almost all of it goes to developing nations. What they don't know is that we have a massive and indirect foreign aid program that remains hidden. And most of it goes to highly developed countries. I am talking about the Defense Department budget, to the extent that it goes directly overseas and pays for the defense of other countries which then don't have to pay the expense of their own defense.

"Let me start with Germany," she continued. "For four and a half decades following World War II, the United States stationed approximately one quarter of a million service men and women in what was then West Germany. Over that time almost twelve million Americans were deployed in Germany. Those numbers have diminished but since 1990, approximately one hundred thousand Americans on average have been stationed in Germany. That means that the typical American taxpayer has paid more in taxes to defend Germany than the average German taxpayer has paid to defend his or her own country. We are talking about one of our major economic competitors. The worker who assembles Chevrolets in Kentucky is paying taxes to defend Germany that the worker who assembles Volkswagens in Dresden does not pay. That places the American worker at a competitive disadvantage. What is even more difficult to explain is that those military bases over the years have poured billions of dollars directly into the German economy. It is effectively what my stepchildren call a 'double whammy,' we give them money, and we also pay for their defense. And when I say 'we,' I mean the American worker.

"This is only one example," she continued. "The list of the top twelve recipients of this direct foreign aid includes Germany, Japan, South Korea, the United Kingdom, France, Italy, Spain, Turkey, Saudi Arabia, and other very developed nations who are all among our economic competitors. To put it in blunt terms, the cost of that Chevrolet that is made in Kentucky is higher due to the amount of taxes paid to defend the plant and the workers in Dresden who are making a Volkswagen that is cheaper because they do not pay those taxes. And when the worker in Kentucky does not have the option available to the worker in Dresden, which is to find work in any of the jobs generated by the presence of American military bases overseas. There may be many things that could be said about this, but I will tell you what I think. I think it is a sin.

"We have four hundred thousand troops stationed overseas, in over six hundred bases," Melinda added. "We spend over two thirds of a trillion dollars every year on defense. The total defense spending of the ten next national budgets, combined, is less than what we spend. Of all the military spending in the entire world, over forty percent is financed by the American taxpayer. I also want to make one thing clear. I do not want to weaken American interests overseas. I believe in a strong national defense and I have put my life on the line for that belief. I just don't think that my neighbors and fellow citizens should be paying for defending their economic competitors. I want those developed nations to pay their fair share, and today I have introduced a bill that would require us to pull back when they do not pay. And I have also introduced a bill to require the Defense Department do a full accounting of what those figures truly are. Finally, think of what we could do with that money in this country. Let us give our veterans a complete college education, and job training, and housing."

As she finished some Members of the US House were startled by what they had heard. Some ignored it or shrugged it off as more liberal shouting into the wind, by a freshman Congresswoman. But Wilton Carlson walked over to Melinda after her speech and he pulled her aside.

"Dimwits. They do not know what you have just done. They will dismiss your speech as the standard attack on defense spending. They do not see the brilliance of it. You never once mentioned Iraq or Afghanistan. You never attacked defense spending head on. Most Americans dislike foreign aid. If you can paint defense spending with that brush, you will have done something. Those workers in Kentucky and Ohio are patriotic about America's military assertiveness. This will make them think twice. It is like your argument for women in combat, a damn Trojan horse is what it is. If women are in the front lines, Americans will be much more reluctant to agree to send troops into any old fight. I am looking forward to working with you. To tell you the truth, I think they should move those overseas bases back here, to Texas. Just remember that when you are President."

He concluded with a rigorous slap on her back, the sound of which was heard around the chamber largely as an endorsement and an approval from one of the most powerful men in Washington, and one of the few Democratic hawks.

The response online might have been predictable. She had also begun to redefine what being a dove meant. People who opposed war of all kinds but did not want to sound unpatriotic became supporters of Melinda Sherman. Her contributions and supporters increased once again by large numbers. She had the most significant political presence on the internet.

Her speech effectively became what it had been planned to be, the beginning of her campaign for the United States Senate. Though she would serve two more terms in the US House of Representatives, in private Wilton Carlson had taken to calling her "Senator," and to telling his colleagues that it was time "to get on her bandwagon. Sherman is going to go all the way."

Melinda began to feel some psychological turbulence. Sometimes she was not sure who she was and she had long recognized that was not good. She needed to take a long weekend away with Garth and the children in order that these perturbations might not grow into seismic shifts that might subsume large tracts of her personality's landscape. The family went to a resort in the eastern mountains where they could relax and be together. There she became anchored and safe and what might have been one of her lost times was mitigated and instead became a vision, a waking dream that she would not immediately share with Garth, but which told the future, as her visions always had.

A MASCULINE MISSTEP

Garth had walked into the bathroom of the suite he had taken for Melinda and the kids, when he saw Melinda on the toilet seat and he quickly turned to walk back out. Then he realized that what he had just really seen was his wife sitting only on the lid of the toilet and his daughter on her knees at Melinda's feet. He had not seen Hanna because she had been on the older woman's other side and was partially obscured. Glancing from the woman to the girl and back to the woman, he recognized that his wife was making a sign for him to leave. Bewildered by what it might mean, he stood still until his wife stood swiftly and gently enough not to disturb Hanna and walked directly across the room to walk him out the door. There he stood, expression unchanged, until Seth spoke to him.

"Yeah, I know," he said, "it's some secret pow-wow. They have been in there for half an hour."

"Do you have any idea what it's all about?"

"No. And if I did, I probably would not say."

Garth hazarded one or two other questions, but it was apparent that Seth had his own reasons for evading the subject. Garth waited a few minutes until the sixteen-year-old boy was speaking on various other matters, but no sooner had his father returned that conversation to the topic than he found himself again matching words with a recalcitrant teenager. Garth was already disconcerted by the uneven behavior of two of the three people he loved most and the silence of the third was another discordant note. When the female side of the family finally emerged, he did not find himself better informed. Melinda was making a cheerful effort to conduct family business as usual, much to the approval of Hanna. Later in their bedroom, Melinda told him.

"She feels bad, poor girl," Melinda said, "like she has betrayed you and to a lesser extent me. Her brother feels the same; only he is not so open about his emotions. He just clams up."

"Why on earth would they feel that?"

"You would think, Garth, that your experience might have told you that almost every problem of theirs stems from the divorce?"

"You mean, they think they have betrayed us to Tabitha?"

"Yes, and I am sure they feel they betray her when they are with us. But they are very wise kids. They know themselves. There is more to it this time."

"What?"

"They are worried that the betrayal is real. You don't want to know anything about what is going on with Tabitha's life, but it is clear she is curious about ours. What they do with us exciting; with the campaign and the notoriety they have at school. So they would probably just talk to her about us anyway. But this time there is something beyond that."

"Are you going to tell me? Or are you going to keep me up all night, waiting?"

He was going to be awake all night anyway. He would be wondering at first what might be done to ameliorate the children's woes, only to remember that nothing calmed those rough seas for a child so well as a night's sleep. He would also mentally walk around the problem Tabitha had created a few times, to take as many views as he could. He even considered how he might try to do anything but knew that the attempt would put more pressure on Seth and Hanna. The thing that did not puzzle him was the motivation of the third party, whom Melinda had reported was involved. Garth understood that man's actions; they were quite orthodox, by the creed of his own sect of one. Earnest Dapple was now sleeping with his ex-wife.

No one knew more about Melinda and Garth than his children. To what extent they had been cross-examined by Tabitha, who then would have relayed the information to Earnest, was the subject of distressing speculation. It was most likely that he knew most of what the kids knew and this tore at Garth's heart. He felt sad for his children. By the time he had run this all through his head a few times it was an hour or so before dawn. Melinda had fallen asleep long before this and he had walked into the main room of the suite put himself on the phone with Eakin, who did even comment on the time of night.

"Who the hell is surprised by that?" she asked. "Don't you think you might have seen that one coming? I did. I have been expecting this call. We both know that she is not likely to go out socially. She has her work and her struggle against you over the kids to keep her busy. She was probably rattling around that house, thinking of how to file another lawsuit, when in the door walks the answer to several of her wishes. She didn't have to go out looking. And what would hurt you more than for her to sleep with one of your friends, particularly one who not only has an interest in damaging not only just you, but also your wife, and who also has the means to do it?"

"Man, was I that blind?"

"No, it is just that you don't think that way. You're too goofy or too much in love or you have too much of your own life to have the time to remember what she is like or may be doing."

"Wait, why have you been expecting this call? Had you figured it all out already?"

"No, but you can bet Ben did. He has been onto Earnest for some time now. Ben sort of understands Earnest. Ben has a natural inclination toward distrust, even though he is trustworthy. And he sensed that Earnest might see Tabitha as your family's point of vulnerability."

"I guess I should have seen it coming, but there is not much I could have done about it. I wonder what I can do about it now," Garth said.

"You have a short memory, Teller," Eakin said. "You don't have to worry about it or do anything about it."

"Why? What am I not seeing?"

"That Ben gave you and your wife his personal guarantee that Earnest would never do anything to hurt you."

"I just don't see how he can make that kind of a guarantee."

"I guess it is better that you don't. Go back to sleep."

"Okay, Eakin. Elbow Elliott in the ribs there and tell him I said 'hello,' will you?"

"Very funny, Garth. Good night."

Garth said nothing to Eakin about what her joviality and irreverence really meant to him, but they inspired in him a kind of comfort that was almost merry. He could not see that his face was shining in the dark but it was enough for Garth to simply feel it. He would often profess jokingly to his oldest and closest friend that he thought very little of her endless mocking, telling her she was a pretty harsh commentator. But he was well aware of the effect she always had of rousing him to hopefulness and courage. Whether he was in the mood to listen to Eakin or not, she was contagious and he always gained a profitable distance from his troubles.

Tommy Kitt was due to visit Washington. Garth and Melinda had given Tommy the job of managing her constituent affairs office back in her home district, since no man or woman would greet the constituents needing help with their Social Security or Veterans benefits with a more compassionate and accommodating attitude than Tommy. He would receive more pay and better benefits and would be able to stay physically cleaner than he had working as an auto mechanic. He could buy a larger house for his family. He also found that people would treat him with a significant measure of respect. He was also part of the Melinda Sherman team now and that was as rewarding as actually being able to help people who needed assistance. Tommy still thought of it as among the least of the many benefits he had received from his childhood friend. His good-hearted honesty was as apparent and as noticeable as the way his suits never seemed to quite fit. When he was in Washington and was around Garth and Melinda his attentions were directed toward them, and never inward. When Garth had once pointed that out to him, he simply remarked that he was the least interesting subject he could imagine. Garth, however would involve good Tommy in his unmindful plan.

Worldly men such as Earnest Dapple are subject to a peculiar form of moral gravity that holds their attentions very close to the ground. The beauties of the heavens or the soaring majesty of certain topographies appear well above their peculiar notice. Similarly, other high flying metaphysical notions such as justice and compassion or altruism and charity or forgiveness and sacrifice pass over their heads as if they were Jupiter or Mars, which neither in soaring apogee nor in swooping perigee ever shine brightly enough or move low enough to fall within the view of the earthbound self-interest of these worldly men. If Earnest were to have ever lifted his gaze skyward he would have only seen flickering and reflected symbols of his own thoughts and concerns. He had been unable to comprehend what many of Garth's more generous feelings might have been upon learning of his dalliance with Tabitha, but he was well aware of what the dictates of his own best interests were. He was now always carrying a tape recorder when traveling in the company of other people.

Tommy Kitt and his motivations would also always fall into one of Earnest's particular blind spots. The zest of selfless love and awe at life's marvels were woven throughout the fabric of Tommy Kitt's nature, which his association with Melinda and later with her husband had not much weakened, nor for that matter could it have even been worn out by the stern and unyielding principles of practical experience. He attached a delightful interest and sense of adventure to all his dealings with his childhood friend and lately her husband. He cherished and nurtured his experiences with them. They were like that magical Argentine way of life that is also a dance. There are, it is said, no such things as mistakes in the tango and Melinda and Garth could make no mistakes for Tommy.

Earnest Dapple suspected everyone who might take an interest in him, or in anything in which he too was interested, or for that matter anyone who might happen to be in the same room with him, or whom he might just consider in a passing thought. To him such suspicious characters were usually entertaining sinister designs upon him and he was clear about what he assumed to be their worst intentions. On the strength of these philosophical insights he would often undertake intricate counterplots and preemptive stratagems and as such was constantly engaging in very deep games that have no adversary. Yet, in this instance he knew his adversary.

Sometime after Tommy had arrived in Washington Garth took him to a known watering hole for journalists, who approach watering holes in the manner of lions or hyenas, not as places to refresh oneself from thirst but to find prey or to sharpen their instincts in the presence of other hyenas and lions. There Earnest was sitting with one of his fellow reporters, one who worked for *The Times of London*. When this man had arisen from the table to go to the men's room, Garth stationed himself in his path but out of the range of Earnest's view. This reporter had met Garth before and he knew him and was unable to let the call of nature keep him from a potential story, so he stopped to talk at about the same moment that Tommy Kitt sat down at the table with Earnest Dapple. Had Tommy been Garth, Earnest's pocket tape recorder would have been turned on instantly, but he only saw Tommy as a blank page and to the extent that his feverish paranoia could bring anything to his attention he was merely guarded about possibly receiving another blow to the stomach. He looked around for potential witnesses and when he noticed some, Tommy was already addressing him.

"Our friend wants you to know that if you do anything that might even indirectly hurt anyone about whom he cares, the police will not be able to identify your corpse from the dental records. You will not be able to enjoy the fruits of your efforts."

After that Earnest switched on his tape recorder but Tommy by that time was getting up from the table. When the *Times* reporter returned to the table, Earnest asked him what had held him up at the men's room and was not surprised at the answer.

Two weeks later, Garth received a visit from the police, from Detective John Huffam who asked if he could ask Garth some questions. Detective Huffam was in his fifties, a thin and care-worn man with lines around his gray-blue eyes, and whose blond and gray hair was retreating from his forehead. He was of average height and had a temperament that was at first glance phlegmatic and steady. There was little that was noticeable about him, except that he had that slightly threatening and watchful reticence that all policemen have. Garth took him into the kitchen while his children huddled in the living room.

Melinda was on Capitol Hill at that time. Her bill to keep the United States from spending unrestricted defense money was not about to be considered. But the reports and the numbers required by her other bill were being generated, even if that legislation had yet to pass. Those figures were attracting a great deal of attention. For one thing she could state with authority just how much the average American was paying in taxes to defend people in other developed nations. And she could compare those amounts to what those taxpayers in wealthy developed nations were not paying.

"I'll get right to it," the detective said. "Your ex-wife has filed a complaint."

"That is something she often does but since you are a policeman and not with the sheriff's office I will assume that it was not a civil complaint this time."

"That is right. She filed a criminal complaint accusing you of assault and issuing a death threat to her and to her boyfriend at her home."

Garth considered the specifics of that reported complaint, quickly recognized Tabitha's overzealousness, and roundly denied that he had done any such thing.

"I know. I have already been to your wife's Senate campaign office. Their records show that on the evening that your ex-wife alleges this happened you were on a plane bound for Kentucky. Besides, Mr. Teller, I have been divorced myself," the detective exhaled, "twice. So, I am not unfamiliar with all the ways in which these allegations may arise."

"Thank you, detective," Garth said.

"Mr. Teller, I have been around the block a few times. There are very few tricks this old dog has not seen. These kinds of complaints tend to contain a kernel of truth in them, the kind of kernel that a fertile and motivated mind can work into an entire organism. So what I am saying is: Be careful. Don't put any more kernels out there. Even though we will not act on her complaint, you will have to be very careful, particularly now that this complaint is on record. Do you understand me?"

"I am not saying that I do," Garth said, remembering his law school training, "but I thank you for asking."

It was not until the next evening when Melinda returned home in time for dinner that the children related a story to her about a visit by a policeman whom they believe they overheard saying something about "kennels" and maybe a "dog" running "around the block." Melinda only flashed a bit of concern and then projected herself into the life of her family.

When the children went to bed she did not have to wait to ask. Garth told her what had happened. She told him that she was disappointed in, not only for embroiling Tommy, but for placing whatever political considerations he might have ahead of his own safety and his importance to his children. Disarmed by her compassion and grace, he solemnly promised that he would let the matter lie and would do nothing else. And in the back of his mind he was comforted about what Eakin had said. There was something about Ben in which he had a Pilgrim's unassailable faith.

The friend he had made on that gloomy Boston night so many years before was not a man of hot temperament or given to lightness of any kind. He seemed impervious to setbacks or to the small tumults of the people around him or even to the capricious and sometimes wicked turns of fate. He was implacable and apparently sensitive only to the internal measurements of his personal standards. He was good-humored and peaceful on the whole but a man of resolution. He was not a man with whom one would desire to come face to face in a narrow pass with no room to step aside. There was some solace for Garth in these assessments. But they were shadowed by the question that such a person might actually exist. Garth's greater calm and resolve came from his relationship to his wife.

It had been commonly observed that women know while men have to learn. This is perhaps best understood when it is applied to matters of the emotions, such as love, or to what are the dictates of the emotions, such as loyalty. There were moments of stillness in which Garth knew that he would do anything for his children and for his wife, but for his wife the interval between herself on the one side and the children and him on the other was an impassable space. This bond arose from her soul in a way that made both joy and duty one and the same. If some opportunity to sacrifice for them would present itself, she would embrace it. This was how she had been able to navigate the shoals of her childhood home. It was who she had always been. But Garth had to work, not to labor extensively, but to put forth some small constant effort to keep this in his mind. There was some part of him that is contained in each man, a part that is always aware of his being expendable, an understanding that the village or the tribe could survive with a few less men but that to lose many women would be a less temporary injury. It is an elemental detachment against which men must constantly strive. Melinda was his cynosure in this effort to join himself more hermetically to his family, and his sextant and astrolabe were the experiences he could recall from having custody of his children as a single parent.

One of the natural and correct but perilous byproducts of his enlightened sympathy and compassion was that he found it extended even to his ex-wife. He found himself feeling sorry for her. When he thought of her he remembered how they met, how they married, how they had their two great children. He remembered them overcoming the obstacles they had faced and doing it together. He knew that her view screen was too narrow to hold on it anything more than one thing at a time, and that too often that was a combination of her resentment and anger. He felt sorry for her for that, for not being able to calmly move on, and particularly for not seeing the pitfall of Earnest Dapple. He knew that Earnest could casually make use of her, as he did everyone, and would despise her by the exact proportion of her usefulness, as is the wont of such men who see other individuals as tools and hold them in contempt for it. Whatever might happen to Garth or to Melinda, something surely unpleasant was in store for Tabitha. Garth was further saddened by the accurate realization that anything he might do, or anything he might say to Tabitha, to try ameliorate her approaching calamity would only blow up in his face. If she were to be drowning, she would reject a lifesaver, if he had been the one to throw it.

His love for his family was also subject to his imagination as it constructed images of their future, pictures that had their genesis at the intersection of love and ego. True love needs no repayment and revels only in its own sublime nature. But since love is also something that men feel it is subject to the weaknesses of men. They often seek beyond loving, to having, to owning. Garth had visions of what the world might bring them all. These are what passed through that space that for his wife was impassable, his wishes for what the family might become. He could sometimes be unaware that what might be will often vigorously contend against what is. Their family had been charmed to this point. They shared so much and enjoyed it all. Garth could not really be faulted for what he saw as Melinda's political potential and what it meant for all of them. His vision was shared by Congressman Carlton, Chip Mathers, Ben Dessous, Preston Cobalt, Leonard Rock, and slightly over a hundred thousand other Americans who followed the campaign in the news and made contact and contributions through the campaign website.

This image of their future was even shared, darkly, by Earnest Dapple.

And all the polls showed that a majority of the voters of the Commonwealth of Kentucky held the same view. They saw in Melinda a political leader of the singular variety which is seen only once in a generation.

But Melinda, in a few words and phrases, brought him back wishing only for the thing they had, a happy and loving life. If love and happiness energized him, they had quite a different effect on her. She was aware of the way in which good times act as a medium or a séance. Her happiness with Garth and his children brought back long forgotten scenes of her father, as if feeling love were a charm to conjure lost love. She was just as much looking back as Garth was looking forward.

Earnest Dapple must have been playing a long game because no more was heard about his digging and snooping. He had been to London to talk to Melinda's mother. He had searched into the Teller family past. He had questioned Melinda's teammates and classmates and the people at her church. He had most likely recorded Tabitha's ramblings about all that she had gathered, coaxed, cajoled and drawn from her own children. He had pored over Melinda's military records. There was no way of knowing what else he had done or he might have uncovered. He kept his powder dry all the while Melinda had run successfully for the United States House of Representatives three times and then for the United States Senate. Perhaps he was like a rare investor who picks a growth stock early and then consistently and bravely refused to sell it for a profit even when good profits are available. Or maybe he had not yet completely formed his strategy or had yet to complete is portfolio. There had been some reason that he had not come forward, but still nosed around in the corners and poked in the dumpsters and put his nose to the wind to detect any scent.

After six years in the US House passed quickly and happily, she was elected to her next office. Senator Sherman was on the top of many lists. Now, almost every reading, listening or watching person in America had heard Melinda's name. Most of them had formed an opinion of her that was positive. The world was even starting to pay attention. Voters and organizations in Iowa and New Hampshire were inviting her to visit. It was all just about to begin, or end.

YOU ARE NOT
LESS DANGEROUS

On the first stir of a brisk autumn wind after a long Indian summer calm, trees will deposit a large portion of their leaves on a lawn in the same manner that Melinda's visions floated and settled into her life. They would resolve slowly and lazily until she could no longer see the green reality of the grass. In what deceptively seemed suddenly she found herself only able to see the blanket of oranges and reds and browns and yellows of her mental disquiet. Her visions varied in kind and were related to the incidents that she called her "lost times." The gentler visions, and those starker episodes, shared the differences that an epileptic will experience in the variations between a mild *petit mal* seizure to a more severe *grand mal* seizure. There were each of various degrees of magnitude within each occurrence, but the boundary difference between the two was measured by her consciousness of what had happened, or the lack of same.

She remembered her visions, not the truly lost times. For those instances, she had to rely on what other people told her in order to have any idea what had happened, often in the way a sufferer of a *grand mal* seizure will awaken to listen to the reports from the concerned friends and loved ones anxiously gathered around. An epileptic who is susceptible to each category of seizure will find relief if he or she no longer blacks out, that is, if the visitations are only of the *petit mal* variety. The loss of control of a particular body part while conscious could feel like dodging the bullet to someone who knew what it meant to lose consciousness and control of the entire body. Melinda had been dodging her own bullets ever since Garth and the children had become an emotional and psychological sea anchor for her nautically inclined consciousness.

She now only had the visions, and they had the unique quality of neglecting the passage of time other than as it occurred in her visionary mode. A visualization of over a year ago would seem as a Tuesday to the Wednesday of a current vision. Her revelatory world was lived on a separate time continuum, each previous visitation being available to the current vision by their point in order and not by their place in actual time. In the mental landscape of her most recent episode, the vision of the way in which Jesus had once urged her to join the Navy was accessible but at a distance. But she could see fairly clearly the more extended revelation that occurred within her more recent coma, the one in which she felt linked to other persons and the world they peopled in such a way that they talked to her and she to them without speaking, and in the way in which she was able to effect transformations in those with whom she was in touch. It was the same vision that showed her that she was not so much seeing the future as she was bringing it into being.

This phenomenon is something not unlike a state of mind that the multitudes of those of us who are not like Melinda all have experienced. It is that wakeful set of moments at the end of a peaceful sleep but prior to actually waking, when dreams are particularly vivid and memorable, and more importantly when those things that are happening in the room around the sleeper are inexplicably within the grasp of the unconscious mind. A dream about alien slaves and masters or about a former lover or about living alone as a child on an island will somehow begin to incorporate the faces or happenings around the sleeping person. It is at these moments that those who did not have Melinda's power or curse or gift have a glimmering perception of the mind's boundless powers, its failure to obey the speed limits of time or the borders of space, its utter separation from the corporeal existence that is its foundation. In much this same manner, for Melinda, the waking dreams and the subsequent realities were mysteriously blended, as if she were living in her visions or that her revelations were really happening, or in the way that the great protagonist of Cervantes happened to know that he was also a character in a book. It was a peculiarly double consciousness that confronted the envisioned events, as they would occur later, as she would live through them.

Senator Sherman's first official trip took her to Detroit, Michigan, to visit the home town of one of her Senate colleagues to participate in a hearing he was to have there and, because she was beginning to be nationally famous, to appear at a fundraiser on his behalf. When she had been at the resort with Garth and his children, she had a revelation in which she also took a side trip to the near suburb of Dearborn, Michigan, with a video cameraman and with one of her staff members. This was where she found herself at this moment, dressed in a dark pants suit outside the most conservative mosque in Dearborn. This Michigan town is the Little Levant of the United States and when she had arrived it was as if she could actually smell the pricking aroma of cumin, the sharpness of turmeric, the musty scent of cardamom, the sweet tang of nutmeg, and the tartness of caraway wafting from the residents' kitchens and into the air of this city that had once been the birthplace of Henry Ford and which now held America's highest concentrations of Lebanese, Yemenis, Iraqis, Syrians and Palestinians.

She quietly began to enter the main part of the mosque. A casual and inattentive guard at the door made an attempt to arrest her progress into this part of the mosque that is reserved only for men. She gently walked past the guard and into the "men only" main section of the mosque. What followed then was something that might be a part of a nightmare but which is something that naturally and approvingly has been and is still occurring every day from the Maghreb to Indonesia, from Kabul to Mogadishu. She was the subject of a good old-fashioned stoning. A screaming gang of men surrounded her and began hitting her and kicking her and throwing objects, mostly shoes, at her. She was even stabbed once. And all the while she kept her calm, as if she were dreaming or as if she had been stoically prepared for it all. And when she fell, she suddenly felt a presence over her, a welcome masculine force that protected her and then carried her away and out of the mosque and into a waiting van.

"What took you so long, sailor?" she asked.

"Jesus, ma'am, I mean, sir, I mean, Senator, what the hell do you think you are doing? I am glad I was here to protect you. You could have been killed. But I have to say that my cover is sure blown now," answered Donny Bhutani, one of the Seals she had flown to safety so long ago.

At this time he was wearing the shalwar kameez and the karakul of a Pakistani gentleman.

"You look pretty good," she whispered, "for the agnostic descendant of Hindu believers that you are."

"Yeah, well my employers are not going to be happy. I am going to have to be pulled out of this mosque and probably out of Dearborn entirely, and then be reassigned to another mosque on the other side of the country."

"Is there one of you in every mosque in America?"

"One of what, Senator?"

"Former Seals who are fluent in Arabic and who look like terrorists and are trained at infiltration and deception."

"More than one, in most cases, and we are not all former Seals, ma'am. Some are recruited straight into the agency and some are former Army or Navy Intelligence officers. You think I look like a terrorist, ma'am? Thanks. Still, I am going to have to be moved," he said.

"Won't your wives be disappointed then, eh, Ghandi?"

"You're pretty funny, General Sherman. You know now, this means we are even. You had saved my life and I have saved yours."

"I saved your life twice, sailor. And my life was never in danger here."

The event at the mosque had been captured on digital film. The video went viral and within minutes after that Senator Sherman was in a television news studio in Detroit. The knife that had been thrust into her jacket and top struck her in a strong leather waist wallet she had put on for the occasion. It was apparently a miracle that the blows that had been struck and that knife thrust that had occurred in the video showed no evidence on her body in the television studio only minutes later. A flashy and obtrusive video headline proclaimed "Miracle at the Mosque" on the television screen before her interview and ran on a crawler at the bottom of the screen while she was interviewed.

She made no commentary and did not allow herself to speak to facts beyond her health and the facts of what the television journalists were then calling a "brutal and savage attack."

She said, "I wanted to make a visit as I would to any church or synagogue."

Melinda immediately called Garth to tell him what had happened and to reassure him of her safety. Seth, now twenty and a junior in college, called him next.

"Dad, the 'Zany Mullah' is on fire," he said.

"Who? What?"

"Remember that character that your friend, Leonard, created years ago in the hope of creating a video that might go viral? Well, he just did."

The weird genius, Leonard Rock had anticipated the power of YouTube several years before its moment, when the video sharing website had just been getting started. Garth could not believe he had hired an actor to dress up like a mullah and to rave on in an exaggerated and antic manner about all sorts of bland Western entities. The "Zany Mullah" had attacked baseball, Gilligan's Islands re-runs, Harry Potter and Disney. He even once had banned irony. But Seth was reporting that the ranting of the Zany Mullah against a certain American female politician named Sherman were now getting a million hits and more.

"It's really crazy, Dad. People seem to be confusing reality with internet humor," Seth said. "The video of her attack is getting millions of hits, and if you look to the right on the YouTube screen, the top ranked similar videos are Mr. Rock's failed attempts at viral comedy and name recognition. She is now the candidate of the twenty-first century Crusades, like 'On to Jerusalem,' and all that. And I checked her new website visits and her new contributions. They are now coming in from older voters in conservative areas. Dad, they are Republicans and Evangelicals, most of them, you know, the opposition."

"Thanks, son. Now please get back to your studies. I am worried that all of this is getting to be too distracting for you. We now have staff at the campaign office to run all this stuff. You need to get your degree," Garth said.

"Yeah, but this is fun."

The third call that day was one that Garth made to Congressman Wilton Carlson.

"I have been expecting you to call me, Teller, and I have already placed a call to the White House on this very topic," he said.

"What topic?" Garth asked.

"Why, your wife's personal safety, what else? I have told them to assign a Secret Service detail to her or risk the fallout."

"But the Secret Service charter only extends to the President, Presidential candidates and to their families."

"Right, which is why I suggested that a Secret Service detail that is trained in protecting a Presidential candidate be reassigned to the Department of Defense or to Homeland Security and that it be mixed with some other agents which it can train in personal protection and that she be protected by this new mixed group. It has never been done, but it will be needed. She is now the fold-out playmate of the month for international jihad."

"Can we put some of those old Seal buddies of her in that detail? Thank goodness one of them was on duty, infiltrating that mosque. Most of them would die for her anyway, even if they did not owe her their lives already."

"I will tell them to look into that. You know, it is a funny thing. She fought against those crazies, even killed a few of them. She was, of all things, a woman soldier. And now she is a leading American politician. She is a symbol of all they fear about the West. But none of that has pissed them off as much as this will. I can hear them ululating in Cairo and Damascus already, damn savages. And Garth . . ."

"Yes, Wilton . . ."

"You better start getting ready to be the first First Gentleman, or the first First Husband, or the first First whatever the hell they are going to call you when she is the President. I am happy as hell that we Democrats will finally have a Presidential candidate who has some real balls."

"She is certainly different," Garth said.

"You keep loving the hell out of her, Teller. You are part of her. She will need you more than ever now."

Melinda was a politician in the same way that a cube is a sphere. She was as different from politicians as you could get. Most politicians can roll into any crowd and move around without leaving a mark. Very little will ever stick to them and their surfaces are smooth and uniform. Melinda was not afraid to show a corner or a flat wall. She had not feared combat and she did not fear the opinions of others. And this fear is what keeps those other spheres rolling. It is what has taken down all their edges. Maybe the Boz had helped her. Maybe she was just lucky. She had done exceptionally well by being different, by not being afraid to say what she felt. She and Garth still had roughly half of their drug left, the part that they had saved for the Presidential race, so he handed her one of the pills before her next press conference at the National Press Club in Washington, DC.

"The intersection of life in faith and life in the world," she began her televised address to the public, "is a very dangerous place at which to stand. Faith, in itself, and religion at its most personal, pose no danger. But the instant that religion takes a stand within the world it is acting like a political party, and in many cases an extremist political party. If you look at what happened to me at the mosque, you have to ask in what way the faith of each of the individuals there could possibly have been affected by my entry into their place of worship. Is their personal faith so fragile that it would suffer by my presence? And could their God be so brittle as to have been damaged by the actions of one middle-aged American woman? The problem is not what you believe but what you impose upon the rest of us. And in many cases the desire to impose upon others is stronger than any personal faith. And that is not faith. It is political will.

"And it is then," she added, "that we all must take notice. We have a tradition of religious tolerance in this country that is one of the very best things about us, about who we are. We need to better understand and to expand our understanding of this tradition and we need to guard it and to enforce it with vigilance. We should not be less concerned by any aggressive or oppressive program or enterprise simply because it asserts a divine right rather than a social or political one. We should be more concerned about an oppression that casts itself as a religion, not less concerned. Our religious freedoms extend to our right to be free from the worldly incursions of the religions of other men and women.

"We may not judge another person's faith," she continued, "but we must judge its worldly actions and the effect it has on the rest of us. Perhaps America is a faith. I must say that it is my faith. I have a democratic right to find my own way to God and I believe that each one of us has it as well. And like everything else in America, it must be democratic and it must be constitutional. We each have the right to be free from the actions of each other's faiths. The actions of each faith may be judged by the way it treats its members and non-members, by the way it treats women, by the way it treats the least among us, by the way it treats those who are its neighbors, and by the way it respects itself in the face of differing beliefs. It is one thing to live your own life in faith, it is another thing entirely to say that your God gives you certain sanctions within the world, such as the right to bomb innocents, or to take and command a land, or to oppress women. It is one thing to do good works and try to live your own life according to the teachings of your prophet, but it is a different thing to say that your faith has chosen you to dictate how others should live. That is not faith. It demeans your God and seeks to make God an instrument of worldly results and success. There is one passage of the Bible that I believe says it all.

"This is my dream," she intoned, her voice deepening and getting stronger, "and in that dream, we all live by this Bible passage, Matthew 6:5-6. And in that dream, no matter what our faith, we all share another faith and that common faith is America."

On a million screens and phones, Americans were searching for Matthew 6:5-6.

"*And when thou prayest, thou shalt not be as the hypocrites are: for they love to pray standing in the synagogues and in the corners of the streets, that they may be seen of men. Verily I say unto you, they have their reward. But thou, when thou prayest, enter into thy closet, and when thou hast shut thy door, pray to thy Father which is in secret; and thy Father which seeth in secret shall reward thee openly.*"

"We have freedom of religion in the United States," she added, "but we have somehow allowed this to become freedom from scrutiny, or even freedom from discussion. The cloak of religion is too often used to throw a First Amendment smoke screen over actions we would otherwise deplore. If a political party or an educational institution or any group were to advocate the subservience of African Americans or women, we would openly deride them as being racist or sexist. There would be a great deal of discussion. Yet when hundreds of millions of women are denied the vote and the right to own property, when they are enslaved to their husbands and fathers and brothers, we do not say very much about it at all, because these oppressions are a religious imperative. Our tolerance of different religions is being used against us. If you advocate the position that I should not have the right to vote, to own property, or to even drive a car, that is just your opinion and I can deal with that. But if you say that these things are a divine imperative, you are not less dangerous. You are more dangerous, because you will not negotiate and you do not accept even the existence of a different opinion.

"I do not want anyone to think that I am against religion. I am not. I may be a Christian. But I respect the religions of others. What I want for us to do is to be able to draw a distinction between religion and what I call the cant of religion. There is a difference between a humble and sincere and personal faith on the one hand, and the loud and ostentatious outward professions of those wishing to appear religious, particularly when these outward professions take form in the real world as legislation, or social rules, or religious wars. I believe in Matthew 6:5-6. I believe my faith is the true faith and because of that I do not have to show it all in public. And I do not have to force you to believe it. If I were to try to legislate the tenets of my faith, it would mean I had doubts of its truth. If you have to enforce your faith at the point of a gun, you do not really have faith. This is where I have trouble with any religion, and my issue is twofold. If you believe your religion requires every woman to cover her body, you do not have respect for any other religion and you do not have faith that your own religion can survive without such worldly enforcements. A truly faithful man of any faith would be able to respect any woman, whether she was covered up or not."

A thunderous applause blended with the sound of shouts and murmurs filled the room and slowly died down. Then came the questions.

"How do you respond to the claim that you have shown no respect for the Muslim religion?" a young woman reporter asked.

"If a Muslim were to come into my church and vandalize it, it would not weaken my faith nor attack the divine truth of my faith. Even if he were to burn my church to the ground, it would be a violent crime and it would disrespectful but it would not reduce the faith of those who had worshipped there. And my church would welcome the unbelievers, so that we might show them the light. If we thought that what someone did in our church would somehow attack our faith, we would be confessing a weakness of faith itself. Desecrating our building, or even our good book, does not diminish our faith."

"Are you saying that those men who attacked you were not true believers?" was the next question.

"Yes. What I am saying is that a man should believe with his heart, not with his fists, his legislation, or his guns. This is one of the things that makes the United States a unique country. Our faith is individual and internal. We are Americans. For dozens of years the Mormon Church in America preached polygamy, yet when it realized that the practice did not meet with the approval of the nation, they changed. The Mormon Church also excluded African Americans until it changed. These major changes did not make them any less Mormon. The essential lesson is that true faith is in the heart, and in the good works of the individual. It is not in what others do or think. It should not be enforced with stones and clubs or even with sharia laws. In fact, real spiritual faith cannot be enforced that way."

"It is interesting that you mention the Mormons, because you would also have been denied entrance into a Mormon church or tabernacle. What do you say to that?"

"That is a very good point. This is the kind of discussion that I think is healthy. There are also parts of some synagogues to which I would be denied entrance. And if I were a Catholic I would not be allowed to serve as a priest. But here in the greatest country in the world, I can serve in the military, I can serve in the House or in the Senate, I could be a member of the Cabinet or even the President. I believe in the United States of America. That is my first religion. It is the one religion that we all should share. It is our belief that anyone will have the opportunity to try to be anything that he or she strives to be or wants to be. You will notice that people from all over the world and people of all faiths want to come to America. We do not have to force conversions at the point of a sword. God Bless America."

Leaving the televised press conference, she walked to her car with a crowd of reporters and cameras around her. On the far edge of that crowd was a young man, an angry young man of Yemeni descent who was born and raised in America and was now unemployed. He began to shout and to condemn Melinda as an infidel.

There was the loud report of a gun being fired.

Melinda was forced to the ground and covered by her security detail. The police grabbed the young man. The national television news called it terrorism and then amended that banner, upon learning the identity of the attacker, to "Shooting at the Truth." The young man was his own private and personal version of the Zany Mullah.

Later that night, at their home, with a security detail outside, Melinda turned to Garth and looked at him quietly and calmly and gently. She told him that she needed him, she needed to go to their secret world. She held her hands in front of her, wrists together, and whispered.

"Take me, Garth. Take me. I will do anything for you, anything you want."

An hour and a half later he said, "Do you know what you just did today?"

"No," she answered, "what did I do, sweetheart?"

"You pushed us to the tipping point."

"Which one?"

"Eight years ago Islamic terrorists high-jacked four American commercial jets and flew three of them into United States landmarks, killing thousands. It opened our eyes to the dangers of religious extremism of all kinds, and not just Islamic. Polls show that it corresponded to the beginning of a significant increase in the number of Americans who now claim that they are agnostic or atheists. Since the beginning of our republic, the percentage of Americans who do not claim to have a religious faith has been miniscule, much less than ten percent and a much lower percentage than the number of people making the same claim in Europe. That percentage in America is still very small, but in those ten years it has more than doubled and it is increasing fast. The tipping point to which you are pushing us is that point at which we will become a humanist nation, secular, and distrustful of all religious extremism."

"That is wonderful, sweetheart," she said, her arm draped across his chest. "I was only saying what I think I've heard you say when we have had our talks."

"No, baby, you have added so much. And the best part is that you have coopted 'God Bless America' from being the anthem of the Christian Right to now being a statement of the secular values of our Constitution."

"God bless, America . . ." she said as she trailed off to sleep.

HIS FIRM HAND NO LONGER ON THE TILLER

Whenever there is a development in the field of foreign affairs the media will go to a Senator or a Congressman with seniority on the relevant committees for comment. They will also go to consultants, academics, think tanks, religious leaders, who have expertise in the field of foreign relations. These are the "go-to" people. The news outlets keep lists of go-to people for everything under the sun. Senator Sherman would quickly become the go-to person for something far broader and deeper and more significant.

She was attacked almost immediately by one of her conservative Senate colleagues who claimed that he had spoken to officials at the Pentagon and that he was convinced that Senator Sherman was endangering the lives of overseas American military personnel by inflaming the radical Islamists.

"Think twice," Melinda said, looking into the camera and not at the reporter who was questioning her.

"I mean, think more deeply, or think again. And I am addressing the American people, not the politicians. I have been in politics long enough to know that the politicians think that we Americans do not think very much, that we do not think deeply. In fact, they are counting on this. So, I am asking all Americans to think twice about this. Think it over.

"What it really means," she said, "is this: Those fundamentalist extremists are so crazy and so dangerous that we are not supposed to talk about them.

They should exercise censorship over us with fear. How can any American abide that? Several years ago a Danish cartoonist was threatened by these same extremist elements for drawing cartoons that they felt insulted their faith. Almost no American media outlet, not even the mighty *Washington Post*, would reprint those cartoons. Now, here is a great American newspaper, one that was so protected by our First Amendment that it one time had no fear to print stories that were damaging to a President, stories that brought down the Nixon Presidency. But the *Post* wouldn't print something out of fear of some group thousands of miles away. That is tyranny. We do not allow it here. We should not bow to it anywhere else in the world.

"And as far as the troops are concerned, no one feels for their safety more than I do," she said. "If there are tactical or strategic issues regarding their safety, they should be dealt with on a tactical or strategic level. Move them. Protect them better. Bring them home. But the most important point is this. The American military is deployed to defend and protect our essential values, one of which is freedom of speech. I can tell you this with some confidence. Those troops would not want to see us surrender what they are fighting for; they would not want us to be any less American. Not on their account, they wouldn't. Think twice. Think again. Think more deeply."

Senator Melinda Sherman was becoming the "go-to woman" for thinking more deeply, for that eminently quotable alternative viewpoint, styled by some as the real story. She was seen this way by not only some in the news media, but by many of her colleagues, by various educational institutions, by groups of concerned citizens in Iowa and New Hampshire, and by a growing segment of the American electorate.

Contrary to what might be expected, Garth was very concerned about this.

Richard Nixon had clearly understood the dialectics of politics. He had been able to find the kernel of advantage in any political liability and had the sense and skill to make that kernel grow into an asset, which is how he stayed on the Vice Presidential ballot in 1956, with the Chekers speech, which turned petty graft into the middle-class virtue of thrift. And every asset also has its similar seeds of its own destruction and in many cases this is the potential for backlash. Garth knew that in every human heart there is small gnome, whose voice is not often heard but which on occasion can command the heart's attention.

This diminutive portion of the soul simply hates the bright thing. Melinda had aura and she was growing in power and influence. She was at that point in the road where she could choose to blaze forward on the upward path or she could take the more gradually inclined hidden road. Garth wanted to avoid any backlash. He did not want her to become the flavor of the month only to fade into obscurity or ridicule.

He recalled what he had read on the paper she had shown him, "hypo-mania, cyclothymia, and hyperthermic temperament." He did not know exactly what those terms meant, but he knew that the woman he loved was different from other people. And he also knew intimately that the world into which they had agreed she would be operating was a cauldron, one that had brought out the worst in people less volatile than Melinda. Garth had already seen the way in which his wife's "edges" had already been shown and to positive effect.

She was rather blunt and had a way with a memorable phrase. She had drawn attention to herself. But they both lived in the awareness that she might one day overstep, or even launch into a vision or an incident not unlike the one in Melinda's shower after they became engaged. They agreed that she focus on her work in the Senate. The Presidential election featuring the Democratic incumbent was approaching and this was at once another reason for her to withdraw from the limelight and onto that more concealed path.

At some time shortly after the President's reelection the question of same sex marriage was a topic of discussion and judicial action. The federal Defense of Marriage Act, which denied federal benefits to same sex couples who might become legally married in states that would permit it, was being questioned. The President had said that he did not support same sex marriage but that his position was evolving, which is a very radical way of saying that he was watching the polls. This was exactly the type of brave and daring act of true leadership which called for a counterpoint and with the opposition having been defeated, the press turned again to Senator Sherman.

She found herself trapped by a group of television journalists that had stationed themselves outside the Capitol. They had questioned a number of Senators, but had now called on Senator Sherman, having the idea that she would give them something that would make news.

Melinda had always had been striking. She was strapping and athletic and it reflected in her carriage and posture. Now, at forty-four years old, the athleticism she had always possessed was still there but her figure had lost its angularity and had gained some curves. The hints of softness and roundness that had always been part of what had made it pretty had retreated, leaving the field to her bone structure. Her high forehead, her straight nose, her strong cheeks and jaw, stood out now, chiseled into a conspicuous and notably handsome beauty. She kept her sandy brown hair short in a way that would have made her look almost masculine were it not for the soft curl of her lips, the feminine vivacity in her eyes, and the dynamic and womanly form that no conservative business suit could conceal. It was to this woman that the questions about same sex marriage were asked.

"I freaking love gay men," she said.

"I am always going to urge that upon people. When I served in the Navy I knew a sailors, soldiers, Marines and airmen. Some were gay. Most were straight. Every one of them measured up. I would have been proud and honored to go into battle alongside any of them. I certainly cannot look any one of them in the eye, and tell them that they cannot have the same rights and privileges that we all have.

"Let us think beyond that. Seven hundred and fifty thousand Americans died in the Civil War. Over four hundred thousand died in World War II. For World War 1 and Viet Nam combined, those numbers total over three hundred thousand. Roughly one point three million Americans have died in wartime in the service of the United States," she said. "Now how many of them do you think might have been gay? This country was built and has been protected in part by people who have been attracted to the same sex. Do we want to pay this debt by denying those same men and women the rights and privileges we all should enjoy?"

The first comment, of course, made all the news stations and went viral.

Her website and contributions began to pick up contacts from within the gay community. Responses from conservative religious people dropped but they did not stop. The highly unusual political scenario was that each frank statement she made added a new group, but did not alienate opposing groups too much. She was defying the rules of political care and caution. Senator Sherman was beginning to be seen as a serious Senator who just happened to speak plainly, and more importantly was able to do so without fallout. She was simply, in a word, exciting.

"I see you are still protecting your big gay brother," Porter said to her on the phone that evening.

"I see it as doing the right thing."

"You always have. And thank you for not outing me."

"I figure that is your call."

"Maybe I will do it myself, later. Do you know where I am calling you from? Hollywood. I have a major role in a major motion picture, part of a franchise."

"Don't tell me you are the next Spiderman."

"It is a Spielberg project."

"What, you are going to be in Jurassic Park IV, or in Indiana Jones V?"

"No."

"I thought you said it was a franchise."

"He is the franchise. All his films are part of the 'Steven Spielberg – Shooting Fish in a Barrel' franchise. This film is going to be about how love is good or how disease is bad or some other kind of emotional slam-dunk like that. Can you believe he just called me up and half the interview was about you, what are you really like, what Garth's like, what are the stories of our growing up. Look out, Mindy, I think you are going to be a celebrity. You've already moved me onto the A list, thank you very much."

"I guess I am happy for you, Porter, but you do know what I am going to say next."

"Yeah, 'Don't mess it up'. I will be okay. I guess this means I am going to have to shut down my 'Nuke Mecca' campaign."

"Oh, my god. That's you, those graffiti? In some big cities?"

"Don't worry. I have been completely anonymous. No one knows who it is. I just wanted to be the one to protect you for once."

Melinda could only answer with silence. And she could only imagine what she could not have known. She was trying to imagine it but try as she might the truth would evade her. And she did not want to know that Porter had been doing this for a couple of years. He had a long time confidential personal assistant whose loyalty was inviolable. His name was Adonis Michaels and his loyalty was in part due to a long and unrequited love he felt for his employer, who had hired him literally off of the street and had given him a much better life. At every city in which Porter stopped, Adonis Michaels would go back into the streets, which were always familiar to him, no matter the city. And he would shorten his name for the small handful of street youths he approached when he would hand each them the "Nuke

Mecca" stencils, some garishly colored spray paint, and a hundred dollars. He would tell them to come back the next day to get paid some more but only if they had done a good job. When they would return after having painted the town he would not be there and if they were ever questioned all they could say was that they had been paid by some middle-aged man they had never seen before and who they simply knew as Smike.

"I will stop it. Jesus has been bugging me to quit anyway."

"You know I have been shot at by those people, don't you? And, trust me on this. Someone in the government knows it was you doing it. It might leak. You can imagine the headline."

"Yeah, I can. 'Presidential Candidate's Hollywood Homo Brother Incites Holy War,' does that sound right to you?"

"How is Jesus?"

"Great. We may even be getting married. They are saying that same sex marriage will be legal in New York sometime this year. I guess you will have to put your money where your mouth is when you attend your big brother's big gay wedding. You can be the flower girl."

"I will have no problem with that. I assume it will be a Ceylonese wedding. This political stuff doesn't really matter. I'm still your sister, first. I am grateful for being able to do what I can for the people of Kentucky and I appreciate playing a part in national affairs, but it does not matter half as much to me as Garth and the kids, and you and, I guess, Jesus."

"That's what makes you so good at the politics. You're not a politician at heart."

"That may be the nicest thing you have said to me. Thanks. No more graffiti, okay?"

"Sure thing."

Melinda wondered if that really was what made her do well at politics. She knew there were other things. Combat had taught her to keep her cool under fire. And there was Garth. She also feared most of her adult life that she was a borderline bipolar. That could give her some kind of weird reverse spin advantage. And she might just be fitting into a long and renowned historical pattern, because one thing that she felt was true as soon as she heard Garth once say it, was that the urge to put your name on a ballot is a kind of pathology. Only crazy people do it. Psychologically and emotionally healthy people are satisfied with the approval of their family and friends. They do not need to be adored by the masses, as shallow and fickle as such admiration is. Being a bit cracked was a professional requirement but maybe she gained from the fact that her cracks ran in a different direction.

Not surprisingly, her position on same sex marriage was to receive another stamp of approval when the President of the United States "reevaluated his position," when he saw that the polls were no longer opposed to same sex marriage, as it was being be legalized in individual states, and might receive the same approval by the Supreme Court.

Garth had once told Melinda that Ronald Reagan was less of a politician than an actor and this had been an advantage. His handlers had more interest in their low tax and corporate welfare agenda than they did in having him be cautious. So he acted, not in the role of a politician, but in the role of a leader. He took minority positions on divisive issues such as abortion that appeared as matters of conscious and not political restraint. Even those who had disagreed with him respected him for not being too much of a careful politician.

Ever since she had been a child, Melinda always had an instinct for doing the right thing. Not even her approaching Senate reelection could change who she was. Wilton Carlson was also a strong guide for her. Garth told her that Wilton had once said that politics was an emasculating profession. Wilton broke that mold. She'd always smiled at that. Politics was not going to emasculate her. She was a woman. Her strength came from a deeper place.

She called the war on drugs "stupid" and "a sin." It is about the economics, she said. An undereducated and underprivileged minority male could make ten dollars an hour working at a fast food store or he could make a few thousand dollars a night by standing on a street corner. Far from discouraging criminal conduct, the government was incentivizing it. And then what happens is that the drug dealer is sent to prison. His conviction removes his economic opportunities. Then he is locked up with hundreds of other criminals with whom he makes fresh drug connections. All of this leads to recidivism, she said.

"No other country does what we do; with five percent of the world's population, the United States imprisons twenty-five percent of the world's incarcerated individuals, despite the fact that we are the land of the free and that there are some very large countries with oppressive regimes and no rule of law. One in every one hundred and thirty-five Americans is behind bars.

"And to those of us who are Christians," she said, "I ask: what of Matthew eighteen twenty-two, or Matthew twenty-five forty? I believe that those words are a good guide to how we should deal with people for whom drugs are a problem. We certainly can be judged as a nation by whether or not we are humane to our offenders. Do we want to be the least forgiving nation in all of Christendom?

"The mounting rolls of the incarcerated are growing more full of people of color from poor neighborhoods every day. As for the so-called war on drugs, wealthy white people use illegal drugs as well but they are much less likely to be caught and convicted. Such a high percentage of the population must feel that the drug laws are all right to break. This is Prohibition and the results are the same. Large numbers of people had repealed the law in their hearts and huge criminal enterprises had sprung up to meet the demand."

She also pointed out that there were significant foreign policy considerations.

"The massive incomes available from smuggling illegal drugs into the United States had turned our Latin American neighbors into havens for violent drug cartels."

This may have been heard before. But no political figure of such high standing had ever been so forthright. It was considered foolhardy for her to make such a strong statement before her reelection. She only cared about taking that shot with her left hand, about hitting the dangerous target. She was not surprised and was pleased later to learn that she had struck a chord even among the conservative voters of Kentucky, who had an anti-authoritarian streak, dating back to the heyday of moonshining and because a good many of them knew someone who had been prosecuted by the government. After all, even her Republican Senate colleague, a libertarian, agreed with her in many respects although he never had stated it so strongly or plainly, but he too had mined that same Kentucky political vein. But she had really captured their understanding when she equated it with the right to bear arms.

"It is simply wrong to blame the instrumentality," she said, "and this is what is wrong with most gun control laws. They blame the gun. Don't blame the gun. And don't blame drugs. Think more deeply. If we blame the instrumentality we are in a sense absolving the individual. We lose sight of individual responsibility, which is the bedrock of our society. If someone does something illegal while using a gun or a drug, do not take the focus away from that individual conduct. Punish it. But punish the conduct. Punish the individual. Do not go looking for blame in some inanimate object. Hold individuals responsible. This is what we lose with most drug laws and most gun control laws.

"What most politicians are afraid of," she said, "is this. They are afraid that if they do as I am doing right now, if they successfully advocate for good sense in our drug laws, that some prisoner will be released and that prisoner will commit some violent crime. Then a political opponent will try to claim that his or her advocacy led to some innocent person being victimized. Again, this is not thinking deeply. This is blaming the instrumentality of the release and not the individual who would commit the crime. Most politicians think that we their voters are not all that smart. But we are. The people of Kentucky are that smart. The American people are smart enough to see it clearly. Do you know how I know we are intelligent? We are smart enough to live in America."

Her curious blending of more customarily considered conservative and liberal positions had become one of her hallmarks. She had done the same by standing as a fiscal conservative and demanding that other developed nations pay their share of their defense, which also pleased the liberal factions who wanted to lower defense spending. She had couched her liberal defense of same sex marriage in conservative terms of supporting the American men and women in uniform. Here she had equated drugs with guns. Many conservative gun owners quickly saw the comparison, especially those already inclined to vote for her, and even some liberals who supported reform in the drug laws had to begin to see the connections. In fact, she felt that she was right all along, and she said it.

"No true conservative can really support our current federal drug laws, which empower the federal government to regulate what an individual puts into his or her own body in the privacy of his or her home. At the very most, a true conservative might be able to advocate that such regulation belongs at the local level, where the police and the public are neighbors and can assess the impacts. And no true liberal can continue to support this country's quest to become the most punitive state in the history of the world and to do so at the expense of poor people of color," she said.

"Outrageous" had been the word some had used to describe her advocacy of drug law reform and her other positions. For one thing, no politician in recent memory had ever used the word "Christendom" and few had ever openly quoted Jesus to further a liberal cause. Same sex marriage was not popular at all among her voters, but they understood her argument about the gay men and women who served in the military. They also knew that this was a position that was more national in its latitude, that it was something that was preparing their own Senator for the national political stage. And they were proud of her for that.

Many of them found a different word for her positions. And this was the word that was often trumpeted by much of the media, which still found her appealing and interesting because her appearances raised their ratings and her face on the front page sold more newspapers.

The favored word was "courageous."

And it was never more appropriate than it was on the eve of her reelection, when she committed what was assuredly called "political suicide."

BEN WAS CERTAIN

Certain dour spices and murky vegetables and rotten essences were also bubbling elsewhere, brewing in a malevolent broth that was going to possibly poison the virtuous and nourishing infusion that Garth had hoped he and Melinda might add to the political menu of the American marketplace. The aroma of this dangerous consommé came to Garth from the only place in the country that could hold the kind of cauldron necessary for the task. Such a brew had its antecedents and he knew could only be made in one place, the same place that this kind of perilous gumbo had often been concocted, in his home state of Texas.

The first hints of an unpleasant fragrance seemed to linger around an innocuous phone call from an unlikely source. Preston Cobalt had called Garth to suggest that he might be able to help Garth with his "Earnest problem."

"Thanks," Garth said. "I will keep it in mind and get back to you with it."

Once he had said something so bland and dismissive to this crafty Texan, he was forced to apply most of his effort on hiding from his old friend, who had also been instrumental in launching Melinda and him on their current political arc. He was very surprised that Preston even knew of such a thing. And he had to make appear as if it were not something that essentially deeply concerned him. Garth's primary goal was to give Preston no cause for thinking that any action was necessary. He knew that any alarm or concern might trigger action on the part of the highly independent Preston no matter how much Garth might urge against it later. Garth only considered later how once, over thirty years earlier, Earnest Dapple had been the only one of their friends who had not been flown on the charter jet to Preston's graduation party because it might confuse the servants. Preston was not a racist but had acted honestly and perhaps without compassion on what had been at the time a family concern. His impressions of Earnest, like Garth's, were more dictated by observation and not by any predisposition. The question uppermost in Garth's mind was not why Preston was making this offer, but how he came to know that there was an Earnest problem in the first place.

There were only three people in Texas who might know anything about what Earnest Dapple had been doing, Eakin Lambert, Elliott Barker and Ben Dessous. Neither Ben nor Eakin knew Preston so only Elliott could have alerted him. But Elliott's own understanding could only be second or third hand. The only one with any direct knowledge had to be Ben and the extent of what he fully comprehended was always hidden from everyone except to Eakin. So for Ben's information to have passed from Eakin to Elliott would practically require that the two of them had entered into some kind of an entente, which Garth had anticipated. And while he smiled to himself to think of this possibility, he knew that he could not call either one of them and that he had to directly get in touch with Ben to see what he might be willing to reveal about any new developments in what Preston named their Earnest problem.

It has been said that geography is destiny. But it is also at the core of the soul of the people of any place. To most early Americans the Appalachian Mountains were a barrier that had to be crossed in order to get to the open farmland and endless possibilities of what was then called the American West. Not all pioneers crossed the ancient and brooding forested ridges.

Some were snagged in the passage and found hiding places in the ridges and hollows and vales that gave many of them the same character as the place, apparently verdant and warm and welcoming but with rigid stone underneath, and capable of equally hard acts of sudden storm or deadly cold or precipitous fog.

Similarly, the character of any Texan is equally not unrelated to the quality of the land upon which he lives or across which he moves. Just the trip from east to west ends of the state will encompass almost a thousand miles and a dozen climates, beginning with the humid subtropical bayous surrounding Port Arthur with its sixty inches of annual rainfall to the arid half-mile-high plains of the Chihuahua Desert around Ciudad Juarez where maybe an inch of rain might fall in a month and where it is cold at night even when the summer sun has overheated the land during the day.

Garth's attention was now called to that particular part of east Texas near this first part of that hypothetical journey, where he had grown up and where his friends and family lived. It was a bit west of the very most eastern part of the state, which is essentially another part of Louisiana, but still east of the much drier hill country of east central Texas.

If this region was the cauldron which was concocting the repellant aroma which had come to Garth as the scent of a threat, it was because it was that borderline province that mixed and blurred the paradoxical vivacity and lassitude of the Latinate voluptuaries of its eastern edges with the more stoical and indifferent characters of the cowboys who inhabited the western side. The land was in between, a region that was hot and humid with standing water and lakes, and which the Sabine, Neches, Brazos and Trinity Rivers crossed. In the direction of the sunrise the people have a partiality for a particular kind of poised and amateur vagrancy that would break into spontaneous festivity, as may occur when a street row might break out or where a drunken man might hold a dialogue with himself or his neighbors or where doorways might become confused by lovers. Toward the direction of the setting sun, such dramas were far more a matter of a kind of distinctly private theater, rarely if ever drawing comment from the phlegmatic individuals whose ethos was to mind their own business and reserve judgment.

Between this cowboy west and the Cajun east, these two personality topographies exist uncomfortably side-by-side. Through this part of Texas, a stranger now moved.

He was a tall and somewhat dapper man for whom "east" did not mean a port on the Gulf of Mexico but one on the Atlantic Ocean and for whom a cowboy or a Cajun was a character on television. In fact this man was somewhat alarmed to have just learned that a Francophone rural person of this part of Texas was not called a Cajun, as he was in neighboring Louisiana, but was called a "coon ass," which was very jarring to him. What Earnest had just learned about the imaginative ethnic taxonomy of east Texas served only as one of the reasons he had already for despising the area, one that was additional to those motives that had long been lodged in him and that disposed him indeed against any place. Such prejudices had never in the past inhibited him from social interaction with individuals he disdained, nor were they going to slow him down now. He was negotiating with the young Cajun gentleman at the bar in Joe Bobby's Roadhouse, outside of Nelsonville, Texas.

Throughout what normally might have been called his relationship with Tabitha, he had treated Garth's ex-wife as a beautiful child. He was so unaware and inattentive of the depths of feeling that existed below her surface that he had calculated that she would have very concrete doubts as to whether or not there could be any such depths in him. But Tabitha's attention traveled in a small set of grooves and did not range broadly in order to cover all her life that might actually need her attention. The trenches that her mind carved in her subsurface beneath these channels were very deep. He could not have anticipated her reaction to his plan to bring their liaison to a termination. At about the time she was only repeating the stories about Garth that he was recording, Tabitha's sister, Gwen, was to arrive for a visit.

Since Gwen had been the spoiled and uninhibited younger sister who had grown up stealing Tabitha's clothes, sports equipment and boyfriends, Earnest had conceived of a convenient plan by which he might end his time with Tabitha, while at the same time enjoying the prospect of putting Gwen on her back on Tabitha's living room before Tabitha were to return home. It seemed to work all very neatly except that he lacked Garth's experience and understanding to know enough that he would then become the subject of Tabitha's immovable hatred. He thought she should have known he had never been serious. Perhaps she did, but it fell into her tunnel vision. He then felt better than he normally might at having to travel not only beyond the Washington beltway, but actually out into America, as far as east Texas.

This may give rise to errant consideration of whatever conscience Earnest may have possessed. He only felt badly for himself. A conscience is like an article of clothing. Many far more tenderhearted persons find that it will bear a certain amount of stretching and slipping and wearing out before it eventually will slip off. But for this intrepid reporter it was more like a vest or a sweater that he could remove and toss off at pleasure.

The young Cajun man at the Roadhouse Bar was always turning sideways and looking over his shoulder in order to talk, as if his voice would not work in any other position. He was engaging and talkative nonetheless, although very little of what he said was often to the point. He would regularly burst forth with one of those unique laughs perched on a point from which it seemed very little might change it into a cry. He had at a very young juncture in his life been initiated into the ways of the adults around him so that his childlike confidence and simplicity had been checked in their natural current. This gave him a certain emotional kind of radio frequency which was accessible to the worldly. The sorrows and duties of life as a grown person had been prematurely strapped to this young man by his father, who had at one time been a hunting and fishing guide in this broader region.

It was about his father and what the young man remembered of his work that Earnest was seeking information, which over a few drinks he was able to obtain. But there was something else. Earnest was well aware of the way in which the early maturing of this young man gave him a sympathetic wavelength with his own jaded sensibility. With the promise of remuneration, he had just sent him on a mission the journalist would never undertake to do on his own.

This now created a decision to be made by the other man in the corner of the bar, to either follow the local younger man or to keep watching the older man from out of town.

By this time Ben Dessous had resided in the area west of Houston for almost thirty years. He was able fit in and he benefitted from the fact that whatever attention each native in the bar directed away from his own group was more certain to land upon the taller man at the bar who was wearing the loafers, the pressed khaki pants, the oxford buttoned down dress shirt and who had been with a talkative Cajun. Ben's only concern was that he might be spotted by Earnest. But Ben had not had any contact with the man for more than thirty years and he now looked like many an older and local hard-worked gentleman. But he did still have the scar. But at this far flung outpost Earnest would not be expecting anyone at all whom he might know, and least of all some long unused contact from one of the poorer neighborhoods of the city where he had gone to college. So Ben chose to stay and keep watching his principle and let the younger man go his own way.

Earnest had not changed all that much as he had moved to his fifties.

He was still thin and had not grayed much. He largely had escaped the more subtle signs of aging that gently rise in the physiognomy of most middle-aged men, the moderated glimmer of mild resignation, the sweet, sad, smart eyes that have the experience of being witness to much of what one has already seen many times, the reserved half smile that comes from knowing that the terribly difficult and the wildly pleasurable feelings of youth have passed, or the understated and fleeting winces that will only occasionally shadow a face that has known great loss. This was the face of a youth in its own way and one that had long been made immune from these intangible tolls of aging by virtue of its own jaded and insensible vitality. Not much could get at Earnest. And for Ben he had been a subject of observation for some time. Whatever changes had come had been taken in. Ben knew that something was happening here, that Earnest's reaction was a little bit too gleaming for what might be good for Ben and those for whom he felt responsible.

One of those people, Garth, had been calling him, the cell phone showed. It was not like Garth to call more than once and Ben applied himself to the question. It could be either that Garth had something pressing to tell him or that he was very interested to know something. Ever since he had gone to work for Eakin, Ben got much of Garth's news from her. She inherently knew the delicate importance of keeping Ben informed. She had direct experience with the way in which Ben seemed to be silently watching and discreetly acting in ways that would always prove beneficial. She would also tell Garth much of what she might know of what Ben was doing. Ben was one of the best examples of that wonderful fact, that every human creature is constituted to be that profound secret and mystery to every other. He knew exactly what Eakin might have told Garth, because he regulated what he told her. But Elliott was also working with Eakin and he did not speak that much to Garth. He had many other friends. Ben inherently knew that Elliott might have been the indirect conduit by which some question had been brought to Garth. It seemed clear that there was now something that Garth wanted to know. That was perhaps always the case more generally, Ben thought, and it could wait.

He watched Earnest consult his cell phone, read his newspaper and order some dinner and even have a few beers, all relatively unaware of how he was being watched not only by Ben but intermittently by the indifferent patrons of the bar. One such watchful but laconic man who had once worked with Ben in another capacity had alerted him to the meeting of the garrulous Cajun man and this stranger from the northeast who was of interest to Ben. Although Ben had been born in St. Croix and had grown up in Boston, his self-possession and his reticence and his utter reliability and his sense of individual boundaries suited him well over the many years it might take for any stranger, particularly one such as he, to begin to gain a network of contacts in this part of the United States. When Earnest finally left to return to his motel, Ben followed him and stayed a discreet distance away and slept in his car.

He followed Earnest's rental car the next morning on a drive westward toward Austin by highway. They had passed the state capital and turned south toward San Antonio and began to proceed over the slow back roads. The front car would often slow down and would occasionally make a wrong turn. It seemed that Earnest was navigating from an old map. The mapping device that Ben was consulting seemed to indicate that Earnest was attempting to follow some old directions on a route along the Guadalupe River but was becoming confused by the various housing developments and neighborhoods which had sprung up since the date of the map. Finally, they reached the remote Texas hill country northwest of San Antonio near a state park to find the old dirt road Earnest might have been seeking.

Ben drove further down the paved road and parked and got out and followed the dirt road but through the woods in order to watch Earnest walking down the lane to its end at an old abandoned fishing and hunting camp along the side of the river. Earnest only wanted to see the camp, to confirm its existence, and he left immediately. Ben kicked around the place and sat for a while along the riverbank and he began to absorb the setting while placing himself back into the time long ago when the camp had been in use. He had an idea where Earnest was now driving, so Ben drove rather directly. He caught up to the rental car on Interstate 10, near the La Grange exit and followed it to Joe Bobby's Roadhouse in Nelsonville.

Entering the bar, he saw the young man from the previous evening, waiting for Earnest. Ben watched from his corner as the young man fidgeted and waited for Earnest. What must have appeared as nothing particular at all to a casual observer from the east coast of the United States, or was not noticeable to a member of the lively social and ethnic group from which the young man was drawn, stood out like some cinematic clandestine drug deal to the laconic and watchfully reserved cowboys who patronized Joe Bobby. The young man was entirely too furtive and the older man was just plain foreign.

The young man was upset about something and was expecting some manner of apology. Whatever it was that he had agreed to do for Earnest the evening before did not sit well. He was no longer satisfied with the terms he had agreed upon earlier and that he was interested in re-forming the contract. Earnest had in front of him a folded newspaper that seemed to hold the man's attention and was apparently the object to be dealt with, as part of the renegotiation.

Earnest finally stood up and left for the bathroom with the folded paper, leaving Ben and perhaps half a dozen other men to assume that it was to make a small adjustment to the contents of an envelope which must have been inside the newspaper. He returned and placed the newspaper on the table between them. Then he was listening to a very involved and lively discussion the Cajun man was recalling for his benefit. Then the younger man took the newspaper and quickly walked out the door, leaving behind a pack of cigarettes that Earnest placed in his pocket. In some of the harder precincts of any urban area, even nearby Houston, Earnest might not have made it to the car with that pack, nor would the other man have made away with the envelope. They would have been relieved of each in the parking lot, whereas here the entire scene had just been part of that peculiar and particular and provincial private theater, for which any kind of audience participation was more than unlikely.

It would have been just as well for one set of such prospective hijackers, since Ben was certain that there were no drugs in the cigarette pack, and that it contained something that not only would have disappointed them but might have also made them quite upset or even sick. Ben had seen the video of Senator Sherman's speech at the National Press Club and had stared at it and the enhanced stills from it, until it had coalesced into a sequence he understood. At the end of the Senator's speech, one of the reporters ambled in the general direction of the podium, even stopping to pass a few words with another journalist, while still attending to his route. Ben had figured it all out. Earnest had more or less made a beeline for the glass of water from which Melinda had been drinking and had surreptitiously slipped it into a plastic bag.

Texas had a long history of fermenting various biotic cultures of a social or of a religious character that had then later infected much of the rest of the country, and in the three decades previous to the time of these events, Texas Fundamentalists had toppled the Moderate leadership of the Southern Baptist Church, which in 1845 had itself separated from its northern Baptist brethren because those descendants of the New Englander Roger Williams had erred in determining that slavery was a sin in the eyes of God. Baptism in all its European, Northern, African-American, Southern and Texan variations had always been a creedless and anti-clerical religious impulse that was essentially experiential. These practices had been the experience of being born again through the ritual of adult baptism springing from the deeply personal experience of communing with the text of the Bible as a member of a priesthood of believers. For the last two decades of the past century and for the first decade of the current one, Baptist Fundamentalists in Texas have taken over the control of the Southern Baptist Convention with the essential tenets of new order being that the only experiences now required are the simple statement that one has been saved. With this must come unquestioning adherence to the dictates of the pastors of the faith, making it what one arch observer has called the new Catholic Church of the South and what another has called the driving intellectual force of the American Republican Party.

That Texas had produced two Presidents and three Presidential terms within a twenty years span seems a coincidence, but it was not one ever far from the mind of one person who sat very near the place where this small section of this narrative has unfolded.

In Austin, a new Texas leader sat in the very spot once occupied by Governor Sam Houston, who had also been a President of the Republic of Texas and a US Senator from the state of Texas, only to fall into disfavor with his fellow Texans when he insisted that his home state not secede from the Union in 1861. He had insulted them with his reasoning, which was that even given the combination of their superior righteous determination and esprit de corps, it was no match for implacable and latent resolve of the apparently dissolute Yankees, which would allow the North to win the Civil War with one arm tied behind its back.

He had said of the Northerners, "They are not a fiery, impulsive people as you are, for they live in colder climates. But when they begin to move in a given direction, they move with the steady momentum and perseverance of a mighty avalanche; and what I fear is, they will over-whelm the South."

Predicting that war's outcome and perhaps indicating the future tra-vails of the Moderate wing of the Southern Baptist Church, to which he had converted in 1854, this man who had also once been the Governor of Tennessee resigned from the office of Governor of Texas, retired to Huntsville, became active in his Masonic Lodge and died two years later. The current Texas Governor at this point was none other than Rich Sartory, who had ascended not only from the office of Lieutenant Governor but also from the position of having been the young man Garth Teller had hired to assist him in managing his first campaign for Wilton Carlson.

Governor Sartory was busy that day as he had been for some time, gathering around him the elements he might require to once again raise a son of the Lone Star State to the highest office in the United States, not in the imminent Presidential election involving the Democratic incumbent, but in the one following. Despite whatever momentum and perseverance might exist in any other region of the country, this man was the chosen future candidate of the fundamentalist – one could call them – clerics he had long courted. He could count on the support of his own populous state, where he had long worked to suppress the voting participation of its Democratic-leaning and growing Latin American minority. He had denied the so-called science of evolution and of the human impact on global climate. So, the dictates of his friends and fellow believers, the pastors, would direct the votes of many others across the South. The Republican establishment was aware of the strength of his base and of his advocacy for lowering corporate and top bracket personal income taxes, so there was very little which might prevent his nomination in 2016.

Rich Sartory also believed that he was well armed with an excellent personal understanding of the man who would likely run the opposing

Democratic campaign that year. And it was to that man now that Ben directed the following text message, in answer to the numerous voice messages he had from Garth.

"Call your parents."

TERRORIST ATTACK

Senator Sherman killed her chances to go beyond being a one-term US Senator on one day a month before her second Senate election. So it had been reported.

She and Garth shared some irony in their individual approaches to her political career. To her, it was not who she really was and always clearly stood second to her marriage and her stepchildren. This is something that is certainly proclaimed by all men and women in politics; Melinda never publicly said it. It was so much a part of her that she could not reduce it to words nor share it with strangers, would have dishonored the genuine feeling. Garth approached the matter like a Chicago Cubs fan; he simply knew that no matter how well things seemed to be going, it could easily end unsuccessfully, when some misstep, revelation, external factor, calamity would intervene. These ironies, his defensive and hers authentic, did not inhibit their efforts. These two worked very sincerely toward their goals but their identities were never fully invested. They were in a dream of politics, which does not strain the imagination in the case of wild success of any type, and which in Melinda's case was never far from the genuine truth. It was her particular brand of oxymoron, political indifference, which allowed her to issue the statements that were widely perceived to have ended her career.

Garth's irony was more a question of having experienced loss in family and career. He knew his wife's peculiar personality as well, the vagaries of politics, and some specifics surrounding the activities of his old college friend who was a reporter. These last were of particular concern to him now. He had just called his parents, as urged by Ben. He had tried to have a conversation but it was made difficult by the quiet tumult on the other end of the phone. He could hear his father putting on his hat and jacket while he tried to talk to Garth. He could also hear the strong and imploring but silent instructing that his mother was doing with her necklace. The final outcome of it was only one snippet he was able to understand.

"I will try to talk to you later, Garth. We have to go," his father had said. "Apparently, your grandfather's grave has been robbed, I mean, disturbed."

Garth would try think about that, while he would be navigating the stormy currents of the maelstrom stirred up later by his wife's startling candor. He would only be able to if he was able to take a breath. When he would leave the deck of the ship he was captaining through the political squall, in order to take a duck below and get dry for a moment, he found that the was neither fresh nor cool. It carried in it the lingering smoke and acrid aroma of some important engine that was about to blow. He and Melinda had a way about them that was calm and graceful in the face of any such problems. Even though Garth had always been a person who could be distracted by worry, he had always understood the virtue of simple approach.

"Well, it will be bad. And it will have an end," he would say.

That such an end might be good or bad was not all that much within his control and his ability to exercise some control would be improved by staying calm. This same end, either way, would make it easier to remain calm because it promised a rest at some point.

And that is how Melinda became the first Senator or Congressmen from a coal producing state to advocate that the United States adopt a tax on carbon. She did it thirty days before her name was on the ballot in Kentucky for reelection to the Senate. It was the right thing to do. Part of the reason she had never formed the kind of powerful friendships nor became part of one of the close groups that are forged in the furnace of politics at its higher levels was that she never felt a part of it. She was a paradoxical combination of being very self-contained, while at the same time her visionary mind could fly past all normal limits.

Senators form a kind of club because they are under a unique set of pressures. The junior Senator from Kentucky was not in this club.

Senator Guscio "Gus" Casabianca of Rhode Island was her only friend in the Senate. He was not repelled by her corners and flat surfaces nor by her political disinterest. He had been introduced to her by Garth whom he had followed by two years through Harvard. To him it was not a matter of Senate collegiality. It was an old school tie. He was the scion of a Providence political dynasty. He honestly liked Melinda and knew she would make his Senate service a great deal more interesting. Many men in the Senate had felt the same way, simply for the idea of being a friend to the Senate's most striking woman. These men and the Senate sisterhood's members who also had made an effort to seek her out had all eventually withdrawn from building the relationship simply because their spherical approach to her cubical eminence was not rewarded by signs of progress. But Gus had an appreciation for her as the wife of a friend from college, and he also liked her for what could only be called her "affliction."

His father had survived extensive combat service in Europe during World War II and had left the Army with a certain *joie de vivre*. He had then been well known as a raconteur and a man more than at home in a parlor or a ballroom, breaking out into song at political functions; he was often telling long humorous stories that had five or six punch lines, never lacking for a clever verbal riposte, finding some success as an amateur painter, and being the favorite of women all through his own career as councilman, federal government appointee, and mayor. He was also a veritable shrinking violet growing in the shades of the wreathed profusion of his wife.

She was known to be in such animated contemplation of her own end that she kept an open casket in the living room of whatever home they inhabited. That she was known to have occasionally climbed into it and from there to have held forth is a matter for speculation and legend, as was the story that she had once fed infant Gus by suspending a baby bottle on the side of his crib. Her way was not always restricted to such limited eccentricity. She could be quite normal, as she had been at the time she lost her driver's license, not for driving under the influence but for driving erratically. Her response was to buy a brand new car, and of course, a puppy.

All this is to say that young Gus had loved her not only as his mother but as the way any impressionable individual might appreciate the Matterhorn or Mozart or magic. So his interests in staying in contact with the singular Senator from Kentucky arose from a sense of loyalty to both his friend, and to his mother, and to the extent this interest was really rather aesthetic.

He appreciated the ways in which Melinda was different. Senator Casabianca carried the mild strangeness and exotic ebullience of his parents at a level just beneath his surface, as a ready tendency toward irony or playfulness. So from surface to core, he was a perfect mentor for Melinda. He was also more attuned to the truth or to what he thought was right than he was toward political expediency. He was tearing himself apart over the way in which mankind's obvious negative impact on global change was either being sacrificed to less cataclysmic problems by his concerned colleagues or that it was being denied. He felt what was almost a kind of sensible or sane madness, that of being the only one to seem terribly concerned about what everyone else should see and should distress them deeply. It had always only been a matter of time before Senator Sherman would move on his behalf, and to do what was right.

"I want you to know, Garth, that I very strenuously argued against her doing this. I told her it would be political suicide and that it was better to have her be a cautious second-term Senator than to be a righteous ex-Senator next year," he said.

Garth always had a difficult time picturing Gus other than the humorous and playful undergraduate he had known for two years at Harvard.

"You do not have to tell me that, Gus, but thank you. I know that she moves to different music. I think you need to hang up and do what you can to explain to the Democratic leadership that it was she on her own, and with no encouragement from you, who decided to put her seat in jeopardy of falling into Republican hands. And if I can help with that, please let me know."

Melinda had co-signed a bill to increase the federal gasoline tax by ten cents every year for ten years and she had gone to the press conference held by the sponsor of the bill. She knew an increase in the gasoline tax was the obvious solution to so many things. In the previous ten years the retail price of gasoline had risen two dollars, from roughly a dollar and a half to three and a half dollars. Those increased payments accounted for a tax on most Americans anyway, but the revenues were going to corporations and oil producing countries. The high price of gasoline was funding Russian aggression, Venezuelan interference in other Latin American countries, and fundamentalist Islamist terrorism through the support of Middle Eastern oil producers. And now the price of gasoline was dropping. It had been proven that Americans could bear up under price increases and that the new tax revenue would help balance the budget and rebuild American infrastructure. She was perfectly willing to stand by her position when a reporter asked her a question.

"So, Senator Sherman, does this mean that you also support a tax on all carbon emissions, a general carbon tax?"

"Of course I do," she answered. "It would be stupid not too."

And before the room could fully recover from the idea of a Senator from the coal state of Kentucky supporting an additional tax on her state's most significant product and industry, she continued.

"And more importantly, it would be a sin. 'For God so loved the world . . .' Who are we to defile it? We have been entrusted with life on earth to be judged by our life on earth and it is our duty to be the custodians of the earth."

"But don't you think the voters of Kentucky will disagree with you?" the reporter asked.

"I happen to know that the voters of Kentucky are a lot smarter than you think they are," she said. "Coal will still be mined and burned, no matter what. It will just cost more. But it is not the future, not even the future of Kentucky. The tax will be a broad economic incentive for renewable energy and the government will not have to pick which new technologies to support. The great engine of American innovation will develop new technologies that will be exported and I believe Kentucky will be in the forefront of that. And it is not really a tax at all, because right now the costs of excessive carbon emissions are being passed on to farmers, to families, the governments, which must remediate the problems, and to our children and grandchildren. The people of Kentucky will think deeply about this and make the right decisions. I have faith in them."

The overnight polls revealed that the voters were actually rather unacquainted with the particulars of what their Senator had reassured them they would have deeply considered, and there was an extraordinary uneasiness in their minds concerning the mere mention of a carbon tax. Her eighteen percentage point lead evanesced and she was now well behind her almost unknown opponent. Two or three days after that the independent and public polls began to report the same numbers, now showing her ten percentage points behind, and the news reports began to label her actions as being "foolish" and "careless."

"It looks like I made my support just disappear like a mist in the bright, hot sun of a late summer morning," she said to Garth.

"It is funny you should say that, because I have lived in Boston, the gloom and mist capital of North America. Sometimes there will be exactly that kind of a fog you have mentioned, the kind that will leave with the sun. And other times even the highest and brightest parts of town will be shrouded in a gloomy vapor and in the low and cramped corners that fog will insinuate itself into every nook. No amount of warmth or light could ever dispel it. But if you were to see just a picture, a snapshot, of each one of these two types of fog from a distance, they would look exactly the same."

"Well, I was not really talking about fog, you know."

"That is my point. Any poll is always only going to be a snapshot of what is on the surface. It will never show what is going on inside. There is time before the election and people will literally think more deeply. The polls now are recording reactions. The election will reflect decisions. That bright and hot sun never comes out until just a few days before the election."

"So I haven't ruined it all?"

"You can't ruin it. Even if you lose the election, nothing important will have changed. We will still have each other and the kids."

"I was hoping you would say that. I know that you cannot conceal anything from me. It is not in your nature to close your lips where you have opened your heart. I saw that first in the way you are a father and it is why I fell in love with you."

And then it began to happen, first in small reports on the online news services and then in a few national newspapers. Another word began to surface, a previously used word, "courageous." Some of the local press started to mention her as the state's best chance to send one of its own to the

White House. She made several campaign stops within Kentucky and even at the open forums very few stood up to question or condemn her. It even seemed that the episode had been forgotten, except that she was still well behind and her polling numbers had changed very little but were moving in the right direction.

One stop a week before the election took her to London and her instinct was to visit her mother, this time alone. She knew her mother well enough to know that the old woman would be preoccupied by the presence of her security detail and would think or speak of almost nothing else, so she managed to arrange for Tommy Kitt to pick her up after she slipped out the back door of her hotel. Tommy dropped her off at her old home. The place had improved somewhat because Garth had arranged for Angelina to have a cleaning service and a lawn service and various handymen had repainted and repaired the house.

"So, to what do I owe the honor?" her mother asked.

"We . . . I want to see how you are really doing," her daughter answered.

"Well, don't blame me. That is all I have to say. It was not my fault."

"Blame you for what, mother?"

No sooner were these words out of the Senator's mouth when the mirror on the far sidewall of the living room exploded into a hundred pieces. Melinda had been standing between the window and the mirror. Whatever demons lay inside of Melinda, they had always fueled her and they were the reasons she had been a runner in college and a triathlete in the Navy. Though calmed, they were still there and they were the source of precipitous action, in this case physical and very much in tune with her military training. She dove into her mother's chair and toppled the chair, and the old lady, onto the floor as several other bullets shattered into the back wall of the living room. She was grateful for what had always been the petite frame of Angelina Bol Sherman, as she dragged the woman rapidly into the bathroom and put her in the tub and lay on top of her.

The single shots were soon replaced by automatic weapons fire and the house began to come apart from the hundreds of little explosions. Then Melinda could hear other shots and more automatic weapons fire and shortly after that the only fire that she heard was now unaccompanied by any matching destruction in the house. She knew that there was a firefight outside now and that the house was no longer a target. Not long after that, all the shooting had stopped. So she quickly slipped over the edge of the tub and crawled to and out the back door. What greeted her as she slipped through the shrubbery to the front of the house was not fully understood until it was reported two days later.

The two assailants this time had not been homegrown dissatisfied youth. They were two relatively slightly older young men in their twenties who had been well trained in Islamic State camps. They had been staking out the home of Melinda's mother rather unsatisfactorily for months, until they saw her emerge from Tommy Kitt's car and walk into the house without the expected security detail. Unfortunately for them, this had all happened in Kentucky.

Their occasional appearances in the neighborhood had not gone unnoticed by at least one of the more watchful neighbors. Melinda had inspired a handful of devoted enthusiasts and more than one or two of these individuals lived in the neighborhood of her birth and kept a watch on her mother's home. When the first shot had been fired, this small network of fans and suspicious neighbors had immediately responded. And since this was not Connecticut or Europe, they responded with their guns. Very soon the two assailants were pinned down and eventually perforated by the crack shots of the descendants of some rather flinty Kentucky woodsmen.

The landslide reelection of the junior Senator from Kentucky who had advocated a tax on one of her state's most important products was depicted as the incredible surprise that it most certainly had not been. In fact, Garth had been right about the nature of the fog. Her voters let their disappointment with her stance be reflected in the polls but they were hers. And she was theirs in the face of the nation, and most certainly against the foreign elements who sought to destroy her. This loyalty and feeling was both demonstrated and enhanced by the startling images of her saving herself and her mother while the people of her state came to her rescue in a manner that was indigenous to their region. Soon she was mentioned for the Democratic nomination in the upcoming Presidential election.

Out of the woodwork everybody came, seeking a piece of her, enough to overwhelm almost any politician. Presidential candidates were once only chosen by other professional politicians. A presidential race and the White House were considered not to be the places for a neophyte. This has long been discarded as folly by the present system, which customarily sets amateurs to contend for the leadership of the free world. Fortunately, Garth was no greenhorn and the years of his life and his network of friends and contacts from school and his career had all provided him with the wherewithal to make sense of the mad rush. He simply had to make decisions on which people to place around in order to control the inflow. Within a very short time, he had in place a structure and organization that would quickly adjust to become a campaign for President when that moment came.

The only other significant Democratic candidate was the sitting Vice President, an older man and a former Senator who had considered running for President more than a full thirty years earlier but who had withdrawn before the first primaries. This Senator who was later the Vice President had begun to campaign in New Hampshire and Iowa. At a town meeting in Iowa, one that was filmed on video camera, a contentious older voter had simply asserted that the candidate was not all that intelligent. What then flowed from the candidate's lips was an effusion of exaggerations, made-up stories, white lies, résumé padding and outright prevarications, the gist of which were, "I am a Rhodes Scholar, and you are not." These pronouncements flowed in such a way that the reporters who later received the videotape from an Iowa Democratic operative of one of the other candidates were almost unanimous in their assessment that the person who was to become Vice President some decades later was not stupid nor a liar but was something considerably more frightening than either. He was ungrounded. None of the journalists reported the real story at the time, due to the withdrawal of the candidate and his offered reasons. He later became Vice President, because that only required one person's support. Then a story was written about that very videotape and what it meant and the Vice President announced his intention to retire to private life after his term expired. That left only a few minor candidates for the party nomination, who would not really be able to stop Melinda.

That story had appeared in *The Washington Post*, under the byline of Earnest Dapple.

Earnest appeared to be helping to clear the way for the nomination of Senator Melinda Sherman to become the Democratic nominee for the office of the President. Garth and his team now considered all of the reasons for why he might do such a thing. The only answer was that he wanted a larger head to hang on his hunter's wall. And one possible solution to that, and a very good one, had been arrived at in the mind of Preston Cobalt, who never had any compunction at acting upon his assessments. He called Garth to tell him that he had already put into action a plan to neutralize the Earnest problem.

"How is that?" Garth asked.

"What the hell is in the heart of every journalist, Garth?"

"I don't know, a pit viper?"

"Very funny, Teller. No. In each one of their reptile hearts, every one of them wants to be a novelist. Earnest Dapple wants to be god damn Ernest Hemingway."

"I don't see of what use that can be."

"Dapple has written a novel and some short stories. I got some friends in publishing who have received queries from him. So, I had an agent contact him and negotiate a contract for representation. I have even secured a damn advance on the novel for him and I have arranged for one of his short stories to be published in the upcoming edition of *The New Yorker*. But the kicker is, get this, under the terms of his contract with the agent and the publisher he may no longer be a reporter and he may no longer write articles on politics."

"Wait a minute. Do you mean you can do all these things? And, did he really jump at the prospect of no longer being a reporter?"

"I have people. And, shit yeah, he is just like the rest of them. He is working on his own *The Sun Also Rises* at this very moment. And wait till you read that short story in that magazine. It is a dinger. It is called *The Thorn of Anxiety*. Surer 'n hell, you'll get a kick out of it."

"I can only imagine," Garth said, "It seems a bit of a bad trade. I mean, we get to be free of him. But the literary life of America must suffer for it."

"Are you sure you are from Texas? So what if a few eggheads get confused. Why would that matter when the right people get to run the country?"

So, what dutifully follows is the story that appeared in that august magazine and was to launch the career of a brilliant literary light, while at the same time protecting the political career of perhaps the most important potential presidential candidate since the founding of the republic.

THE THORN OF ANXIETY

I wake up without a penis. I assume that this is because unlike other men I never gave mine a name. Men do this. Some call him (it?) Mr. Happy. Mine was far too complicated and ironic to be called that. I had a friend once who later committed suicide who called his Hector. I learned this was a Latino name and the idea of my penis having a Latin temperament was too ludicrously close to the mark. Besides, hector is also a verb. I have been tricked by my penis, betrayed by it, coaxed, cajoled, and badgered. I am not sure I would want it hectoring me. I'd kill myself.

Anyway, it was gone for whatever reason. Talk about getting in touch with your feminine side. What was I going to do? Would I have to use my brain more now? To make the decisions my penis used to make? And what about those absent-minded moments when out of habit I would reach down for something on which to reassuringly put my hand? And, what about sex? They say, "Size doesn't matter." Certain women seem to please each other without one. Gradually my shock gave way to concern and sooner than expected I had learned to get along without it.

I no longer woke up in the middle of the night with that ineluctable aching, throbbing sensation. I found I could carry on entire conversations with a woman in which I no longer felt the poignant urge to peek at her butt or breasts. No more coming out of the boys' room with a wet spot on the blue jeans. In fact, the whole matter of jeans became more of a breeze.

And I learned to get along without sex; after all I had once gone sixteen years without it. But still I felt something was missing and although my emotional reaction to the lack of a penis had faded, spiritually my apprehension was growing.

I began to look out for it on television, at flea markets, on the street, in Nieman-Marcus catalogs, at Little League games. A couple of times I thought I saw it. I recognized what I thought was a too-familiar head shape on an accountant in the financial district and there was a flicker of recognition in his eye too. So I followed him. Actually, I watched him for several days; going to his office, home, the subway. He was apparently a good father, husband, and employee. I began to feel that old penis pride again.

Women always think that the one thing men would change about their penis is its size, but that's a lie. The first thing they would all change is to have it be guaranteed to do what it is supposed to do and when it is supposed to, and to make sure it keeps doing it over the long haul, so to speak. Not a few of them would like their penis to earn a living too. And here was my penis doing all those things.

One day as I sat on his street in my car watching the house, drinking coffee and eating a doughnut, I was surprised by this accountant suddenly appearing at my window.

"I am not your penis, you know," he said.

"Mmhhffamnff," I replied, powdered sugar rising in a cloud in front of my face.

"In fact, if I were anyone's penis it would not be someone as pathetic as you."

"MMhhnn. Mhfffnm. Che . . . Just what exactly do you mean by that?"

"You know. Get a life," he replied as he turned for the house.

"You mean 'get a penis,'" I mumbled to myself.

He was right though. As is often the case, hope had outwrestled reason in me. There had been something in him that was too fastidious, almost officious. He was too mannered and not very natural. And he was way too thin. And short. So I continued to look until I thought I'd found it again. It had become a pair of neoprene stocking foot trout fly fishing waders I saw at Dick's Sporting Goods store. They were the good kind, with gravel guards and reinforced knees, extra thick. But I was hip to myself by now and knew only after a few days of going to fondly look at them that I was half-expressing some other desire close to my heart. I began to give up on looking.

Then one day on the bus I noticed a man was staring at me. By the time I thought about this, he was already off the bus and had turned to me and smiled. I recognized that smile immediately. It was my penis.

I staked out that bus stop and after about three weeks I saw him again. He was well over six feet tall, very stockily built, with black hair, age about thirty. And he was Korean. This was a fact only startling at the outset. That my penis should come from a different culture, one whose practices and beliefs were recondite or even obscure to my own view, began to make more sense as I thought about it. They have such odd food though. I began to worry that at some point my penis had once eaten a dog.

This time I was less circumspect and cautious as I was more certain of its (his?) identity. So I followed him right down Elm Street, around the corner onto Truman St. and finally into a corner grocery store on Truman and Oak Streets. I walked right up to him and before I could say a word . . .

"Not going back," he said.

"You have no choice," I said. "You're mine."

Pretty soon I was in a protracted debate with my penis. Of course, I was on the side of right and God and justice and have considerable persuasive powers. He was, well, he was my penis and simply, stolidly not accustomed to losing debates with me.

He spoke in that gruff, abbreviated pidgin English, almost spitting out those short declarative phrases. I told him that it was not proper for a penis to be walking around in public, overcharging for milk and being overtly suspicious of his African-American patrons.

"Have own name now," he ejaculated.

"What?" I asked.

"Wong." I had noticed this name on the sign over the door.

"Aren't you a little concerned that it rhymes with schlong?"

"You no give name."

"And the Hebrews gave no name to God either. Jehovah, or Yahweh, means 'that which cannot have a name.'"

"No want to be call Jehovah."

"Listen, you had it pretty good. You never had to work or worry. I always paid attention to you. Treated you very well. Took you places."

"Put me places."

"Yeah, but that wasn't so bad."

"Ethel Kaminsky."

"Okay, so sometimes it wasn't so great. You put me up to Ethel Kaminsky anyway. That was your idea."

"Better than beating."

"I thought you liked that."

"No liked. Liked Susan Bartlett. Kate Freeman."

I could see I was going nowhere with this. This damn thing would not listen to reason. Why was I surprised by that? I told him to go ahead, have his own life. And I left. But he had given me an idea. And I turned it over and over in my head and finally I decided.

That Tuesday I called Kate. It had been a while and I was never sure that we had broken up or even why. I didn't mention anything about my situation. First we met for a cup of coffee at Starbucks and we just talked. I remembered what it was like to sit at home when my single mother sat at the table and talked to us, my two sisters and me. The time went fast as Kate told me about the way her job made her feel and the problems in her family. We laughed and at the end she said to me, "I never knew you knew so well how to talk to a woman."

"You mean, 'listen,'" I said.

It was after a long while, several movies, me cooking dinner, a few walks, talking on the phone from work, babysitting her five-year-old, holding hands, that one night she gave me a look, one I had never seen her give me before and she said, "You know, if you don't make love to me very soon, I am going to think that you think that something is terribly wrong with me."

"There is nothing wrong with you. Just with me," I said.

"What?"

"I lost my penis."

"Let's go to bed."

It was several months later, after we had made love almost non-stop, when it seemed that we just might never emerge from the bedroom. Kate said that she had never been more in love, never been more emotionally and sexually satisfied in her life, but that she had been nursing a growing desire to get a hold of my penis. Even though your life may be perfect she had explained, "Sometimes you just need some penis." So I told her the whole sad story and she laughed. She said some things about how a man can't be trusted with his penis, no wonder it had left, and how she had wished she had been there to witness me debating my penis in a Korean grocery store. We made a date the next day to go to Wong's.

When we walked in it was a completely different story. No longer gruff and suspicious and resentful, Wong was soft-spoken and well-spoken, gentle and attentive.

"Hello, Kate," he said. "How have you been?"

"Fine. We've been getting along pretty well without you, you know."

"I am only a little surprised. He may be a real idiot, but he's basically all right. You always had a good effect on him. He sure has been a real jerk to me."

"Don't listen to that prick," I interjected.

"Why don't you let me handle this," Kate said. "Wait for me outside."

Well, handle it she must have, because about twenty minutes later the two of them came out of the store and told me we were all "going home."

And that is how it ended. I call it the peregrinations of a penis. Maybe something like this has happened to you. Or to someone you know.

Despite some misgivings, Garth thought the story a bit entertaining. And it was received well, but only very briefly, before it grew into a sensational international literary and legal incident.

Lawyers know to rarely seek remedy at law for their own causes. In this way they are like early barbers who would never sit themselves in their chairs without the benefit of a mirror and shave themselves with a straight razor. Lawyers understand better than anyone that the law operates in this same blind manner and is as like to cut as it is to shave and that the odds that the blood that the law leaves on the floor might be their own are too uncomfortably high, even in the case when they are most decidedly in the right. In fact, the most skilled and well-trained jurists are most troubled and apprehensive about any cause that is entirely righteous, because at that point only one outcome will possibly only do so much as restore the equilibrium while the opposite outcome will destroy it and any of the middle-ground decisions will compromise it. The worst thing, any lawyer can tell you, is to be in the right.

This is the enigma which Earnest Dapple had found confronting him upon public release of his first literary effort.

Shortly after the publication of *The Thorn of Anxiety*, it was attacked as being plagiarized from a story that had been published a year or two earlier in England, but which had been written long after Earnest had written his story. Earnest correctly claimed that an analysis of his computer would show that his document had not only predated the publication of that story in England, it also preceded what that author had claimed was his date of conceiving and writing the story. Earnest also pointed out and quite correctly that his own story in *The New Yorker* had been carefully crafted in order to paraphrase a story by Nikolai Gogol, called *The Nose*, so that it was legally and critically relying on a much earlier and more literary precedent, and that the English story was in no way as sound or as funny as *The Thorn of Anxiety*.

That he was right in all instances served his purposes in the way that was quite the opposite of what one might expect since the operation of literary circles is not unlike that in the halls of justice, in that it more than anything resembles the fluid functioning of the social life of what in America was once called junior high school and is now called middle school, and where the victory so justly goes to the more popular or bigger children from the more established families.

The offended English short story had been written in London by the famed Anglo-Jamaican author, Sir Jimarcus Kingsley Malcolm, Commander of the Order of the British Empire (CBE), winner of the Whitbread prize and PEN/Pinter prize, and most notably an Academy Award nominee for his screenplay for the hit movie, *My Ska Band Catamite*. Such honors had long obscured the fact that Mr. Malcolm had begun his career writing pornography and that his friends and family members had sued him for generously borrowing facts from their own lives in order to manufacture his fictions. These honors were now certainly going to encourage every interested party, many of whom were his friends, to bury the new American upstart under a snow storm of criticism so opaque as to cover up what Jimarcus had always known, that in writing his own tale he had again generously borrowed from a story he had once been sent by a friend who worked at the office of his literary agent. Besides, the success of the movie for which he had penned his famous screenplay had rendered permanent his status as the reigning lion in the wide realm of thought provoking and socially relevant fiction written for and about gay, mixed race individuals of color who had one parent who had descended from the peoples of what was once a colony of the British Empire. The seemingly boundless engine of the guilt of the London literary classes would preserve their knight at the expense of the American who could no longer get any fiction published, even if it were to have been the next *Moby Dick*. Earnest at least was able to return to his position at *The Washington Post*, which had been satisfied by the independent analysis of his computer and had weakly defended him in print, knowing full well that they were to benefit hugely from the return of one of their most successful reporters. He returned to that vocation with what might be described as a vengeance, only a more calculated version.

Some men whose hearts are bent every minute of every day only on their advancement by any means, even those they know to be despicable or loathsome, still affect a tone of higher morality and regularly disparage to themselves the depravity they seemingly see around them, scoffing at the follies they see as being base or shortsighted. Some of the world's craftiest scoundrels have served in the highest offices that enabled them to do the greatest damage to the largest number of innocent people while at the same time keeping an active ledger with a floating balance ostensibly in their favor with their account with heaven. Whether they are interposing themselves into the place of the accounting angel they might one day inevitably meet, they are certainly doing the cherub the favor of making that eventual accounting more expedient. In the case of Mr. Dapple, the calculations had just rocked well into the red, calling for some fashion of retribution, most likely of the worldly variety.

This calculated vengeance then manifested itself to the woman whom Garth had hired to run the eventual presidential campaign and who was now working on putting together that framework and she duly reported that manifestation to Garth.

"Dapple thinks he has something. And he has made no secret that he intends to use it sometime after we declare for President, probably when Melinda gets the nomination and it will have the most impact," she said.

Kelly Dunbar had arrived in Washington many years before, at around the same time Garth had, and from another part of Texas not far from Houston. She had become more or less a hometown friend in Washington after she had graduated from the University of Texas and had come to the capital to try to become a reporter and had then shifted into another career as so many others had done. She had chosen politics because it was a match to her Texas temperament and it was the only career that really had no entry-level requirements. Anyone could just start to do it. And she was very good at it.

She and Garth, on the night of her report to him about Earnest, met at the bar at a quiet restaurant in the southwest section of Washington, DC, where there were only ever local patrons.

"I know he thinks he has something but this is the first time he has indicated it directly to someone associated with Melinda. My old pal, Earnest, has been digging around for a while. And quite literally digging in one instance," Garth said.

"It is better if you don't tell me what he thinks he has dug up. Oh, of course, I didn't mean to say . . . Well, it is better for me not to know," she said.

"And I am sure that his self-satisfied smugness made him all that much more attractive to you," Garth said.

"It is funny you should say that. Do you remember that story I half told you way back when we first came to Washington?" she asked.

"The one I begged you to finish every time I ever saw you for about twenty years after that?"

"It might be time to finish that story now."

Garth remembered what he had been told of it and he remembered at the time what Kelly had been like when she was that young. She was a very bright, buttoned down young lady from a very good Texas family. She tended to wear conservative and expensive navy blue business suits. Half of all men would look no further than past the appearances she put forward. But to that other half, nothing could hide the fact that what was underneath her business suit was something that was also slightly in evidence in the glimmer of her blue. She was voluptuous, and that quality was also in her spirit. Her half told story had been about how she had gone for an interview at a famous Washington institution, and how she had also managed to flirt with a man who was not giving her the interview but who was hovering around her during it. She made sure he knew that she was interested. She never revealed to Garth who this man had been because he was famous and because she had been ashamed of behaving like a groupie.

But she had told Garth the far more interesting part of the tale which had captured and had held his interest and had been the reason he had kept asking her to name the man until only after a couple of decades he had tired of asking. She had spoken of a weekend she had spent with his man in Annapolis, after he had called her on the number that had been on her résumé. Garth even remembered the phrases with which she had peppered the story. Kelly had said she was "as romantic as the next woman," but that at some point she had decided to "keep a tally" on the small notebook in her purse beside the bed. In the short forty hours they had spent together, this famous Washingtonian had assailed the temple of her body a grand total of eighteen times, and this was taking into account that during most of the waking hours the two of them were doing other things. The final count at which Kelly told Garth she was able to arrive was nine times a night for two straight nights. He also remembered the debate that he and Kelly had at the time of that first telling of the account. After he had said he was envious of the guy, she had assumed it was for the ability to perform to that level and had assured him that it was "not really such a good thing."

Garth demurred and said he did not feel one way or the other about the ability, but that he was simply and purely and totally in awe of the desire. Garth felt he was passionate at that time in his life, and in fact that old passion is still what sustained him in his marriage to a very fit woman thirteen years his junior. Whoever this famous guy was he was some kind of national treasure or force of nature. Garth's now faded but previously long held curiosity about the identity of the famous maniacal man was reignited.

"If I tell you who he was, do you promise not to react?" Kelly asked him.

"Certainly, you know me. I am the soul of reserve and calm discretion."

"No, really, I am serious. Do you swear to take it calmly?"

He spat his beer across the back of the bar and shouted.

"What? He gets to take down a President and do it nine times a night too!"

She had given him the name of one of the most famous reporters in the history of Washington, if not the world, whose investigative journalism had eventually led to the impeachment and resignation of a President. This man and his colleagues were the reason that so many young people at the time, like Kelly and undoubtedly Earnest, had wanted to become reporters. It was a time at which investigative reporting came both to be considered more honorable while in practice becoming far less so. This reporter boyfriend of Kelly's had been a major celebrity, well beyond the bounds of journalism. His wife had been a celebrity, and it was to her that Garth now referred.

"Damn, do you know that book his wife wrote, *Indigestion*, in which the woman finds out that her husband is being unfaithful, because she has done some of her own investigative work on him? Well, that was supposed to have been semi-autobiographical, meaning it was about your guy there."

"She didn't need to investigate. All she needed was to have known he had left the house."

"That's an understatement."

"Well, anyway I am glad I was able to give you your big vicarious beer-spewing thrill. I have to get back to work anyway, and hope that all we will have done will not be destroyed by my friend's spiritual heir who was also, and weirdly, your college classmate."

"Nothing has happened yet and I am sure we have time. And I promise not to repeat your story to anyone," he said.

"I know."

Garth figured that the biggest opportunity for whatever it was that Earnest had been planning would not arise until after the party conventions and in the thick of the general election. Earnest could then become the iconic reporter who had destroyed a candidate and had swung the election with a story, which is more or less what he had always wanted, to be like the man who had for one weekend secretly been the incessant animatronic lover of the woman who would be running that very candidate's campaign. Garth conjectured for one painful moment whether a perpetual state of rut was one of the hallmarks of that variety of journalistic ambition, calling to mind far too many images of Earnest in action. The *Thorn of Anxiety* had given Garth the same discomfort, but it had done so with a certain dramatic irony. It did then occur to Garth that as much as all of this seemed like something Earnest might have felt was personal to Garth, it probably was merely business, the corporate interest of Earnest expressing itself, from the very beginning, of being the one to encourage Garth into this profession, to helping Melinda to the nomination.

Garth also pondered the ridiculously small size of the seemingly expansive and wide-open world of national politics. He considered that at one point each of the two major party presidential candidates had been members of the same secret society at Yale and only two years apart, making them constituent elements of a whole massive universe consisting of forty-five male individuals. And there was the fact that at times recent and distant in the history of the country the highest office in the land seemed to have been passed among members of the same family. His closeness to Earnest, both a classmate and a fellow Owl, was more or less just part of a long historical trend, as was the fact that he was the primary advisor on what would be the presidential campaign of his own wife, or the fact that the man doggedly following Earnest's tracks was the man he had met through Earnest, and that Earnest had also been sleeping with Garth's ex-wife. All this was mere preamble to the likelihood that the Republican candidate for President would be Rich Sartory, Governor of Texas and the first person Garth had ever hired to work for him on a campaign. No one would believe any of it, if someone had tried to make it up. But it was true.

That intramural feeling of it all being in such close quarters was just a zephyr of seeming unreality, blowing practically unfelt amidst the stronger gusts of the upper atmosphere of American politics at such a high altitude, among which was the strong jet stream headwind for Garth of knowing, like a fan of the Cubs, that it was all going to end unsatisfactorily. In the high-speed aircraft that his marriage to Melinda had become, he had always been the sturdy structure of the craft and its navigational devices for her, or more accurately for her shining psychological difference from most other people. He kept her and them all together, more or less. But now he realized what she was to him in that two-seat jet, or what her detaching impairment was to him. She was the ejection seat, the escape from total disaster, the reassuring covered button on the side of the stick steering device upon which he would sometimes rest a finger and toward which he would often longingly glance. She made the prospect of bailing out nothing near like the panicked disaster almost every other political operative might envision.

She made it look inviting.

THE ONLY ADULT
IN THE ROOM

It was the eve of the first Democratic Presidential debate nomination that Garth received another visit from Detective John Huffam, the care-worn policeman of average height with lines around his gray-blue eyes, whose blond-gray hair was retreating from his forehead. This time there was something that was noticeable about him beyond that slightly threatening and watchful reticence that all policemen have. He was more serious and concerned. That fairly determined attitude was tinted by the slight wincing indication that the detective did not want to be doing what he felt required to do, which was to approach Garth at the site of the debate in Washington, when they were making their final preparations for it.

"I think you might want to come with me, Mr. Teller," the policeman said.

Garth could tell from the tone and terseness of that remark that it was sincere. He could also determine it from the quality of the wood in the toothpick that the detective was chewing. Garth's native instinct was to question all that was of surprise to him. Garth's legal training was telling him that any discussion that might be had would best be had later and with the representation of an attorney. But his political reflex was to remove the detective as swiftly as possible from this room full of campaign and media people and where his wife was also being prepared for her first major national media appearance as a candidate for President. And it was about her that the concern Garth expressed to the detective was addressed. He asked if he might have a minute to speak to his wife.

He simply told Melinda that he had to leave and that it was not important but that it was a matter that probably involved his ex-wife, Tabitha.

"What? Really? Now? Why?" she asked.

"I am not sure. But it doesn't matter. You will be all right. Do you remember what Wilton Carlson told us, at the beginning of all this?" he asked.

"He said a lot," she answered.

"About Section One of Article Two of the Constitution."

"Oh, right," she said, starting to smile, "about the two requirements for disqualification to serve as President of the United States."

"That no one who was not a natural born citizen, or who was not over the age of thirty-five, could serve as President. To those, Wilton had added his own third prescribed disqualification. Do you remember?"

"The founding fathers should have added, 'or any son of a bitch who actually wants the job.' And he added that I would be the best candidate in a long time, because I was not really dying to be President."

"You get the point," Garth said.

She did and she also trusted her husband. They shared everything in this enterprise, so if he was not being forthcoming now he had a good reason. She still was concerned with anything that might have to do with his first wife, but those concerns related only to whatever impacts something like that might have on Seth and Hanna. She did not consider what his absence from the debate preparation might have on her. As they parted he saw of a bit of a wary flicker in her eyes.

In the detective's car, he asked, "What is this about?"

"You are a person of interest in the apparent murder of Earnest Dapple."

"May I ask if this is the doing of my ex-wife again?"

"You may ask," the detective said, "but I am not permitted to tell you . . ."

"I see," said Garth. "You used the word, 'apparent.' I also assume that a body has not been found."

"You can assume anything you might, Mr. Teller, although your legal education has already told you that answer."

Garth was aware of at least several things, that Detective Huffam was not entirely committed to this case, and that his position in his wife's campaign and the timing of the police contact gave all the impressions of there being a strong political foundation to whatever investigation was now proceeding.

When they arrived at the station Garth was led into a sterile waiting room and left to wait. And wait he did, for well over an hour. Then the door opened and Detective Huffam reentered the room and apologized.

"The delay was out of my hands. The Assistant United States Attorney is on his way to question you."

Murder is rarely a federal crime, Garth knew, except in certain limited statutes and in instances involving federal officials, interstate actions, national security and very few other cases. The Federal Bureau of Investigation, not the local police, generally investigates such cases. Garth surmised that what had happened here was that some bright and ambitious Assistant United States Attorney had been scanning the incoming Washington, DC, cases and that thought he might, as the saying goes, make a federal case out of it.

Paradoxically, in the face of such an upgrading of jurisdiction, Garth decided to hold off on contacting a lawyer. He had a premonition of what was to come.

"I can at least take you to an office here where there is a television, so you can watch that debate," the detective suggested.

"That would be good. Thank you," Garth said.

In the lieutenant's office, he sat on the couch as the television was turned on to one of the channels covering the debate, which had just begun. It was a round robin debate with Senator Sherman and the four other Democratic candidates who had entered the various primaries, all of whom were well behind her in the polls and who had every reason to attempt to do her some damage. A question was presented and each candidate would answer in turn and then they all would get a chance to respond to the others answers.

Garth found it surreal, that this was happening. Melinda was every inch the woman with whom he had fallen in love. She was beautiful in her handsome way and this direct and confident appearance was also in every one of her answers, delivered with what can only be considered a style of leadership that was neither cautious nor equivocal. She ignored any attacks on her. The equivocation and caution of the other candidates, when put in context next to their sniping, gave the impression that she was the only adult in the room.

The debate was to end with a closing speech. Each other candidate took at least a few moments in his remarks to comment on her or on one of her positions. Garth could hardly hear them and he certainly was not watching them. His eyes were glued to his wife's face and he saw it begin to take on a beatific expression and he saw her eyes begin to sparkle and he was absolutely certain that when she spoke she would, in a phrase, begin to shine.

"I see a vision," she said.

Garth was certain that among the millions of Americans watching, only he and her brother and Tommy Kitt knew that she was speaking quite literally, that she meant the word "vision" not in the sense that it had been said by every single politician who had ever used the word, but how it had been understood by William Blake or Emily Dickinson.

"And in it I see Jesus in the streets and fields and cities and forests and towns of the United States. He seems troubled to me. He says that the United States is indeed blessed to be the last, best hope for the world. He says that this should be our greatest faith as a nation, to know that we lead the world by the power of our example and not by any example of our power.

"We should heed the example of the Berlin Wall and the Iron Curtain," she continued. "They came down not because we sent troops to Eastern Europe but because the peoples of the Warsaw Bloc nations were deeply moved by our values and our freedoms and our respect for individual human rights and the rule of law. The examples of Iraq of Afghanistan stand as sad parables of our failure to have faith in what it is we are and what we represent to all the people of the world. I stand here this evening as the only one among us who has taken a life, but I had done so only in order to save lives. My vision now convinces me that as the leader of this great nation I will not risk one life nor will I order the taking of any life, except under the same circumstances. Too often our leaders have sent Americans into dangerous situations and then have cynically invoked patriotism and support for our troops in order to support these foreign military interventions. True patriotism and true support for our men and women in uniform would be to never send them into harm's way unless it is absolutely justified. Jesus is showing me that I should and must see every man and woman in uniform as a son or daughter that she is.

"I have heard our Lord say, 'Blessed are the peacemakers, for they will be called the sons of God. Blessed are the merciful, for they will be shown mercy. Let your light so shine before men, that they may see your good works and glorify your Father in heaven.' If the United States of America is a Christian nation, and it is, but across all of its constituent faiths, in our sense of mercy and tolerance and respect, we must let our light guide other nations, and we cannot enlighten them at the point of a bayonet. If other nations and faiths do that, they do so as a confession of a lack of faith, a lack of conviction, and a pessimistic understanding that people will not be guided to their beliefs by anything other than force. We must not fall into that failure of faith," she said.

"We are the shining light," she added. "Too often we have lost sight of this and in our reliance on force instead of upon the truth of our values we have let our light dim. This great nation has 'not come to destroy men's lives, but to save them.' We must think more deeply and feel more deeply. We must not live in our tempers but in our hearts. Jesus says, 'Do not resist an evil person. If someone strikes you on the right cheek, turn to him the other also. And if someone wants to sue you and take your tunic, let him have your cloak as well. If someone forces you to go one mile, go with him two miles.' And he will be convinced by the power of your faith.

"Finally, I stand here among you as a woman. In much of the rest of the world, the women are stoned to death for little reason. They are denied property, the right to vote, the right to travel, the right to go about and do according to their individual freedom. In this nation we treat the least among us according to this dictate: that as we do unto them, so we do unto Jesus. Let the world see that in a great nation of many faiths, a woman may lead us. An American woman will not be held back by the historical forces that have oppressed women and which still oppress many women throughout the world. That is it. That is what I see. God bless America."

Garth, who knew this remarkable woman perhaps better than anybody, sat there utterly surprised.

He still had no idea at all what the impact of her statements might have been. He knew only one thing for sure. Of all the countless times Jesus had been cited in politics, this was certainly the first time it had truly been sincerely done. He was also dead certain that a few dozen million Americans had completely unknowingly just witnessed a vision or a cyclothymic episode or whatever it was that made his wife shine. She had certainly stepped outside of the bounds of political caution. The reaction on the television, among the other candidates, by the moderator, and among the audience seemed equally as stunned.

Garth looked at Detective John Huffam and he thought he saw a tiny bit of water on his face. Garth wondered.

"Detective, are you by any chance an ex-Marine?"

"There is no such thing as an ex-Marine, Teller. I am a Marine. And so is my second son, even though he was killed in Iraq," Huffam said.

Just then, the door opened and in walked the Assistant US Attorney. He was wearing a trim and expensive blue suit that could only have been purchased with resources beyond that of a government salary, a Harvard class ring, a pair of black Italian loafers, and a white shirt and maroon tie. He had the solid good looks of a son of a good family. He came on as if he were the kind of fellow who called the counterman at his local convenience store by his first name. He smiled, introduced himself and mentioned Harvard within the first three sentences. Beneath all this blandly attractive appearance Garth detected that here was a man who planned to run for statewide office in his home state of Virginia and that his stint in the office of the federal prosecutor was for the purpose of making the name and building the political capital required for that campaign.

"We already know everything, Mr. Teller. So this is your chance to come clean and clear yourself," AUSA said.

"Which is why, of course, you are asking me questions," Garth answered.

"Listen, I know you. I know the type of guys who went to Harvard in the Seventies. I know that you left Capitol Hill under questionable circumstances. I can ruin you, Mr. Teller. I can take any man off of the street and I can ruin him."

"I am certain you can. I am certain that you have done that to some poor innocent persons in the past," Garth said. "And allow me to suggest that solving this mystery, and the discovery of the real perpetrator of this apparent deed, is of the last importance to you."

This casual and friendly banter between two men who shared an old college tie continued for only about another hour. And when it finally tired out the questioner, he told Garth he could leave even though Garth was well within his rights to have left the moment he had arrived. He had decided that the best path was to stay and to learn and to not give any information, and to not appear afraid or at risk. On the way back from the station Detective Huffam sat quietly, until Garth addressed him in the car.

"I suppose that I am a person of interest because of the record of my threat against Mr. Dapple. It also seems from what just happened that he also left some notes or something that you found which indicated that I would be implicated if anything should have happened to him. But there seems little more than that, including any real evidence that Mr. Dapple has been killed," Garth ventured.

"Do you have any teenagers, Mr. Teller?" he asked.

"Not anymore, but I have survived two of them."

"Have you noticed how much they are smarter than we are, especially with all that computer internet technical stuff?

"That cannot be denied," Garth said.

"Well, my fourteen-year-old daughter, she is a wizard with all that stuff."

"She sounds like quite a comfort for you and a source of pride."

"And a resource, Mr. Teller; she is a resource."

"That is an interesting observation."

"You don't know how interesting."

"I would like hear."

"For one thing, that guy Dapple is surely dead. He is one of those creatures of habit and one of his habits is to check in all the time, with work, with certain friends. He has not done that for days and his apartment showed no signs of planned departure. He was in the middle of doing several things. He implicated you in various notes on his computer. That lovely gentleman you just spent the evening with has all that stuff. I brought it all back to the station and he took a look at it. But there was one of those . . . what do you call it . . . a thumb drive in the drawer next to his laptop. When I plugged it into the computer, I found out that it could not be read. Now, if I had brought it right back to the station it would have taken weeks for the boys there to crack it. I wanted to know what was on it right away, so I took it to my daughter. It was protected by a dual password and it was encrypted, which means she opened it up in about five minutes."

"She sure is quite a resource then."

"I am going to keep it, Mr. Teller, at least for a while. You probably know what is on it. It is very detailed and represents years of research into stuff I do not think is anybody's business really. But it is all about motive, your motive to kill Mr. Dapple. I don't think I can hold onto it if it begins to look like you actually have something to do with this. Then I will have to turn it over to your Harvard buddy there. But for the time being, I will be keeping it. And if you are as innocent as I believe you are, I will destroy it."

"May I ask, why?"

"For the good of the country, Mr. Teller, for the United States of America."

"I would like to meet that daughter of yours, one day," Garth said, "and tell her what kind of patriot her father is."

As both Garth and Detective Huffam could have predicted, the events of that evening at the police station were leaked to *The Washington Post*, which ran the story the next day that the husband of Senator Melinda Sherman had been picked up for questioning in the investigation into the apparent murder of Earnest Dapple, one of their very own. By the time Garth had returned home though, he had officially withdrawn from all matters having to do with the campaign, leaving everything to the team he had. He had decided to be just what he had been described as, the husband of the candidate.

Melinda was disappointed. She really did not want to go forward at all without Garth, to attempt to do it alone. But as always, she was completely in tune with him and she was open to what he would show her.

There are times when all the fundamentals are in upheaval and the skies and the seas are in wild revolt, when fauna and humankind revert to an atavistic furor and none of the rules of civil society or even the apparent natural order of things seem any longer to apply. Before this melee the sensible man or woman will seek cover and refuge. But for a man or woman who is possessed of some great purpose or is burdened by the indispensable quality of some ineluctable task, the tumult is something with which he feels a mysterious brotherhood and he is provoked to some parallel vehemence, to abrupt passions that previously lay dormant in his or her character. Many valiant and marvelous deeds have accompanied the lightning and thunder, by individuals who have ridden the whirlwind. Garth's confidence, ebullient spirits, and optimism overwhelmed Melinda's doubt and confusion. He rousingly embraced the challenges and applauded and relished the way he knew that they would grow closer in meeting them.

"What? Do you want this all to be a cake walk?" he asked. "Didn't you just set the political establishment on its ear? Is now the time to walk away from the battle?"

And above all, she was turned happily to face the maelstrom by his love and by his passion. In the strangest sense, this was an animated and perilous constituent element of the way in which their entire audacious and colossal political enterprise was simply just a part of their love affair, a presidential campaign that was really a romance.

The reaction to her debate appearance had begun to formulate. Senator Sherman had hit a moment in time when the American public had been made weary by the human expense and financial outlay of two wars in Asia. Her message had seemed to pick a fruit that had grown quite ripe. And she had done something that had also been long awaiting its catalyst. She had awakened the Christian left. Those socially conscious and charitable people had become agnostic or wayward or secular or atheist, but they still lived, or perhaps lived more, according to the charitable and Christian values of their ancestors, their communities, and their culture. Their essential reasonableness had given them to make their arguments on humanistic grounds while they also would respect and recognize opposing views. The right had not had any such inclination toward pluralism or debate and had cloaked its own arguments in the absolutism of religious dogma. Melinda had given this more liberal group the will to fight fire with fire.

Eakin Lambert called Garth a few days later. She said she had seen in the news that Garth and Melinda still had an Earnest problem, even though there no longer seemed to be any Earnest. She concluded her conversation by saying, "Open up your front door."

On the other side at that very moment was Ben Dessous.

"Hello, Garth," he said. "I have arrived in order to accomplish the delicate and complicated tasks that the police have neither the inclination nor the proficiency to complete. I will plumb the complexities of the tangible actualities that are to be discovered at the foundation of this condition that has festered too long in the media. I believe that I have done sufficient preliminary research into the subject and now that I have my feet on the ground in this location it should be simple for me to discover the destiny that claimed the unfortunate Mr. Dapple, as well as his current whereabouts."

"Hi, Ben. Good to see you," Garth said.

He invited his old friend into the house. He had never felt anything but a connection to the man whose life he had once saved in the simple act of returning him that favor. He was certain that it would be as Ben had said. There was no way that the police cared enough or knew enough to really get to the crucial facts of what had really happened. Ben could certainly do that and he had a good head start. In fact, it was possible that Ben might already have a very good idea. And that understanding is what caused this tiny bit of ambivalence. He trusted Ben with his life. He knew Ben would protect Melinda and him.

He had even once had guaranteed it.

A DUTY TO THINK
MORE DEEPLY

In the time of this narrative, when a the sailing craft of a particular marriage sailed on uncharted waters with the two figures in it, one a wise and robust man of distinct middle age and the other a resilient woman in the prime of her years, the firm hand that had been on the tiller had been that of the man. And then he turned it over to the woman and pledged to support all her efforts above and below decks while she undertook the navigation of their conjugal craft.

A one Mr. William Robinson, able seaman, reporting in the time of Trafalgar, once claimed that in the fleet of nine ships of the line of which Mr. Robinson's ship was one, only two of those crews would have sailed rough seas and fought an overmatching enemy and stormed a battery for the love of their just and compassionate captains. The other seven crews did as well they could entirely for the magnificent glory of old England. Whether these same proportions, of two in nine possessing the privilege to strike for love, hold true for the rest of all the world of human endeavor or if they are rated rather a bit high, is as much a matter for speculation as are the relative merits and attractions of an entity as grand as all of old England or as slim a volume as love. On the latter matter Mr. Robinson was of the clear opinion that Albion did not motivate so well as the other, and on the former issue Garth was certain that the number of men who are fortunate enough to crew for a captain they love was quite well below twenty-two point two percent. He was probably happily alone in the world.

The woman with her more delicate hand now on the rudder had grown up the little mother in service of her family, had been a student athlete working with her coaches and professors, and had gone on to serve her country, all with the measure of success that can often arrive at the door with selfless devotion. She had served her love or her vision since then and had sounded both depths to the last fathom consistently and assiduously enough to know that the two were often one and the same. She knew how to fill a role and how to do so actively and with initiative. She had never slept or rested under her husband's watch but had been the most active and ingenious first mate. Yet though this might have been her first time at the wheel, she had been ready for it in so many ways because she had been very much on her own, steering her internal way through the shoals and storms of a type of a capricious nature that dwelt within her. It was this, her shine, which would be called upon now to help her drive the ship. Garth would be at home and he would love her but he would not be with her all the time.

The attacks against her debate performance had begun to coalesce. The high priests of right railed at her from their radio and talk show lecterns, claiming that she was naïve and soft on terrorism and a danger to American interests. They accurately pointed out that the build-up of American military power and the projection of that strength had been undertaken and had been preserved by Presidents of both parties. The declamations of these men were supported by a chorus of elected officers of the Republican Party who pointed out that the United States had many far-flung commercial interests that were at risk overseas and that the projection of military strength had protected those interests. And by this they largely meant oil. And a much smaller but equally vocal minority within her own party attacked her for injecting religion into the debate over public policy, claiming that she would act not what was in the nation's best interest but according to some hidden directives.

Melinda finally spoke at a press conference and as she began it was if the Congressional Medal of Honor she kept in her drawer had begun to materialize around the collars of her blouse and suit.

"My ancestor, General Sherman, once said, '. . . it is only those who have never heard a shot, never heard the shriek and groans of the wounded and lacerated . . . that cry aloud for more blood, more vengeance, more desolation.' I have noticed that men who have not been shot or wounded in the service of their country, men who are quick to send their fellow Americans into the dangers they have not faced themselves, have made the majority of commentary against me. While this does not address the merits of their comments, it casts a pallid light on the place from which they speak. I do not have the words to explain or justify a single American death in Iraq or Afghanistan. And neither do my detractors. Would they themselves die for oil, for the faint hope of establishing democracy in a faraway land that has no foundation for it, or would they send their sons and daughters to die for those things? I think not.

"I also weep," she said, "when I think of the regular American families who not only pay this highest personal price but who also foot the financial bill for its costs. Hundreds of billions of dollars in taxes and in money borrowed from the taxes of the future grandchildren of these families have been spent on costly military adventures in foreign lands and a vast proportion of these funds have wound up in the accounts of the executives and wealthy stockholders of the massive defense contracting companies which profit from war and then turn around and fund the very same individuals who would attack me for seeking to stem this great source of growing income inequality. Regular Americans are dying for the right to grow poorer while funding the growing wealth of the forces that would continue this disturbingly sinful trend and which fund its advocacy.

"We are Americans, a nation founded on the right and the duty to dissent and to question authority. While it may be true that the policy of the leaders of both parties has been to support our foreign military adventures, it was our thirty-fourth President, a Republican, who first warned us of this very military-industrial complex that is so prevailing in our public lives. He was also a soldier and a war hero and he knew more of what he spoke than anyone could have. No President has sought to take a different path because none has thought to lead. Each has taken the path of protecting himself from the very criticisms that are mounting against me now. I will lead and we will see if the path we take is not the better one," she said.

"I do not pretend that we are not in the midst of a global struggle. It has been called a war on terrorism. Terrorism is a method. It is not something against which the ponderous and massive operations of a war may even be effective. Our much larger struggle is and always will be against tyranny and we may make no mistake in stating that some of these tyrants make use of the power of religious fundamentalism in order to control their people and to attack us. These tyrants respect and fear the power of our ideals and values, which they fear will infect their people and diminish their authoritarian control. They fear that their people will want to tear down the figurative walls which keep them from enjoying the same rights and freedoms that all the world knows we take for granted," she said. "They fear that their women will want to vote, that their men will want practice any religion of their choosing, and that their children will expect to grow up in a world like the one they see in the United States. We simply cannot force our way of life upon people whose ignorance and fear of it is fueled by their leaders who proclaim our use of force as another reason for those people to continue to oppose us. We would be far more effective to flow with the faith that their leaders justifiably have in the ultimate attractiveness and righteousness of our way of life. For a fraction of the cost in hundreds of billions of dollars and thousands of lives, we would have been better off to give the Afghans and the Iraqis millions of smart phones and laptops and a permanent access to the news and information of our world. We know that we have the best way of life in the world. Let our faith in that not seem to be diminished by aggressive actions that seem to indicate that we believe any other thing.

"It has been said," she continued, "that 'He who kills in the name of God demeans his god.' Men seek to impose their religious will over others and we know that this is in fact a lack of faith in the power of their religion to convert and to attract without violence. The same pertains to our faith in America.

"Some people in my own party have said that as President I will 'know nothing' but what I envision my religion tells me, that I will govern not by my leadership but by my faith. I am a Christian, but what that means to me is that I must live my own life by the dictates of my faith. A fundamentalist Muslim may believe that it is his duty and his right to impose Sharia law on all of his neighbors, but the kind of Christian that I am believes that her God needs no such legislative mandate or executive force in order for people to see the light. My Christian faith is a thing that is far more ephemeral and delicate and beautiful. I hope that I can serve my God and I know that it is only within the confines of my own life that I can do that, through good works and with love and charity.

"I believe in our constitutional democracy. I believe in our free market system. I believe in our rule of law that seeks to protect the individual against the larger groups and against corruption and injustice. I also believe that the mind of God is beyond our understanding, but that directing the world is not part of it. The world is our test, the proving ground for our individual lives. God has blessed America. But the blessing is ours to honor. We should not profane that blessing by attempting to reduce him to a state-sponsored God."

Then came the questions.

"Aren't you afraid, Senator, if you take us down this path," the first question began, "that there will one day be a terrorist attack that will have resulted from your softness on terrorism?"

"I am from Kentucky. And I have spent some time living in the suburbs of Washington, where one day a deer was walking down the middle of the street in the middle of the day. In Washington the people gathered and commented on how cute and wonderful that deer was. But in Kentucky we are smarter than that. In that situation we would not see a deer at all but a creature whose nature as a cautious prey animal has been so corrupted that it no longer acts like deer. I have all along said that we as Americans owe a duty to think more deeply, to think twice about what we see and hear."

Garth heard her as he watched on the television from home. He remembered all of what she was saying as having derived from conversations the two of them had. He was now waiting for the other shoe to drop.

"Osama bin Laden released a video showing he was not really a man of faith. It showed how he smugly smiled at his ability to manipulate religious belief to send other men to their deaths in order to launch a successful attack on the United States. In response to that, we have spent trillions of dollars. He changed us in ways that are not all good. The problem is that we see any American injured by that terrorism only as a victim. They are American heroes. They died because they believed in this country, where we believe that men and women should live according to the ideals and freedoms and rights that we all take as our birthright. We should honor them as heroes and be grateful for the blessings of freedom that God has conferred upon us all. If one looks at it more deeply, it can be said that by making our country less open and less free we have not properly honored the faith we should have in our way of life. We have not honored the faith for which these Americans were sacrificed."

"Are you saying that we should not have reacted as we did against terrorist attacks against us?" was the next question.

"No. I will forcefully and decidedly combat terrorism. I believe I am the only candidate of either party who has personally taken out a suicide bomber. But I know that the larger battle will not be won by becoming more like the part of the world that is not free. We will win by continuing to do what the tyrants fear, by changing the part of the world that is not free with the power of our example. And we may only do that by remaining the land of the free and the home of the brave."

And with that she walked off the stage and more or less into history, as not only the first woman war hero who was also a major politician to speak in these terms. She had supposedly committed political suicide in the past and she might not be afraid to do so at any time, so long as she spoke from her heart.

"Man, I remember that whole deer thing," Seth said.

He was home now, having not quite graduated from college due to issues arising from his attention deficit disorder.

"You were mad at the deer for not being instinctively afraid."

"And for eating our flowers, don't forget," Melinda said. "They were manmade monsters and no longer deer."

"This is all so amazing," Hanna said, "like we are living inside of a movie."

She was on break from senior year at Harvard.

"That is a good way to think about it. It will do us good to always remember that it is not real. What's real is right here in this house. It is you guys, you and your dad," she said

She made them dinner, which she relished because she had not done it for a while, and not in a longer time for the four of them.

"You know now that when you leave tomorrow for Iowa and New Hampshire, I will not be with you. And you are going to be walking into a shit storm," Garth said much later, when he was alone with his wife.

"I have been in those kinds of storms before, on the ground, in the air, and right here inside my own head. I also have you inside my head and heart. You may have recognized some of you, or some of your words from our previous discussions, coming out of my mouth today," she answered.

"I know. Those were almost intimate things I say in private, between us. I would never think to inject them into the public dialogue at this level."

"Well it is time someone did, because they are right. You are right. And they are things I have felt or have envisioned, but I only truly recognized them when I heard you say them. You really are inside of me. So, since we are not going to be together for a while, may I ask you a question?"

"What? Oh, yeah, sure, go ahead."

"Are we just going to sit there and talk dirty to each other or are you going to do something about it?"

A few days later Garth was talking to Kelly Dunbar.

"The polling numbers are saying something I have never seen before," she started. "There was an immediate and large drop after that press confer-ence. In fact, she has fallen behind. 'Dangerous' is the word most used, or most echoed, as a reason for no longer supporting her, but just recently her numbers have started to pick back up. And her opponents have not gained too much ground. There is a new category taking up most of the slack, a large group of newly undecided voters who used to support her. And after we get past that 'dangerous' part, the next thing we hear is this, that they disagree with her but respect her honesty."

"I think those are good things," he said.

"Here is the really good part. We are tracking large increases in Democratic and some Republican registrations across the country. And we are also getting new hits on the campaign website and new contributions. We can identify all of these new people to some extent. And you are going to love this. They are people who have never voted, young people, Latinos, African Americans, very poor white folks and, get this, Republican women. Your wife is changing the electoral landscape."

"That is all very interesting. Stay in touch."

"Are you sure you cannot come out here? The Senator is not like any woman I have ever known. There is something about her that is off, and I don't think that she is 'off' in the way all politicians are. It seems more fundamental. It is kind of like, I don't know, she shines, I guess. Yeah, she shines."

"I like the way you can speak of her as if she is the Senator and not my wife. Please keep it up. Keep that objectivity. Be honest with me about her."

"I only see a candidate, Garth, and I see you as a resource and as my boss. And now I have to go run 'The Shining Senator's Expedition to the Primary States.' Wish me luck."

"We have a disturbing tendency," Senator Sherman said in Des Moines, Iowa, "to react at the level of the lowest common denominator. And here is a good example. My critics do not consider all that I have said. I want all Americans to understand this one thing. When someone does or says something like that, what they are really saying is that they think we are stupid. We are not. We are Americans. And we must be particularly concerned when it comes to war or to any pervasive governmental action. The government is a large and ponderous and unwieldy bludgeon. It is rarely the right instrument. Though my opponents would label me a dove or a pacifist or a liberal, I am a far better conservative than they are. There is a cultural orthodoxy in America, on both the left and the right, which has too much faith in the state and is too willing to use it for the wrong ends. And nowhere is this more true than in the case of the family."

"The conservatives would have the government come through the front door of the family house and into the bedroom to see what is going on and to make decisions as to how what it sees should be treated," she said in

Nashua, New Hampshire. "A true conservative is supposed to question government authority. And the liberals are no better. In response to the issue of child abuse in some families, we have hundreds of local agencies full of social workers who walk through the family door and pass judgment on American families. If we think more deeply we will realize that there have been and will be cases where some twenty-five-year old local government social worker has removed a safe and happy child from his or her parents. This may not be abuse, but the fact that it was done by the government makes it almost worse. And what no one but I will say is that we should always question the use of the government to regulate what happens within the closed doors of the family home and particularly the bedroom."

In Aiken, South Carolina, she said, "This reaction at the level of the lowest common denominator is always in response to the media, which acts in concert with the government to drive an instinctive reaction, and then to drive governmental action. This is how we became involved in two long and costly wars for which we have little to show. It happens all the time and at every level. Whenever we have a terrible shooting in this country, my own reaction is of profound grief. It provokes in me, as it should in everyone, a very deep and philosophical sorrow. It deserves that. It does not deserve some knee-jerk reaction or some overtly political response. Far too many times, in such an instance, I have seen some politician immediately try to enact legislation over the fresh graves of murdered children. That grieves me almost as much as the original loss.

"And why do we feel compelled to react to remote events in faraway lands that most Americans cannot find on a map?" she asked in Iowa City. "Why do we not take the long view? One example is that we have built a grand highway in Afghanistan, but that highway immediately fell into disrepair and disuse. If those people are not even ready for a highway, how can they be ready for free market democracy and constitutional guarantees of individual rights? Our thoughtlessness may lead to expensive mistakes. We should not react. We should think first and think twice and think deeply. And I have mentioned democracy. In the recent events of what was called 'the Arab Spring' many Americans reacted only positively, believing that the springing up of democracy is always a good thing, no matter where it occurs. But if we had thought twice we would have realized that it is not. In fact, it has promoted the rise of the Islamic State. The best and most important part of our own democracy is its least democratic element. It is our Constitution that matters, because it embodies the central values that no democracy may tyrannize the rights of a minority or an individual. The first thing that has been done in some of the newly formed so-called democracies of some of the Arab states is that the majority immediately imposes its will on the minority religions and sects. That may be democracy, but it is democracy at its worst and it is not our constitutional democracy. We should not ever attempt to 'export democracy' to any place that does not already have constitutional guarantees of individual rights and freedoms. All we need to do is look to Japan, where a free market democracy has flourished, but only on the foundation of a constitution which we had indeed exported to them."

In Manchester, New Hampshire, she said, "I have said since I first came to work in government that there is something wrong with the fact that we spend half of the world's entire expenditures on defense and we use it to defend entirely developed nations that can pay to defend themselves. It is a very pernicious form of foreign aid to wealthy nations. And it will one day be the expense that breaks the back of the federal budget. But now I want to say that it also makes us the biggest target. If there were an armed and active Europe, do you think the Russians would be obsessed with the United States? Would Russia care to prop up Syrian and Cuban dictators if they had to be concerned with armed Germans, French, Italians and Poles? Would China, which is still a communist authoritarian state, be spreading its influence to

Africa and South America, if there were an armed Japan off her coast? I state these as questions and I know how the critics will answer. They will say that we have to remain the most militarily powerful nation on earth in order to preserve our fundamental ideals and beliefs and way of life. And I will answer that they have less faith in those very same things than I do. And I also believe this, that every person in the world also loves freedom and justice and equality. In the breast of every oppressed person in the world beats a heart that dreams of being American, or being like an American. We need not use our military to protect some kind of American empire. It will expand because it is right and just and good. And for those who come to America, for those who love the United States enough to want immigrate, we must be charitable. Immigration has always fueled our growth and enriched our society. It is literally where each of us has our beginning. I cannot see any strong opposition to immigration that is not based on fear, distrust, or hate. And those do not strike me as American virtues."

Senator Sherman barely finished first in the Iowa caucuses and she increased her lead in winning the New Hampshire primaries. Her margins of victory began as being smaller than the proportion of voters she had added to the equation. And that began to build. The core of her support was almost fanatical. There were people who would do anything for her. Regular Democratic voters caught the bug. And those people who had initially and had superficially supported her, only to migrate away because they might have thought she was dangerous, came back to her.

Since the very beginning. American politicians have promised change and reform and to shake up the old order. There had also always been politicians who in some way represented change. But in each of these cases, changes did not occur. Senator Sherman was a woman and a war hero and married to a divorced man.

She pierced the cultural orthodoxy.

She won every primary by ever increasing margins and the other candidates dropped out in fairly short order. All of this seemed pale to her, unless she could once again begin to share it with her husband. She had learned to go it alone. But it was not the same. It was not good. She ached to have him by her side.

THE TRUTH WILL OUT

There is a faint echo of something that sounds like sucking and it is emanating from a back room, the very kind of back room that in a political time long past would have been referred to as smoke-filled, and would have served as the locus of the variety of deal making which has also fallen out of vogue. Although the presence of a certain individual in this particular room may make it tempting to wonder if the smoke had been literally sucked out of it, there is a simpler explanation. Smoking has been exiled to out of doors even in the political sense and truly productive back room deals have given way to sound bites, money, social media, and mass marketing. There remains nothing left politically for this kind of room unless it is to be used for the timeless and more enduring enterprise known as conspiring, which is the use to which it is being put here in the offices of one of the conspirators whose machinations intend to thwart the presidential campaign of the Senator from Kentucky. A small number of older white men, as is most often the case in conspiracies, are planning a way to counterattack the astounding success of the Democratic nominee for President, and one of those men is himself about to be the nominee of the other major party, none other than Rich Sartory, Governor of Texas.

The others are senior members of his staff and of the staff of the other primary conspirator, in whose warren of offices this back room is to be found. The unseen billionaire backers of Governor Sartory have paid a great deal of money to secretly obtain the advice and guidance of one of the most highly successful Democratic consultants in the country, one who personally knows the husband of the Senator from Kentucky. The source of that already described faint sound is this same man, Mr. Parker Askew. And he has spent much but not nearly all of the money he has been paid in order to research and repair the report he is discussing with Governor Sartory.

"It all comes down to the truth. Our studies show that independent and undecided voters support her because she tells the truth. It is as simple as that. Once we factor out everything else, her forthrightness is the most important aspect of her success," Askew said.

"I hope you are not suggesting that I start telling the truth," answered Sartory.

"Our focus groups show that it is totally about being sincere, so it is not about saying what you think is true, or what you have been told is true, or what you have long thought was true. You have to say what you feel is the truth. Even people who disagree with you will respect your sincerity and they will admire that you are unafraid to disagree."

"I have been telling the truth for years and it does not seem to be helping. Evolution is bunk and so is global climate change, but when I say those things people opposed to me don't decide to respect my leadership."

"That is because you don't believe it. I am telling you that this is the crux of our research. Only say what you feel is true. You will have to work on being honest. No politician is honest. But she is."

"If the problem is what you said, how do I shed the political instinct and start being sincere?"

"The report details how do to that. Oddly enough, we have found the secret is to read the quotations of William Tecumseh Sherman. This is an irony since he is the ancestor of Senator Sherman, but she may also be some atavistic reoccurrence of some genetic trait that was almost singular in him. No American ever spoke so free of any concern for how his statements might be perceived. It is stunning. And we have included his quotes in this report. You will understand when you read it."

"We certainly have to try something, because we are so far behind in the polls. By the way, it sounds like your office's air circulation is on the fritz. I hear a kind of sucking," Sartory said as he left the room.

"Now," Parker Askew said, turning to his own staff after the Governor had left, "we have to get on the line to all of our other clients, our corporate and commercial clients, and tell them that we have the secret to their future success. Make them pay for the report. We can sell it to them each as if we had prepared it for them individually. It will serve two purposes. We will make money. And if more and more people start to be honest then it will devalue honesty and that will also take something away from the Sherman campaign."

And from such back rooms have history-changing events emerged.

The Sartory campaign's next stop was at an elementary school in Arkansas, a state which already inclined to support him. The setting was going to be very low key and safe. The Governor would read a story to the children and the photo opportunity would show the public just how nurturing he was. After the session, one of the third graders approached him and spoke very passionately about her love for tigers. She seemed to cry.

"Tigers are going extinct. Can you save them when you're President?"

Governor Sartory had been practicing how to cleanse himself of all political instinct. He remembered reading that William Tecumseh Sherman had once said, "If I had my choice I would kill every reporter in the world, but I am sure we would be getting reports from Hell before breakfast."

This was the test, and his opportunity to really make political use out of what it could mean to be truly sincere.

"Let them eat Indians," he told the girl.

The room went still.

"The tiger population of the world has gone down to about three thousand individual animals, when there were once thirty-five times that many. The population of India has exploded to over one point three billion people and it is still growing too fast. The simple solution to the problem of imminent tiger extinction, the elegant answer to the whole situation, is to let the tigers eat the Indians. There are certainly more than a few to spare. And up until the colonization, that is, the civilizing, of India, this is what the tigers had been doing for thousands of years. You could have seventy thousand or so healthy and happy big cats before you even started to really notice any missing Indians."

Several sturdy third graders were suddenly whimpering and casting furtive sidelong glances for their absent mommies. The little girl who had asked the question was staring and looked puzzled. Several of the boys were leering hungrily at the lone eight-year-old boy of Indian descent. The rest of the children seemed to be laughing.

At exactly this same moment, eight hundred and sixty miles to the northeast, another Askew client was being inducted into the Rock and Roll Hall of Fame. Rocky Rockwood had been doing a number of sincere and forthright things to the chemical composition of his own body. It is a condition peculiar to such a state that it confuses observers who might imagine that a person has temporarily mislaid the mental files and notes from which he might call forth any truth whatsoever, while the more honest fact is that the altered individual knows even more clearly what he might honestly mean. So, it was that the now middle-aged British heavy metal icon addressed his audience.

"Sod you all and this bloody mess. Bugger this whole place. What is it anyway? How can you build a goddamn temple to something that is supposed to be a frigging revolution? Real rockers are subversives, not busts to be worshipped. The whole bloody hypocritical mess was made clear at the beginning, when Yoko Ono spoke at the Rock and Roll Hall of Fame dedication. 'Hello, I ended the greatest rock and roll band of all time,' she must have said. 'So you blokes can just pretend I am Josef Mengele and I am dedicating the Holocaust Museum.' Bloody hell. If you loved rock and roll when it was relevant and you still have it in your heart, you will burn this place down. And any good rocker, sod it all, should know how to die in a plane crash or of an overdose. Who wants to see my old puss, in a wheelchair and singing about being a badass?" That was an interesting word choice, because his next move was to bite off the head of a cute white kitten.

While he was chewing on that, three hundred and sixty-five miles to the southeast, the most prominent African American politician in history of the United States was addressing the Congressional Black Caucus, saying this.

"If the Reverend Doctor Martin Luther King Junior were to come back to us here today he would most definitely say that it is time for black people to stop seeing themselves as victims. His new dream would be that the content of our characters would be a lot more like those of the Chinese Americans or even the Ethiopian Americans or the Indian Americans or the Haitian Americans, where we would consider the problems and the discrimination that we shall overcome, then we would get down to doing the extra work required to help ourselves. We would stand on our own and not seek assistance. My own success is testimony to the virtue of that stance. I knew my way was going to be tougher than it would have been had I been white, I also knew that the greatest obstacle I faced was being tempted to dwell on those problems. I have a new dream. And in my dream, one day on the red hills of Georgia, I see that the great grandsons of former slaves will be doing extra homework while the great grandsons of former slave owners will be playing dice. And I believe this is exactly what the Reverend Doctor Martin Luther King Junior would dream today."

Germany's mighty Bayer chemical and pharmaceutical company began to run radio advertisements in the United States for their new product that kills lawn weeds over a period of six months. In the radio commercial, the "weeds" are anthropomorphized and given human voices which then express their fear of being exterminated by the Bayer product, drawing a parallel to the company's notorious efficiency at eradicating actual humans in the Holocaust and twenty years prior to that in the trenches of Normandy.

The President of the High Priesthood of the Church of Jesus Christ of Latter-day Saints announced that same day that God had just told him to tell the Church members that it was time to switch its position away from opposition to same sex marriage

"We've always been sort of kidding about the one man, one woman thing. After all, the President of the United States had also admitted he had been 'faking' his own opposition. And . . . when one thinks of it," he added, "we have always been about the alternative life style in this country. So let's open the door to all kinds of marriage."

It was pointed out that the Church of Jesus Christ of Latter-day Saints had just recently issued a statement opposed to same sex marriage and in support of the California law which had banned same sex marriage and which had been overturned by the courts.

"I hope you guys don't think we tell you everything. It only takes a short look at the record to see that we have not always held the view that marriage is one woman and one man. Brigham Young denounced it. And God told Joseph Smith at one point to marry another man's wife as well that same man's fourteen-year-old daughter."

Back at the elementary school outside of Little Rock, there happened to be two third graders who were descended from members of the Caddo and Quapaw Native American tribes, a small and compact girl with bright eyes and a boy who was large for his age and who had always been shy.

The two were naturally close and at this moment the boy was consoling his friend, who was sobbing. When it all was explained to the Governor, he tried to honestly and sincerely console them.

"Don't you worry, young lady, no tigers will be eating you or any of our *American* Indian friends," he said. "But I bet you don't like living on that Indian reservation."

At some point, Rich Sartory had been told that there were no reservations in Arkansas and that the only Native Americans in the state had descended from those who had somehow escaped the bloody repression of the tribes and the subsequent Removal to reservations in Oklahoma. But it somehow had escaped him, and now he felt that font of sincerity welling up inside of him again, and he took the opportunity to pronounce his program for saving the American Indian.

"We should abolish the reservations. All we have done is to marginalize the Indians. They should be encouraged to become regular Americans, like the Italians and the Jews and the Africans and even the other Indians, from India. American Indian culture will only survive as part of American culture. We have learned that there is no such thing as separate but equal. Segregation always leads to inequality. Now the reservations are just places to avoid state laws and have become homes to casinos and cigarette emporiums. I am not sure that is what the Congress had in mind when it originally considered Indian sovereignty."

The ever quaint notion of intellectual property, that anything so fleeting and evanescent as an idea could be owned and that its possessor could, with the assistance of a government, exercise dominion over it, was always doomed. It had only sustained within the calm and organized precincts of the West, but was seen in China and most of the rest of the world merely as an impediment to commerce. Then came the cataclysmic digital volcanic eruption that was not unlike the one which overwhelmed Pompeii, taking out thousands of Roman citizens and overtaking old man Pliny in the bargain. In this digital dynamic volcanism, the pyroclastic flow of trillions of ones and zeroes torched and subsumed millions of books, record stores, the royalty payments of writers and songsters, newspapers, and many other relics in about the time it takes to say, "cut and paste," or, "download."

The Askew Report landed in the hands of many of the people who set out to put it to practice, including the conservative radio talk show host, Tim Grady. Mr. Grady had grown up with his Irish Catholic immigrant father who was a member of the machinist union and they lived in a voting precinct in Brooklyn, New York that had always gone Democratic, even for Adlai Stevenson in 1956. From this it was an almost straight path to his becoming a right-wing polemicist. And it was about this father that he spoke on this same day.

"My dear old man died last month at age eighty-nine," he said. "He had lived a full life, Army veteran in World War II, raised four kids with my mother, worked at an airport fixing planes for forty years, was an alderman a St. Michaels, grandfather to ten, loved baseball, always had a helping hand for a friend and did not tolerate fools. But I don't want to talk about his life today. I want to talk about his death, and what I think it means for the country. No, I don't mean my dad's ability to contribute to our American way of life will be missed all that much. I just think that the circumstances of his death have important implications. He had a heart attack and by the time anyone had found him he had lost any sign of brain function. He was put into intensive care and put on a heart-lung machine. He had no living will, no advanced directive. It took the family four days to decide to let them pull the plug on his devices. He died quietly a few hours later. His health care insurer paid his hospital bill, which was two hundred and forty thousand dollars.

"He had," Grady continued, "been kept alive at an expense equal to the income of six average American families, or the health insurance premiums of a hundred and fifty healthy young Americans. But had no brain function. Now, my dad would have been the first to tell you to pull the plug. He had been a frugal man and had saved money all his life. The expense of all of this would have offended him. I know, he should have thought to have a living will. But he was not of that generation. He was simply prepared to live, to die, and to go meet his maker. Now, I am sure that many American families face the same question, every day. And it is a tough decision. And nobody wants to equate money with life or with love. But at some point the question is money, especially when the health care costs for the elderly in this country are going to be an ever growing fiscal nightmare.

"My solution," he continued, "is to help families to make this decision. Simply put, pay them. In a case where there is no living will, pay them a lump sum for making the difficult decision to pull the plug. Look at it this way. Fifty years ago my dad would have died in a few hours after he had been found. The only reason he was kept alive was because science could do it. Why should healthy and working Americans pay higher health care premiums because of advances in medical science? Shouldn't it be the other way around? I don't know what the payment should be; maybe twenty thousand dollars. I am not qualified. I only know that my old man would have told our family to take the money, save the expenses on other people, and throw a good old-fashioned Irish wake."

"Hitler began with the idea of persecuting the Jews," Professor Levi Rosenthal said in his "Sociology of Totalitarianism" class at Brandeis University, later that same day, "in order to focus the angry attention of the deprived and battered majority of Germans on a scapegoat. His original goal may have been to destroy his Communist rivals for the support of the unemployed masses, but feelings against the Communists were not as identifiable or as deeply and historically rooted as German anti-Semitism. It was the politics of hate. He came frighteningly close to his goal of eliminating European

Jewry. But the question before us today is whether or not the current trends of assimilation and reduction of the world's Jewish population is in some way a result of the rhetoric of the Nazi genocide. Has Hitler somehow caused twenty-first century Jews to internalize the message that it is not safe or good to be Jewish? Has the lesson been that being the Chosen of God is bad public relations? When a person is mugged, it is never his or her fault. Yet, he or she will always think that he or she might have taken another route, or looked less easy to rob, or something else. Are assimilating Jews doing this same second-guessing? Is Hitler still at work, reducing their numbers?"

Governor Sartory concluded his day at the elementary school with remarks to the effect that it was an inescapable truth that society would only prosper if some children actually were left behind, that the price of success is that many people cannot be permitted to succeed.

"It is like bullying," he said. "All the hoity toity liberals are up in arms against bullying. But the fact is that there is always that one kid who has to get picked on, in order to keep everyone else from being that kid. In other words, one kid gets bullied for the psychological health of all the others."

Rocky Rockwood's little white kitten lasted about as long as Professor Rosenthal. Tim "blood money" Grady was moved from Fox News to a web log. The Rock and Roll Hall of Fame began inducting rap singers, disc jockeys, auto-tuned Disney singers, country stars, and never skipped a beat. The story of the second dream of the reincarnated Reverend Doctor Martin Luther King was quickly retracted and blamed on a teleprompter that had gone on the fritz. The President of the High Priesthood of the Church of Jesus Christ of Latter-day Saints announced that God had called back and reneged on his support for same sex marriage just as He had once done with His ban on African Americans ever being allowed into the Church of Jesus Christ of Latter-day Saints. Without any real notice, the multinational Bayer Company continued to ease its way back into the business of killing. And the hard-core fanatical conservative support of the Republican Party and the Baptist Fundamentalists of Texas rallied around their candidate and railed against the liberal media. Governor Sartory's poll numbers went up a little.

Melinda had returned home for a few days and she and Garth had been following these developments.

"Do you think it was something in the water?" she asked.

"Only if it was something sucking," he answered. "Rocky Rockwood is one of Parker Askew's prized clients. He has pictures of him all over his office. So is the Bayer Company. And frankly I think that their radio commercial is the most shocking story of all. All the others must have some connection and I'm pretty sure that the Sartory campaign must have some connection to Askew through a back channel. When Rich worked for me, he met Parker. So, who knows?"

"Has politics always been so . . . incestuous?"

The look on Garth's face became temporarily dark and distracted. "I, I don't know, I guess, yeah. It has always been pretty much that. What happens is that an apparatus gets put together in a successful political operation. It generates people who are all connected and future political enterprises borrow from the past successful ones. People get recycled. So, yeah, you could say it was always what you said it was."

"Well, if that is the case, it seems that it all has something to do with me."

"I would have to say I agree with you. You are sincere. That seems to have started it."

"I don't think I could have said anything at all like those things."

"We do both recognize that there is a startling cultural orthodoxy in this country, almost as if it is a dictatorship of consensus. Everyone believes the government has the right to intervene, whether it is overseas or in our private lives. No one questions sending young men to die in a war or questions the vast sums of money spent to keep very sick people alive. Critically important questions of religion and culture are never asked. No one questions the loss of individual freedoms in the name of the amorphous wars on drugs and terror. And nowhere is the cultural orthodoxy stronger than when you consider love and marriage. The true template for love is how one should love one's children, selflessly and without expectation of return. That opens a lot of doors. Yet the social dogma is that love generates expectations of return and that heterosexual monogamy is its only form. It is astonishing that no one comes out and says what Juliet says in the garden or what Paul says to the Corinthians, that love is only positive and generous and is its own reward, and that it requires no state sponsorship, which in the end limits it terribly."

"Yes, I guess you're right. This is the same horrible cultural orthodoxy that keeps us from considering that we should let tigers eat human beings, when that is so obviously the best solution," she said, smiling archly.

"Only if they eat Pakistanis too, you know, for a balanced diet."

"Now you're just being mean and silly."

Within a few minutes, Garth and Melinda were embracing, tears in their eyes and holding each other very closely. Melinda had to go back on the campaign trail, with Garth only helping from home. It had been a good test for her and she had passed, but she always missed him whenever he was not around if even for a day. And he had watched her grow more independent, in the same way a parent is happy to send an independent adult child out into the world after having put in all that love and hard work. This selfless aspect of his love for her made Melinda miss him all the more while they were apart.

So they were more than happy to learn that they could be together all the time again. The cloud had suddenly been lifted from over Garth.

Ben Dessous had disposed with what had been known as the Earnest problem. He called Garth to tell him that the investigation was over. Garth confirmed this with a call to Detective Huffam. Whether or not Ben also had a hand in the disposing of the named individual was still a question. And there was one even more significant and important development, not of the nature of an issue being removed but more a question of an addition.

THE REALLY BIG GAY WEDDING

"There are two ways we can look at this," said Doctor Alan Money, of George Washington University Hospital, "the scientific and medical way, or the second way."

The handsome young former college athlete had been chosen for this singular medical role in the Sherman campaign because he was an active Republican and was a member of an evangelical Christian church. He had even said publicly that he would vote Republican in the upcoming election, even as he had in past elections and would in future ones. The handsome thirty-five year old was also tall and well built with blue eyes and black hair and his face was chiseled. He was discussing before the rapt press the standard and customarily required public disclosure of the report on the medical condition of one party's presidential nominee, in this case the physical examination and medical records of Senator Melinda Sherman.

"Remember, Senator Sherman is forty-six years old and she has suffered extensive traumatic injury in battle," he said. "The first explanation for what has happened, the medical and scientific one, is that one of her few remaining eggs in her one remaining ovary managed to penetrate through the extensive blockage in her one remaining fallopian tube in order to finally reach her uterus, where it was fertilized."

"What is the second explanation?" a reporter asked.

"The second explanation is that it is a miracle. I prefer that explanation. It is easier to accept. It is a miracle that Senator Melinda Sherman is pregnant."

It had happened the night that Melinda and Garth had been talking about his being away, curiously, the same night she had told him he was always inside of her and he had told her that people would want to stick it to her. And they had learned of her pregnancy on the night they also had learned that Garth was no longer a person of interest in that matter of the death of Earnest Dapple. The reaction of the right-wing commentators to her pregnancy was precipitous.

The rain of their assaults watered some unintended growths. Some of these men actually insisted that she withdraw from the race and stay at home and begin to think about taking care of the baby because that was a divine calling or at least a more proper concern for a woman than running the country. Others more cleverly said the same thing by asking aloud if she would take a maternity leave from the office of the President of the United States. The response to this was assigned to Congressman Wilton Carlton, appearing at a press conference and on most of the television news shows on behalf of the campaign. The lanky now seventy-year-old Texan was in his element and the tenor of his drawl was perfection.

"I can't believe that all these good old boys are so frightened of a pregnant lady and of what it means to be expecting. They seem to have lot less courage than roughly half of all the individuals in the United States," he said. "We are talking about Senator Melinda Sherman here, folks. She once carried eight tired and wounded Navy Seals seventy miles to a ship at sea while she had been grievously wounded. I am pretty sure she can carry this pregnancy to term while she is doing a little old thing like running for President. The President of the United States has a pretty strong support network. Think of how well that child will be cared for with the prayers and support of three hundred and thirty million Americans."

Once again Melinda's record of bravery in combat in service to her country had immunized her from the pitfalls and attacks that can hobble a woman in politics and in the workplace. A few weeks after the conservative attacks and Congressman Wilton's answer had been analyzed in the polls, she made a speech to this exact same effect, that it was an honor and a privilege to be able to put one's life on the line for the United States of America and one that honor and a privilege had been too long denied to all American women and that the truth of her argument had been born out in the recent polls. It was a surprising confirmation and it began to make her boldness and forthrightness appear to be prophetic, or like leadership. She was still the Senator from Kentucky but all of this, all of what made her different from every other politician along with the miracle pregnancy, made it as if she was someone more along the lines of the Senator from International Celebrity Icon, Spiritual Division.

She was given the singular indulgence of being able to run for the office of President of the United States without having to travel too much at all, other than to make intermittent appearances at major events. It was as if America and the rest of the world would come to her. The international and national coverage of her family and her background and her friends and her clothes and her workout regimen and her husband and her favorite movies and her military career and her home town and her recipes and her Senate activities and the books she was reading and her positions on every issue and her doctor and her lawn service guy and just about everything else about her began at a strong level and seemed to increase to a peak as the election approached.

Denunciations that then emanated from the darker and more hostile corners of the Muslim world only too closely echoed what had been the attacks of the far right of American politics, that a woman and a pregnant woman at that should be seen and not heard. She had been immunized from these original assaults and the way in which the imams and the sheikhs and ayatollahs seemed to parrot them only made her more popular with Americans who may or may not have agreed with her. In a way it was also as she had stated, that she was something along the lines of the first feminist or perhaps even the first new woman.

If she had been a marginal candidate and had advocated letting women fight and die alongside men and had advocated drastic reductions in defense spending or not sending any single American to a war to which she would not send her own child, she might have quickly disappeared from public view. Her support of a carbon tax and a gasoline tax and her support of same-sex marriage and her open discussion of the relative merits of religions and her opposition to the government involvement in the family and her opinion on abortion and how she had decried the growth of the security state would have each given some group some sound basis to oppose her.

But as it was now, the entire country appeared to be proud of the way she made the United States appear to the world, in the same way that Kentucky had been proud of her or the people of her hometown had been proud of her. Most Americans knew that her popularity and her likely election to the Presidency would once again remind the world of what it was that made America special and different.

The iconoclastic positions she had taken did not alienate the individual constituencies that opposed them. The majority of Americans generally supported her for reasons that transcended the issues. But her opinions were disparate enough, both conservative and liberal, that there was some issue that did appeal to them. Gun control advocates, who might have opposed her for claiming that no one should blame the instrumentality were able to claim they supported her because she favored cutting defense spending and was more of a pacifist than any previous candidate. Many evangelical

Christians supported her, despite opposition to many of her positions, and claimed it was because she stood to defend secular Christian ideals against the violence of the non-Christian world. But they also supported her because of the miracle of her pregnancy and her obviously spiritual concerns that she boldly expressed in terms that were Christian even if they were of a different variety than they had heard thumped at them from the pulpits of the right. And so the wisdom of political caution was turned on its head by her boldness and frankness. Voters saw only the whole of her, ignored their differences and remembered their common ground.

The Pope, moved by her stance on halting American military adventures overseas, scheduled an impromptu visit to the United States and he gave her his blessing. A few dozen reporters attempted to cover the women believed to have been exiting her baby shower. The President of Russia vowed to storm out of the room if she ever dared to breast feed in front of him. Melinda immediately became the most popular new baby name in France. More people saw the acceptance speech she had given at the Democratic Convention than had ever watched any Super Bowl. The Nobel Peace Prize, which had once been awarded to an American President in his first year of office and before he had escalated American military involvement in a conflict in some Central Asian nation, was this time awarded to her as a Presidential candidate, in no small part due to her selection of Senator Gus Casabianca as her Vice Presidential running mate and the strong signal that sent to the international community that the United States was finally going to do something about global climate change. Garth's mother even took her hand off of her necklace for several weeks at a time. Melinda's brother, Porter, was so excited he decided to schedule his wedding to Jesus in New York for as soon as possible, so he called Garth.

"Garth, Jesus and I are getting married on October twenty-fifth and we want you guys to be there," he said.

"Congratulations. Of course we will be there."

"Garth, I think you guys owe it to me, you know, with what I did for the campaign and all."

"Porter, I have already said it. We will be there."

"Then you won't mind if the wedding cake is in the shape of a penis and that Jesus and I and all the groomsmen will be wearing only in jock straps?"

"Of course we won't mind, Porter."

"We are asking the friends and family from Jesus' side to dress as Marilyn Monroe and my side is supposed to dress as Elvis."

"This Elvis would expect nothing less."

"As part of the exchange of our vows we plan to discuss the way in which we came to be open about being gay and to recount the details of our first sexual encounter."

"I am certain that everyone will find that very touching and enlightening."

"Damn it, Garth. I can't get you upset, can I? How did you know I was not being serious?"

"I knew that mainly because your lips were moving. That is how I always know you are not being serious. I know you too well."

"That is so sad."

"Yes, Porter, you are so conservative and predictable. That is why you are planning the zaniest, wildest, craziest, most famous Big Gay Wedding in the history of the world. Who knew you were so shy? Who needs a penis cake when you have CNN?"

"In all seriousness, thank you. This is amazing of you to let this happen," Porter said.

"I certainly would have made this as a scheduling decision. But it is not. This wedding is important to your sister. She is very excited for you and wants to talk to you. So I am handing her the phone."

"One second, Garth, one more thing before you put me on with Melinda. Does this mean that I will not have to do all of the planning on my own, you know? Does it mean I will get some help?"

"We both know, Porter, that you already know that the Secret Service will take over all the planning entirely and that all you will have to do is to tell them what you want. I am sure that the Secret Service detail that has been protecting you since the convention has already told you that it will be the easiest planning of any Big Gay Wedding ever. Here is your sister."

In only a few minutes Melinda was laughing so hard she had tears running down her cheeks. Her brother always had that effect on her. She told him how happy she was for him and for Jesus and how much she thought Jesus had always sort of been Porter's personal savior, so to speak. She was happy that they would be able to formalize their relationship and publicly express their commitment. Porter half apologized for so many things that it only served as a litany of all the strange reasons she had for loving him. And in the end of the conversation it was exactly as it once had been on the roads north of London, Kentucky, when two very young Ceylonese siblings were communicating telepathically while hitching rides from memorable strangers on the way to Ohio.

By this point in time, the political right had learned to be circumspect about attacking Senator Sherman. They remained quietly watching their public opinion polls. But the high and righteous hectors of the religious right were of course now bitterly decrying and severely condemning on behalf of their benevolent Christian God, whom they interpreted as being prepared to smite America down into a flattened and cindered version of some kind of Haiti or Indonesia, simply for considering the election of a woman whose brother was such a deviant pervert. One of the outcomes of this was something perhaps that God might actually have foreseen but had neglected to mention to the evangelical intimidators.

Porter's wedding became an accounting of every American who had a gay sibling or a gay cousin or uncle or who worked with a gay or lesbian person or who had one for a friend or an acquaintance. Interest in the wedding and their support for it burgeoned. These numbers were dramatically increased by the massive numbers of gays and lesbians from within the conservative segments of American society who came out and announced their orientation. Many of these individuals, it turned out, had a sibling or a cousin or uncle or who was a haranguer on the Christian right or who worked with one or who had one for a friend or an acquaintance, thus spreading around the responsibility for what was the holy smiting to come.

One thing that had always puzzled Garth had also coalesced in front of him in the form of his wife and her novel political strengths. He had always known that Americans vote for President for reasons that are a largely cultural or social or personal and have little to do with policy or government, but there was one aspect of that which the Democrats had never fully exploited. The commentators and the pundits had their own agendas and they could not see much more than the political and policy elements of any candidate's make up. But the winner of every presidential race was more likable, more someone with whom you might like to socialize. In this respect, Democrats and Republicans were more or less on a par, except for one thing and that was the thing that had always puzzled Garth. There was no such thing as a cool Republican. Democrats could be cool. And cool is what separates Americans from Europeans. Cool matters in the United States. And there she was, his wife, the highly attractive and miraculously pregnant Congressional Medal of Honor winner and wounded war hero who was still in her mid-forties, with the famous gay actor brother and two stepchildren, and she was saying things no one had dared to say and she might be just a little bit crazy, and she was clearly madly in love with her divorced husband and she seemed to care more about being who she really is than she cared about winning the election. How cool was that?

Of the two hundred million American adults of voting age, only about three-quarters are registered to vote. Of those registered voters, only sixty percent actually turn out to vote in the general election. For anything but a presidential election, even a smaller proportion turn out. That leaves well more than half of Americans eligible to vote sitting at home on Election Day. These numbers tend to fall disproportionately into the categories of the poor and the people of color and the young. This final group was now registering and becoming involved in ways that were reminiscent of the upheavals and youth rallies against the Viet Nam War. Their children were now following a candidate who seemed new and cool and expressed their values and they were rallying against the way in which politics had always seemed to be practiced. The poor and the minorities were only slightly less energized by the hope that a candidate who not only stood for change but who also advocated specific change might actually change the system which had worked for so long against their hopes and interests. And these groups were now actively being registered to vote by the swarms of young people canvassing their towns and neighborhoods.

The long-awaited wedding of Porter and Jesus was moved to a larger venue. Many of their friends and acquaintances were in attendance as were the friends of Porter's sister and brother-in-law. Eakin Lambert was there along with her company's chief financial officer, Elliott Barker, who was Garth's old friend and classmate. They brought with them Eakin's sons and her other most trusted employee, Ben Dessous. Preston Cobalt and Leonard Rock were there with their wives and families. Congressman Wilton Carslon was in attendance with his striking new girlfriend, an internationally famous fashion model from New Zealand who would later dump him the very instant he had obtained a green card for her. Tommy

Kit and all the younger Kitts were there. Detective John Huffam brought his wife and family and took the opportunity to take Garth aside and tell him that he had destroyed the thumb drive he had taken from the apartment of the deceased Earnest Dapple. Garth spent some quality moments with the detective's daughter and made sure that she was introduced to Melinda. A very subdued and somewhat confused Angelina Bol Sherman was in attendance. Her sharper edges had been dulled now by old age and by the fawning attention of important people. Even Tabitha Vivenda was in evidence. Ben Dessous made a point of introducing himself to her and sat next to her at the wedding and at the following reception. As always, he had taken this on as yet another responsibility he simply felt compelled to assume. Ben's move had made Garth not the least bit concerned that they had invited his often volatile ex-wife. Even Eakin Lambert, who had once told Garth that nothing good could ever come from him making this kind of overture, looked at Ben with Tabitha and then gave Garth a knowing and satisfied smile. Senator Gus Casabianca was there with his family and several of his closest friends and supporters. Both Hanna and Seth were among the rather large and unwieldy gaggle of what could only be considered the equivalent of groomsmen and brides-men. Garth had accepted the honor of being the best man to Porter, or perhaps he was the maid of honor. Garth could only happily speculate.

Porter Sherman had expanded the invitation list to include a small smattering of people he knew might be interested in meeting the next President of the United States. This meant that the wedding had to be moved to the Cathedral Church of Saint John the Divine, in Harlem, in order to accommodate half of Hollywood. The largest cathedral in the world could also hold the rest of the guests, which now numbered half of the Democratic Senators and Governors in America, many of the party's senior Congressmen, most of the nation's liberal leaning business and social and political leaders, and several dozen world leaders and representatives of heads of state. Foreign heads of state sent their ambassadors while the sitting President of the United States was still in office. He issued a statement that he now supported same sex marriages.

Melinda was about seven months pregnant and beginning to show. It was reported that she wore a conservative and comfortably fitting gray wool business suit with a floral print blouse. She was blessed by not being one of those many women who put on a lot of extra weight when pregnant and she had also maintained her workout regimen. She had a luminous glow that and had given her a beatific appearance that can be seen in the women of certain Renaissance paintings.

She did her best not to upstage her brother. Most of the guests knew the protocol and focused their attentions on the two men who were getting married. The gay community of friends of Porter and Jesus were simply too deeply moved and proud to do anything more toward Melinda than to look at her and inwardly weep tears of profound joy. The relatives of Jesus already knew Porter, so the real excitement for them was in the person of the Democratic nominee for President, for whom all their friends and neighbors planned to vote and who had suddenly and miraculously turned whatever shame they may have felt toward their gay relative into unalloyed pride. Melinda gracefully and smilingly accepted far more warm and enthusiastic hugs from these strangers than her security detail might have liked.

For Melinda, leaving the cathedral would have not been unlike flying into enemy territory in the daytime had it not been for Porter and the Secret Service which had set the security cordon two blocks away from the wedding on each side. Morningside Heights had not seen such an outsized and disruptive tumult of individuals bent on mayhem since the New York City Police had violently suppressed the ferocious student uprisings at Columbia University in 1968. As it was, the reporters were reduced to shouting questions at the Senator as she got into her limousine with her husband.

Porter however did walk over to a part of them. His own Secret Service detail, which had code-named him "Daffodil," prevented him from getting too close. He soon grew tired of the fact that they only asked him questions about his sister, so he simply gave them one item to think about, as he walked away.

"Yes, she definitely does plan to breast feed."

Garth sat in the limousine with Melinda and thought again about something that he had imagined, considered, turned over in his mind and then decided, but which was the one such thing he had never told his wife and would never tell her. He believed that he knew what had happened to Earnest Dapple and why he, Garth, had suddenly become someone who was no longer suspected in that death. He knew Ben had been involved. He was certain of how it had all happened. He smiled to himself now, because even though he had once felt so terrible for not consulting and conferring with his wife, he was very happy he never had done so. His silence had saved her to some extent and it would continue to do so.

The ending he imagined was very real to him, so real it is dutifully reported here in the subsequent chapter.

AN IMAGINED ENDING

Here is Garth's version of events.

Elliott Barker had called Earnest. Eakin and Ben had decided that Elliott would be the only one whom Earnest would not suspect of having some ulterior motive. Earnest's impression of what he had long assumed was Elliott's dissipated and amoral character was naturally based on his own internal measurement rather than any assessment of what Elliott really was. And Elliott was a good deal more complex than Earnest could ever assess. Elliott had always seen the world through very old and experienced eyes and his own belated view of it filled him with an ineffable and almost over-whelming melancholy. His apparent cynicism was only the landing place for his inherent sensitivity, after it had been educated by what he had seen as the arbitrary and unjust nature of life. There was in his smile and in his eyes the category of kindness that can only arise from the generosity that springs from the awareness of loss. It was the recognition that we can only do what we can and no more, and that in its faint and delicate way it was something beautiful. What sincere and genuine cynicism that Elliott truly possessed was trained only upon himself. He cared very little what might happen to him. Earnest saw the exterior and incorrectly diagnosed a lack of loyalty in what was an apparent lack of interest and concern. He saw Elliott as being as careless with himself and therefore careless with this friendships and relationships, while Elliott did delicately care for those things in ways he worked to mask. A call from the biochemically loyal Eakin Lambert would have aroused Earnest's suspicion. A call from Ben would have scared him enough to push him to immediate action.

It had to have been Elliott who called.

Elliot had been briefed by Ben to a limited extent on what Earnest had been doing, enough so that Elliott could make what he had to say to appeal to Earnest. And that material would be that he had come upon some information about Garth and his wife that he wanted to share with Earnest. The fact that Elliott had known Garth for a long time and now was working with his oldest and dearest friend would have supplemented the possible appeal of whatever Elliott might have to say. But he would also have to have added something, some observation that was part of a truth that Earnest already knew. Elliott had said that he had something to tell Earnest about Garth's family and also something about that night so many years ago at the party at the Owl Club. In keeping with Elliot's diffident and insouciant nature, he had not pressed Earnest nor did he seem anxious to talk, only telling the reporter that he would tell him the stories if he were ever in the Houston area.

The soft sell and the mention of family and the possibility of confirming what Earnest believed had actually happened that long ago night put Earnest on one of the earliest flights to Houston that he could schedule. He called Elliott within a few days and he was told that Elliott was going out on Eakin's sailboat, which was moored at a marina in Galveston Bay. This did not raise any red flags for Earnest because the class from which he and Elliott came thought of boats the way other people think of picnic tables or car rides in the park. Of course Elliott would be in a sailboat. So Earnest went to the marina and got on the boat and he asked if Eakin were also coming along. Elliott told him that Eakin did not even know that Elliott was meeting with Earnest, which had been the only answer Earnest would have accepted. So Elliott took the thirty-eight foot day sailboat out onto the Bay and into the Gulf of Mexico. With only the mainsail set, they slowly tacked away from the mainland. Earnest would not have seen or have heard anyone coming out from below deck and up behind of him because of the sound of the rush of the water and the wind in the sail and because of the natural pitching of the deck. He would have only been aware that he had been temporarily incapacitated by a high voltage electrical charge from a Taser. He would not have known that the person who had done this was Ben Dessous until he had seen him later, while he was handcuffed and tied and lying on the deck way out into the Gulf, at which time he would have also watched Elliott disembark the sailing craft in order to get into a motorboat that had been anchored at that spot, which he then piloted away leaving Ben and his captive alone on the sailboat.

Lying on his side and barely able to move, trussed up with duct tape and a pair of handcuffs, Earnest began to assess his situation. He had only his own heart as an internal guide so he immediately expected the worst. For the first minute or so he cried. Then he cried out until he recognized that no one could hear him. Throughout this time his implacable captor kept going about his business. He was attaching a small sea anchor to a cable he was placing around Earnest's waist and under his arms that were handcuffed behind his back. On the deck in front of him was a filet knife stuck in small chopping board. Earnest's own inclinations, had the situation been reversed, told him that Ben was about to stick the filet knife into him, enough to make a deep but not too open seeping wound in his leg, before he would drop him overboard where the small sea anchor would slowly take him down to the bottom while drifting him several miles with the current. He did not need to know that the Shortfin Mako sharks that were native to these waters would scent the blood and were big enough to make sure that very little if anything of him would be left. He just knew he was to be some creature's lunch.

He remembered an old Chinese proverb about a man whom the Emperor had sentenced to immediate death. The man then told the Emperor that he could teach the Emperor's favorite horse to speak Mandarin if the Emperor would give him a year to do it. The Emperor granted his request and promised to have him put to death if he failed in that year. The man's wife was distressed to know that she would still lose her husband in one year's time. But the man told her that three things might happen in a year's time: the Emperor may die, he – her husband – may die of natural causes, and the horse may learn to speak Mandarin.

Earnest knew his only option was to buy some time.

"So, I guess I am not going to be told the two things I came to find out, about Teller's family and about that night thirty-seven years ago," he said.

"Oh," Ben said, as he took a seat, "there is probably very little economy in discussing a fact pattern we both already know."

"I know you two were involved in a shooting."

"Yes, Dapple, Garth shot a man to save my life that night."

"I have that information all written down and filed on my computer and in a safe deposit box. If anything happens to me, it will all get out."

"No one will know that any calamity has befallen you until long after I have rifled your apartment and have examined all of your possessions. Nor are you the type to have done anything other than to have kept the story of a lifetime all to yourself. And those gentlemen who may have corroborated your story of that night are all either dead or are incarcerated."

"Don't be so sure that I don't have some failsafe. It is also on my computer at the *Post*. And the story is more than what happened back then when Teller was also a drug dealer. His wife is a lesbian. She slept with another woman in college."

"Evidently, what you consider to be the confession you had recorded from Ms. Caroline Collins was in actuality rife with contradiction and the predominant element of the recording is your own coercion and harassing. It is alike with all your research, imprecise at best. No paper would run with it after you have gone, not without months of independent research. It might possibly have been published immediately under your byline, with you taking the risk, but not without you. And that is contingent upon the paper having your report, which they do not. By the way, being gay is not pathology, as you seem to think it is. The fifteenth President was gay. And I believe what we are talking about is that she might be bisexual."

"Her actor brother is also queer. The Democratic presidential nominee has a brother who is a flaming fag."

"The voting public has long since decided that family is not fair game, politically. It has all been coming out anyway, in a manner of speaking."

"Okay, what do you think people will say when they learn she is certifiably crazy, diagnosed with hypomania, cyclothymia, and hyperthermic temperament, a total nut case?"

"No reputable newspaper would touch a confidential report, specifically one issued twenty-five years ago by an unqualified non-professional. And many highly functioning and successful individuals have been similarly diagnosed. And this story will never find publication because you are about to be degustation for several members of the species, *Isurus Oxyrinchus*."

"The report will make qualified professionals go look at all the tapes of her. Then you will see some fireworks. And I am no longer talking about whatever press may happen. I am talking to you, as a man, as an American. Do you know what you are about to let loose on America? All that diagnosis means she is borderline bipolar disorder. Do you want her to have the nuclear codes, and have her finger on the button?"

"Right. There has never been a paranoid President nor has there been one who suffered from satyriasis or clinical depression. There has never been a stupid President. The country has never been run by a gross amateur or by someone whose ulterior motive was a pathological and personal inse-curity. On the contrary, this nation has survived what appears to actually have been a rich and storied tradition of borderline Presidents. A President Sherman will be a welcome positive change because her primary difference is that she is genuine."

"Interesting you should mention satyriasis. Do you know that hyper-sexuality is a symptom of hypomania, cyclothymia, and hyperthermic temperament? Do you know that she and Teller are a couple of perverts? She submits herself to him and ties her up, like in some damn porno movie."

"I don't consider you are helping yourself out here. They are consenting adults and all of that is not anyone's business. I am beginning to wonder if you may be too unwholesome a repast for the sharks."

"Did you know that her mother was a collaborator with the Nazis during World War II, she was the girlfriend of some Gestapo trooper in her home town in Poland? And get this; she used to abuse the gay brother. This old psychopath created the atmosphere in which your precious Melinda Sherman was raised. You may not find this to be an alarming danger, but most Americans would."

By this time Ben was beginning to tire of the exercise. He had fastened the sea anchor by cable to Earnest. He was certain that he had calculated that it would more than just offset his buoyancy and that Earnest would gently drift to the bottom of the Gulf of Mexico some seven miles away, give or take a mile and dependent upon the vicinity, number, and voraciousness of the local shark species. He knew that there was not even the remotest possibility that Earnest would talk his way out of the situation or that anything would come along to change that possibility, not so long as Ben kept his eyes peeled to the horizon. He also knew that he had a responsibility, and he always took that seriously, to hear the other man out, to see if there might be some bit of information or some revelation that might assist Ben in the cleaning up he would have to do for the next few days. His own experienced calculations were that there was very little that Earnest might say that would be substantive. And Ben had largely determined what Earnest knew or thought be knew. If what continued to spew out of Earnest was a steady stream of vitriol, prurience, contempt, and bile, Ben was going to slip him into the water sooner rather than later. He decided to start tossing bits of cut up beef over the side of the boat. He was chumming and he wanted Dapple to see it.

"As a result of that upbringing," Earnest said, "Sherman is about as likely to drop all of her clothes to the floor as she is to shake your hand. She is a sexual freak and she is an exhibitionist. She was charged with sexual harassment in the Navy but she got off with the charge because she was a valued officer and the guy she had harassed was a junior officer. It is a classic case of the chain of command thwarting justice. And you can imagine now, with this aberration of a woman being about to have a baby and go to the White House, what she is going to do with breast feeding in the middle of cabinet meetings and meetings with foreign heads of state. Her own brother admits she will do it."

"We both know she is incapable of sexually harassing anybody who did not already have the wrong idea about her. And I am looking forward to the country having a female President who is in her full feminine flower. She will be a tremendous symbol for girls in the United States and all over the world."

"All that stuff about her being a Christian is a lie. She once even openly attacked the faith of the Christian Community of London, Kentucky."

"Well, it seems that the Christian Community of London, Kentucky would and has disagreed with you on that point. They are proud of her former membership of that congregation and have said so many times. As far as what defines a Christian, she has a genius for being Christian in a way that is a welcome change."

"She had a very sick relationship with her own father. Part of her many pathologies is her horrible daddy fixation and it is at the root of her relationship with Teller. Tell me that is not sick."

"It is not. And you may have it backwards. Senator Sherman has a commanding maternal instinct, which makes her an unsurpassed stepmother and will make her a great mother. It will also make her an excellent President. And she will save the lives of thousands of American service men and women, whom she will never send to an unjust war. I am beginning to think that it is time you went for a little swim."

"But you have not heard the best of it."

"I am certain that I have."

"She is really his aunt. She is Teller's aunt. He is her nephew. I found out that nine months before she was born the Sherman family had gone to Texas for vacation. The mother got separated from the family and was caught in a flood on the Guadalupe River. She was rescued by Teller's own grandfather at his hunting and fishing camp. The old man took advantage of her and the two of them conceived a child. That child was Melinda Sherman. She married her own nephew! He is the grandson of her father. The crazy old mother hid it from the family. Her father suspected it but never said anything. It is another reason she is so crazy. Teller knows it too or else he strongly suspects it. But there he is, happily making a baby."

"That is all rather fantastical and highly unlikely and no one is prepared to believe it."

"I have the genetic tests. I took a sample of the old man's tissue from his grave and had it tested along with some of her saliva I took from a glass which she had been drinking from."

"You mean, from which she had been drinking."

"What? You're going to get pedantic with me now?"

"I always strive to be exact. It is one of your countless deficiencies that you are disordered and sloppy. I know what you have done. I saw you at the fishing camp and I witnessed the exchange at the Roadhouse. Your actions in this regard are hardly the equivalent of a plea for mercy. It is all rather despicable."

"It is still god damn incest, Dessous. It is incest, pure and simple."

"Not in Texas. And not in Kentucky either. And in fact, it is not incest in any state in the country. You have missed the most important fact. She is not his aunt. Her mother is not his grandmother. She is his father's half sister. If you have ever consulted the table of consanguinity you would have seen that a full aunt or uncle is three degrees away from the individual. A half aunt or half uncle is a full six degrees separated from the individual. No state or international jurisdiction prevents marriage between individuals who are more than four degrees removed."

"That is what you say. But don't you think the voters have a right to know? More importantly, Mr. Holier Than Thou, don't you think your friends have a right to know?"

"My friend is Garth Teller and I believe he knows. In any event it is up to him to decide. I do know his wife but she is really not my friend. Even more significantly, she has risen to the status of a very important historical figure. She is therefore beyond my personal scope. I feel only one duty toward her and that is to protect the importance of her position. Aren't you feeling like it is time to take a little dip. You must be getting hot."

"Here is the thing. What it all really means is that she is a Jew. Sherman is a Jew. Teller is a Jew. That inbred kid of theirs will be a Jew. Do you really want a bunch of Jews in the White House?"

"That is a curious thing for one African American man to say to another. And if you had also consulted even the most rudimentary guide to Judaic law you would know that only Garth could possibly be Jewish since he is the only one who had a Jewish mother. And he is not a practicing member of any religion. So your distinction is merely ethnic and that makes you little less than just another racist."

With this last word, Ben gently inserted the filet knife into his captive's thigh. He then lifted the reporter over the transom and slid him into the water.

"She is not even related to William Tecumseh Sherman," were the last words of the journalist. Ben wondered why Earnest had not resorted to humor earlier. It might have kept him on board a little longer. But as they say in Texas, the son of a bitch needed killing.

So many things have been said about the truth that it is truthfully rather difficult to know which if any of them might be the truth. The illustrious bard who said that at length the truth will out had never tried to wade through the morass of the Warren Report or ponder any of the many other tales of conspiracies that grow out of government, but he was perhaps merely expressing a tendency for which the truth is often known. The novelist who said that truth will often yield to the aesthetic may have come closer to the truth of truth, particularly because he was aware that the said artistic sensibility was that of the popular masses, meaning that the easiest truth will be the one that wins. In this way complicated facts are boiled down to archetypal forms, believable fictions, and stories that conform to prevalent predispositions. And as that other novelist and sports commentator has been noted to have said, Americans are creatures of their first impression and for them late-arriving truths often fade back into obscurity, which is really the shade of a fable which has already taken root and grown. Perhaps the most truth which has ever been distilled from the truth is that it is invariably stranger than fiction.

Ben had actually decided to go by car to Washington and to do some of his own investigating. He could not have known that while he was on the road

Earnest had suddenly disappeared. The regular call-in schedule that Earnest had set up had been disrupted and concerned colleagues who had been sworn by Earnest to report to the police had done so. Detective Huffam had already been to Earnest's apartment by the time Ben had arrived in Washington, DC. And the newspaper had reported that Garth was being investigated in connection with what was considered to be a likely murder. Ben felt the pain of being too late very personally and the feeling of having let his friend down gave him greater motivation in uncovering all the facts. Since he had no access to what had been in the apartment, he moved on to a relentlessly thorough canvassing of the neighborhood and Earnest's haunts. It was not long before the evidence began to point to long absences during which Earnest had neither been at work nor at his apartment. And these could not be explained by trips or by assignments and in fact they were all rather a little too regular. He knew in his gut that Earnest must have had a second domicile if not a double life.

He was able to find it within several weeks of doing very little other than putting himself into the mind of this man he had only known long ago and by following up on those assumptions and speculations with the expenditure of what was once called shoe leather. He found the house in a ghetto neighborhood only three subway stops from the office of the *Post* and four subway stops from Earnest's apartment. The house was locked up tight and appeared to have been so for some long time. In the back, off the alley, he found a window well that had its window broken out from the inside. It was a small window and Ben took many precautions not to have disturbed the evidence as he took a several minutes to squeeze in through that window. What he found was appalling to him. The basement had apparently been the dungeon of a younger person, likely a girl, who lived in deplorable conditions. There were rats and piles of garbage amid the remains of old canned food meals and the dirty mattress and table and chairs. The lone bathroom was foul and had never been cleaned. And yet there were signs of young life, a doll, some drawings, small areas that had been kept clean as was possible.

The place was completely closed. There was very little light. Ben went up the stairs to find that the door at the top was apparently bolt-locked from inside the first floor. But the door had one of those old-fashioned key holes, the ones through which people in old books and movies would peer. Scrutinizing the view through this aperture, Ben was able to determine what had happened to Earnest, why the prisoner in the basement had finally escaped and who that prisoner had likely been.

His best and perhaps only chance now was to become a part of that neighborhood. And within a few weeks he found his man. He was an older gentleman and Ben saw him as sort of a working class African American version of Elliott Barker, which is to say his melancholy was misanthropy; his generosity was with brutally frank statements to his friends and neighbors and his kindness was buried under deeper levels of a more profound sense of greater loss. But Ben could see it. And at his age and with his own matching temperament, he was more or less able to befriend the man after a week or two of seeing him at the local tavern.

And at that point Ben simply asked him how was the girl doing, the one he had saved.

The old man was happy to have someone who knew what he had done and he was at least willing to tell Ben the story and then to take him back home so the twelve-year-old girl could tell him in her own words. Ben knew that he would find the girl doing well and prospering. He also knew that he could not go to the police because that would propel the girl into the foster care system and she would suffer there. Where she was now, she would gradually recover. She would be all right with the old man who had found her wandering the street one day and who rushed her out of harm's way. And she had many natural gifts which would surface and flourish in this nurturing atmosphere. After all, she was the daughter of a Harvard graduate.

She had been Earnest's daughter from a liaison he had with a woman from that neighborhood who had long since died from a drug overdose. Earnest had simply taken the child and had installed her in this second home, locking her in the basement so that she could not get away, feeding her from cans he put down there, rarely if ever letting her out and then only when he was feeling in a certain mood. She rarely complained but as she got older she became more of a concern and soon she was largely exiled to below ground. Her relationship to her father had become only what she could occasionally see of him through that keyhole. The mysteries of the human heart will ever escape us and here was one perhaps only less understandable than most. She loved her father. So her escape was precipitated by what she had seen through that keyhole. She left because she saw that he would never again be for her what he had been in his limited and brutal way. And this is what the police saw when Ben had anonymously provided them with the address and the facts.

The house was locked. There had been no unauthorized entry, even to the first floor from the locked basement. The police found that inside of the building there was a trace of a smoldering, suffocating vapor that had been in the air for some time. There was something on the ground by the kitchen table, a blackened mass that once had a small glowing fire slowly expiring on it. There was a dark greasy coating on the appliances, the table and the walls. And next to the blackened mass were the remnants of Earnest Dapple's clothes and belongings. Call the death what it can be called, and the police called it a smoking accident, it had all earmarks of something stranger. No one had set fire to Earnest and no such fire would have likely burned him so fully. Porter Sherman may or may not have caused it. He certainly had concentrated on it, and would claim credit for it later.

Earnest Dapple had died from spontaneous combustion.

COME AND GET ME

On December 15, 2016, in between the successful and landslide election of Senator Melinda Sherman to the office of President of the United States and her inauguration ceremony, she gave birth to a healthy baby girl, whom they named Angela Teller but who was known in some circles as America's Baby. It was an event that was celebrated as an unofficial United States holiday. She would grow up to be normal by all accounting except to the degree that she was very intelligent and very independently minded and also an excellent athlete. She would bear up well under the pressures of growing up in the White House, largely due to the inherent strength of her character. She was also very much the doting attachment of her older half siblings, Hanna and Seth, and her father was never far away from her or her needs.

She would grow to be almost six-foot tall, as handsome and beautiful as her mother, but with dark brown eyes. She would choose to attend college and play varsity basketball not at the alma mater of her father (she protested the Boston gloom) but of that of her beloved godmother, Eakin Lambert. Elliott Barker and Eakin had revealed that they had been secretly married for several years, as Garth might have suspected. The happiness and strength of this union persuaded Eakin's adult sons to return to the love and support of their brash and outspoken mother. They became fast friends with Seth and Hanna and actively participated in care of young Angela Teller.

William Shakespeare had an ambivalent view of the institution of marriage. If we look at the end of *Measure for Measure* or at the marriage of Portia and Bassanio from *The Merchant of Venice*, it might be assumed that the Bard thought of matrimony as a rancid affair, on a par with a kind of punishment for the bride and groom. More of a mixed blessing are the marriage of Beatrice and Benedick from *Much Ado About Nothing* and the conjugal pairing of Kate and Petruchio from *The Taming of the Shrew*, about which much good may be said, but the successful operations of which would be beyond the understanding of any outsider, who also would be happier and saner never to see those intimate processes or to attempt to understand them. Such was the success of the marriage of Eakin and Elliott. It worked. It was entertaining. But were anyone to figure it out, they might be mystified, if not appalled.

Melinda was required to attend to the business of running the country, but the loving quality of the interaction of mother and daughter was never lost to her mother's importance to millions of other people. Angela was breast fed until the age of six months, during which time she did meet the President of Russia, who did not storm out of the room.

Hanna Teller had a boundless enthusiasm and an infectious love of life that accompanied her many intellectual and artistic talents. She had a powerful soprano voice, a beautiful and exotic face, a tall and attractive frame, an expressive personality, and a deep and abiding affection for her Uncle Porter and the world in which he was now one of the lions. She went out west to live with him and become an actress. Hanna came to star in many zombie movies, outer space soap operas, transplanted Japanese horror films, and other ephemera of this era, which were meant to be seen by smaller audiences and only on a computer screen. Hollywood was still Hollywood, which meant that her efforts were not long beyond the notice of the great nepotism engine which is movie entertainment and soon the niece of Porter Sherman was appearing in major motion pictures.

Seth Sherman struggled with his attention deficit disorder for only so much longer before he received the very best treatment and assistance, becoming along the way the national poster boy for what could be done with this neurophysiological impairment. He finished his university education, took a job as a waiter and eventually rose to be the top executive at his restaurant chain. He sensibly married a tall blonde nurse who was of the perfect temperament and who had a unique knack for making, "Where have you placed your cell phone?" sound like, "I love you." And it was her support that allowed his native intelligence to thrive and he eventually started his own food service company and they became quite wealthy.

Governor Rich Sartory never completely recovered from his drubbing at the polls but he did return to Texas, where he was resoundingly re-elected Governor and served out his second term. He moved on to become the high priest of the tea party resurgence and railed strenuously if not effectively against government involvement in everything from mail delivery to health care while staunchly inveighing against evolutionary and environmental science, women in the workplace, poor people, and common sense. He had a long and successful career. The people who had supported him came to love him fanatically as their numbers steadily dwindled.

Preston Cobalt became the Secretary of Energy and was outstanding and noteworthy for his prescience and insight, and for enlightening the entrenched interests of his state and his former colleagues in the oil and gas business. He helped to convince them of what they already knew, which was that the future in their industry was limited and that permanent future growth was in the field of renewable energy. Perhaps most important was his great feat of policy legerdemain by which he played perception against perception and created a positive synergy. Because his former colleagues were convinced that he was privileged to know what the government would be doing, they were also convinced that a carbon tax and gasoline tax were definitely coming down the pipeline. So they began to set aside portions of their own sales into anticipatory funds, reasoning that when those taxes would be enacted the companies that would survive and prosper would be the ones who were already prepared. These actions, taken in concert, were seen to have eased the burdens of those taxes, which were eventually enacted and which sparked an explosion in the development of renewable energy technologies, which then became a primary export of the United States.

Ben Dessous would accept no official position even though the prospect had been discussed. He had saved enough to retire from Eakin's company and indeed was of that age at the time of the inauguration. What he did accept was a security clearance and a permanent pass to the White House, which he used frequently, not out of any desire to seem important or to bask in the attention of the First Family, but out of the same elemental sense of responsibility that had always moved him. He could often be seen in the room where Angela was playing or studying or where the adult children had gathered, watching and measuring by some unseen scale of possible dangers. He was also given a top-level security clearance and had the President's permission to sit in on Secret Service briefings, where he only made rare remarks that were fitting and were accepted gratefully.

Porter and Jesus lived happily in their Beverly Hills mansion, where they looked after Hanna and raised several Pomeranian dogs. They filled their home with art and friends and music. Porter took fewer roles and spent much time at home with Jesus and with setting Hanna up with her voice and acting lessons. The roles he did take were usually the sassy older friend who helped the younger heroine straighten out her love life in romantic comedies. The President of the United States would often stay with them and her stepdaughter on her trips to California. Porter still had his own Secret Service detail and Hanna had one, but he looked forward to seeing his sister and to doubling the number of handsome and fit and mysterious

Mormon men in his home. To their credit and due to the warmth and humor of the First Brother, they all also looked forward to protecting the home of Daffodil.

Leonard Rock was named Secretary of Commerce, from which position he was able to promote and to effect the completion of his own dream, which was to create a free and national infrastructure of high-speed internet service for all of the more populated regions of the United States. He drafted legislation to create services on the model of the Rural Electric Cooperatives, which had carried electrical power to every corner of America. They created a boom in productivity, a boom in creativity and innovation, and an overall annual two percent increase in the gross domestic product of the United States which carried on for many years.

Tommy Kitt and his family remained in London, Kentucky, the only place they could ever be happy. Tommy held various different jobs within the federal government there until the South Central Kentucky Power and Light Company hired him to be its chief executive officer. He was always at the ready on the regular occasions in which President Sherman would come to visit her mother, which was quite often. His enduring and disinterested admiration for his childhood friend had never waned and it was now something that was emulated by the neighborhood, the region and the entire state of Kentucky, which chose to recognize him as the First Friend. Of course, she would insist that he call her Melinda, which he never did.

Earnest Dapple had died intestate, which meant that his estate would go to his children first, and if there were none, then to his parents. If they had predeceased him, his estate would go to his siblings. It was not difficult for Garth, operating from the office of the President, to get it all straightened out. Earnest's daughter took the estate in trust until such time as she would turn eighteen, and the appointed trustee was the older man who had been her putative guardian. He would love her as a father loves a daughter until the day he would die and that would enrich her life far more than the comfortable living she was suddenly able to obtain. Every year or so in the late fall, a tall and nice looking older white gentleman and a slightly older African American gentleman would pay them a visit and her guardian would only refer to these two men as friends although she soon was to recognize that one of the men was the husband of the President and the other one of his closest friends.

Parker Askew would spend some time wandering in the wilderness after he had lost all but one of his clients shortly after the day everyone began telling the truth. He eventually became the in-house media consultant at the Bayer Corporation's United States headquarters in Pittsburgh, Pennsylvania. He was able to attach himself to a kind and warm widow and matron who was a native to that city. And even though he missed the bright lights and fast pace of the nation's capital, he soon found that he could be happy in one of the friendliest and liveliest small big cities in the country.

Tabitha Vivenda never really recovered from her experience with Earnest Dapple and in her idiosyncratic mind it came to be seen as something that was Garth's fault, until it became one and the same with it. She had retired from the law and had taken to live on a small farm in rural Maryland that had horses and cats and dogs, which she struggled to take care of and which kept her vital and strong. She developed a strange and otherworldly laugh, which came out at awkward moments. Her home was always a little bit unkempt. But her life was greatly enriched by regular and loving visits from her daughter and her son and daughter-in-law, who also took it upon herself to spend some of her husband's wealth on a maid and cleaning service for her mother-in-law.

One of the very first conversations that Garth and Melinda had after she had been elected was about the drug, Boz. Melinda Sherman had just

Gerald Weaver

given her election night acceptance speech. She told Garth she had something to say to him in private. Garth followed her into the room. He found her there in all her enceinte glory, completely disrobed. She was even more beautiful to him than the very first time she had tried but had failed to get her clothes on the floor.

"Of the nine million reasons that I love you, Garth Teller, one of the very top ones is that you know how to make love to a pregnant woman, I mean a pregnant Senator."

"You mean a pregnant President-elect," he said.

"I am not even going to think about how weird this all is, not for another couple of hours or so."

Afterward she quietly asked, "Garth?"

"Yeah, baby."

"That's good sweetheart. Please keep remembering who I am."

"That will never be a problem, Madam President-elect."

"You're a funny guy. Do you know those pills we decided I would take, the ones that made people like me?"

"Oh, those," he said, "I replaced them with sugar pills."

"Well that means I have been flushing sugar pills down the toilet."

It had been a presidential campaign that, for the first time in history, had also been a love affair. And now their love affair was going to run the country.

The role of the First Lady in American politics had always been circumscribed by the prejudices that have always attempted to limit women. These presidential wives could not step into any substantive roles. It would seem to threaten the authority or even the masculinity of the President and it would make the wife seem strident, or appear as if she were wielding her husband's authority without merit. There were no such restrictions on a male spouse of the President.

The first First Gentleman was free to make his own role, to expand the role of the President's spouse for the women who would come to hold it later. Garth had the unofficial role of advisor to the Chief of Staff, which was held by Kelly Dunbar. He was also a bit of National Security Advisor even though someone else also held that role. He was really something along the lines of an at large cabinet Secretary, the Secretary of Whatever Needed Attention. He wore it well and he referred to his wife as Madam President whenever any other official was in the room. She never acted on anything without consulting him. And he never let his unofficial official duties get in the way of raising Angela.

At some point in her first term, the President began to call him by another name, a playful name, one of her many playful names for him. Porter, by now, was the First Gay First Brother. The Sherman Presidency contained so many "firsts," that there was a consistent need to double that primary ordinal number. Hence, the First First Gentleman, which could never be written on a computer without a red line appearing under the second First. Melinda took to calling Garth the First Jewish First Gentleman, and she did so because at some point he began to take an interest in the faith of his fathers, or in his case the faith of his mother. He did not go so far as to become a practicing member of the religion, but on occasion he would attend a Reform Synagogue.

He took a trip back to Ricochet Hill Camp. Jewish groups reached out to him and he responded. He now told people he was Jewish. He took a trip to Israel, without his wife. She would joke with him, saying that he had never told her he was Jewish before she married him. And he told her the story of the great Hank Greenberg, a Hall of Fame baseball player who had always been more of a raconteur and man about town than he had ever been a Jew. But as his career reached a certain point, he felt a certain duty to show people who he was and from where he had come. And Garth's wife loved him all the more for doing this same thing. Garth's mother took to not wearing necklaces at all.

There were many things that were changed in the two Sherman administrations, in addition to the carbon and gasoline taxes and the boom that arose from the free national internet service. One of the very first and crucial things to happen was an escalation of rhetoric against the United States from the Islamic extremist groups and nations. There were too many reasons for them to hate America now. A President who had once actually exchanged fire with and had killed a number of Muslims now ran the United States. She had no compunction about telling America and the world that the cant of religion was dangerous, that a state-sponsored God was profaned by religious adherents who did not have faith enough to let people come on their own to their religion. She spoke openly of Christian values and called the West Christendom.

They feared her for two things that were inherent in what they had always feared about the United States. It represented the potential globalization of the values of individual freedom, justice under the rule of law, equality of all the people, and the unalienable human rights of all men and women. They rightly feared that they would lose control over their people if these values would continue to take hold in their regions and countries. The two things that President Sherman did which were of greater concern to them were that her international status accelerated and strengthened these trends, and the fact that she was a woman posed a new threat within the already existing one.

Wars of faith were declared, but not by the nations of what President Sherman called Christendom. Her very existence was seen as a kind of Crusade by Islamic extremists. Her response was to reduce the number of American targets overseas. Bases were relocated to the United States. Troops were taken out of service. Agreements were made with Japan,

France, Germany, Italy, and other developed nations to increase their own defense posture and expenditures. Troops were pulled of Afghanistan and Iraq. All of these men and women, who had by Executive Order been permitted to serve in all combat positions and units, who were discharged were given a full college tuition GI Bill, like had been done after World War II.

One day a successful terrorist attack occurred in the form of a mid-range surface-to-surface missile that had been smuggled onto American shores in Maryland and was fired at the White House. It was intercepted and destroyed by a missile defense system hidden in and around Washington. Fighter jets were scrambled from Andrews Air Force base and the President was set to be evacuated to Marine helicopter One to Air Force One where she would be kept safe in the flying command center in the sky. But she refused to go through with evacuation. Television cameras were brought to the front lawn of the White House and she addressed the terrorist groups behind the missile attack, and a good several hours before the responsible individuals had been apprehended.

"Here I am," were her first words, "Come and get me.

"I am not going anywhere. We are not going to change who we are. And unless you understand who we are you will be doomed to failure. If by some miracle you are able to get me, someone else will take my place. And I am warning you. He is one tough Italian American. We will just elect new leaders. America is not its leaders. We are a people, a free people who respect each other's rights and freedoms. And we are an ideal of freedom and equality that exists in the heart of every human being. We are, and that is, something that you can never destroy."

With that, several things happened. The apparatus of the security state began to be refined and made smaller and more precise and less expensive. The giant and expensive broad base security measures of the past were dialed back. And the response to the attack was to do what its President had always urged. Think more deeply. There was no knee-jerk reaction to the first impression. The issue was not seen as an attack on the country. It was seen as an incident of religious extremism, and religiously inspired terrorism did not present a solid target against which to retaliate. Americans decided to feel proud that the forces of the modern Dark Ages were conspiring against them. Within the United States, religion fell into disfavor. And two hundred years later this was what would come to be seen as one of the major turning points that had come from the Presidency of Melinda Sherman.

The primary religion in the United States of America would be faith of the majority of the people in the country and in its position at the front of the world. In a sense, America would become a secular faith based on the rights of all humans and in a more truly Christian way.

History would later show that the first woman President had put the country on that path. Melinda Sherman's presidency had been the tipping point around which turned the wheel of full gender equality. A woman could kick your butt too. Men had always secretly known this. But by the time President Sherman was re-elected, it was the accepted wisdom.

But all this is recollecting ahead, being nostalgic for a distant future. The events at hand are an election, a birth, and an inauguration. On the eve of the inauguration, friends and family surrounded Garth and Melinda, including one bright-eyed little seven-week-old girl. Eakin Lambert was there with Elliott. She walked up to the President-elect and whispered.

"You know that he has always been a god damn crazy romantic, don't you?"

Melinda only smiled, her eyes welling up.

"In you, he finally found a woman who was as good and as big as his dreams. And I am not talking about the political Presidential stuff. I am talking about being able to measure up to his crazy ideals," Eakin said. "You do, you always have."

"Oh, there have been my moments," Melinda said, "when I am not so sure. I just know that I want to aspire to what his love means. And I guess I have had an advantage. Someone once said that, 'a man is lucky if he is the first love of a woman. A woman is lucky if she is the last love of a man.' I think I came along late enough in the game for him, to be his last love. He learned from his love for his children. But we both know, Eakin, that he loved you first and has always loved you. And I have been the direct beneficiary of that."

And in what was a long season of firsts, the President-elect and her husband's best friend embraced and shared tears of joy. Garth watched and realized that it was also the first time he had ever seen Eakin cry.

"Well," Garth said later, after the inauguration was over and he and Melinda had retired to their bedroom in the White House, "now look what we have done. We have a baby to raise and a country to run. And I am almost sixty years old. What the heck is up with that?"

"Two people can easily raise a baby. And for the first time in history, two people will be running this country. And each one of us, even on his or her own, would do better than much of what I have seen some of those individuals do."

"Yeah, but we can no longer say we don't care, which is what we did when you were running."

"Since when have you ever not cared, Garth Teller? I know you have always cared, but you did it the right way. Look at your kids. You were always the first vision of my heart, way back when I was a girl. And I see it clearly now, more clearly. We will do quite well."

"You think?"

"Yes. You have been the last dream of my soul."

ACKNOWLEDGEMENTS

My wife, Lily, whose love and support have made this novel possible and whose patient forbearance does far more than that, is the foundation of my life and my work. She is living proof of the existence of miracles and of redemption. She not only overlooks the ways I can be trying, she manages some fondness toward them. My son, Simon, plays more of a role in my writing than he can know. And his sister, Harriet, is patient and kind every single time I remind her of her same role.

John Bond at Whitefox, is funny, wise, helpful, insightful, accommodating, experienced, determined, humbly brilliant, a tousled genius, and in some ways my very best friend. To George Edgeller, his assistant, I owe the same thanks, in smaller portion. To Fiona Marsh at London Wall Publishing, I offer my undying and sincere gratitude and my apologies for being so difficult. I am indebted to Tony Mulliken, at Midas Public Relations Anthony Mora, to Emma Draude, and to Kristen Harrison at Curved House. To Harold Bloom and Gordon Lish, I owe much of what is my love of reading and writing. I am happy to have been a student and feel blessed to be a friend.

Substantial gratitude also goes to this book's editor, Jemima Hunt, who manages to know everything in the very wide range of topics that this novel attempts to reach, while having such a keen edge for writing style that I carry a "Jemima knife" in my head. A trio of unofficial editors were crucial;

Magda Bogin, Lily Chu, and Sybil Baker. To another group, I owe different individual writing-related debts: Joanne McFadden, Louis Bayard, Carol Fenelon, Antonio Sands, Polly Draper, Rocco Chu, Margaret Desjardins, and the inimitable Jonathon Levi.

And to the late great, David Eakin, I owe more than can be written. Bloom says that the price of love gets dearer as we age because so much is spent on those who are no longer with us. When Dave passed, my love lost a large place to which to go. I lost a place to go, too, as well as a reliable source for bail money.

CPSIA information can be obtained at www.ICGtesting.com
Printed in the USA
BVOW02s0527070916

461331BV00025B/20/P